a hunger artist

A Hunger

TWISTED SPOON PRESS
Prague

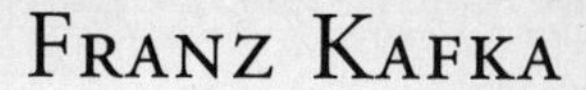

ARTIST

translated by
KEVIN BLAHUT

illustrated by
HELENA VLČNOVSKÁ

ISBN 80-902171-1-7

Contents

a hunger artist

FIRST SORROW

A trapeze artist — it is well known that this art, practiced high in the domes of the great variety theaters, is one of the most difficult attainable by human beings — had, first just in striving for perfection, and later also as a habit that had become tyrannical, arranged his life so that, for as long as he worked at the same enterprise, he remained on the trapeze day and night. All of his needs, which were very minor anyway, were seen to by servants who watched from below, working in shifts and using specially constructed containers to pull up and down everything that was needed above. This way of life did not create any particular difficulties for the world around him, though it was a little disturbing that he stayed up there, as was impossible to conceal, during the other performances, and, although he usually remained still at such times, a glance from the audience would occasionally wander up to him. But the different managements forgave him this because he was an extraordinary, irreplaceable artist. And of course people understood that he did not live this way out of malice, but because this was the only way he could remain in constant practice and preserve his art in its perfection.

And besides, it was healthy up there, and when, during warmer times of year, the side-windows in the lantern of the dome were opened and the fresh air and the sun penetrated powerfully into the brightening space, it was even beautiful. Admittedly, his dealings with humanity were limited; only sometimes did one of his gymnast colleagues climb up to him on the rope ladder, then both of them sat on the trapeze, leaned to the left and the right on the rope-holds and conversed, or laborers who were making improvements to the roof exchanged a few words with him through an open window, or the fireman checking the emergency lighting on the highest gallery called out to him something respectful, though scarcely audible. Otherwise it remained quiet around him; only sometimes did an employee who had wandered into the empty theater during the afternoon look up to where, at a height almost vanishing from view, the trapeze artist, having no way of knowing that he was being observed, practiced his art or rested.

The trapeze artist could have lived this way undisturbed if it had not been for the inevitable journeys from place to place, which he found extremely aggravating. It was true that the impresario took pains to see that the trapeze artist was spared any unnecessary extension of his suffering: race cars were used for the journeys in the cities, whenever possible at night or in the earliest hours of the morning, and they would chase through the empty streets with all possible speed, though admittedly too slowly to satisfy the trapeze artist's longing; in trains, an entire compartment would be reserved, where the trapeze artist would spend the journey up in the luggage rack, which was a miserable substitute for his life at other times, but nevertheless a substitute; at the site of the next performance the trapeze was in its place long before the trapeze artist's arrival, and all the doors that led to the auditorium were thrown open, all the corridors kept free — but the most beautiful moments in the impresario's life were still the ones when the trapeze artist put his foot on the rope ladder and, in no time at all, was finally hanging up on his trapeze again.

Although the impresario had succeeded with many such journeys, he still found them unpleasant, because the journeys, disregarding everything else, were always damaging to the trapeze artist's nerves.

So it was that they were travelling with each other again. The trapeze artist was lying in the luggage rack and dreaming. The impresario was leaning in the corner by the window and reading a book. Then the trapeze artist addressed him softly. The impresario was immediately at his service. Biting his lips, the trapeze artist said that, instead of one trapeze, as he had used for his acrobatics up until now, he would now always have to have two trapezes, two trapezes opposite one another. The impresario agreed with this idea immediately. However, the trapeze artist, as if he wanted to show that in this case the impresario's agreement meant as little as a refusal would have, said that he would never again and under no circumstances perform on one trapeze. He seemed to shudder at the idea that it might ever happen again. Hesitating and observing, the impresario explained his full agreement once again, two trapezes were better than one, and this new arrangement was also advantageous because it added variety to the performance. Then the trapeze artist suddenly began to cry. Deeply disturbed, the impresario leapt up and asked what had happened, and when he received no answer, he climbed up on the bench, caressed him and pressed his face to his own, so that the trapeze artist's tears would flow over his face as well. But only after many questions and flattering words did the trapeze artist say, sobbing: "Just this one bar in my hands — how can I live!" Now it was already easier for the impresario to comfort the trapeze artist; he promised to telegraph the site of the next performance about the second trapeze as soon as they reached the next station; reproached himself for having allowed the trapeze artist to work on one trapeze for so long, and thanked him and praised him highly for finally having called attention to the mistake. Thus the impresario gradually succeeded in calming the trapeze artist, and he was able to return to his corner. But he himself had not been calmed, and with grave concern he secretly regarded the trapeze artist from over the top of his book. When such thoughts had begun to torment him, would they ever completely stop? Didn't they have to constantly increase? Weren't they existence threatening? And the impresario really thought he saw, in the apparently quiet sleep in which the crying had ended, how the first wrinkles began to etch themselves into the trapeze artist's smooth, childish forehead.

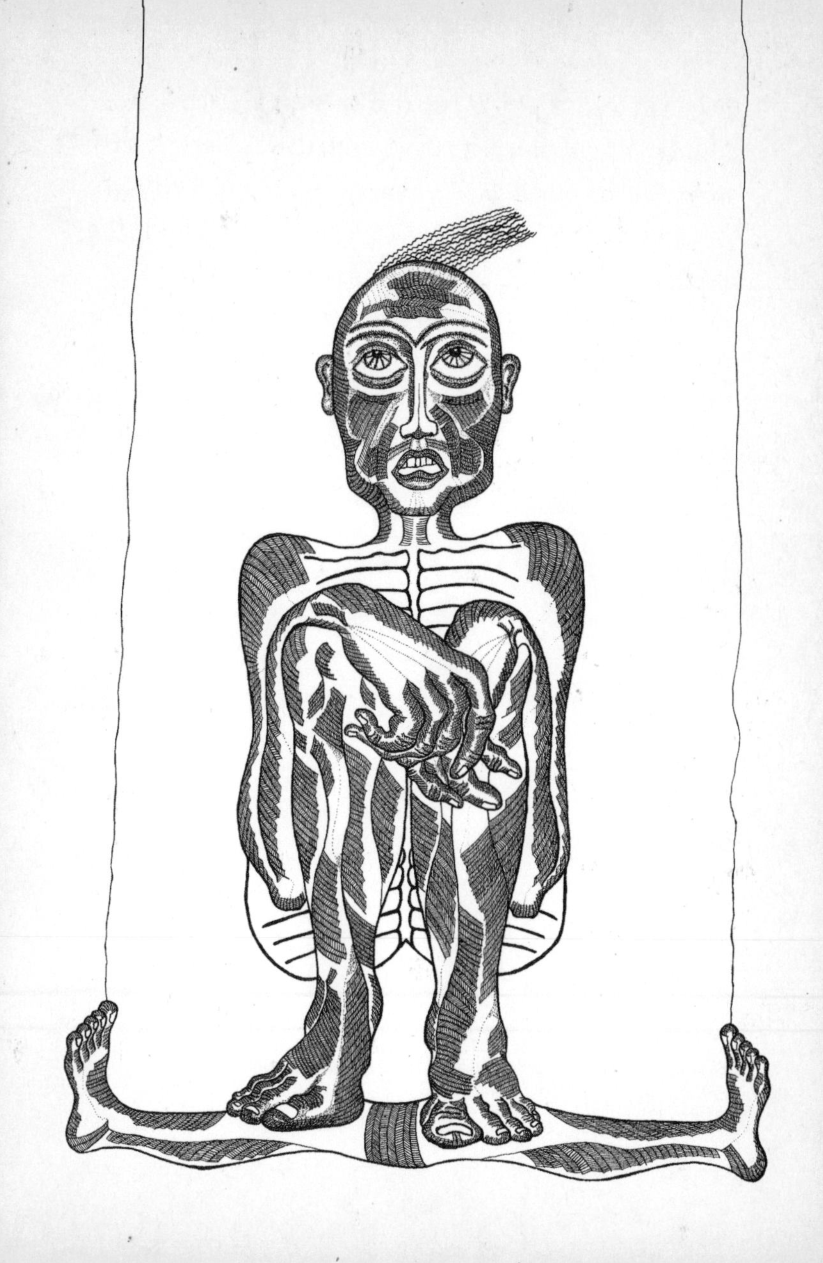

A LITTLE WOMAN

She is a little woman; quite slim by nature, she is tightly bound; I always see her in the same dress, it is made from a yellowish gray fabric that in a certain way resembles the color of wood, and is decorated with tassels or certain buttonlike fringes of the same color; she never wears a hat, her dull blond hair is smooth and not messy, although she wears it very loosely. Although she is tightly bound, she is quite flexible, and she exaggerates this flexibility; she likes to put her hands on her hips, and, surprisingly quickly, turn her upper body sideways with a single movement. I can only reproduce the impression that her hand makes on me by saying that I have never seen a hand in which the fingers are as sharply divided from one another as hers. However, her hand is in no way an anatomical peculiarity; it is a completely normal hand.

This little woman is very unhappy with me, there is always something about me that she finds objectionable, some injustice is always being done to her because of me, I annoy her at every step; if it were possible to divide life up into the smallest possible pieces and judge each piece separately, there is no doubt that every little piece of my life would annoy her. I have often wondered why I annoy her so much; it could be that everything about me contradicts her sense of beauty, her sense of justice, her habits, her traditions, her hopes; such contrary natures exist, but why does she let it cause her so much suffering? There is no relationship between us that would cause her to suffer because of me. She need only decide to view me as a complete stranger — since this is after all what I am and since I would have nothing against such a decision — she need only decide to forget my existence, which I never have and never would force upon her — and all her suffering would obviously be over. In this I take no account of myself or of the fact that her behavior makes me uncomfortable, I ignore this because I recognize that this discomfort is nothing compared to her suffering. Of course I am completely aware that it is not a loving suffering; it has nothing to do with improving me, especially since everything she objects to in me is not of such a nature that it might prevent my success. But my success does not worry her either, what worries her is precisely her personal interest, namely, to take revenge for the torment that I cause her, and to prevent the torment that threatens to come from me in the future. I once tried to show her the best possible way of putting an end to this incessant annoyance, but in so doing I caused such an outburst of rage that I will never repeat the attempt.

It could be said that I share a certain responsibility, even though this woman is a stranger to me and even though the only relationship that exists between us is the annoyance that I cause her, or rather, the annoyance that she allows me to cause her. Apparently she also suffers physically from this annoyance, and this cannot be a matter of indifference to me. Now and then — and lately with increasing frequency — I hear reports that, in the morning, she has appeared pale, without having slept, tormented by headaches and almost incapable of working; she worries her relatives, they search here and there for what might be responsible for her condition, but until now they have found nothing. I alone know; it is the old and always new annoyance. Of course I do not share her relatives' concern; she is strong and tough; whoever is capable of becoming so annoyed is probably also capable of overcoming the consequences of the annoyance; I even suspect that she — at least in part — only presents herself as suffering in order to make the world suspicious of me. She is too proud to state openly how much my existence torments her; she would consider it degrading to appeal to others because of me; she concerns herself with me only because of revulsion, because of an infinite revulsion; to discuss this unseemly affair in public would be too much for her sense of shame. However, because of the constant pressure the affair puts on her, she is also incapable of being completely silent about it. And so, with her feminine cunning, she seeks a middle way; silent, she brings the matter before the judgment of the public only through the outer signs of a clandestine suffering. Perhaps she is hoping that, once the public turns its full gaze upon me, a general public annoyance with me will result, and that, with its great mechanisms of power, the public will condemn me much more quickly and powerfully than her private annoyance, weak by comparison, would be capable of doing; then she will withdraw, sigh, and turn her back on me. However, if this is what she hopes, she is deceiving herself. The public will never have so infinitely much fault to find with me, even if they examine me with their strongest magnifying glass. I am not as useless as she believes me to be; I don't want to brag, and certainly not where this is concerned; however, if I were not considered particularly useful, I would certainly also not be seen as the opposite; I appear this way only to her, to her eyes that practically flash with whiteness; she would not be able to convince anyone else of it. So can I therefore be completely at ease regarding this matter? No, certainly not, for if it becomes known that my behavior actually makes her sick (a few of her protectors — precisely the ones who are most diligent about conveying news of her — are already close to realizing it, or at least act as if they were), and the world comes and asks me why I torment the woman with my incorrigibility and if perhaps I plan to drive her to her grave and when will I finally be reasonable enough and have the simple human decency to stop — if the world were to ask me these questions, I would have a hard time answering. Should I admit that I don't take these signs of illness very seriously, thereby creating the unpleasant impression that, in order to rid myself of this guilt, I cast the blame on others and moreover in such an indelicate manner? And could I perhaps say openly that I would not feel the slightest sympathy even if I believed she were really sick, since the woman is a complete stranger to me and the relationship that exists between us is entirely her creation and is maintained entirely from her side? I do not want to say that I wouldn't be believed; actually, people would neither believe nor disbelieve me; they would never get to the point where belief would be discussed; they would simply register the answer I had given regarding a sick, weak woman, and this could not be to my advantage. With this answer as with any other I would run across the stubborn inability of the world not to arrive at the suspicion of a love affair in cases such as this, even though it could not be any clearer that no such relationship exists and that, if one were to exist, it would be more likely to originate from me, since I would be capable of admiring the little woman for the power of her judgment and the tenacity of her deductions if these merits were not constantly being used to punish me. From her side, however, there is not a trace of the possibility of her having a friendly relationship to me; in this she is staunch and true; in this lies my only hope; but even if it would fit into her battle plan to make such a relationship believed, she would not forget herself to the extent where she would do anything of the kind. However, the public, completely obtuse wherever things of this sort are concerned, would cling to their opinion and always decide against me.

Therefore the only option left open to me would be — at the right time, before the world intervenes — to change myself to such an extent that the woman's annoyance is not eliminated — which would be unthinkable — but is at least to some degree mitigated. And I actually asked myself on several occasions if I was so content with my current situation that I would not want to change it in any way, and if it would not therefore be possible to undertake certain changes in myself, even if I were not doing it because I was convinced of their necessity, but only in order to placate the woman. And I attempted it with all sincerity, not without conscientiousness and effort, it even suited me, I found it almost enjoyable; individual changes became apparent, were clearly visible, it was not necessary to call the woman's attention to them, she noticed all of them before I did, she even noticed the expression of purpose in my being. But success was not granted to me. How, after all, could it have been? Her dissatisfaction with me is, as I now understand, fundamental; nothing can eliminate it, not even if I were to be eliminated; her fits of rage at the news of my suicide would know no bounds. However, I cannot imagine that she, this clever woman, does not comprehend just as well as I do the hopelessness of her efforts as well as my innocence, my inability, even with the best possible intentions, to meet her demands. Of course she understands it, but, being of a fighting nature, she forgets it in the passion of the fight. Correspondingly, it is my unfortunate nature — which, having been granted to me as it is, I cannot choose otherwise — that I want to whisper a soft warning to someone who has gone completely out of control. Clearly this is no way to reach an understanding. Again and again I will leave my house with the happiness of the first hours of the morning and see this face, distraught because of me: the sullenly pouting lips; the glance that, no matter how rapid it is, overlooks nothing, examining and knowing the result even before the examination; the bitter smile that bores itself into her girlish cheeks; the complaining glance to the heavens; the putting of her hands on her hips so that she may fortify herself, and then the paleness and trembling of her indignation.

Recently, and for the first time, as I understood with surprise when it happened, I made a few suggestions to a good friend about this matter, just in passing, simply; with a few words I conveyed the impression of the whole affair, as small as it basically is for me, but still without telling the entire truth. It was strange that my friend did not ignore me, but in fact embellished on the affair on his own account, and held to this point, refusing to be diverted from it. However, it is even more unusual that despite this he underestimated the affair on an important point, for he advised me quite seriously to go away for a while. No advice could have shown less understanding; the facts are quite clear, anyone could understand them by approaching closer, but they are not so simple that my departure would settle it all or would settle even the most important thing. On the contrary, I must beware of departing; if there is any plan at all that I should follow, it should be the one that keeps the affair within its narrow bounds, which do not yet include the outside world; that is, to remain quiet, to stay where I am, and to allow no great, conspicuous changes to be brought about by this affair, which also involves not mentioning it to anyone. However, all of this not because it is a dangerous secret, but because it is a minor, purely personal affair, and as such is easily borne and should remain that way. In this my friend's remarks weren't useless; they taught me nothing, but they reinforced me in my basic opinion.

As is revealed by more careful consideration, the changes which the state of affairs seems to have undergone over the course of time are not changes in the affair itself, but are merely the development of my view of it, insofar as this view becomes calmer and more masculine, approaching the core. On the other hand, however, the series of constant tremors — which, however slight, manage to stay with me — has produced a certain nervousness.

I am becoming calmer in regard to the affair in that I believe I recognize that a decision, however close at hand it seems at times to be, will not come after all; one is inclined to overestimate considerably the tempo with which decisions arrive, and this especially when one is young; at one time, whenever my little judge, made weak by the sight of me, sank sideways into her armchair, holding herself steady with one hand against the back of the chair while the other nestled against her corset, and tears of rage and despair rolled down her cheeks, I always thought that the decision was now at hand and at any second I would be called to account. But there was no decision, no calling to account; women often feel faint, the world does not have time to give its attention to every incident. And what, after all, has occurred over all these years? Nothing, except that such incidents repeated themselves, sometimes stronger, sometimes weaker, thus making the sum total greater. There are also people who hang around in the vicinity, who would like to intervene if they were to find an opportunity. But they find none. Until now they have only trusted a scent, and it is true that a scent is enough to occupy them abundantly, but to others it is not worth anything. However, it has basically always been this way; there have always been these people standing on corners, these people who do nothing but breathe the air, who always excused their proximity through an overly clever reason, preferably through being related. They have always been watching, their noses have always been full of this scent, but the result of all of this is only that they are still standing there. The only difference is that I have gradually come to recognize them, and can distinguish between their faces; I used to believe that they would come gradually, from many different places, and that the dimensions of the affair would continue to expand and this itself would force the decision; today I think I can be sure that all of it has been there from the beginning and that it has very little or nothing at all to do with the approach of the decision. And the decision itself? Why do I call it by such an important name? If it should ever happen — and certainly not tomorrow or the day after and probably never — that the public should concern itself with this affair — which, as I will continue to repeat, it is not competent to do — I will not emerge from the proceedings unscathed, but it will certainly be taken into account that I am not unknown to the public, that I have lived in its full view for as long as anyone can remember, both trusted and trusting, and that therefore this suffering little woman, presenting herself only much later on — who, by the way, someone other than me might have long since recognized as a bur and, as far as the public was concerned, silently crushed beneath his boot — that this woman, even in the worst case, could only add an ugly squiggle to the diploma with which the public has long since declared me to be one of its respected members. That is the present situation, about which there is little that might make me uneasy.

That I have in fact become a little uneasy over the years has nothing to do with the actual meaning of the affair; it is simply impossible to bear being a constant annoyance to someone, even if one recognizes the groundlessness of the annoyance; one becomes uneasy, one begins, in a certain sense only physically, to await judgments, even if, rationally, one does not believe that they will ever come. However, in part it is only a matter of something that appears in old age; unpleasant details become lost in youth's endless well of strength; if someone has rather shifty eyes when he is a boy, it is not held against him, it is not even noticed, not even by him; however, the things that survive into old age are remnants, each one is necessary, none will be renewed, each is scrutinized, and the shifty eyes of an aging man are quite clearly shifty eyes; they are not difficult to see. Yet even this is not a real, objective deterioration.

Therefore, from whichever perspective I consider it, it remains true — and I hold to this opinion — that if I only keep this little matter slightly covered with my hand, I will be free for a long time to continue living my life as it has been up until now, undisturbed by the world, however enraged the woman might be.

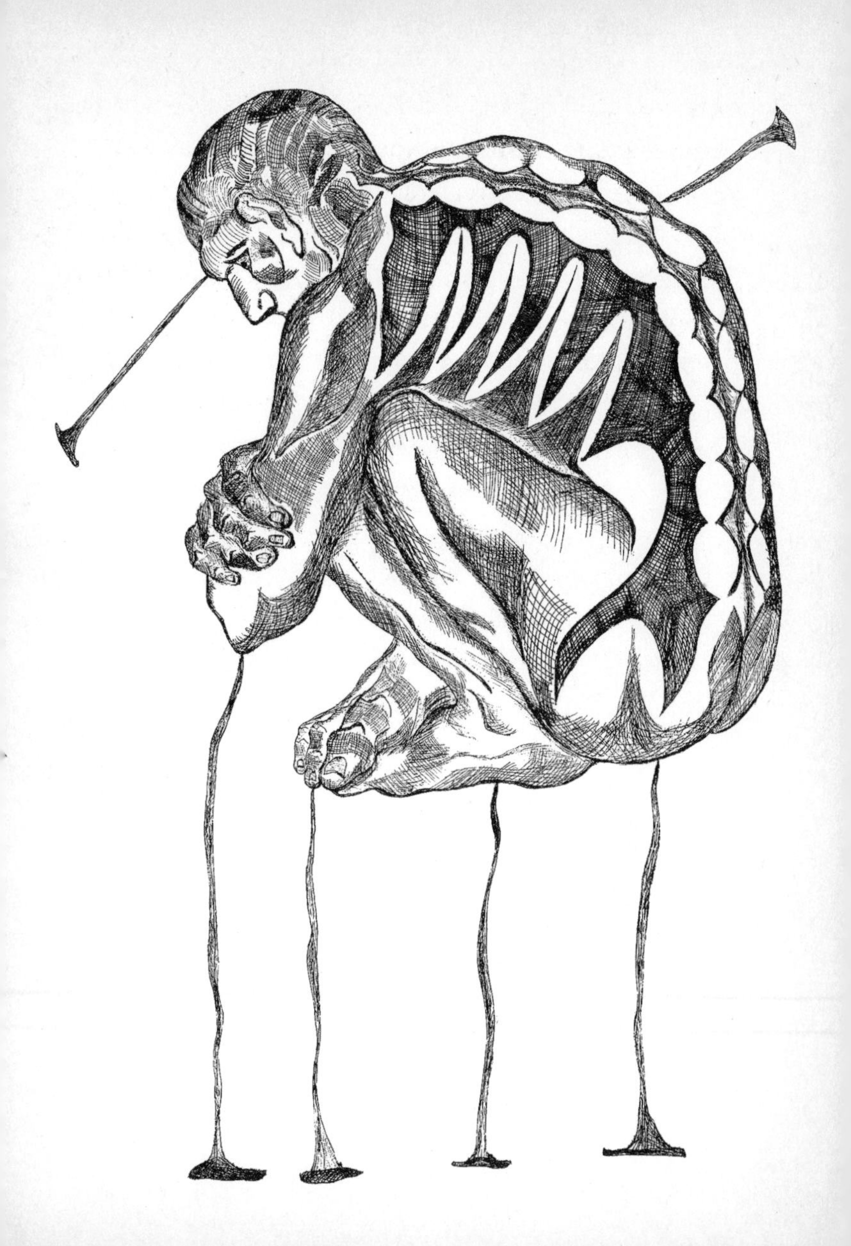

A HUNGER ARTIST

In the past few decades the interest in hunger artists has declined considerably. While it used to be profitable to organize exclusive productions of such performances, today this is completely impossible. Those were different times. Back then the entire city would be interested in the hunger artist; attendance would increase from one fast day to the next; everyone wanted to see the hunger artist at least once every day; as the fast progressed there were subscribers who sat in front of the little cage all day long; viewings also occurred at night, with torches used to heighten the effect; on pleasant days the cage was brought outside, and the hunger artist was displayed to children in particular; while for adults he was often just a diversion in which they took interest on account of fashion, the children watched with amazement, open mouthed, holding each other's hands for reassurance, how the hunger artist, pale, in a black leotard, with powerfully jutting ribs, scorning even a chair, sat on the straw that had been strewn about, nodded politely and maintained a strained smile as he answered questions, and stretched his arm through the bars so that people could feel how thin he was, but then withdrew completely into himself, paid attention to no one, and not even to the striking — so important to him — of the clock that was the only piece of furniture in the cage, but only looked straight ahead with eyes that were almost closed and occasionally sipped water from a small glass to moisten his lips.

In addition to the constantly changing group of spectators, there were also permanent guards who had been chosen by the audience, usually butchers, oddly enough, who, always three at a time, had the task of watching the hunger artist day and night to make sure that he did not nourish himself in some secret way. It was, however, merely a formality introduced to placate the masses, for the initiates knew well that during the fast the hunger artist would never, under no circumstances, have eaten the smallest thing, not even if coerced; the honor of his art forbade it. Of course, not every guard could understand this, at night there were sometimes groups of guards who kept their vigil very laxly, intentionally sitting in a distant corner and becoming engrossed in a game of cards, with the obvious intention of allowing the hunger artist some small refreshment, which they thought he could take from a secret reserve. There was nothing more tormenting to the hunger artist than such guards; they made fasting horribly difficult for him; sometimes he overcame his weakness and sang during these vigils for as long as he could in order to show the people how unjust their suspicion of him was. But this was not much help; they simply wondered at the skill that allowed him to sing even while he was eating. He much preferred the guards who sat close to the cage, were discontent with the murky lighting of the hall at night, and instead illuminated him with electric flashlights leant to them by the impresario. The harsh light did not disturb him, he was unable to sleep anyway, and he could always fall into a stupor, regardless of the lighting and the hour, even in the overcrowded, noisy hall. When such guards watched over him he was quite happy to spend the night without any sleep at all; he was prepared to joke with them, to tell them stories of his nomadic life, and then to listen to their stories, all just to keep them awake, to show them again and again that he had nothing edible in the cage and that he was fasting as none of them could. But he was happiest of all when the morning came and, at his expense, an enormous breakfast was brought to them, into which they threw themselves with the appetite of healthy men after an arduous, sleepless night. There were, however, people who saw this breakfast as an improper influence on the guards, but this was going too far, and when others asked if they would like to take over the vigil simply for the sake of doing it and without breakfast, they would disappear, but they held to their suspicions nonetheless.

This, however, was among the suspicions that could never be separated from fasting. No one was in a position to spend all his days and nights keeping a constant watch over the hunger artist, and thus no one could know first-hand if the fast was observed correctly and without interruption; only the hunger artist himself could know, and thus he was the only spectator who could be completely satisfied with his fasting. But, for other reasons, he was never satisfied; perhaps fasting had nothing to do with his being so emaciated that many, to their regret, had to stay away from his performances because they could not bear the sight of him; perhaps it was dissatisfaction with himself that made him so emaciated. For he alone knew, as no other initiate did, how easy fasting was. It was the easiest thing in the world. And he did not keep this a secret, but no one believed him; in the best case they considered him humble, but most thought he was greedy for publicity, or even a fraud for whom fasting was easy because he knew ways of making it easy and even had the nerve to half-confess it. He had to put up with all of this, and had grown accustomed to it over the years, but inwardly this dissatisfaction was always gnawing at him, and never, after no period of fasting — this had to be said on his behalf — had he left the cage of his own free will. The impresario had set forty days as the maximum duration of the fast, and he never let the fasting go on longer than this, even in the metropolises, and for good reason. As experience had shown, the interest in a particular city could be stirred up by increasing the number of advertisements over a period of about forty days, but then the crowds fell off, a considerable decline in popularity was apparent; in this regard there were of course small differences between the different cities and countries, but the rule remained that forty days was the maximum time. Thus on the fortieth day the flower-wreathed cage was opened, an enthusiastic audience filled the amphitheater, a military band played, two doctors entered the cage to take the necessary measurements of the hunger artist, the results were reported to the hall using a megaphone, and finally two young ladies arrived, happy that their lots had been chosen, and tried to lead the hunger artist a few steps down from his cage, where a carefully chosen convalescent's meal had been served. And at this moment the hunger artist always protected himself. It was of his own free will that he laid his bony arms into the outstretched hands of the ladies who bent down to him, ready to help, but he did not want to stand up. Why should he stop precisely now, after forty days? He could have endured it longer, infinitely longer; why stop precisely now, when he was in his best form for fasting, or rather, before he had even reached his best form? Why did they want to rob him of the glory of continuing to fast and becoming not only the greatest hunger artist of all time, which he probably already was, but of surpassing even himself and entering the realm of the incomprehensible, since he felt there were no limits to his ability to fast. Why did this crowd, who acted as though they admired him, have so little patience with him; if he could endure fasting even longer, why didn't they want to endure it? He was also tired, was happy sitting in the straw, but was now supposed to rise to his full height and go to the food, the mere thought of which caused him nausea, which, out of respect for the ladies, he struggled to keep down. And he looked up into the eyes of the ladies who seemed so friendly but in reality were so cruel and shook his overly heavy head on his weak neck. But then what always happened happened again. The impresario came, lifted his arms mutely — the music made speech impossible — over the hunger artist, as though inviting heaven to behold its work here on the straw, this pitiable martyr, which the hunger artist certainly was, but in an entirely different sense; he seized the hunger artist around his thin waist, using exaggerated caution to illustrate that he was handling something delicate; and handed him over — not without secretly shaking him a little so that the hunger artist's legs and upper body swayed back and forth uncontrollably — to the ladies, who in the meantime had become deathly pale. But the hunger artist tolerated everything; his head lay on his breast as though it had rolled off and was inexplicably hanging there; his body was hollowed out; his legs pressed together firmly at the knees in an instinct of self-preservation, scraping the ground as though it were not the real one and it was the real one they sought; the entire burden of the body, small though it was, lay on one of the ladies, who, looking for help, her breath racing — she had not imagined her honorary position to be like this — first stretched out her neck as far as it would go in order to keep it from coming into contact with the hunger artist, but then, when this did not succeed and her more fortunate companion did not come to help her (but instead, shaking, was satisfied with carrying the hunger artist's hand, this little bundle of bones, out in front of her), she broke out in tears amid the crowd's delighted laughter, and had to be replaced by a servant who had been prepared long in advance. Then came the food. The impresario poured a little down the hunger artist's throat while he was still in the midst of a half-sleep that resembled a fainting spell, amid jovial talk that was supposed to divert attention from the hunger artist's condition; then another toast was made to the audience, which the hunger artist had supposedly whispered to the impresario; the orchestra emphasized everything with a great flourish, the crowd broke up, and no one had the right to be dissatisfied with the proceedings, no one, except for the hunger artist, always him alone.

He lived this way with short, regular intervals of rest, in apparent splendor, honored by the world, but nevertheless usually in a bleak mood, which became increasingly more bleak because no one knew how to take this mood seriously. What could anyone have used to console him? What more could he possibly wish for? And when a good-natured person came along who felt bad for him and wanted to explain that his sadness probably came from fasting, it could happen, especially if the fast were at an advanced stage, that the hunger artist became infuriated and, to everyone's horror, began to shake the bars like an animal. But the impresario had a method of punishment he liked to use for such situations. He apologized for the hunger artist in front of the assembled crowd, admitted that only the irritablity caused by fasting, incomprehensible to well-fed people, could excuse the hunger artist's behavior; in connection with this he also came to mention the hunger artist's claim that he could fast even longer than he did, which could be explained in the same way; he praised the ambition, the good will, the great self-denial that were certainly also contained in this claim; then, however, he sought to refute this claim by showing photographs (which were also for sale); in these pictures one saw the hunger artist on the fortieth day of a fast, in bed, almost extinguished by weakness. This distortion of the truth, well known to the hunger artist, but still unnerving every time he heard it repeated, was too much for him. The result of the fast's premature end was portrayed as its cause! It was impossible to fight against such incomprehension, against such a world of incomprehension. He had still listened to the impresario eagerly, in good faith, at the bars of the cage, but every time the photographs appeared he let go of the bars, sank back into the straw with a sigh, and the crowd, who had been reassured, could approach again and look at him.

When the witnesses of such scenes thought back on

them a few years later, they were often unable to understand how they had acted. Because in the meantime the aforementioned reversal occurred; it had happened suddenly; there may have been deeper reasons, but who cared about discovering them; in any case, one day the spoiled hunger artist found himself abandoned by the pleasure-seeking crowds, who preferred to flock to other shows. Once again the impresario hunted through half of Europe with the hunger artist to see if the former interest still existed in a few places; all in vain; a virtual aversion to show-fasting had developed everywhere, as though by secret agreement. Of course, in reality this could not have happened so suddenly, and now, after the fact, one remembered quite a few early indications that, in the intoxication of success, had not been given sufficient consideration and had not been rooted out, but now it was too late to do anything about it. Although it was certain that the time for fasting would come again, this was no comfort for the living. What was the hunger artist to do? He, whom thousands had cheered, could not display himself in showbooths at small fairs, and he was not only too old to take up another profession, but also too fanatically devoted to fasting. So he said goodbye to the impresario, his comrade in a career without equal, and found an engagement with a large circus; in order to spare his feelings, he did not even look at the terms of the contract.

A large circus, with its host of people and animals and equipment constantly balancing each other out and complementing one another, can use anyone at any time, even a hunger artist, though his demands must be appropriately modest, and besides, in this particular case it was not only the hunger artist who was being taken on, but also his old, famous name, and, because of the peculiarity of this art, the quality of which did not decrease as the artist grew older, no one could say that a depleted artist, no longer at the height of his powers, was trying to flee into a quiet post in a circus; on the contrary, the hunger artist guaranteed that he could fast just as well as before, which was perfecly believable, and he even claimed that, if left to have his way, which was promised to him immediately, he would, for the first time, legitimately earn the world's astonishment, a claim that, given the mood of the times — quickly forgotten by the hunger artist in his enthusiasm — only made the experts smile.

However, essentially the hunger artist did not lose sight of how things were, and accepted it as self-evident that he and his cage were not put in the middle of the ring as a main attraction, but instead were kept outside, near the menagerie, in a place that happened to be quite accessible. Large, brightly painted posters surrounded the cage and proclaimed what was on display there. When, during breaks in the performance, the public forced their way to the menagerie to see the animals, it was almost inevitable that they would come upon the hunger artist's cage and stop for a while. They would have spent more time there if it had not been for the people behind them, who longed to see the animals and pushed forward along the narrow path, not understanding this delay and making longer, undisturbed observation impossible. This was the reason why these visiting times caused the hunger artist great anxiety, even though he also wished for them because they were his reason for living. In the beginning he could hardly wait for the breaks in the performance; he had watched the crowd with delight as it rolled toward him, until, too soon — even the most stubborn, almost conscious self-deception could not withstand the experience — he convinced himself that, again and again, without exception, they were all going to see the animals, or at least intended to. And this view from a distance was always the most beautiful. For when they had reached him, he was surrounded by the screams and curses of groups that were constantly forming, those who — they soon became the more embarrassing ones to the hunger artist — wanted to look at him at their leisure, not because they understood, but because they were capricious and defiant, and the second group, who wanted nothing but to reach the menagerie. Once the great crowd had passed, the stragglers came along, and these people, to whom the possibility of stopping was no longer denied, hurried past with long steps, almost without glancing to the side, in order to reach the animals while there was still time. And it was not a very common stroke of luck when a father came with his children, pointed at the hunger artist, explained at length what this was all about, talked about earlier times, when he had been to similar, but incomparably more fantastic performances, and though inadequate preparation from life and school kept the children from understanding — what was fasting to them? — the radiance in their searching eyes betrayed something of future, more merciful times. Perhaps, the hunger artist said to himself occasionally, everything would have been a little better if his cage were not so close to the animals. This made the choice too easy for people, not to mention that he was hurt and constantly oppressed by the smells from the menagerie, the restlessness of the animals at night, the carrying past of raw pieces of meat for the predators, and the cries at feeding time. But he did not dare to complain to the management; he still had the animals to thank for the crowd of visitors, among whom a supporter could occasionally be found. Besides, who knew where they would hide him if he were to remind them of his existence and that he, strictly speaking, was merely an obstacle on the way to the animals.

A small obstacle to be sure, an obstacle that was becoming smaller every day. People became accustomed to the singularity of this anachronistic attempt to claim attention for a hunger artist, and when this happened his judgment was pronounced. He wanted to fast as well as he could, and he did it, but nothing could save him now, and people passed him by. Try explaining the art of fasting! Someone who does not feel it will never understand. The beautiful posters became dirty and unreadable, they were torn down and no one thought of replacing them; the little board with the number that told how long the fast had been going on, which in the beginning had always been carefully updated, had been the same for a long time, since even this small task had become wearisome to the personnel after the first few weeks; the hunger artist fasted on, as he had only dreamed of before, and, without effort, he succeeded exactly as he had predicted, but no one counted the days, and no one, not even the hunger artist himself, knew how great his achievement already was, and his heart became heavy. And when once during that time an idler stopped and made fun of the old number and said it was a fraud, it was the stupidest lie that indifference and inborn malice could invent, because the hunger artist was cheating no one, he was working honestly; it was the world that was cheating him of his reward.

But many days passed and even that came to an end. One day a supervisor noticed the cage and asked the servants why this perfectly serviceable cage had been left standing there, unused and full of rotten straw; no one knew, until, with the help of the board with the number on it, someone remembered the hunger artist. They moved the straw with sticks and found the hunger artist inside. "You're still fasting?" asked the supervisor, "aren't you ever going to stop?" "Forgive me, everyone," whispered the hunger artist; only the supervisor, holding his ear to the bars, understood him. "Of course," said the supervisor and put his finger against his brow to indicate the hunger artist's condition to the workers, "we forgive you." "I always wanted you to admire my fasting," said the hunger artist. "And we do admire it," said the supervisor obligingly. "But you shouldn't admire it," said the hunger artist. "Well, then we don't admire it," said the supervisor, "but why shouldn't we admire it?" "Because I have to fast, I can't do otherwise," said the hunger artist. "How odd," said the supervisor, "why is it that you can't do otherwise?" "Because," said the hunger artist, slightly raising his little head and, with lips pursed as though for a kiss, speaking right into the supervisor's ear so that nothing would be lost, "because I couldn't find the food I liked. If I had found it, believe me, I would have stuffed myself like you and everyone else." Those were his last words, but in his broken eyes there remained the firm if no longer proud conviction that he was continuing to fast.

"Now clean this up!" said the supervisor, and they buried the hunger artist with the straw. In the cage they put a young panther. To see this wild animal casting itself about in the cage that had been barren for so long was a recovery perceptible to even the dullest sensibility. The panther had everything. Without hesitation the keepers brought it the food it liked; it did not even seem to miss its freedom; this noble body, furnished almost to the point of bursting with everything it needed, seemed to carry freedom around with it; freedom seemed to be lodged somewhere in its jaws; and happiness with life came from its throat with such force that it was not easy for the spectators to resist fleeing. But they overcame this urge, crowded around the cage, and never wanted to leave.

JOSEPHINE, THE SINGER
OR
THE MOUSE PEOPLE

Our singer is called Josephine. Whoever has not heard her does not know the power of song. There is no one who is not swept away by her song, which is that much more impressive since our people as a whole do not love music. Our favorite music is quiet peace; our life is hard, and even when we have tried to shake off all our daily cares, we cannot rise to things, such as music, which differ so much from our life at other times. But we do not complain about it much; we never get that far; we consider our greatest advantage to be a certain practical cunning, which we of course need in the greatest possible degree, and we are in the habit of using the smile of this cunning as a consolation in regard to everything, even if we should have the longing for the happiness — but this doesn't happen — that might come from music. But Josephine is an exception; she loves music and she also knows how to mediate it; she is the only one; with her demise, music will disappear from our lives, who knows for how long.

I have often wondered what this music actually does. We are completely unmusical; how is it that we understand Josephine's song, or, since Josephine denies that we understand, at least believe we understand. The simplest answer would be that even the dullest senses cannot resist her, but this answer is unsatisfactory. If this were really true, one would first of all, and in every case, have the feeling of something extraordinary in regard to this song, the feeling that something came from this throat that we have never heard before, something that we are not even capable of hearing, something that Josephine and no one else enables us to hear. But in my opinion this is not what happens; I do not feel it and have not observed that anyone else does either. In intimate circles we admit openly to one another that, in and of itself, Josephine's song does not represent anything extraordinary.

Is it song at all? Despite our unmusicality we have a tradition of song; in the early days of our people there was song; legends speak of it and some songs have even been preserved, though of course no one can sing them. Because of this we have an idea of what song is, and Josephine's art does not correspond to this idea. Is it song at all? Is it perhaps only whistling? And whistling is something all of us are familiar with, it is our people's only skill, or rather, it is not a skill at all, but a characteristic expression of life. All of us whistle, but of course no one ever thinks of presenting this as art, we whistle without paying attention to it, in fact without noticing it, and there are even many among us who do not know that whistling is one of our characteristics. If it were true that Josephine doesn't sing, but instead only whistles and perhaps, at least as it seems to me, scarcely goes beyond the bounds of ordinary whistling — perhaps her strength is not sufficient even for this ordinary whistling, which an ordinary laborer is capable of doing all day long, in addition to his work — if this were true, then Josephine's alleged artistry would be refuted, but the riddle of why she has such a powerful effect would still have to be solved.

However, what she produces is more than mere whistling. If one stands far away from her and listens, or even better, if you put yourself to the following test: if Josephine is singing among other voices and one sets oneself the task of recognizing her voice, then, without fail, one will hear nothing but a normal whistling, a little striking at most because of tenderness or frailty. But if one stands before her, it is more than just whistling; in order to understand her art it is necessary not just to see her but also to hear her. Even if it were just our everyday whistling, there is first of all the peculiarity that someone solemnly presents himself to do nothing but the ordinary. Cracking a nut is really not an art, and therefore no one would ever dare to call together an audience and crack nuts in front of them in order to entertain them. If he does it anyway and he succeeds in his intention, then it can certainly not be a matter of nut-cracking alone. Or it is a matter of nut-cracking, but it becomes clear that we have ignored this art because we have mastered it too completely and this new nutcracker shows us its true nature for the first time, in which case it might even be useful for the effect if he were even less skilled at nut-cracking than most of us.

Perhaps something similar is the case with Josephine's song; we admire in her something we do not admire in ourselves; what is more, she agrees with us completely on the latter point. I was once present when, as naturally happened quite often, someone pointed out to her the common folk-whistling, and in fact quite humbly. However, for Josephine even this was too much. I have never seen such a bold, arrogant smile as the one she put on then; she appeared positively mean, she, who on the outside is actually perfect tenderness, remarkable even among our people, among whom there are many such female forms; in her great sensitivity she herself must have also noticed it right away, and regained her composure. In any case she denies any connection between whistling and her art. For those who are of the opposite opinion she has only contempt, and probably unconfessed hatred. This is not normal vanity, for this opposition, to which I myself half belong, certainly admires her no less than the crowd, but Josephine wants not only to be admired, but to be admired precisely in the way she has prescribed; admiration alone means nothing to her. And when one sits before her, one knows: what she whistles is not whistling.

Since whistling is among our unreflected habits, one might believe that people also whistle while listening to

Josephine; her art gives us a sense of well-being, and when we feel this way we whistle; but the people in her audience don't whistle, we are as quiet as mice; as though we had been blessed with the desired peace, from which our own whistling excludes us, we are silent. Is it her song that charms us or is it not rather the solemn peace that surrounds her weak little voice? It happened once that, in all innocence, a silly little thing also began to whistle during Josephine's song. Now, it was exactly the same thing we were hearing from Josephine; there in the front the whistling that was still shy despite all the routine, and here in the audience the unselfconscious childish peeping; it would have been impossible to indicate the difference; but we hissed at the intruder and whistled her down, even though this would not have been necessary, for she would have crawled off in shame and fear anyway, while Josephine struck up her triumphant whistling and was completely ecstatic, her arms outstretched and her neck fully extended.

She is, incidentally, always like this; every trivial detail, every accident, every show of resistance, a crack in the parquette, a gnashing of teeth, a failure in the lighting, she considers a suitable occasion for heightening the effect of her song; in her opinion she sings to deaf ears anyway; there is no lack of enthusiasm or applause, but she has long learned to live without what she considers to be genuine understanding. Because of this she finds all disturbances very convenient; every-thing that comes from outside and opposes itself to the purity of her song, and is vanquished in an easy fight, or in fact without a fight, can serve to awaken the crowd and teach them appreciative respect, even if understanding remains out of the question.

If small things can serve her so well, then how much more can great ones. Our life is very restless, every day brings such surprises, fears, hopes and terrors that it would be impossible for the individual to bear all of them if he did not always, both day and night, have the support of his comrades; but even when this is the case it is often quite difficult; sometimes a thousand shoulders tremble under the burden that was actually meant for one alone. At such times Josephine thinks her time has come. She is already standing there, this delicate creature, quivering alarmingly, especially under her chest; it is as though she had collected all her strength in her song, as though everything about her that did not immediately serve her song, every strength, almost every possibility of life, were extracted, as though she were laid bare, sacrificed, turned over to the protection of benevolent spirits, as though, fully extracted from herself, living in her song, she could be killed by the passing of a cold breeze. But precisely at such a sight we so-called opponents are in the habit of saying to ourselves: "She can't even whistle; she has to go through such horrible exertions to force out something that is not song — we are not talking about song — but is more or less ordinary whistling." This is how it seems to us, but, as already mentioned, no matter how unavoidable this impression is at first, it is superficial and passes quickly. Soon we are also immersed in the feeling of the crowd, who listen warmly, body against body, breathing anxiously.

And in order to gather together this crowd of our people, who are almost always in motion, rushing back and forth between destinations that are often not very clear, Josephine must usually do nothing but take up the attitude that indicates her intention to sing — her little head is leaned back, her mouth half open, her eyes directed toward the heavens. She can do this wherever she wants, it needn't be a place visible from far off: any hidden corner, chosen on an accidental, momentary impulse, is equally serviceable. The news that she wants to sing spreads immediately, and soon it draws in processions. Now, sometimes there are obstacles; Josephine likes particularly to sing in times of excitement, many cares and afflictions force us to take different paths, even with the best intentions one is unable to assemble as quickly as Josephine would like, and if she should stand in her great pose for a while with an insufficient number of listeners — then admittedly she becomes angry, stamps her feet, curses ungirlishly, and even bites. But even such behavior does no harm to her reputation; instead of making some effort to contain her demands, people do their best to meet them; messengers are sent out to round up listeners (this is kept secret from her); on the paths one sees posts set up in the vicinity, waving to the people who are approaching that they should hurry; all of this until a reasonable number of listeners has finally gathered.

What causes the people to go to such trouble for Josephine? A question that is no easier to answer than that of Josephine's song, to which it is also bound. One could cross it out and combine it entirely with the latter question, if it were possible to claim that the people were unconditionally devoted to Josephine's song. This, however, is not the case; our people have hardly any familiarity with unconditional devotion; this people, who love harmless slyness more than anything else, the childish mumbling, the admittedly innocent gossip that moves only the lips, such people cannot dedicate themselves unconditionally, and of course Josephine feels this too; it is this she fights against with all the effort of her weak throat.

However, one cannot take such generalizations too far; the people are dedicated to Josephine, but not unconditionally. They would, for example, not be capable of laughing at Josephine. One can admit to oneself that there is much about Josephine that invites laughter; in and of itself we are always close to laughter; despite all the suffering of our lives, a soft laughter is, to a certain extent, always at home with us, but we do not laugh at Josephine. Sometimes I have the impression that the people understand their relationship to Josephine — this frail being, in need of protection, somehow set apart, in her opinion set apart because of her song — as though she had been entrusted to them and that they must take care of her; no one knows the reason for this, but the fact seems to be undeniable. One does not laugh in regard to that which one has been entrusted; to do so would be a breach of duty; there is nothing more malicious than what the most malicious among us inflict upon Josephine when they say: "Laughter abandons us when we see Josephine."

Thus the people look after Josephine in the manner of a father who adopts a child that has extended its little hand — one is not sure whether pleading or demanding — to him. One would think that our people would not be capable of fulfilling such fatherly responsibilities, but in reality, at least in this case, they meet them in an exemplary fashion; no single person would be capable of doing what in this regard the people as a whole are in a position to do. Of course, the difference between the people's strength and that of an individual is so enormous that it is enough for them to pull their charge into the warmth of their proximity for him to be sufficiently protected. Still, no one dares to speak to Josephine of such things. "I whistle at your protection," she says then. "You can whistle all you like," we think.

Besides, it is really not a refutation when she rebels; it is rather the way of a child and a childish expression of gratitude, and the way of a father is not to bother about it.

However, something else plays a role in this affair, and it cannot be so easily explained with reference to this relationship between Josephine and the people. Josephine is namely of the opposite opinion; she believes that she is the one who protects the people. Her song allegedly saves us from a bad political or economic situation, it brings about nothing less than this, and if it does not drive away the misfortune, it at least gives us the strength to bear it. She does not express it in this way, nor in any other. Overall she says very little, among the blabbering mouths she is silent, but it flashes from her eyes, and it can be read from her closed mouth (there are few among us who can keep their mouths closed, she can). At every piece of bad news — and on many days they overrun each other, among them those that are false or only half-true — she rises immediately. Though at other times she gravitates tiredly to the floor, she rises and extends her throat and, like a shepherd before a thunderstorm, seeks an overview of her flock.

It is true that children present similar demands in their wild, undisciplined manner, but Josephine's demands have a basis that these other demands are lacking. Of course she does not save us, nor does she give us strength; it is easy to present oneself as the savior of this people, who are accustomed to suffering, unsparing of themselves, quick in their decisions, well-acquainted with death, only seeming to be anxious in the atmosphere of wild courage in which they constantly live, and moreover are just as fertile as they are daring — it is easy, I say, to present oneself after the fact as the savior of this people who have always found some way to save themselves, even if there were also some victims, in regard to whom the historians — in general we neglect history completely — are paralyzed with horror. But it is nevertheless true that in times of crisis we listen to Josphine's voice even more attentively than at other times. The threats that hang above us make us quiter, more modest, more submissive to Josephine's dictatorial tendencies; we are happy to assemble, happy to press against each other, especially since the reason for the gathering is so distant from the torment of the real issue; it is as though, quickly (yes, haste is necessary, and

Josephine forgets this all too often) we collectively drank one more glass of peace before the battle. It is not so much a vocal performance as a popular gathering, and yet a gathering that is completely silent except for the little whistling at the front; the hour is far too serious for anyone to think of wasting it with talk.

Of course, such a relationship could never satisfy Josephine. Despite all the nervous discomfort that fills Josephine because of her position, which has never been fully clarified, she is blinded by her self-assurance, and because of this there is much she does not see; without any great effort it is possible to make her overlook even more; to this end, which is to say, to a generally useful end, a mob of flatterers is always at work — however, Josephine would certainly never sacrifice her song only to sing off to the side, unnoticed, in the corner of a popular gathering, even if this in itself would hardly be a trivial matter.

But she does not have to, because her art does not go unnoticed. Although we are essentially occupied with completely different concerns, and the silence hardly exists for the sake of the song alone, and many do not even look up, but instead press their faces into their neighbor's pelt, and Josephine's exertions up there seem to be in vain, some of her whistling — this cannot be denied — inevitably penetrates to us. This whistling, which rises where silence has been imposed on everyone else, comes to the individual almost like a message from the people; Josephine's frail whistling in the midst of grave decisions is almost like the pathetic existence of our people in the midst of the tumult of the hostile world. Josephine, this non-entity in terms of voice, this non-entity in terms of achievement, asserts herself and finds a way to us; it does one good to consider this. Should there ever be a true vocal artist among us, we would certainly find him unbearable at such times, and would unanimously reject the senselessness of such a performance. May Josephine be spared the realization that our listening to her is a proof against her song. She certainly suspects it — why else would she deny so strenuously that we listen to her? — but she continues to sing, and whistles past her suspicion.

But even if it were otherwise, there would still be something to comfort her: to a certain extent we do genuinely listen to her, and probably in much the same way that one listens to a vocal artist; she achieves effects that a vocal artist would try in vain to achieve with us, and which are granted solely to her insufficient means. This is primarily connected to our way of life.

Among our people there is no youth, and scarcely even a brief period of childhood. Periodically, demands are made that the children be guaranteed a special freedom, a special exemption; they have a right to a little freedom from worries, a little senseless romping around, a little play, and one would like to acknowledge this right and help to fulfill it; such demands are made and almost everyone approves of them, nothing could be more deserving of approval, but, given the actual circumstances of our lives, nothing is less likely to be granted; one approves of the demands, one makes efforts toward this end, but soon everything is as it was before. Our life is such that as soon as a child is able to walk a little and make out a little of its environment, it must immediately care for itself like an adult; the regions in which economic considerations force us to live dispersed are too large, our enemies are too numerous, the dangers which have been prepared for us too difficult to foresee — we cannot keep the children from the struggle for existence; if we did, it would mean their premature end. Still, in addition to these sad reasons there is an elevating one: the fertility of our species. One generation — and each is numerous — puts pressure on the others; the children do not have time to be children. If the children of other peoples are carefully looked after, if schools are established for the little ones, if children, the future of the people, stream forth from these schools every day, for a long time, from one day to the next, they are always the same children who emerge. We have no schools, but the vast hordes of our children stream from our people at the shortest possible intervals — joyously hissing or peeping, as long as they cannot yet whistle, writhing, or rolling further on because of the pressure, as long as they cannot yet walk, awkwardly sweeping everything along with them because of their sheer mass, as long as they cannot yet see, our children! And not, as in those schools, the same children, no, always, always new ones, without end, without pause, scarcely does a child appear than it is no longer a child — behind it press the childish faces, rosy with happiness, indistinguishable in their number and their haste. This admittedly also has its positive aspects, and others might justifiably envy us because of it, but we are unable to give our children a real childhood. And this has its consequences. A certain residual, ineradicable childishness permeates our people; in exact contradiction to our best quality, our infallible practical understanding, we sometimes behave quite foolishly, and exactly in the same way that children behave foolishly: senselessly, wastefully, magnanimously, carelessly, and all of this often just for some trivial amusement. And if our joy at this naturally cannot have the full force of childish joy, something of it certainly remains. Josephine, moreover, has always profitted from our people's childishness.

But our people are not only childish; in a certain sense we are also prematurely old; among us childhood and old age arise differently than they do among other peoples. We have no youth, right away we are adults, and we are adults for too long: because of this a certain fatigue and hopelessness runs through the essence of our people, who as a whole are so tenacious and optimistic. Our unmusicality is probably also connected to this; we are too old for music, its stimulation, its upswing are not suitable to our gravity; we tiredly wave it aside; we have retreated to whistling; a little whistling now and then, this is what is appropriate for us. Who knows if there is any musical talent among us; if it did exist the character of our comrades would repress it before it even began to develop. On the other hand, Josephine can do just as she likes: she can whistle or sing, or whatever she calls it; this doesn't bother us, we find it appropriate and are able to bear it; if it should contain something of music, this is reduced to the greatest possible triviality; a certain musical tradition is being preserved, although we do not make the slightest effort toward this end.

But, although the people feel this way, Josephine gives them even more. At her concerts, and especially during serious times, only the very young are interested in the singer as such, they are the only ones who watch with amazement as she puckers her lips, expels the air from between her pretty little front teeth, swoons in admiration for the notes that she herself brings forth, and uses this fainting spell to spur her on to new results that she finds more and more incredible. However, as is clearly discernible, most of the crowd have withdrawn into themselves. Here, in the sparse pauses between the battles, the people dream; it is as though the group released the individual, as though the restless one were allowed, for once, to stretch out in the large, warm bed of the people. And within these dreams one sometimes hears Josephine's whistling; she calls it effervescent, we call it irritating; in any case it belongs here as it does nowhere else; otherwise music hardly ever finds an appropriate moment. Within it there is something of the poor, short childhood, something of the lost happiness which will never be found again, but also something of today's working life, of its small, incomprehensible and nevertheless enduring and inextinguishable cheerfulness. And all of this is really not said with great notes, but lightly, in a whisper, confidentially, and sometimes a little hoarsely. Of course it is a whistle. What else could it be? Whistling is the language of our people, often someone whistles his whole life without knowing it; here, however, whistling is freed from the restraints of everyday life, and for a short time it frees us as well. These performances are certainly not something we would want to miss.

However, it is a long way from here to Josephine's claim that she gives us new strength at such times, etc., etc. For normal people, it should be noted, and not for Josephine's flatterers. "How could it be otherwise" — they say with unbridled audacity — "how else could one explain the great draw, especially with the threat of immediate danger, when the performances have sometimes even prevented the sufficient, timely defense against precisely this danger." Now, the last part is unfortunately true, but it does not contribute to Josephine's glory, especially if one adds that, when such gatherings have unexpectedly been broken up by the enemy and many of us have been forced to sacrifice our lives, Josephine, who is responsible for the whole thing, yes, and has perhaps attracted the enemy with her whistling, was always in possession of the safest place, protected by her followers, and very quietly and with all haste was the first to disappear. But this is basically known to everyone, and nevertheless they hurry forth the next time Josephine, as she chooses, rises to sing. One could conclude from this that Josephine stands almost outside the law, which allows her to do whatever she wants, even when she endangers the people as a whole, and that everything is forgiven her. If this were true, Josephine's claims would also be completely understandable; yes, if the people gave Josephine this freedom, this extraordinary gift which is given to no one else and which actually refutes the law, one could, to a certain extent, see in this an admission that, just as Josephine claims, the people do not understand her, helplessly admire her art, do not feel worthy of her, use positively desperate means to compensate for the harm they do her and, just as her art is beyond their comprehension, also put her person and her wishes outside their power to command. Now, this is completely untrue; perhaps the people capitulate to Josephine too quickly in regard to individual details, but they capitulate unconditionally to no one, and also not to her.

For a long time, perhaps since the beginning of her artistic career, Josephine has been fighting for an exemption from work because of her song; she should be relieved of the care for her daily bread and everything that is connected with our struggle for existence, and the burden should be shifted — probably — onto the people as a whole. Someone quick to enthusiasm — and such people exist — could discern the inner justification of this demand from its peculiarity alone, from the state of mind that is capable of coming up with such a demand. However, our people draw other conclusions, and simply refuse the demand. They also do not exert much effort in refuting the grounds for the petition.

Josephine points out, for example, that the strain of work harms her voice, that while the strain of work is modest in comparison with that of song, it still takes from her the possibility of sufficiently resting after a song and strengthening herself for the next song; she must exhaust herself completely, and under these conditions she can never attain her best performance. The people listen to her and disregard her. This people, so easy to move, sometimes cannot be moved at all. Sometimes the rejection is so severe that even Josephine stops short; she seems to obey, works in the proper fashion, sings as well as she can, but all of this only for a while; then she takes up the struggle with new strength, of which she seems to have an infinite amount.

Now, it is clear that Josephine is not actually striving for what she literally demands. She is rational, she has no aversion to work, the aversion to work is completely unknown to us, even after the fulfillment of her demand she would certainly live no differently than she does now, work would not stand in the way of her song, and her song would not become any more beautiful — she is striving simply for the public, unambiguous acknowledgment of her art, an ackowledgment that will last through the ages and rise above everything that has been known up until now. However, while everything else seems attainable to her, this is stubbornly refused her. Perhaps she should have directed her attack in another direction from the very beginning, perhaps she herself now sees the mistake, but she can no longer retreat, a retreat would mean she was being untrue to herself, and she must stand or fall with this demand.

If she really did have enemies, as she says, they would be able to watch this battle with amusement, and without lifting a finger. But she has no enemies, and even though some of us occasionally raise objections against her, this battle amuses no one. Even if only because in this case the people appear in their cold judicial stance, which one otherwise sees very seldom. And even if one might condone this stance in this case, the mere thought that the people might act similarly regarding oneself excludes any possibility of joy. The rejection is similar to the demand in that it does not concern the thing itself, but rather the people's ability to decide against one of their own comrades so inscrutably, and that much more inscrutably considering how they usually care for these same comrades, paternally, and more than paternally, humbly.

If an individual stood in the people's place, one could believe that this man would have surrendered to Josephine all along, only to end his beneficence when she made her last, incessant, burning request; he would have surrendered a superhuman amount in the firm belief that his generosity would nevertheless find its proper bounds; yes, he would have surrendered more than was necessary just to accelerate the matter, only to spoil Josephine and force her to constantly new demands, until she raised her last demand; then, abruptly, because he had prepared it so far in advance, he would have produced the final rejection. Now, this is clearly not the way things are, the people do not need such tricks; besides, their admiration for Josephine is sincere and proven, and Josephine's demand is so extreme that an unbiased child could have predicted the result; nevertheless, it could be that such conjectures also play a role in Josephine's perception of the affair and add a bitterness to the pain of the rejection.

But even if she makes such conjectures, she does not let them scare her away from the battle. And recently the battle has become more intense. While before she only conducted it with words, she is now starting to use other means, which in her opinion are more effective, but in our opinion are more dangerous for her.

Many believe that Josephine is becoming so insistent because she feels she is getting old, her voice is showing signs of weakness, and because of this it seems to be high time to conduct her last battle for recognition. I don't believe this. Josephine would not be Josephine if this were true. For her there is no growing older and no weakening of her voice. When she demands something, she is not brought to it by external factors, but by inner necessity. She is reaching for the highest garland not because it is hanging a little lower for the moment, but because it is the highest; if it were in her power, she would hang it even higher.

Nevertheless, this disdain for external difficulties does not prevent her from using the most undignified methods. To her, her justification seems beyond doubt; therefore, what does it matter how it is attained; in the world as she imagines it, dignified methods are precisely the ones that must fail. Perhaps it is also because of this that she has shifted the battle from the realm of song to one that is less dear to her. Her followers have circulated remarks by her, according to which she feels capable of singing in such a way that it would be a genuine pleasure for everyone at every level of society, including the most clandestine opposition, genuine pleasure not in the people's sense, since they maintain they have always felt this pleasure at Josephine's song, but pleasure in the sense that Josephine longs for. However, she adds, since she cannot falsify the high or flatter the base, things must remain exactly as they are. But it is different with her battle for an exemption from work; though it is also a battle for the sake of her song, she does not fight directly with the precious weapon of the song itself; every means she uses is therefore good enough.

Thus, for example, some people spread the rumor that she would shorten the coloraturas if her demands were not met. I know nothing about coloraturas and have never noticed any trace of them in her song. However, Josephine wants to shorten the coloraturas. For the time being she will not do away with them, but will just shorten them. Supposedly she has made good her threat, but I for one have noticed no difference from her earlier performances. The entire people listened as always, without saying anything about the coloraturas. And the treatment of her demand has not changed. Moreover, just as there is something truly charming about Josephine's form, there is undeniably something charming about the way she thinks. Thus, for example, after that performance, as though her decision in regard to the coloraturas had been too harsh or too sudden, she explained that next time she would once again sing the coloraturas in their entirety. But after the next concert she reconsidered, and now the great coloraturas are gone for good, and they are not to return until a decision is made in Josephine's favor. Now, the people ignore all these explanations, decisions and changed decisions just as an adult deep in thought ignores the babbling of a child, essentially benevolent, but beyond reach.

Josephine, however, does not give in. Thus, for example, she recently suffered a foot injury at work which makes it difficult for her to stand during her song; yet, since she can only sing while standing, she must now shorten her songs. Although she limps and lets her followers support her, no one believes that she has really been injured. Even admitting the particular sensitivity of her little body, we are a people of workers and Josephine is one of us; if, however, we decided to limp because of every bruise, the entire people would never stop limping. But even though she lets herself be led around like a cripple, even though she appears in this pitiful condition more often than she does otherwise, the people listen to her song with gratitude and delight, just as before, though they make no fuss over the shortening of the performance.

Since she cannot continue limping forever, she invents something else; she pleads fatigue, irritability, weakness. So in addition to the concert we also have drama. Behind Josephine we see her followers, begging and imploring her to sing. She would like to, but she can't. They comfort her, flatter her, practically carry her to the place where it has already been decided that she should sing. Finally, with incomprehensible tears, she gives in. With what is obviously an extremity of will she tries to begin singing, faintly, her arms not extended as usual but hanging lifelessly from her body, giving one the impression that they might be a little too short — she tries in this way to begin singing, once again it doesn't work; this is indicated by an involuntary jerk of her head, and she collapses before our eyes. But then she struggles to her feet and sings, I believe, not much differently than at other times; perhaps if one has an ear for the subtlest nuances one might discern a little unusual excitement, but this only improves the performance. And when it is over she is actually less tired than before; she departs with a firm step — to the extent that her scurrying tripping can be described this way — refusing any help from her followers and regarding the crowd with cold glances as they respectfully clear the way for her.

That was how it was last time. However, the most recent development is that, at a time when her song was expected, she has disappeared. Not only her followers are looking for her; many people have been enlisted in the search; it is all in vain; Josephine has disappeared, she doesn't want to sing, she doesn't even want to be begged to sing, this time she has left us for good.

It is strange, clever as she is, how badly she reckons, so badly that one might believe she does not reckon at all, but is instead pushed along by her destiny, which in our world can only be a very sad one. She herself withdraws from the song, she herself destroys the power she has won over our souls. How could she have won this power if she knows so little about these souls? She hides and does not sing, but the people, quiet, without visible disappointment, imperious, a well-balanced mass, who really, even if appearances speak against it, only give gifts and can never receive them, not even from Josephine, these people continue on their way.

For Josephine, however, things can only get worse. The time will soon come when she will sound her last whistle and fall silent. She is a minor event in the eternal history of our people, and the people will overcome the loss. Of course it won't be easy for us; how will the gatherings be possible in complete silence? But weren't they silent even when Josephine was there? Was her actual whistling significantly louder and more lively than the memory of it will be? Was it anything more than a memory while she was still alive? Didn't the people rather, in their wisdom, value Josephine's song so highly because precisely in this sense it could never be lost?

Perhaps after all there is not much that we will miss, but Josephine, freed from earthly pains, which in her opinion are prepared for the chosen, will cheerfully vanish in the vast crowd of our people's heroes, and soon, since we record no history, will, in heightened deliverance, be forgotten like all her brethren.

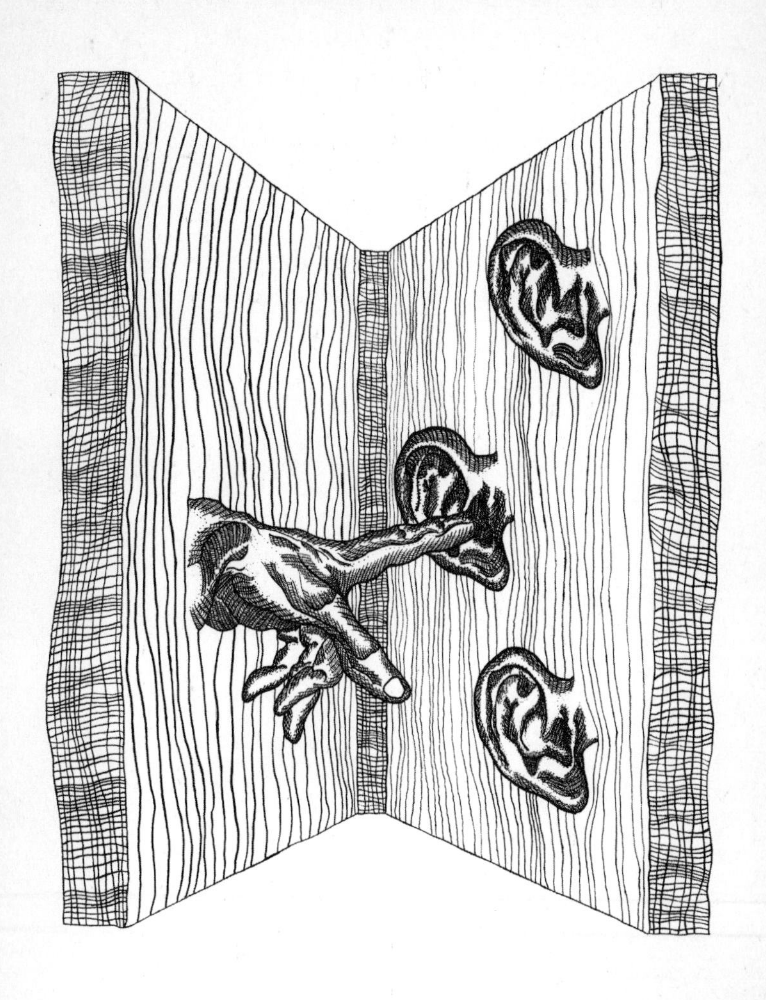

A Hunger Artist
Franz Kafka

originally published in German as *Ein Hungerkünstler*
(Berlin: Verlag Die Schmiede, 1924)

Translated by Kevin Blahut
Illustrations by Helena Vlčnovská

Set in Janson

Published by Twisted Spoon Press
P.O. Box 21 — Preslova 12
150 21 Prague 5, Czech Republic
info@twistedspoon.com
www.twistedspoon.com

Printed in the Czech Republic

Distributed to the trade in North America by

SCB DISTRIBUTORS
15608 South New Century Drive
Gardena, CA 90248-2129
toll free: 1-800-729-6423
info@scbdistributors.com
www.scbdistributors.com

10 9 8 7 6 5 4 3

ECHO

ARCHERS CREEK #1

BY

GEMMA WEIR

Echo

The Archer's Creek Series #1

Published by Hudson Indie Ink

www.hudsonindieink.com

Echo/Gemma Weir – 2nd ed.

ISBN-13 - 978-1-913769-92-5

Karen,

For Martin, Sophie, Eddie & Myles.

I finally stopped talking about it and just bloody well did it!

#welcometoarchescreek

E ♡ xx

ONE

Olivia

"Fuck, fuck, *fuck*! I fucking hate Texas," I cry, slinging my backpack to the floor. The heavy bag lands on my foot and shooting pain explodes up my leg. "Bollocks," I hiss, scowling at the godforsaken backpack before giving it a kick with my uninjured foot. "Stupid fucking bag. Stupid fucking bus."

Muttering angrily, I lean down to grab my bag but the sound of a raspy chuckle from behind me makes me freeze to the spot.

Ass in the air, bent at the waist, I turn my head to find the source of the sound. Starting at the tarmac, my gaze glides over a huge tyre, across shiny chrome, then slowly tracks backward till I find a huge leather boot. Realising how absurd I must look, I straighten, awkwardly tugging at the fabric of my tank, before I slowly turn around and face him.

My eyes widen as I take in the full image of the biker god in front of me. Jesus, he's huge. His strong, thick thighs are spread astride a badass Harley motorcycle, the polished chrome sparkling in the morning sunlight. A tight white T-shirt stretches taut over his bulging muscular chest, partially hidden by a soft looking black leather vest. I eagerly take in the tattoos that look to cover his arms down to his knuckles and peak tantalizingly out of the neck of his shirt.

His hair is dark, almost black, short at the sides but longer, shaggy and tousled on the top. It's the type of hair you pull when you're mid orgasm and god, I want to reach out and run my fingers through it just to see if it's as soft as it looks. Forcing my hands into my pockets, I finally allow myself to focus on his face. A silent gasp falls from my lips because he's beautiful. Somehow both masculine and pretty at the same time, with perfectly chiseled cheekbones, a strong jaw, and full lips that are spread into an amused grin as he watches me check him out.

Embarrassed at being caught, I feel heat bloom in my cheeks. "Hi, err, can I help you?"

"No thanks, darlin', I'm happy watching," he says, pulling a long drag from his cigarette and lazily blows the smoke into the air as his eyes unashamedly glide over my body.

My skin heats under his appraisal, but I fight my instant sexual reaction to him and raise my eyebrows snarkily. "You having fun over there?" I snap, mimicking him, as I rake my eyes over his ripped jeans, pausing on the visible bulge beneath his zipper. Oh my god, is he hard?

"Sugar, I'm enjoying every minute," he drawls, the corner of his mouth twitching into a cocksure grin.

My lips part, as instant arousal pulses to life in my stomach. This guy, this biker god, has literally made my panties wet with his smooth as whiskey southern accent and his grin that promises all kinds of dirty, sweaty fun. Jesus, if this is how they make the men in Texas I wish I'd come here earlier.

Shaking my head, I pull in a deep breath, hoping enough air will dissolve this lust haze I'm in, and put my brain back in charge. "Okay, show's over, buddy, so buh-bye," I say sardonically, willing myself to turn away from his magnetic gaze, but knowing that I won't.

He doesn't move.

For some reason his inaction, brings all of the anger and annoyance I was taking out on my stupid backpack before he arrived surging back to the surface. "For god's sake. I'm having the day from hell, so can you please just fuck off and let me be pissed off in peace?"

Instead of leaving, or at least saying something, he leans forward onto the handlebars of his motorcycle and chuckles indulgently, like I'm just the cutest thing in the fucking world.

Incredulous anger ignites in my stomach. "Are you serious? Where the hell is all this Southern charm and Texas hospitality I was promised?"

Grabbing my bag from the floor, I turn to leave, but before

I get two steps, his hand on my elbow stops me and my flesh tingles where his skin touches mine.

Biker Boy's off his bike and beside me, so close his woody, clean scent surrounds me as his body heat warms my skin. "I'm sorry, sugar. Tell me what's happened, and maybe I can help," he drawls.

I glance down at his tattooed hand, his thick fingers wrapped around my arm, his thumb stroking caressing circles across my skin. Slowly I lift my head, and our gazes lock, intensity sparkles in his sea-green depths and his stroking movement stops, as he slowly trails his hand down my arm, reluctantly freeing me at the tips of my fingers.

Stepping back, I release the breath I hadn't realised I'd been holding. "My bus broke down this morning. I went to get coffee, and now it's gone and I'm stuck here. Wherever the hell here is?"

Biker Boy lifts his hand to his head, running his fingers through his hair. "Shit," he hisses.

I close my eyes, a short, bitter laugh escaping me. "Yep. Shit. That pretty much sums it up," I sigh, opening my eyes, feeling the warm sun above me as it beats down on the barren roadside. The sounds of crickets chirping, and the small town behind us bustling with life filling the silence that's hanging between me and the gorgeous stranger.

"Where were you headed?" he asks, his voice pulling my attention.

Staring at his full, pouty lips, my mind blanks and I have to shake my head, to clear the haze his presence seems to create. "El Paso."

"You on vacation or is El Paso home?" he asks.

"Neither, I'm travelling," I reply.

"Travelling where?"

"Wherever takes my fancy. It's all part of my great American adventure," I say, smiling widely.

Biker Boy rubs his bottom lip with his thumb, his lazy movement so effortless, I can't take my eyes off him. God, he's the hottest thing I've ever seen, and the cheeky tilt of his head and the twinkle in his eye says he knows exactly what I'm thinking.

He smirks at me. "Well, sugar, welcome to Archer's Creek."

An unwelcome blush spread across my cheeks and his smirk changes into a predatory grin. "What's your name?"

"Olivia."

Knowing smirk still firmly in place, he steps towards me, reaching out to gently trace my jaw with the tips of his fingers. "Olivia. That sure is a pretty name," he says, trailing a path along my cheek, until his thumb is beneath my chin, keeping my eyes fixed firmly on his. "Sugar, the way you're looking at me right now, like you wanna lick me. You need to stop it, else I'm gonna strip you naked and spread you out like dessert in about two seconds. I got no problem with that at all, but it seems as though I should give you fair warning."

The pad of his thumb pulls down on my bottom lip and I swear, I can actually hear my brain shouting at me to beg him to do exactly what he just said. But I can't fuck a random biker I just met, can I?

Reluctantly stepping backwards, his fingers fall from my face and I slowly edge away from his magnetic pull. "Okay. Well, this has been interesting," I whisper, forcing myself to take another step away from him. "Texas, and you, have certainly made an impression, but I'm gonna go now," I motion over my shoulder towards the small town, "and see if there's any way of getting to El Paso by the end of the day. So, er, bye," I mumble, turning away as warm fingers touch my skin again and his hand on my elbow stops me.

Like a moth drawn to a flame, I risk a glance over my shoulder and my gaze meets his.

"Echo. I'm Echo," he says.

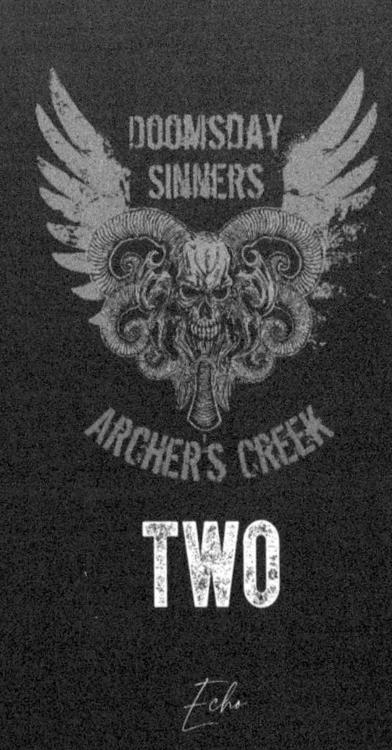

TWO

Echo

Fuck.

My cock's so hard it's trying to force its way out of my jeans.

I should have ridden past and ignored the crazy person screaming and swearing like a sailor on the side of the street, but one look at her never-ending legs and those perfect fucking tits and I couldn't keep my eyes on the road. When that first "Fuck" fell from her lips in that sexy British accent, my dick was hard and I was hitting the brake and pulling over to watch the show.

This bitch is a walking wet dream, she screams sex, all angry attitude and fire. Fuck, it's been a long fucking time since I've seen pussy this hot.

Her dark hair's curly and kind of a mess—perfect to bury

my fingers in and pull while I pound into her from behind. She's built like a pinup girl, curves that just won't stop and a body that was made to fuck. I don't remember the last time I was this turned on by a woman who was fully dressed and my mind is overflowing with all the dirty things I want to do to her.

She's hot for me. I can see it in her dilated pupils and her rock-hard nipples that are straining against the fabric of her shirt despite the heat of the day. Her body's screaming at me, showing me just how turned-on she is.

Her body turns, walking away, but I can't let her, I have to fuck her and I can see she feels the same.

She wants me, and I want her; it's simple. Sex doesn't have to be complicated, sometimes it's just naked, sweaty fun. Get in, fuck, get out. No strings, no drama, and no commitment.

I'm not against relationships. I see the boys at the club who are still hot for their old ladies ten years on. Some so hot for each other we find them fucking all over the club, but I've never found pussy who can keep me interested enough for a second round, let alone a permanent commitment.

But Olivia is one seriously hot fucking bitch, and I want her in my bed as soon as fucking possible. Before I even realize what, I'm doing, my fingers are wrapped around her arm, and her scent and potent arousal is surrounding me.

Leaning into her, I breathe her in deeply, committing the smell to memory. "Echo, I'm Echo," I tell her, as my already hard cock kicks against my jeans, eager to introduce himself too.

With my grip on her arm, I try to turn her towards my bike, but she tenses and tries to pull from my grip. I want her, but maybe here on the side of the road isn't the best place to get naked.

I'm moving too quick, acting like a sex starved fucking caveman, so I force myself to release her arm and take a step back from her. "I'm real sorry, sugar, but there isn't another bus heading out of Archer's Creek to anywhere until tomorrow afternoon."

THREE

Olivia

"Fuck," I hiss as the reality of his words settles over me.

"Hell, sugar, anyone ever tell you that you've got a foul mouth?" he snaps angrily, glaring at me.

Clenching my fingers into my palms, I turn to face Biker Boy, aka Echo, and force my lips into a sardonic smile. "I'm so sorry if my language is offending you, but I'm afraid my quota for polite conversation's been used for the day," I hiss. "As much as I appreciate you pulling over to comment on my use of the great British fucking language, I actually have more important things on my mind than what a hot stranger thinks about me swearing. You see I had a free ride to California lined up *if* I could get to El Paso today, but it appears that won't be happening now, and I'm pretty fucking pissed off. So again, I apologise if my foul mouth has affected *you*," I say, my words dripping with sarcasm.

Echo's face darkens, and I step back instinctively. "Sugar, you need to watch your tone or I'm gonna find something better to do with that mouth of yours," he growls.

I shudder, appalled by what he just said, but somehow still turned on, as the low rumble of his voice vibrates straight to my clit. He steps towards me, closing the gap between us, his eyes narrow, his broad shoulders pulled back so he towers over me. Everything about his body language screams dominant, alpha male, and I should be intimidated. Shouldn't I?

But I'm not scared of him. Instead my mouth waters and my tongue bobs out to lick at my suddenly dry lips. I stare at him, unable to move, frozen in the heat of his gaze as my mind floods with erotic images. I imagine taking that final step to him, until we're touching chest to chest. Then I'd sink to my knees at his feet and look up at him, watching the excitement dance in his eyes while his fingers stroke my cheek lovingly before his thick cock slides into my mouth.

"Olivia." At the sound of his voice, I squeeze my eyes closed as the filthy daydream evaporates like mist, replaced with mortified embarrassment.

A low soft chuckle coaxes my eyes open and my gaze moves to him, a heated, knowing look flashing through his eyes as he chuckles lowly, all of the scary, dominant alpha gone, replaced by amusement. "Come on, sugar, let me buy you a drink, and we'll see if we can sort you a way to El Paso tonight."

Lazily stepping forward, he curls his arm around me and pulls me into his side and I let him, hypnotised by his intense maleness. Without thought I lift my hand to his chest, the leather of his vest, warm under my fingertips as I allow him to steer me towards his bike.

One step, two, three, I allow him to guide me, prepared to go where ever he wants, still dazzled by his hotness and the intensity of want I'm feeling for this guy. Then the bright Texas sunlight, bounces off the shiny paintwork of his huge Harley and I freeze to the spot, suddenly aware that we're standing right next to the massive, intimidating motorcycle.

Echo throws his leg over the huge black motorcycle and chuckles to himself. His gaze burning a path along my skin, taking in every detail of my body before he pats the leather seat behind him.

"I'm not getting on that thing with you," I hiss, staring at the metal beast as if it's going to launch itself at me.

"Well now, that's a real shame, sugar," he drawls, the muscles in his arms bulging as he twists the throttle and the engine roars to life. Tilting his head to the side, his eyes take me in as a wry smile spreads across his face, then he winks at me, tipping his chin, before he turns the bike and rides away.

What the hell. A wave of disappointment and an overwhelming sense of loss rips through me as I watch the bike, until he rounds a bend and disappears. He left. All that flirting, and he just left.

Grabbing my bag with a little more force that necessary, I swing it up onto my shoulder, wishing for the hundredth time this trip that I knew how to pack lighter. With one last look in the direction Echo went in, I sigh, then turn around and trudge back up the street, towards the small town and hopefully a bus station.

With each one of my steps I replay the bizarre scene that just played out with Biker Boy. I mean he's hot, seriously hot, but he's hardly the first hot guy I've ever met, though I've never fantasized about giving any of them a blowjob within seconds of meeting them.

Archer's Creek is even smaller than I first thought, just a handful of shops, bars, and a diner, with no signs of a bus station so far. Stopping, I reach into my pocket and pull out my phone, googling for directions to where ever I can buy a bus ticket from, when I feel the hairs on the back of my neck lift.

"Hey sugar," he rumbles from behind me.

Freezing, I feel a swarm of enthusiastic butterflies leaping to attention in my stomach. Spinning around I find Echo crossing the street, his confident stride eating the distance between us until he's beside me and my skin tingles with awareness.

Reaching out, he lifts my bag from my back like it's weightless and flings it over his shoulder. Staring at him, I try to act nonchalant but it's almost impossible when my entire body is sparkling with excited anticipation. I don't know why he's affecting me this way, pulling my bottom lip between my teeth I lift my eyes to his face.

His grin is salacious and full of a lusty promise. “Miss me already, sugar?”

My lips twitch, a smile spreads across my face, and I playfully roll my eyes at him.

Taking my hand possessively in his, he pulls me towards him draping his arm across my shoulders, holding me to his side. The weight of his touch feels natural, like he’s done it a thousand times before, and I glance up at him from beneath my lashes. He towers over my five-foot-eight frame, I’m pretty tall, but I feel dwarfed against his huge, firm chest. He’s a total stranger, but my attraction to him feels instinctive, like it’s so obvious that I shouldn’t fight it.

Mesmerised, I move when he does, letting him tow me up the street until we reach a worn wooden door covered in stickers. Pushing it open, he moves his arm from my shoulders and places his palm flat on the base of my spine, the heat of his touch guiding me into the dimly lit store.

Stepping inside I realise it’s not a store, but a bar, with a neon sign spelling out ‘Strikers’ hanging above a worn wooden bar. A blonde waitress is busy serving customers, but when she spots Echo, she raises a hand in greeting and smiles broadly, her expression becoming quizzical when she sees me. Strong, warm fingers curl around my hip and he leads me to a barstool, lifting me like I weigh nothing as he places me down onto the seat.

Tilting his head to the side, Echo looks at me for a moment, then reaches out, his fingers pushing a loose strand of my hair behind my ear. His touch is intimate, the action of a lover, not a virtual stranger, its unfathomable, but I don't want him to stop.

"What you drinking, sweetheart?" Echo asks.

"Oh, err a beer, please."

Echo's watchful eyes reluctantly turn to the bar. "Brandi, two beers, please."

The waitress grabs the drinks from a cooler and passes them to Echo before resting her hip against the bar and turning her attention to me. "Hi, I'm Brandi," she says, thrusting her hand across the bar.

Reaching over, I shake her outstretched hand. "Olivia," I reply.

Her lips purse and she turns her attention to Echo, raising her eyebrows expectantly. Exhaling dramatically, he rolls his eyes before responding. "Olivia's bus left without her. She's looking for a way to El Paso by tonight."

Her eyes immediately flash back to me and soften sympathetically. "Oh, hon, that's too bad, but there's no buses going out of town until later on tomorrow."

My head falls forward into my waiting hands and I groan in frustration. Strong fingers wrap around the back of my neck, and a shudder of desire breaks through my despair, running down my spine. Echo leans down, his breath warming my skin. "I'm real sorry, sugar."

His fingertips stroke feather-light caresses down my neck to the curve of my shoulder and I slowly lift my head as he cradles my face with his hands. Leaning towards me I can feel his warm, minty breath as it heats a tingling path across my skin. The sound of the bar fades, and the only noise I hear is the loud beat of my own heart.

I stare into Echo's eyes and watch them darken and fill with smouldering desire. In this moment, all I see is him, all I feel is him. All I want and need is him. We're detached from reality, connected and so consumed with each other that we're oblivious to the world happening around us.

Bloody hell, I want him to rip my clothes off and fuck me till I've forgotten my own name, and then do it over and over again for the rest of my life. I don't know what the hell this is between us, but it definitely feels like more than just lust.

"There's a bus tomorrow, hon. Can you get that one?" Brandi's voice shatters my connection to Echo, and the hustle and bustle of the bar returns in a rush, flooding my senses.

Echo's hands slide reluctantly from my face, but his eyes stay locked on mine. The pull to stay connected to him is intense, but I force myself to turn to Brandi. "Nope, tomorrow's too late. I had a free ride lined up, but only if I got there today. A friend of a friend said I could jump on his band's bus and hitch a free ride to California, but they're leaving tonight. I really can't afford to pay for buses all the way across the country to try and catch up with them."

"Oh my God. This. Is. Perfect," Brandi squeals.

Startled, I jump, almost spitting out the beer I'd just

swallowed. I cough, my eyes watering as the beer tries to come back up.

"Have you ever worked in a bar?" she questions excitedly.

I nod cautiously. "Erm, yeah, I worked in my local pub years ago. Why?"

A huge smile lights up her face and she claps enthusiastically. "Problem solved then. You can work here."

I sit up and reply. "I can't work here."

"Why not?" Brandi questions.

Echo's attention moves from Brandi and slowly turns to me. "Yeah, why not, sugar?"

"I'm here on a tourist visa. I can't work, unfortunately. Well, at least not legally, and jail is so not part of the great American adventure."

Echo reaches out and his fingertips gently pinch my chin, tilting my face up to his. "You wanna work here, sugar?"

His touch is distracting, but I force myself to focus and shrug dismissively. "I'd love to work here. God, the money would be amazing, but like I said, tourist visa."

His touch leaves my skin and his perfect face breaks into a breath-taking smile. "Okay, you're hired."

Bereft from the loss of his touch, I snap, "Echo, you can't just say I'm hired. It's against the law. I could be arrested. You could be arrested. Plus, you can't just give me a job; I'm fairly sure whoever owns the bar might have something to say about that."

Echo leans against the bar, relaxed. "Fuck, sugar, take a breath. The club owns the bar, so if you want the job, it's yours."

"What club?"

A dimple pops in his cheek, and I stare at it. What would he do if I licked it?

"The Doomsday Sinners MC."

Laughter bursts from my throat and I laugh so loudly, it takes me a second to realise he's frowning.

"What's so fucking funny, Olivia?" he snaps.

"Are you seriously trying to tell me that this bar's owned by a biker club?" I ask incredulously.

Echo's beautiful face falls into a scowl. "Careful, sugar," he warns. "Yes, the club owns this bar."

I try to swallow past the lump in my throat. "What, like *Sons of Anarchy*?"

Echo nods once, muttering quietly, "Fucking bullshit TV show."

Saliva lodges in my throat. When I finally find my voice, it's small and unsure. "So an actual, real motorcycle club?"

Annoyance is clear on his face, and his gruff voice turns serious. "The Sinners are very fucking real, sugar."

"And you're a member?"

He barks out the one word response. "Yes."

"Well, fuck."

FOUR

Echo

She's getting ready to run. I can see fear in her eyes that wasn't there a minute ago. Fuck, I can't help but love the way she's looking at me, like she's not sure if she should run away from me or straight into my arms.

I want this girl in my bed, and her working for the club is the easiest way to make that happen.

"Olivia." I touch her cheek, but she flinches and backs away from my touch. "Sugar, calm down. The club owns a few businesses in town. Strikers is just one of them."

She rubs her hands over her face, muttering under her breath about not being able to write this kind of shit, and I can't take my eyes off her.

A few seconds later, she looks up, opens her mouth, and then closes it again. She fidgets on her stool, crossing and uncrossing her legs before she finally speaks. "I want to say yes, but what about my visa? If I get caught working illegally, I'll get arrested and deported."

Olivia's big, blue eyes are messing with my brain. Something about her makes me want to help her. I want to promise her that everything's going to be okay, that *I'm* gonna make everything okay for her.

Pulling at my hair, I force my fucked-up protective instincts out of my mind. I throw Olivia a cocky smirk. "Sugar, things run a little differently here in Archer's Creek. You and that fine ass of yours don't need to worry about the cops, or working under the table without a visa. If you're working for the club, we'll make sure the sheriff doesn't bother you."

I can see the reluctance to believe me on her face, and I watch the myriad of emotions pass across her features while she thinks over my offer.

Cupping her chin lightly, I wait for her to look at me. "I promise I won't let anything happen to you." Holding my breath, I fight the urge to pull her into my arms and just kiss her till she agrees to do what I want.

There's just something about this fucking woman. I can't take my eyes off her. I can practically see her thinking, as her trusting blue eyes search my face to see if I'm telling the truth.

Then she nods, surprising the hell out of me. "Okay, why the fuck not? Let's add working for an MC to my CV. When do you want me to start?"

I wasn't expecting her to agree, but I can't dull the bright smile that covers my face at the thought of her staying. Olivia working at the club's bar is perfect, at least until I've fucked her senseless and got rid of all these messed-up feelings she's provoking.

Fucking her is exactly what I need to do. It doesn't matter that she makes my heart bang in my chest in a way that's freaking me the fuck out. It doesn't matter, that I'm forcing myself to walk away from her right now, because if I don't, the urge to sit and watch her perfect fucking ass sway as she works will keep me frozen to the spot.

Fuck, what's wrong with me?

FIVE

Olivia

Echo left, and an hour later, I'm behind the bar wearing a Strikers tank top and staring into space, when a hand touches my shoulder, I squeal and jump.

"Sorry, doll, just thought I'd check on you." Brandi says, smiling, her infectious enthusiasm a welcome change from Echo's charged intensity.

Once I'd accepted the job, Brandi quickly showed me the ropes then left me to serve customers. The bar has finally quietened down, and it looks like it's time to get to know my new co-worker.

"You're from England, right?" she asks.

I laugh at the question I've been asked a thousand times since I got to the US and nod. "Yes."

Brandi props her hip against the wooden bar. "So were you only going to El Paso for the free ride?"

I shrug. "No. Texas was always on my list of must-see states. It's just a happy coincidence that's where the ride was."

"So no boyfriend waiting on you? The guy in the band?"

I shake my head and chuckle. "No, I'm off men."

She pulls over a stool and points for me to sit before hoisting herself up onto the bar. "Okay, so no men. You on women now?" she asks matter-of-factly.

I laugh. "No, I haven't moved onto the fairer sex, I'm just taking a break from men for a while."

"Hmm…" She raises her eyebrows. "That sounds like there's a story."

It's been a long time since I've had a girly gossip, and Brandi's instantly likable so I shuffle, getting comfy on my stool. "My ex decided that I wasn't for him, that he preferred my best friend."

She gasps, her whole body pulling back in outrage. "What a bitch! I hope you slapped the shit out of both of them."

I laugh. "James, my best friend, really isn't that much of a bitch, and no, I didn't hit either of them."

She slaps her hand across her mouth, her eyebrows lifting almost to her hairline. "Your boyfriend cheated on you with your best friend, a guy?"

I nod.

She jumps down from the bar and throws her arms around

me, pulling into an unexpected hug. My head's squashed against her shoulder; it's a little weird, so I just pat her back awkwardly.

Pulling myself from her grip, I step back to regain some personal space. "It's okay. I was pissed at the time, but I'm over it now. The three of us are actually really close."

"No wonder you're off men. You're probably terrified you'll turn the next one gay too," she says, and then slaps a hand across her mouth. Her eyes widen and her shoulders hunch as she pulls in an embarrassed breath. "Oh my god, I'm so sorry. That came out all wrong."

The giggle that escapes me quickly morphs into a full belly laugh, and I laugh so hard tears roll down my face. After a few minutes I pull in a deep, cleansing breath and fan my red cheeks with my hands, swallowing the laugh that's still trying to escape. It takes a few moments more before I can finally speak. "How did you end up working here, Brandi?"

Brandi's cheeks are stained red with embarrassment. "I've been around the club my whole life, and Sleaze gave me the job here."

"Sleaze?"

Her eyes turn dreamy, and a serene smile spreads over her face before she finally speaks. "Yeah, my man. He's in the club with Echo."

I lean forward, suddenly much more interested in our conversation. "So it's an actual biker club?"

She giggles. "Oh, sweetie, you're so cute. Yes, it's a real

biker club. Don't they have MCs in England?"

"Not that I know of. I mean, maybe, but I've never seen any. Bloody hell, if they do and the members all look like Echo, I'm going to track them down and ask to join," I blurt quickly.

Brandi laughs, smiling. "Everyone in Archer's Creek knows the club, but the guys keep to themselves. It's probably the same with MCs in England."

"So how long have you and Sleaze been together?"

"Since I was sixteen. My daddy was a Sinner, but he and my momma didn't really get on, so she tried to keep me away. She moved us out of Texas hoping that my dad wouldn't come visit." Laughing lightly, she smiles fondly before continuing. "My daddy came to see me every other weekend. My momma hated it. Then one time he brought a prospect with him. Sleaze was twenty-one, and I was fifteen. I was head over heels for him from the moment I set eyes on him, but he barely spoke to me. He came with my daddy every single time he visited for almost a year till I turned sixteen. On my birthday, he kissed me, told me that I was his forever, and that was it. We've been together ever since." Brandi blushes, lost for a moment in a memory.

"Wow."

My voice startles her and she looks at me, her smile serene. "A Sinner man is a force to be reckoned with. Once they fall for a woman, they fall hard and fast. They might be bikers, but they're good men."

Dubious and a little confused, I ask, "So they're not all criminals, like the bikers on those TV shows."

"Jesus, Liv, those bikers on the TV might be hot, but that's not real life. The club, it's more like a family. They have their own set of rules. They're loyal to the club, to each other, and the ride free way of life."

After pausing for a moment, I ask, "So what's Echo's story then?"

Brandi smiles at me, eyeing me knowingly. "I don't know much really. He turned up at the club one day straight out of the army, still in his uniform, and just never left."

The door opens and Echo strides in, his long legs eating up the distance to the bar. The air seems to thicken, and all eyes turn to him as he moves through the room. Every woman in the place sees him. They push out their tits and flick their hair, desperate for his attention.

His eyes search the room until he finds me, then the heat in his gaze pins me to the spot. My nipples pebble and my stomach clenches with excited awareness. God, he makes me want to throw myself at him. Does he have that effect on everyone?

When he reaches me, he slips effortlessly onto a stool and leans over the bar, his tattooed fingers tapping against the wood. "How's it going, sugar?"

Folding my arms across my chest, I try to hide my insanely hard nipples. "Good thanks, what can I get you?"

He reaches forward and his fingers wrap around my arm

and stroke my wrist. Pulling my hand from my body, he gently circles the pulse point. "I'll have a beer please. And you. Grab yourself a drink and get your ass around here and come visit with me a minute."

I slide a bottle of beer across the bar, and he grabs it. "Where's yours?"

I'm saved from replying when a woman slinks up to him. She pushes her breasts against his arm, her red nails tiptoe over his leather waistcoat, and she leans over to whisper into his ear. I can't hear what she says, but Echo responds and her face pales. Snarling, he brushes her hand off him, and she quickly scurries away.

"Brandi, Olivia's taking her break now," he shouts. His eyes dare me to disagree, but instead, I grab myself a beer and walk around to his side of the bar.

"Sit," he demands, motioning for me to take his seat as he pulls out another stool and positions it close to mine. Resting his elbow on the bar, he turns his huge body towards me. "How you liking Strikers so far?"

I laugh lightly. "It's going great. I haven't broken a thing yet."

His smile is beautiful, and I instantly smile back at him. He lifts the bottle to his mouth and takes a drink of his beer. A drop of liquid pools on his lower lip, and mesmerized, I stare until his tongue dips out and licks it away.

"So you're travelling? How long you been out in the States for?" he asks.

I scoff. “Travelling—it sounds so cliché, doesn’t it? I’ve been here nearly three months now. Time’s flown by, and there’s still so many things to see.”

He nods thoughtfully. “Where have you been so far?”

Pulling the elastic band from my hair, I run my hands through the curls. “God, so many places. I started off in New York, but it wasn’t for me, so I didn’t stay long. Then I went to Miami, Orlando, Chicago, New Orleans, and a few others. I’ve moved about a lot.”

“Why didn’t you like New York?”

I sigh and look down at my shorts, pulling at the frayed threads that hang from the bottom. “It was too big. Too full. I’ve never felt more alone than I did in a city that’s so full of people. New York is where I always imagined I’d fit in, but instead, it’s where I realised I’ve been pretending to be something I’m not for years.”

His eyes soften in understanding. “I’m not a big-city boy either. Too many corners, too many places to hide. Have you been on your own the whole time?”

“Yep.” I nod. “I worked hard to fund my trip, and I really don’t have that long here, so I wanted to go wherever I pleased. I’ve had to use free rides and favours from friends of friends where I could, because, god, it’s so expensive out here. But I’d rather be on my own than waste my time on someone else’s schedule.”

I glance down when his hand moves to my thigh. His fingers

spread wide across my skin, his touch possessive. I raise my head, and our gazes clash, intensity flaring in his eyes. "What made you decide to go travelling?" he asks.

I take a long pull of my beer and sigh. "I was floundering at home. Crappy job, living with my parents. Everyone else was getting on with their lives, and I was just… not. I needed to escape and have an adventure before the chance passed me by. You know what I mean?"

When he nods, it's like he completely understands. "So where's home in the UK?"

"I grew up near Manchester in a small town out in the country. But right now, I'm not sure where home is."

His thumb strokes back and forth over my leg and goose bumps pebble on my skin. "So what do your boyfriend and your friends and family think of your adventure?"

"My parents were ecstatic. They sold the house and bought a Winnebago before I'd even packed my bags. They said they'd just been waiting for me to move out so they could enjoy their retirement. Last time I spoke to them, they were touring eastern Europe," I say on a laugh.

Our bodies face each other, and like a magnet, I'm drawn to him. Echo pulls his hand from my thigh, and the connection breaks. I feel the loss of him instantly, my skin trembling as I fight the impulse to beg him for his touch.

"And your boyfriend?" he asks, his eyes narrowed.

I shake my head. "No boyfriend, not for a while. My friends

were shocked though, they didn't see me as the backpacking type."

His hand moves back to my thigh, and warmth radiates through my whole body. "Why not?"

I push out a long sigh and look down at my ripped denim shorts, Converse, and T-shirt. "This isn't who I was back home."

A loose curl falls across my face, and Echo reaches for it, pulling gently then tucking it behind my ear. "So who were you then, sugar?"

I can't seem to take my eyes off his hands. Tattoos cover the fronts and swirl down to the words etched across his knuckles. His touch is intimate—too intimate for someone he just met. Forcing my eyes up they lock with his, and potent chemistry crackles between us. "Different," I whisper.

Suddenly, I'm stifled by his presence; I need to get away from him. Finishing my beer, I slide off the stool. "I should get back to work."

His head tilts to the side like he's trying to figure me out. "There's a party at the club tonight. You'll come."

He's not asking. He's telling me, and I'm nodding before I even realise I'm moving.

"See you soon, Olivia." He stares at me intently for a moment then walks away.

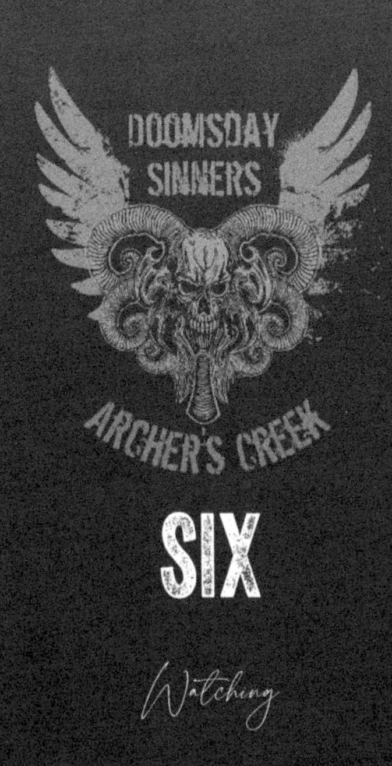

SIX

Watching

I see her.

Watching him.

She's so beautiful.

So innocent.

I want her.

But she's becoming tainted.

I see the stains of impurity bleeding across her skin.

I can save her.

But it's not time yet.

Until then, I'll watch.

SEVEN

Olivia

I watch Echo leave, staring at the door long after he's gone. My racing heart gradually slows, and I scoff at myself.

"Well, hello there, darlin'. You're a new face, ain't ya?"

Pulling my eyes from the door, I focus on the new voice and who it belongs to. He's older than the other guys in the bar, maybe in his sixties or even seventies with a warm, weathered face and mischievous eyes.

"Hi, I'm Olivia." I hold my hand out across the bar, and he takes it in a firm shake.

"Well hello, Miss Olivia, I'm Gus. It's always a pleasure to meet a beautiful young lady," he says with a wink.

I chuckle. "You're a charmer, aren't you, Gus?"

The sound of his deep laugh wraps around me. "It's been a

long while since anyone's called me a charmer, sweetheart. I'll have a beer, please."

As customers flow in and out of Strikers, Gus sits at the bar chatting and drinking while I work. "So, Miss Olivia, where are you from in the UK?"

I hand a drink across the bar to a customer, wait till he leaves, and turn to Gus. "Manchester. It's a big city like London, but no one's ever heard of it."

A knowing smile crosses his face, and he leans forward over the bar. "Young lady, I'll have you know I know exactly where Manchester is. My late wife, Millie, and I spent a lot of time over in England. We stayed several times in a beautiful village not far from Manchester called Disley. Millie loved England. She'd have moved there, but we never got the chance."

My eyes widen in surprise. "Gus, I grew up in Disley. Wow, that's so weird. How on earth did I end up meeting someone in Texas who's visited the town I grew up in?"

Gus sits at the bar, reminiscing about his wife and their time in the UK and I smile happily chatting to my new friend and the closest link to home I've found since I landed in America.

"So, Miss Olivia, what brings you to Archer's Creek?" Gus asks.

I scoff lightly. "I didn't exactly plan to be in Archer's Creek. My bus left without me, so I'm stranded here, at least until I figure out what I'm gonna do next now I'm not going to make it to the bus today." My mouth drops open as my own words sink in. “Oh my god, I don’t have anywhere to stay.” Turning to Gus, I blurt out, “I was supposed to be staying on the bus with the band. But I’m here in this tiny town, and it’s seven at night and I don’t even know if there’s a hotel here.”

Gus reaches out and places a reassuring hand on my arm. “Darlin’, calm down. There isn’t a hotel, but there’s Miss Mimi’s guesthouse.”

“Is that local?”

“Yes, ma’am, just across the road. Miss Mimi’s a little odd, but the rent’s cheap and the rooms are clean,” he says, standing and shrugging on his jacket. “Well, Miss Olivia, it’s been a pleasure meeting you, but my dinner’s calling me, I’ll see y’all again soon.”

“Bye, Gus, it was lovely meeting you too,” I say, waving as he turns and heads for the door. As I watch his retreating back a sigh falls from my lips, Gus reminds me of my grandad, and I fight the urge to chase after him to hug him and see if he smells like mint and soap, like my grandad does.

By the time my shift is over, my feet hurt, I’m sweaty and ready for a shower. Two new waitresses arrive to work the rest of the shift, and I sigh in relief as I walk from behind the bar and collapse onto an empty stool. Brandi crosses the bar towards me, smiling widely and looking unbelievably cool and fresh considering her shift was longer than mine.

“Sweetie you were great, and the next shift will be easier,” she says squeezing my shoulder. “Are you gonna get a room at Miss Mimi’s?” she asks.

"Hopefully. I have no idea what I'm going to do if she doesn't have any rooms available."

"The old crone's always got rooms," Brandi scoffs.

"Oh god, Is she that bad? Is there another motel in town?"

"Nope she's your only option I'm afraid, she's a miserable old bitch who hates the club, but apart from that, the place is okay," she says with a laugh.

"She sounds like a real peach," I say on a groan.

Still laughing, Brandi leans in wrapping her arms wrap around me in a tight hug. "You'll be fine. Go take a shower and we'll come get you in an hour."

"Come get me. Why?"

Pulling her jacket on, she walks toward the door, looking over her shoulder and smirking mischievously at me. "For the party obviously. See you in an hour."

The door swings closed behind her before I have a chance to speak and I'm left staring at the closed door my new enthusiastic friend just left through. Shaking my head, I laugh lightly beneath my breath, then grab my backpack and hook it over my shoulder. Pushing through the exit door, I lift my chin and look across the street to the large house I'm assuming must be Miss Mimi's guest house. The building looks like every scary house, in every Halloween themed movie, I've ever seen. Gothic revival style, a huge archway frames the front door and I climb the steps tentatively, my eyes raking from side to side waiting for something to jump out of the shadows and scare me.

As I reach the front door it swings open just as I raise my fist to knock.

"Welcome to Miss Mimi's guesthouse. I'm Miss Mimi, how may I help you?" A woman wearing pearls and a thick woollen twinset says in a chirpy southern accent.

My eyes widen a little at the stereotypical southern belle in front of me. Her make-up is heavy, and her hair's coiffured into a bizarre halo of backcombed perm. She looks scarily like the pink evil teacher from the Harry Potter books.

Schooling my face into a normal expression I smile. "Hello Ma'am, my name is Olivia Townsend. I was told you might have a room I could rent." The cloud of perfume that surrounds her almost chokes me, and I hold my breath as I wait.

"Well you're in luck dear, I do have a room available." With a flourish, she ushers me into the house and down a corridor to a basic but clean room.

She holds the door open, and I step past her into the bedroom, quickly glancing around the small, but clean space. "This is perfect, thank you."

Miss Mimi smiles woodenly, clasping her hands together in front of her. "Now, Miss Olivia, I have a few rules that I'd ask you to abide by while you're under my roof. These rooms are single sex only, I don't allow any fornicating outside of marriage vows in my home. This is a God-fearing household; I won't accept my guests taking the Lord's name in vain. Pastor Roberts, service on Sunday starts at 9 am, so I'll make room for you in our pew. Breakfast is at 8 am, lunch at 12 noon and dinner at 6.30 pm. Meals are extra, but I don't mind having one more to cook for if you'd like to join us. Here are your keys. The front door is locked from 1 pm to 6 pm, and I'd appreciate it if you were in your room by a reasonable hour."

I nod politely and give her two nights' rent as deposit, waiting patiently as she looks me up and down, then finally turns and leaves. Alone at last, I kick off my trainers and flop down onto the bed. It's been a long day, and the moment my back hits the comforter exhaustion washes over me.

My eyes drift closed and images of Echo flash into my mind.

His scent surrounding me.

His eyes locked on mine.

My breathing becomes shallow, and my nipples harden. My sex throbs as erotic thoughts of Echo's tattooed hand creeping under the waistband of my shorts flash through my mind. Hot and unsatisfied, I squirm against the cool cotton sheets. Fisting the fabric beneath me I let my imagination take over and my fingers become his as they slide down my stomach and into my panties.

His fingers tease my sex, stroking along the sensitive skin. Wet and desperate, my back arches as his thick finger touches my swollen clit, circling it mercilessly. Panting, my hips grind against his hand, the pressure of an orgasm sparking to life deep inside of me. His huge body cages me in, I'm surrounded by him as I beg him silently for more, urging him on as he finally pushed two thick fingers into me, curling them as he tortures my clit. It's perfect agony, absolute bliss, and then my orgasm splinters out of me in an explosion of pleasure.

My eyes crash open.

My chest heaves.

My hand is still inside my shorts as I stare at Miss Mimi's bland white ceiling, my chest heaving as my body tingles, aftershocks of my orgasm still rippling across my skin.

I force my eyes to stay open, if I close them I know I'll lose myself to another Echo based fantasy, instead I drag myself off the bed and pad with shaky legs into the bathroom. Turning on the shower I strip out of my clothes and step immediately under the water, letting it cool my skin and wash away the remains of my orgasm.

Inhaling sharply, I rest my forehead against the tile, exhaling slowly as I let my mind wander over everything that's happened today. My bus broke down, then left without me, leaving me stranded in the middle of Texas. I met the hottest man I've ever seen, got an illegal job working in a bar owned by a biker club and I just got myself off to a fantasy about a man I barely know, in the house of a women who would probably have me smite down by God if she knew what I did on one of her beds.

Once I'm dry and dressed, I stand in front of the mirror and stare at my reflection, taking in how my white dress clings to my body like a second skin. The hem skims my upper thighs, with the fabric dipping tantalisingly low in the back, revealing my entire back almost all the way down to my butt crack. Black leather ankle boots with a chunky heel emphasise my long legs, and my hair is a mass of untamed curls.

Simple yet sexy.

A knock at my door startles me, and opening it, I find a stern-looking Miss Mimi standing in the doorway. "I'm sorry to interrupt you, Miss Olivia, but Brandi and two of those heathens are asking for you. I'd be happy to call the sheriff to get rid of them."

I laugh, assuming she's joking, but her face hardens. "No, that's fine. Brandi's here for me. She's going to show me around," I say quickly.

Miss Mimi scoffs, her face twisting in disapproval. "Olivia, dear, those criminals are not someone a respectable young lady should be associating with. Their sinful behaviour is polluting our town. Spending time with them will only spread their disease into you, like the other disreputable women that associate with them."

Clenching my teeth together to hold back the scathing retort that's on the tip of my tongue, I pull in a slow calming breath before I speak. "Well Miss Mimi, I appreciate your concern and I'll certainly bear that in mind, but if you'll excuse me, Brandi is waiting for me."

EIGHT

Echo

Holy fucking hell.

The front door of Miss Mimi's ugly ass house opens and Olivia emerges wearing a tight white dress; her legs bare, her hair a chaotic mess of curls. As she steps down the steps my eyes are drawn to her nipples visibly pushing against the fabric. Fuck, I want to suck them into my mouth and bite them till she's squirming and desperate.

My gaze drops slowly down the length of her body and I groan, my dick is so hard it's painful. Her dress is short enough to show off her long, tan, sexy fucking legs. Jesus H. Christ, the things I want to do to her, starting with pulling up that dress and wrapping those legs around my waist while I fuck her senseless.

Sleaze's old lady squeals loud enough to pull me from my

fantasy and rushes at Olivia, wrapping her in a tight hug. Sleaze whistles through his teeth. "Would you look at that bitch. That kind of fresh pussy is gonna have the boys lining up to take turns."

I see red and my hands clench into fists. "She's not fucking club pussy, you asshole. None of those stupid bastards are gonna fucking touch her."

I don't know what it is about her, but this woman's under my skin. She's goddamn perfection. I want to fuck her, do all kinds of dirty things with her and to her, but I want more than that too, I want to pull her into my arms and worship her. Sleaze looks shocked. Hell, I've fucking shocked myself. Pussy is pussy, and I've never had a problem passing bitches along to my brothers once I'm done with them.

But Olivia...

Hell. Fucking. No. She's mine.

Mine. What the fuck?

I don't claim bitches. I get my dick wet and then move onto the next. But the thought of one of my brothers touching her makes me itch to claim her, possess her.

This girl is dangerous to me, I need to stay way the hell away from her.

NINE

Olivia

"Hello, Echo," I say, glancing up at the man who was the star of my spank bank less than an hour ago.

Echo's leaning against a shiny black car, his jaw clenched, his hands twisted into tight fists, anger and frustration pouring from him. His eyes seem to blacken and smoulder as he turns his gaze to me, spearing me with furious intensity and I step back, shocked as his silent sneer sends waves of apprehension pulsing through me.

Brandi seems oblivious to the charged standoff Echo and I are engaged in as she hops in front of me, breaking the connection and pulling my attention to the guy standing beside Echo. "Olivia, this is Sleaze," she gushes.

The guy reaches out and hooks Brandi around the waist

pulling her in close. She nestles happily into his chest as he lifts his chin to me in greeting. "Olivia," he says, his voice deep and gruff.

My fingers salute him in an awkward wave, and his mouth twitches into an amused half smile. "Hi," I squeak.

Echo slaps the roof of his car, pulling all of our attention to his scowling expression. "Let's roll. Party's going without us." Then he lowers himself into the sleek black leather seat, his glorious muscles flexing as he moves.

"This is gonna be so much fun," Brandi says excitedly, climbing into the back seat and gesturing hurriedly for me to follow suit.

Laughing I lower myself into the leather seat. "Don't you go to all of the club parties?"

Her smile changes to a grimace. "I go to some of them, old ladies don't really mix with the club whores. Some don't come to the club at all except for the family days," she says, wiggling her hips, dancing in her seat.

I grab her wrist to draw her attention. "Whores, like actual prostitutes?" I hiss, my eyes wide in horror.

"No," she laughs. "They're not real whores, just skanks that hang out at the clubhouse. Girls that want to fuck a biker and don't care which one."

We slow to a stop as we pull up to a high metal gate and a guy bends down, leaning against the car window. "Echo, you're missing all the fun, brother." He's young, maybe nineteen or twenty, when he glances into the back seat and sees me he licks his lips. His eyebrows lift in interest as his gaze drops to eye fuck my boobs. "I see you brought something new and fun back with you. I call dibs on her, she's one fine bitch."

I don't see Echo's arm move until his fist's wrapped around the guy's shirt and he's dragging him through the window and into the car.

"Daisy, I'll cut out your fucking tongue if you ever speak like that about her again. You won't think about her. Hell, if you ever touch her, I'll fucking kill you. You get me?" Echo growls.

Daisy nods quickly, his eyes widening in fear. "Sorry, brother, I didn't know she was yours."

Echo drops Daisy's shirt and pushes him backwards. "Open this fucking gate," he snarls.

"Well fuck, I think things just got interesting." Sleaze chuckles softly.

We pull to a stop in front of a massive warehouse. The building is utilitarian and imposing against the black night sky. Music blares from heavy open metal doors, and people spill from inside, loitering in groups beside the fire pits that are dotted around. I'm grateful when Brandi hooks her arm through mine and leads me into the club.

The room is masked by a smoky haze, but the intense scent of sex permeates the air. Half-naked women dance on the tables as horny men watch with hungry eyes and blatantly hard cocks. My gaze darts frantically around the room before landing on a bald man, his head thrown back in ecstasy, his fingers tangled into a blonde's hair, controlling her movements, pushing and pulling while she sucks his dick.

My heart pounds in my chest with either disgust or desire, but I'm not sure which.

Dragging my eyes from the scene, I look around until my gaze lands on another couple. Unable to look away, I swear I can hear their moans of pleasure mingled with the beat of the music, as a silver fox in a worn leather waistcoat thrusts his hips back and forth, pounding into a curvaceous woman, bent over the arm of a sofa. I can't drag my eyes from the woman's face as she cries out her orgasm, basking in pleasure, completely uninhibited by her audience.

"It's a lot to take in, isn't it?" Brandi says.

I nod, and her hold tightens on my arm.

"Come on, doll. Let's go get some drinks."

Reluctantly I let her pull me forward and we move further into the room. My hands are shaking slightly from the adrenaline that's coursing through my veins and I don't know if it's the debauchery I've already witnessed or just the intense vibe of this place, but I can feel eyes watching me.

Twisting around I glance over my shoulder, searching for Echo and secretly hoping it's his intense gaze I can feel watching me, but he's gone, and a heavy weight of uncertainty settles on my chest.

The guy behind the bar is a beautiful giant. His skin's a warm caramel colour, and his high cheekbones are pronounced like a model's, but his bright, friendly smile dims as we reach him. "Brandi, girl, you know you can't be here on a party night on your own. You know the rules."

Brandi scowls and snaps out, "Smoke, I'm old enough to be your momma, so don't you be telling me what I can and can't do."

Smoke rolls his eyes and shakes his head. "You're barely five years older than me, so cut the bullshit Brandi. You know I've got to call Sleaze and tell him his woman's here. Don't make me do it again, honey, come on."

Brandi throws her hands in the air and shouts, "Oh my god, Smoke, that happened once, nearly three years ago. Sleaze is here, so can we get drinks now?"

"I call bullshit. That man of yours likes your ass pinned to his lap. I don't see him, so go home before you get us both in the shit," Smoke snarls.

She smiles smugly as the crowd parts and Sleaze marches into view. When he reaches us he pulls her into his chest, slinging his arm possessively around her. "Baby, Smoke's refusing to serve me and Liv," she purrs up at him.

Brandi peers around Sleaze's huge body and pokes out her tongue at Smoke before turning back to snuggle into her man's chest, looking up at, her expression so childlike and heartbroken, I have to cover my mouth to hide my grin.

"You refused to serve my old lady and her friend?" Sleaze growls.

Smoke visibly cowers against Sleaze's anger. "I told her she couldn't be here on her own, man."

Sleaze kisses Brandi's forehead affectionately, then turns to Smoke. "You think I'm stupid enough to let my hot-ass old lady come here alone?"

Smoke rubs his mouth with the back of his hand. "No, man, course not."

Sleaze nods stoically. "Now you show my old lady some respect and do your fucking job."

Rising up onto her tiptoes, Brandi leans in and kisses Sleaze sweetly on the mouth. "Thank you, baby," she coos seductively.

An unexpected wave of jealousy washes over me, and I turn so I'm not staring at their intimate moment.

"Well hello, sweetheart." Smoke's purrs melodically, as his gaze roams over my body. "What can I get you?"

"Beer, please," I say, smiling.

Focussing all of his attention on me, he narrows his eyes into a seductive smoulder, his lip twitching into a confident smile. "Is that the only thing I can do for you, sweetheart? I can think of a few more things I could offer that would be more…" he pauses dramatically. "Enjoyable," he drawls, leaning over the bar and running a finger tip across the pulse point on my wrist.

He's so smooth, but his Casanova act isn't really working for me, and I can't help but laugh at his obvious flirting. "Just the beer, please. I think I'm good for everything else," I say, biting my lip to hide amusement.

Obviously delighted by my blatant brush-off, he slaps the bar and barks out a laugh. "Offer's always open, babe. I got loads of suggestions of things I can do for you… or to you." He slides a beer towards me with a wink before walking away.

Carrying our drinks above our heads, Brandi and I weave our way through the mass of bodies till we reach the makeshift dancefloor. The music pulses through me, and I let the heavy bass guide my body. Head back, arms in the air, the rhythm consumes me and my inhibitions melt away.

Several tracks later, I pull my hair from my neck as sweat runs down my heated skin, while my hips still sway to the music. The sensual beat of the song morphs into an energetic bounce, and Brandi and I laugh, twirling around, carefree and happy.

An hour later, my dress is sticking to my damp skin, my hair's a wild mess, and my feet throb. I motion to the bar, and Brandi nods, grabbing my hand and towing me through the crowd, across the room to where Sleaze is sitting. His eyes track Brandi, and as soon as she's within his grasp, he pulls her into his lap, whispering into her ear and holding her close.

While the mountain of a man claims all of my friend's attention, I collapse onto the sofa next to theirs and groan with pleasure. Stretching out my legs, I point my toes and wiggle my bruised feet, glancing up at the bar a few feet away, wishing this place had waitress service. When the sofa cushion next to me depresses, I turn my head and find a man I don't know sitting too close, his presence crowding me. His shoulder-length, white-blond hair frames his angular, beautiful face, his piercing silver-grey eyes assessing me as he tries to draw me in. An intense sense of fear has me edging away from him, my skin crawling at his overpowering energy.

TEN

Echo

I'm desperately trying to ignore her, but I can't take my eyes off her. I've watched her laugh with Brandi and flirt with Smoke. I've watched the way her breasts push against the thin material of her dress and how her ass sways as she dances to the pounding music.

I've watched her, and so has every other horny fucking bastard in the room.

I'm jealous, and I hate it. I want her to be sitting on my lap; I want her dancing with me. Fuck, at this point, I just want to be close to her.

My dick's pressed so hard against the zipper on my jeans, there's an imprint on my cock. I'm a walking fucking hard-on.

I want every horny fucker who thinks she's going home

with him to know she belongs to me.

I need to claim her.

But she's not mine.

I just need to fuck her.

I fight to convince myself that's all I want, just to fuck her. Get her out of my mind and out of my system.

One night of her screaming my name and this desire, this need I have for her, will disappear and she'll be just like the others. A passing fancy.

Puck sits down next to her. Too close to her. Crowding up on her.

He's a sick motherfucker. He likes weird, fucked-up shit. The whores know what they're getting into with him; hell, I think a couple of them even like it.

But not my Livvy. He shouldn't be near her.

I'm on my feet, walking towards her before I've even decided to move, because that fucker just put his hand on her leg. She's not mine to protect, but I don't fight the instinct.

He doesn't get to touch her.

I want her to belong to me. I want to claim her and have her claim me back.

The red mist descends.

He doesn't get to breathe the same air as her.

She's. Mine.

ELEVEN

Olivia

Creepy guy's hand touches my thigh and a cold sense of dread radiates through me. I go to push him off, when I see Echo ploughing through the crowds, shoving people out of his way as he storms across the room. Seconds later, he looms over us, his body tense, fists clenched.

Wrapping his hands around creepy guys shirt, Echo drags him from the sofa and slams him into the wall, holding him in place by his neck. Anger morphs Echo's beautiful face, twisting it into a furious mask and I start to move, compelled to go to him, to calm him but from the corner of my eye, I see Smoke leap over the bar and rush towards us. His arms wrap around me carefully, lifting me from the sofa, and pulling me against his chest holding me in.

All eyes turn to Echo, his voice booming in the now quietened room. “You don’t fucking touch her,” he bellows.

Pulling my head from Smoke’s chest, I slowly turn towards Echo. His body is tense, the muscles in his neck and biceps bulging as he keeps the guy pinned against the wall, his fury making him bigger and more terrifying. Smoke’s arms are banded around me, and I’m unable to move, but I clearly hear Echo’s words.

“You touch her again, and I’ll fucking kill you,” he hisses, his voice a deadly warning, then he releases his hold and the creepy guy slumps to the floor, his hands moving to rub at his neck now he’s free. Echo turns to me and Smoke immediately releases me, stepping back and leaving coldness to replace his comforting body heat.

My eyes feel wide as they take in the man in front of me. Echo’s chest is heaving, his gaze wild and angry until our eyes meet, and then his fury seems to bleed from him. His shoulders slowly relax and warmth returns to his face. He steps towards, me and I struggle to breathe.

“Livvy,” he murmurs, his voice a low rasp.

My friends call me Lil or Liv, but never Livvy, but I don’t mind the nickname on his lips. Everything about this man intrigues and entices me. I’m drawn to him in a way I’ve never experienced before, especially with a stranger. Its purely physical, just chemistry, but my body sways toward him as his eyes compel me to go to him, and I feel a physical pull.

"Livvy." His voice is a command now, all soft coercion gone, replaced with a demand for my obedience.

Silently, I stare at him. I'm frozen, unable to move towards him, but unwilling to walk away, to run without experiencing whatever this magnetic connection is between us. He steps closer, lust and triumph flaring in his eyes as his firm grip wraps around my hand, and I'm pulled into his chest. His hand lifts slowly to my face and he strokes his fingers carefully across my cheek. The room around us fades away and all there is, is this man and me and this moment of silence between us.

It feels like it goes on forever, then time suddenly speeds up again as his eyes leave mine in a blink. He bends and his arms circle my waist, then I'm lifted into the air and hoisted up and over his shoulder.

The room explodes in a cacophony of whoops and cheers I'm carried hanging upside down, dazed and confused out of the room. Before I can even process what's happening, Echo has walked us down a corridor and into a bedroom, slamming and locking the door behind us. Sliding me down his body, my feet hit the ground, and shock and all of the leftover adrenaline from the fight and everything else that's happened tonight pours through me in a rush.

"What the bloody hell was that?" I shriek.

His eyes bore holes into me, but he remains silent.

"Echo, seriously, what the fuck was that?"

He strides towards me, the muscles in his arms and shoulders bulging as his barely restrained anger seems to make his whole body tense. I retreat from his fury, but he pursues me till I'm backed against the wall and his body is caging me in holding me prisoner. My nipples harden in anticipation at his closeness even as his fist wraps into my curls, pulling hard and forcing me to look at him.

My skin tingles; my instinct to run battles with a desperate desire to get closer. Then he touches me. His thumb caresses the pulse point in my neck before his fingers spread wide, encircling my throat.

"Sugar, didn't I tell you to watch how you speak to me?" he growls.

My mouth drops open. Of all the things he could have said, I wasn't expecting him to scold me.

His mouth twists into a snarl. "Pucks a sick motherfucker and I'll fucking kill him if he ever touches you again."

His thumb traces my bottom lip before dipping into my mouth. Closing my lips around it, I instinctively lave it with my tongue before sucking lightly.

"I didn't like him touching you," he admits angrily.

All the air pushes out of me in a shocked exhale as his fingers trail slowly down my neck and over my collarbone before finally drifting across the swell of my breast.

"I didn't like them watching you." His southern drawl drips like honey and I push my thighs together, desperate to ease the ache in my pulsing sex. "I don't share." His voice rumbles through me, and my panties flood with arousal. "None of them can have you." The possessiveness and jealousy in his voice does something to me, and I vibrate with need.

His fingers edge under the top of my dress, slowly pulling the fabric down. My rock-hard nipples tingle, and I arch my back, pushing my breasts closer to him and silently begging for his touch. Leaning forward his lips wrap around my eager nipple, his teeth scrapping against the sensitive tip and I groan in agonised pleasure.

"You're mine," he whispers as his fingers press against my stomach and he guides me to face the wall. "Hands flat, don't move," he says lifting my arms and pushing my hands against the wall in front of me.

The dimly lit room is silent except for my ragged breath and glancing over my shoulder, I see the flash of desire in Echo's eyes before he sinks to the floor. From my position I can't see him, but his body heat surrounds me; his palms warming the skin on the backs on my ankles, scorching a path up my legs as he slowly glides his hands towards my arse.

Rough hands edge my dress up, and cool air wafts across the exposed skin as Echo rises from the floor, and pushes between my shoulder blades, forcing me to bend at the waist. His large thigh parts my legs till I'm spread wide; my skin tingling in anticipation.

"Don't move." His voice is rough and uncompromising, then he sinks back down to the floor, pressing his face into my pussy, making me gasp with need. His groan makes my legs shudder, and I feel my arousal dripping down my thighs.

"Sugar, you smell like the best kind of trouble." His fingers trace a line down my panties. "So wet. This all for me?"

Nodding silently, I moan when his wet tongue circles my clit through the lace of my underwear. Then the sound of ripping fabric fills the air and cool air engulfs my heated pussy. I gasp, then mewl as he blows hot breath across my lips, making my flushed sex tingle with anticipation.

"Look at this pretty little pussy," he coos. "You're fucking purring at me, your cums just running out of you. Ask me to taste you, baby." His voice is raw and pure desire.

"Oh god," I gasp wantonly.

His hot breath brushes against my pussy, he's so close, the warm air heats my sensitive skin as he speaks. "Ask me to taste you, sugar. Beg me."

I shake my head. Even in my desperation, the words won't come. He spanks a sharp slap against the soft skin of my bare arse, and sparks of heat shock my nerve endings.

"You want me to touch you, don't you?" he questions.

I nod furiously. My legs sagging as he runs a finger from my arsehole all the way to my clit, teasing, but not giving me enough to make me feel good. His hand connects with my arse again and I flinch against the sting, arching and pushing back into his hand silently urging him to do it again.

"Sugar, do you need me to take a firm hand with you? You

like it when I spank you, don't you?" He growls the words.

His rough touch soothes the red handprint on my arse, and the words fall from my lips before I can stop them. "Oh god. Yes, I like it."

Finally, he pushes one thick finger inside me, his lips at my ear. "I can tell, baby. You're so fucking wet, every time I tell you to do something, you gush again." He adds another finger, slowly pushing in and pulling out, before reaching up and grasping a handful of my hair, pulling sharply and dragging my head up and back.

Echo leans over me till his body surrounds me. "Oh yeah, sugar, you like it when I pull your hair. Your cum's dripping off my hand."

A third finger pushes into me and I pant with desire, my legs shaking as his fingers increase their tempo till my hips are pushed back against him, meeting his hand thrust for thrust. My orgasm rushes to the surface, teetering on the edge until his voice in my ear whispers, "Come on, Livvy, let me hear you." He bites down on the soft skin where my shoulder meets my neck, and pleasure hits me like a bomb, my legs buckle, and I scream.

Aftershocks pulse through me, and I gulp air as my heartbeat slows. Echo's sure grip holds me up, turning me to face him as he cups my cheeks in his large hands. Leaning in he kisses me gently, his touch reverent, almost adoring, and completely unexpected.

His hands run down my sides to the bottom of my dress, slowly dragging it up and over my head before dropping it to the floor. My bra is added to the pile, and then his ravenous eyes rake over my naked form.

"On your knees, sugar." It's an order, and something in his face warns me to comply. Desperate for him, mindless, I eagerly drop, my knees hitting the cold tile floor. His gaze is focussed on me; there's softness in his eyes when his fingers reach out to trace the side of my face and jaw.

He slowly removes his jeans, the clicking of his zip echoing in the tense silence of the room. When his cock springs free, my mouth waters at its thickness. His velvety long length frames the drop of cum shimmering at the head and Echo wraps his hand around it, stroking up and down as I lick my lips.

One hand on his cock, he grabs a handful of my hair, tugging me towards his waiting dick. "Open up, sugar, I want to feel that dirty little mouth of yours."

Wrapping my lips around his thick girth I sink down onto him till he hits the back of my throat. He tugs sharply on my hair and pulls himself free of my mouth. "Easy, sugar. You're gonna make me come if you carry on like that."

Smiling I focus on his hard cock, licking up the length of him before circling the tip with my tongue, tasting the drops of cum that appear. Opening wide, I take as much of him as I can into my mouth, sucking on the way down, then teasing with a gentle scrape of my teeth on the way back up.

"Jesus," he groans.

I relax my throat, fighting my gag reflex and breathing through my nose as I swallow as much of his pulsating cock as possible. The rush of desire shocks me, and I squirm, pushing my thighs together.

"So good." His encouragement urges me to suck harder, pushing him to lose control. "Fuck." The single word is a plea as his hands tangle in my hair, controlling my movement; forcing his cock deep into my throat, holding it there before pulling back and thrusting deep again.

His grip on my hair tightens, and a spark of desire pulses through me. The hint of pain makes the ache between my legs intensify and I reach down to my pussy and sigh in delight as my fingertip scrapes my clit.

"No." There's no mistaking the order in that single word, and I instantly still, tilting my eyes up to look at him.

My mouth still full of his cock, I swirl my tongue around the head, making him growl in response. Holding my head, he pushes till he hits the back of my throat making my eyes water as his cock fills my airway. His tight grip holds me still, then, yanking my hair, he pulls out of my mouth completely.

I blink up at him, and our gazes lock as he speaks. "On the bed, sugar."

TWELVE

Echo

Fuck.

The sight of her on her knees with my cock buried in her mouth almost had me blowing my load straight down her throat. I've had a lot of blowjobs, but never one that almost brought me to my knees. She's the perfect fucking contradiction, sweet as hell but a dirty little bitch too.

When her fingers went to her pussy, I had to make her stop. Because if she's gonna be touching herself, then I plan to be fucking watching, but with a much better view.

She did exactly what I told her to do. Fuck, she got off on being ordered around. The more demanding I got, the wetter she got.

Pushing up off her knees she slowly rises and my cock

jerks when I get the full image. Crazy hair, pouty lips, and those fucking eyes that I just want to stare into. Her perfect perky tits and rosy pink nipples are hard and waiting to be bitten, her bare pussy glistening with arousal and begging to be filled.

She's all mine, ready and desperate for me, and I already know once isn't gonna be enough with her. I don't know what the fuck it is, but something about Livvy is pulling me in.

I want to own her.

Touch every inch of her skin.

Ruin her for other men.

I sound like a fucking psycho!

It must be her British accent. Maybe that's why she's driving me fucking crazy. I just need to fuck her till I get bored. And I will; I always do.

I don't want an old lady; I don't do commitment.

But then one look at Livvy and I'm all in. I want to own her and claim her as mine. I want to protect her and look after her.

I want it all with her.

THIRTEEN

Olivia

I don't try to fight my response to his command; I want to do what he tells me to.

"Olivia, get that wet pussy on the bed so I can fuck you till you scream," he growls and I scramble onto the bed and lie back on the pillows. He follows till he's hovering above me, and I hear the familiar rustle of a condom wrapper being ripped open. His eyes lock with mine as his thighs push my legs wide, then his cock slams into me in one long hard thrust.

"Arghhh," I scream. The force of his thrusts push me up the bed, and I brace my hands against the headboard, letting my eyes fall closed as I bask in the sensation of pain and pleasure mingling together.

"Eyes," he demands, his voice gruff. I force my eyelids to open and he waits till I focus and our gazes lock. "I own your pleasure, sugar. I want to watch you fall apart."

Grabbing my legs he wraps them around his back and I cross my ankles and hold on tight as he sets a punishing pace. His huge dick stretches me; I've never felt so full. Every time he pulls back and thrusts in, I shudder as his rigid length drags across my heightened nerve endings.

"Oh god," I groan as my orgasm starts to rise, my eyes struggle to stay open, my whole body tense, poised for the explosion of pleasure.

"Eyes," he barks again through gritted teeth.

His voice intensifies everything and my eyelids flutter open. The sensation of pleasure rises from my toes and up through my body till ecstasy rips out of me. "Ahhhh," I shout, my orgasm exploding from me on a desperate cry.

Never slowing his tempo, Echo pulls my legs from his waist and drapes them over his shoulders. "Fuck, sugar, I'm there. I want you with me." His voice is rough, and in this position, he's buried so deep in me I feel every ridge of his cock as he moves.

"Come on, sugar, one more," he orders.

I shake my head, my body languid after the orgasms he's already given me but instead of taking his own pleasure his ocean-green eyes harden, never breaking our connection. "No, no, no, no," I chant and he laughs, slapping my arse then thrusting harder and deeper into me. My body comes to life again, and I tense all over as his orgasm rips through him, and I scream, sending us over the edge together.

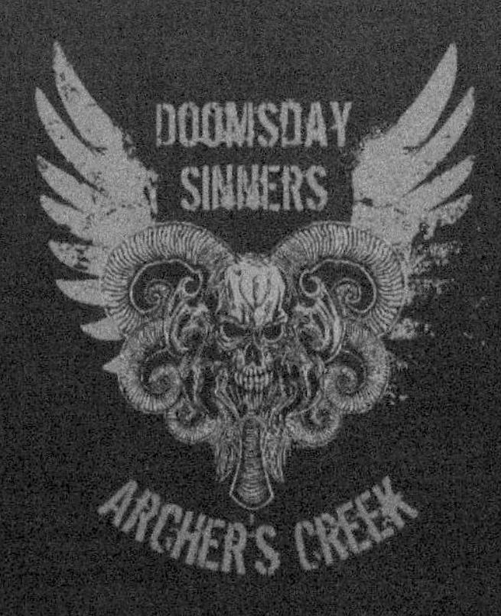

FOURTEEN

Echo

Holy fucking shit, I thought I knew what good sex was. I was wrong!

My heart's beating wildly in my chest, and I struggle to breathe. I can't tear my eyes from her. Her wild hair spreads across my chest, and her hot, sticky body is sprawled on top of me.

I should be rolling her off me and kicking her out. But instead, I'm staring at her and hoping I never have to let her go.

She isn't the type of woman you fuck and fuck off. She's the woman that you spend your whole life fighting to keep.

Maybe it's time for me to start fighting.

FIFTEEN

Olivia

My head rests on Echo's chest, both of us panting and sweaty.

Silent.

My heart's races, thudding in my chest. Do I regret this? Every inch of my skin tingles, and I fight the urge to scratch to prolong the amazing sensation. Slowly, I open my eyes and see the endless tattooed chest beneath my head. His arms are wrapped tightly around my shoulders, our legs entwined, and my head lifts and falls with his steady breaths.

I break the silence. "Tell me about your tattoos."

A light chuckle vibrates from his chest. "What do you want to know, sugar?"

"I don't care, anything. Which was your first one?"

He starts to move, but I wrap myself tightly around his arm, stopping him. "I'm comfy, don't move. Just tell me."

His fingers draw patterns across my back, and I feel him inhale deeply before he speaks. "I got my first tattoo when I was seventeen. It's a protection rune."

"Where is it?"

"On my left shoulder."

My hands trace the lines of the tattoos that cover his chest, absentmindedly following the patterns. "What about the others, do they all have meaning."

Echo laughs. "No, a few are just 'cause they're badass."

"They're beautiful," I tell him, my voice relaxed, my muscles slowly melting into him, as a yawn falls from my lips. We fall silent again, my fingers swirling over his skin and I tilt my head to look at him, and see his eyes are closed.

He's asleep.

I take a moment to stare at his beautiful face and the stubble that coats his cheeks and chin. Awake, he's dangerous and potent. Asleep, he's rugged perfection.

I close my eyes and pull in a deep breath. I don't want to move. I stare at him, and for a moment I pretend I can stay curled up with him till he wakes up and we can start again. But I can't. This is a one-night stand, a beautiful holiday memento that I'll never forget but refuse to tarnish with the awkward morning after. So, with renewed vigour, I lean down and drop a gentle kiss on his chest, then start to untangle myself.

Slowly, I squirm and wiggle, pausing every few seconds,

until I'm free of Echo's arms, then as quietly as possible, I grab my dress and throw on my clothes. Boots in hand, I stand by the door. I can't resist one last look.

I commit the scene to memory. Echo sprawled naked, fast asleep on his rumpled sheets. He'll be the standard all guys will be measured up against from now on.

As I leave, I whisper, "Goodbye, Echo."

Then I shut the door silently behind me.

SIXTEEN

Echo

Stretching my arms I search for Livvy's warm, luscious body but the sheets are cold and my bed's empty. My eyes snap open, anger building in my chest as I walk to the bathroom, but it's empty too.

She's gone.

I rake my hands through my hair. "That fucking bitch!" I shout.

I've hit it and quit it too many fucking times to mention. But I'm the one that kicks out clinging whores. I've never had a fucking woman disappear in the middle of the night.

It's good that she's gone.

Fuck, I don't want to give her the "It was fun but I don't want an old lady" speech.

The sex was good, but not so good that I can't find someone else to scratch the itch.

Who the fuck am I kidding? The sex was fucking amazing and Livvy's fast become an obsession I don't want to quit.

Shit. My cock's hard as steel just thinking about her bent over, my tongue tasting her cream as she got wetter and wetter.

Fuck that. No fucking bitch runs out on me.

I say when we're done.

I claimed her.

She's mine.

I know it. Everyone in the club knows it. I just need her to accept it too.

So hell no, we're not done yet.

SEVENTEEN

Olivia

"Gahhh." My back cracks as I struggle to sit up. This bed's so lumpy it feels like it's filled with rocks. Once my feet hit the floor, I stretch my arms above my head and pad into the small bathroom, catching my reflection in the mirror and finding sex-tousled hair and lust-laden eyes staring back at me.

I look like I've been completely ravished. Teeth marks mar the top of my shoulder, and images of Echo biting me and pushing me over the edge into a bone-melting orgasm flash into my head. My legs sag as I remember his commanding voice and dexterous fingers; I grip the sink tightly to keep upright.

I rush through my shower, washing the scent of sex and Echo from my skin. My body's tired, and muscles I haven't used in years ache, while the dull pulse in my pussy refuses to let me forget how he thoroughly used my body in the best way.

I've had a couple of one-night stands before, but they never made me feel like this. The morning after was always filled with shame and regret, but my time with Echo has just left me aching for more. But I can't pin my hopes on a holiday romance, because that's what this would be.

Echo's the unexpectedly perfect guy, just at the wrong time.

Blowing out a wistful sigh, I throw on my Strikers tank, a pair of denim shorts, and my Converse, and I'm ready for my shift. As I go to leave, my stomach growls loudly, reminding me that the last time I ate was lunchtime yesterday so I head to an old-school diner a few doors down from Strikers and slide onto a chrome stool at the counter. Moments after I order, the waitress drops my pancake stack in front of me, and I drown it in maple syrup, dipping the crispy bacon in the sweetness before popping it into my mouth. The salty-sweet combination hits my tongue and I hum with happiness.

"Ahem." A throat clears next to me.

Swallowing my food, I turn towards the sound and find a real-life cowboy, or at least a guy who dresses like a cowboy, sitting on the stool next to me. His bright white smile glints like a toothpaste ad in the sunshine.

"Good morning, ma'am," Cowboy says, tilting his hat to me in greeting. Heat blooms in my cheeks and rises into a full blush as something about his formal salutation makes me go all girly. I take a moment to check him out, his gingham shirt accentuates his slim but toned arms and shoulders and tight blue jeans that I'd guess might be Levi's and shiny cowboy boots complete his look.

He's a walking, talking, sexy Woody doll.

"Hi," I say with a little wave.

He reaches out his hand, and I take it. Cowboy exudes confidence, so I expect his grip to be firm and decisive, but instead it's weak and clammy.

"Wyatt Anderson, ma'am."

"Olivia Townsend," I reply, pulling my hand back quickly and discreetly wipe my palm on my shorts. His touch has left me with a strange, uncomfortable feeling that only accentuates when the cowboy's eyes slowly look me up and down, his gaze dipping to my boobs.

Watching him appraise me, I snap my fingers in front of his face. "Hey, dickhead, my face's up here," I bark, arching my eyebrows imperiously.

Confident, gleaming eyes rise to meet mine; a self-assured grin is plastered across his lips. "I'm sorry, ma'am, it's just those perfect titties of yours are just so eager to say hi. I don't want them to feel left out." Amusement laces his voice.

A laugh bursts free from me. "You're a dick for staring at my tits, but that's a brilliant freaking comeback."

He holds out his hand. "I apologise, let me try again. Wyatt Anderson, ma'am. It's a pleasure to meet you." His eyes sparkle with mischief as he tips his head from side to side, speaking his next words to my boobs. “And you. And you.”

I giggle again. “Olivia Townsend, and the girls are Bonnie and Clyde,” I say point from my right boob, to my left.

Wyatt laughs, and raising his coffee cup to my boobs, he toasts them. “Ladies.”

He’s cute, in a cocky I-know-I’m-good-looking kind of a way. Fresh-faced, he’s almost a bit too well-groomed. His stubble’s artfully sculpted, and his teeth are a shade too white. Cowboy’s sex on legs, but it feels like it’s taken a lot of time and effort to get him that way.

I turn my attention back to my breakfast and fork a mound of syrup-soaked pancake into my mouth. “Mmmmm,” I moan appreciatively.

“We don’t get many British folk in Archer’s Creek, so you must be new to town?”

I nod. “Yep, just got here yesterday.” I carry on eating, and the moment the pancake hits my tongue I groan in pleasure.

Wyatt laughs. “Miss Olivia, I’m gonna need a cigarette by the time you’ve finished those pancakes.”

My skin flushes red, and I cover my face with my hands in embarrassment. Wyatt touches my wrists, pulling them down. “Don’t be embarrassed. I’m just jealous that it’s the pancakes that are causing those noises,” he says with a wink.

Oh God, the cowboy’s flirting with me. This town’s packed full of hot guys and I should be in man-candy heaven, but all I can think about it Echo. I try to compare him to Wyatt but they couldn't be any more different. Echo's rough and gritty, where Wyatt's polished and smooth. Echo took control and I let him; I wanted him to be in charge.

Flashbacks of last night explode into my head. Echo pulling my hair, making me come again and again. I'm so enthralled by the dirty slideshow, I don't even realise Wyatt's been talking this whole time.

"So how 'bout it, Miss Olivia, can I pick you up tonight?" Wyatt asks, a glint in his eye.

Wyatt's hot, but Echo's hotter. Echo was the best sex I've ever had, and I'd totally do a repeat with the biker boy. But last night was a one-time thing; it has to be.

Fuck it. "Okay, why not, I'll go out with you tonight that'd be nice," I say, then instantly regret it, but it's too late to take it back, so I smile brightly and hope he doesn't notice how fake it is.

Wyatt's grin is smug, like he never had any doubt that I'd agree. "Shall we say eight o'clock tonight?"

I nod. "Sure, I'm staying at Miss Mimi's."

"Auntie Mimi did say she had a new guest. Well, I'll leave you to your breakfast. See you tonight, Miss Olivia." He grins, pulls my hand to his lips with a flourish and kissing the back of it softly.

Oh my god, Wyatt is Miss Mimi's nephew, and Miss Mimi is a judgemental old crone with horribly uncomfortable beds. She obviously hates the bikers and anyone who associates with them. But does her nephew feel the same?

Who knows, maybe nice guy cowboys are better than bad boy bikers?

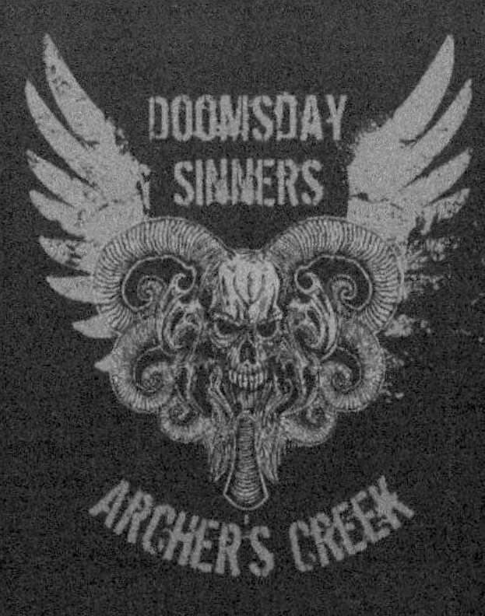

EIGHTEEN

Waiting

I watch her.

She's beautiful.

But she's tired.

Pure.

Perfect.

But she went with the biker scum.

Now she needs to be punished.

Purified.

Saved.

I can cleanse her.

I can be her saviour.

But it's not time yet.

Now I need to wait.

NINETEEN

Echo

It's been a hell of a day.

I planned to track Livvy down first thing this morning, find out what the fuck she thought she was playing at, sneaking out in the middle of the night. But as soon as I left my room at the clubhouse, I got drafted into club shit that couldn't be ignored.

The Sinners aren't classic one-percenters. We skirt the law but don't spend too much time on the wrong side of it. The club owns several legitimate businesses in Archer's Creek and the surrounding towns, but we've also got some under-the-counter illegal shit going, just not enough to make us a target. I deal with security for everything the club has going on. Muscle, intel, surveillance—that's all on me.

The club business has me driving over to Dripping Springs,

a few towns over. We own the only strip club in the town, and I'm forever dealing with the shit that happens there. Leave it to Beavers, the titty bar, is run by the Prez's old lady, Grits. She's an old, hard bitch, and she runs the place with an iron fist, but just lately she's had a few pretty boys in causing trouble and pestering the girls for 'extras'.

Now, as law-abiding citizens of Archer's Creek, we don't condone the strippers offering extra services on the side, but we happily turn a blind eye and make sure that no one gets out of hand.

After spending a long day dealing with het-up strippers, all I want to do is track down my bitch and spank her ass for running.

Miss Mimi is a sour-faced old bag. She hates the club 'cause her old man took off with one of the club whores twenty years ago. The old bitch wouldn't tell me where Livvy was, just said she'd have the sheriff on my ass if I didn't get off her property. I'm not worried about the sheriff, he's been on the club's payroll for years, but the threat pisses me off all the same.

The longer it takes me to track her down, the more pissed I'm getting. The thought of turning her over my knee and reminding her who she belongs to is making my dick rock-hard.

She's mine, and if I need to let this whole fucking town know, so fucking be it.

TWENTY

Olivia

At eight on the dot, there's a knock at my door and I open it to find Wyatt standing in his aunt's hall, a confident grin spread across his face, and despite being a little annoyed by his arrogant appraisal on my body I'm impressed at his punctuality.

"You look hot, Miss Olivia," he says, bringing my hand to his lips and kissing it with an audible mwah sound. I try to speak but end up spluttering with a cringe of embarrassment. "Oh, er. Thanks?"

Still holding my fingers, he lifts his arm and wraps my hand through his elbow, leading me down the hall. The move is old-school chivalry, but instead of swooning, it feels awkward and orchestrated.

Noticing I've left my bag behind; I pause. "Oh, I'm

sorry, I left my purse in my room. Let me just grab it and we can go."

He nods, and I dash back to my room, sighing and wishing I could just stay the moment I'm away from my date. Reluctantly I force myself to grab my purse and leave my room, but when I walk back into the hall, Wyatt and Miss Mimi are standing close together and talking in hushed voices.

"Wyatt, I'm ready when you are," I say. He looks up and smiles, but raises his finger, asking for a minute.

Several minutes later, I'm still standing in the hallway. Sighing loudly I fidget with my handbag, wishing I'd just stayed in my room, while Wyatt and his aunt gossip like old women. "Wyatt, I'm sorry to interrupt, but if this is a bad time, we can always reschedule," I offer, secretly hoping he'll say yes and I can bail on this date before it even starts.

A scowl crosses his face as he turns towards me, and I shrink back slightly in surprise. In a flash, the scowl disappears and the confident smile returns. "Of course not, Miss Olivia, please excuse my rudeness. Shall we go?"

I narrow my eyes at his snippy tone and start to speak, but his perma-smile distracts me as he threads my arm through his again and steers us out the door.

Wyatt's a good-looking guy, but without the hat and the cowboy styling, his hair's dark, short, and slicked into a side part with so much product it looks wet. Does he really think that's a good look? His much-too-skinny jeans and ab-hugging T-shirt are designed to show off his muscles. But it all feels like he's trying too hard.

He walks us across the street to Strikers. Jesus, after working here for the last eight hours, this date is quickly jumping into worst-date-ever territory. Ushering me into a booth, he slides in opposite me and lasciviously looks me up and down again.

"Did I tell you how hot you look, baby?" He drawls.

Flashing him a brittle smile, I swallow down the retort that's on my tongue and instead glance down at my outfit and smile for real. My pale blue summer dress has wide straps, is fitted round my tits to the waist, and then flares out in a cute rah-rah skirt to just above my knee. The material is floaty and patterned with hundreds of little flamingos. My hair's down and curly and I look good, only now I wished I hadn't wasted it on the pig opposite me.

Time drags. We order beers and try to make small talk, but Wyatt's eyes rarely lift from my boobs.

I'm bored.

After two beers, I check my phone and throw out an exaggerated yawn. His head lifts from my boobs for a moment and he looks at me quizzically.

"Oh gosh, Wyatt, I'm so sorry. It's just been a really long couple of days," I say, faux apologetically.

He stands, then walks around the booth and scoots in next to me. Cringing, I move till I'm wedged against the back of the booth, but instead of taking the hint he leans into me, the stench of the seven beers he's drunk and his stale, putrid breath hitting me.

"Baby, you ready for bed?" he purrs.

Oh God, his suggestive tone and the ridiculous exaggerated drunken wink has me holding back laughter. He leans further into me, and I fight the gag reflex that threatens when he breathes in my face and his arm creeps round my shoulders. Sucking in my stomach, I try to move as far away from him as possible, but instead of noticing that I'm trying my hardest to be as far away from him as possible he just inches even closer.

The sound of a door slamming reverberates through the room, and tingles start all along the back of my neck. Wyatt lifts his head, spotting something on the other side of the bar and the colour drains from his face. His arm tightens across my shoulders and his fingers dig into my skin.

"Wyatt?" I say, but his gaze is fixed, his fingers clenching into my arm painfully. "Wyatt, let go, you're hurting me," I say louder, trying to remove his hand from my skin, but he's not paying any attention to me, his head is turning slowly, his gaze following the movement of something across the room.

Prying his fingers from my skin, I shove his arm off my shoulders and grab my purse as I try to push him out of the booth. An ominous quiet seems to have engulfed the entire room and Wyatt's still blocking my escape, but his focus is no longer on me. Peering round his body I find Echo and Smoke standing at the end of the table.

Echo looks pissed, anger evident on his face, but he's not looking at me; all his fury is focussed solely on Wyatt. I look from Echo to Wyatt and back again. The pair are engaged in a silent stare down whilst Smoke stands stoically by Echo's side.

I push at Wyatt's back until he reluctantly stands, and I shuffle out of the booth, smoothing my dress as I straighten. I turn to leave but Echo's hand snaps out, grabbing my arm to stop me.

"Sugar, want to explain what the fuck's going on?" he growls.

"I'm not exactly sure what you want me to explain, Echo. I was just leaving," I say haughtily.

Wyatt's head turns towards me, a sardonic grin twitching in place. "Olivia, baby, where are you going? Our date's not over yet."

I laugh. "Dude, our date's sooo over." I waggle my finger up and down, pointing to his get-up. "All this. Yeah, that doesn't really work for me."

Echo's grip on my arm loosens, so I start to walk away, but Wyatt the douche grabs my shoulder. "You fucking prissy little British bitch. You're lucky I'm interested in you at all after being seen with that piece of shit biker."

I spin round to respond, but Echo has him pinned by his throat to the wall, leaning in close to Wyatt's face. Echo's voice is so low I can't hear what he's saying, but Wyatt blanches and starts jabbering. “I’m sorry. I didn’t touch her. Don’t hurt me. Please don’t hurt me,” he whines.

Echo turns towards me, anger straining his whole body. “Livvy, go stand your ass at the bar and wait for me. I’m not done with you yet.”

He’s not done with me yet. Who the fuck does he think he is?

“Fuck you, Echo. I’m done, and I’m going,” I bite out angrily.

Echo doesn’t respond, instead, he turns to Smoke and nods towards me. Smoke jumps up, slinging his arm over my shoulders, guiding me to a barstool and lifting me up onto it, caging me in with his hands on the bar.

Furious, at being manhandled, I shove at Smoke’s enormous shoulders. “Smoke, what the hell? Move, I’m leaving.”

He looks genuinely sorry, but shakes his head. “Sorry, sweetheart, but Echo wants you to stay, and he’s only gonna follow your ass back to Miss Mimi’s if you leave.”

“I’m sorry too, Smoke,” I say with a shrug, then I knee him in the balls with as much force as I can muster. Poor Smoke drops like a sack of potatoes and I hop down from the stool stepping over his groaning body as I walk straight out the door.

TWENTY-ONE

Echo

When I walk into Strikers and see Livvy—my Livvy—sitting with that pansy fucking Wyatt Anderson's arm round her, I just about lose my mind. From the doorway, I can see she's trying to move his arm, but she shouldn't be anywhere near him in the first place.

And he shouldn't be touching what's mine.

I don't even remember moving from the door but then I'm standing at their table and Anderson's telling Livvy their date isn't over. Furious, blinding jealousy pulses through me. I hate that I've lost even a day with her. I've only just found her, but she's already under my skin.

My heart's thumping in my chest. Anderson's a little prick, one of the pretty boys Grits has been having issues with. He's a bully who doesn't understand the meaning of the word no.

He could have hurt her.

He needs to be taught a lesson, and I'm gonna really enjoy being the one who teaches it.

Livvy's being a pain in my ass and trying to run again, so I give Smoke the nod to watch her while I scare the shit out of Anderson. My hands are around his throat, and he's pinned up against the wall, and hell, maybe I'm enjoying this a bit too much. Leaning in real close I whisper to him, "Olivia's mine."

His face pales.

"She's mine and you touched her."

The poor guy looks like he's gonna throw up. "Remember what we did last time you messed with club property?" A few years back, we broke his nose and one of his arms for getting rough with one of the strippers.

He's shaking, and a sheen of sweat's broken out all over his face.

"Olivia's not just club property. She's my property. So this time, I'm gonna teach you a real lesson, one you won't forget." Letting go of his neck, he drops to the floor and starts to cry.

"I didn't do anything. I didn't know she belonged to the club. I'm sorry. I'm so sorry. Please just let me go. Please," he begs, his voice a pathetic whine.

Laughing, I sneer down at him, curled like a fucking coward on the floor. Bringing back my leg, I kick him in the face, and his nose explodes with a crack and I lean over him, keeping my voice low so only he hears. "Me and the boys will be seeing you real soon."

I turn toward the bar just in time to watch Livvy bring her knee up hard and nails Smoke in the balls. My stomach clenches as he drops to the floor and my little hellion steps over him and walks straight out the door.

TWENTY-TWO

Olivia

My heels stomp loudly as I dash down the street. I don't even know where I'm going, I just need to walk.

"Stupid bloody man." My muttering is perfectly synced with the noise of my heels. "Trying to tell me what to do."

Stomp.

"He's not done with me yet."

Stomp.

"Who the hell does he think he is?"

Stomp.

I get about a hundred yards down the street before strong arms band around my waist. "Uuuufff," I grunt as I'm airborne, hanging over Echo's shoulder and staring at his arse. That's twice in two days that this Neanderthal has manhandled me and

I swear I'm not turned on by him going all caveman on me. Definitely not turned on. Honest.

"Put me down, you fucking bastard," I yell, kicking my legs and pounding at his back with my fists, but his grip never loosens. Echo deposits me on my feet next to his bike and shoves a helmet I've never seen him wear onto my head. I try to bat his hands away from me, but he ignores me, silently fastens the strap under my chin before throwing his leg over the saddle and straddling the huge metal machine.

Crossing my arms across my chest, I glare down at the terrifying motorcycle. "I'm not getting on that thing."

Echo pulls in a sharp, exasperated breath before tipping his face up to the sky. "Sugar, climb on behind me and wrap your arms round me."

I shake my head and start to edge backwards. "Echo, why the fuck are you even here, chasing after me?"

He climbs off his bike, slowly stalking towards me. "I'm reclaiming what's mine."

"What the bloody hell are you talking about?" I shout.

His intense gaze pins me to the spot, and it slowly dawns on me what he means. "What's yours, Echo? Me?"

Heat flares in his eyes, and he squares his shoulders. "Hell yes, sugar, you're mine." He drags me towards him and I start to protest, but his lips claim mine in a punishing kiss that silences me, and I melt into his touch.

"Get on the bike, Livvy."

Torn from the blissful aftermath of his kiss, I open my eyes and pull from his embrace. “No way,” I shake my head dramatically. “Motorcycles may look hot, but they’re death traps, and I’ve got no inclination to die.”

Wrapping his hand around my wrist he pulls me towards him. His voice rough and full of barely contained anger. “Do you think I’d ever put you in danger?”

“I have no idea, I don’t know you. But it’s not you I’m worried about right now. It’s that thing,” I say, pulling from his grasp and pointing at the massive Harley. Somehow he manages to scowl and roll his eyes at the same time as he reaches for my finger, and gently urges me forward, placing my palm over his chest. “Do you trust me?”

“I don’t know you, Echo,” I say on a sigh.

He tilts my chin up to face him. “It takes time to get to know someone, sugar. Do you feel my heart under your fingers?”

I nod.

“Something about you makes my heart race in a way it never has before. I bet if I felt your heart, it’d be beating in sync with mine, because you feel it too, this connection we have. Don’t you?” Echo’s voice is earnest, honest, and I drop my eyes to look at where my fingers are spread across his chest. I feel the thud of his heart, and mine stutters in response.

“Look at me, sugar,” he demands. Lifting my eyes, I swallow. “Do you trust me, Livvy?” he asks again.

My response is instinctive. “Yes, but—”

Smiling, he threads his fingers through mine. "No buts, sugar. Now get on the bike."

"Echo…" I bite my lip.

Turning his head he looks pointedly at the seat behind him, barely hiding his impatience. Exhaling loudly, he leans towards me. "So help me God, if you don't get your fine ass on my bike in the next three seconds, I'll have your panties around your ankles, and I'll spank your ass till it's a perfect shade of red right out here in the open. It's your choice."

My mouth drops open in shock but I quickly clamber onto the bike and wrap my arms around his waist. My legs are spread around his, and he grabs my knees, pulling me forward until my lady bits hit his back. His clean scent mixes with the smell of his leather waistcoat, and I bury my face against his back, inhaling deeply.

Echo starts the bike, and the moment the wheels start to move, blinding fear consumes me. I squeeze my eyes tightly shut, and my fingers clamp onto him in a death grip at his waist. We pull up to the clubhouse just a few minutes later and Echo jumps off his bike, lifting me off and removing the helmet from my head.

Grabbing my hand, he walks quickly, dragging me behind him until I stumble. I yank my hand trying to pull myself from his grip, but he just tightens his hold on me, so I plant my feet and shout. "Bloody slow down. I'm in heels."

He doesn't speak, but his pace immediately slows, and

walking at a normal speed he leads me into the building and through the bar that's full of men, instead of packed with crowds of party goers. If they notice us, they don't pay us any attention as Echo marches forward, pulling me along behind him. Almost to the corridor on the far side of the room, he pauses, then looks back at me. His eyes twinkle with mischief before he turns back towards the room full of bikers.

Releasing my hand, he puts his fingers to his mouth and whistles loudly. The bar silences and all eyes turn to face us. "Yo. This here is Olivia. She's mine. If any of you see her trying to leave the clubhouse, you stop her and bring her back to me."

There's a chorus of yeses and nods of acknowledgments and Echo nods, smiling widely, before he leads me, my mouth dropped open in shock the rest of the way, to his room pushing me inside before turning and locking the door behind us.

TWENTY-THREE

Echo

This bitch is driving me insane.

I've never had to chase down a woman in my life, and yet Livvy seems to run from me at every opportunity.

Well, this shit ends now.

I've never felt jealousy before. I've never felt this anger and possessiveness that I feel for her. I want her, and she wants me, I know she does. I see the way she looks at me, how turned on she is.

She gave herself to me completely, and I want that again.

She woke something in me, and I need it again.

TWENTY-FOUR

Olivia

"Echo, what the hell? You can't just tell a group of bloody bikers that I'm not allowed to leave," I shout.

"Livvy, sugar, you've already proved you're a massive fucking flight risk. If you really want to leave, I'll take you back right now. But I'm not having you sneak out in the middle of the night again."

I glare menacingly at Echo and stamp my foot. "Why am I here?"

His hands are doing that sexy hair-ruffling thing again, and the movement mesmerises me. Back and forth, his fingers drag through his hair, dishevelling it. His lips twitch into a smile as he watches me check him out, then his expression turns serious and his eyes pin me to the spot.

"Want to explain why I woke up alone this morning?" He growls.

I sigh dramatically and roll my eyes. "Look, we had fun, but it was a one-night stand. I wasn't expecting breakfast."

In an instant, he's across the room. "This doesn't feel like a one-night thing to me, sugar," he drawls, his fingers caressing my cheek, so close I can feel his hot breath when he speaks. "You're mine. I want you to be mine, Livvy."

Closing my eyes, I shut out everything and just feel his touch. God, I want this man. I tried to convince myself that this was a one-night stand, just amazing sex, but it feels like there could be something more, something deeper.

"What you thinkin' about, sugar?" he asks, his voice a honeyed drawl.

I force my eyes open and realise I'm wrapped in Echo's arms. I don't remember moving closer to him. "This is insane. I don't know you, Echo. We only met a couple of days ago."

"Fuck, sugar. I know that."

Pushing away from him, I step back. "It's lust. That's all it is, just lust."

"It's not just fucking lust for me," he roars.

I should be terrified, and I am, but not of him. Even after only a couple of days, I already know he'd never hurt me, so I step towards him, the pull to be close to him stronger than any argument I can think of to run away again.

He reaches out and cups my chin. "I've found what I want,

Livvy. You. I want every kiss, every gasp, every moan. I want to know everything about you, your hopes, your dreams. What your happy ever after looks like. Tell me you don't feel it too, 'cause I can see it in your eyes."

His voice is desperate. I've never heard him speak like this before, and I stop and stare at him. I open my mouth to speak, to deny his words, but no argument comes. Then I'm not sure who moves, me or him, but we're chest to chest again.

"Mine," he growls.

I tremble at the possession in his voice.

"Last chance, Livvy. You can leave now and I won't chase you. I'll leave you alone. The choice is yours," he snarls impatiently.

His eyes are dark, anger and desire swirling in their depths. Excitement and fear mix in my chest and I shake. My eyes lock with his, and I see the sincerity of his promise; If I walk away now, he won't try to stop me.

So why can't I move my legs?

"What's it gonna be? I can't force you to stay, so walk away now or choose to stay and belong to me?" Striding across the room he unlocks the door and opens it, letting the noise of the guys in the bar filter in.

"What about them? You told them not to let me leave," I whisper, glancing into the dimly lit corridor.

Echo turns his back on me and moves to the other side of the room. "I'll make sure no one stops you."

Forcing my feet to move I cross the room and rest my hand on the door. I can feel Echo watching me silently from his spot against the wall. Pulling in a deep breath I shut the door, then turn to face him. "So, what are you going to do with me now?"

Rushing towards me he hauls me into the air and strides across to the bed with me in his arms. Calmly he sits, flinging me face down across his lap, his huge hand pressing between my shoulders and holding me down.

My heart's banging in my chest. I'm frightened, but so turned on. "Echo what are you doing?" I ask, my voice breathy and excited.

"You drive me fucking crazy," he laughs. "The other night you loved doing as you were told, you loved me being in control. So this is the way it's gonna work. I woke up alone. I didn't like that. By the time I tracked you down, you were on a date with that pussy-ass bastard Anderson and his hands were all over you. That pissed me off. In fact, from the moment I realized you were gone this morning, all I've been thinking about doing is spanking your ass until you're wet and begging. Now, if you're not down with that, you need to say now."

Gasping in short, excited breaths, I squirm in his lap, making a half-hearted effort to get free.

"Oh sugar, yeah, you want me to spank you, don't you?" he chuckles.

I try to speak, to say no, but nothing comes out.

"I want to hear the words, Livvy. You want me to spank you, don't you?"

Heat blooms in my cheeks, and I close my eyes briefly before nodding. "Yes."

Echo strokes his hand up and down my back before his fingers drop lower to caress my arse. Cupping the cheek, he squeezes tightly before moving to the other side and repeating the action. I'm tingling from head to toe, my breath coming in excited gasps as my fists wrap tightly into his jeans. Terrified, excited anticipation tingles across my skin. I'm more turned on than I've ever been in my entire life.

Lifting the hem of my dress he flips the fabric up so the skirt rests against my back. His fingers run along the edge of my panties, slowly pushing them to the side so he can gently stroke along my wetness, his fingers teasing my entrance but never dipping any further.

My pussy is pulsing, my mind silently begging him to do something. Touch me, spank me, anything. "Echo, please," I beg.

He pulls down my panties, and I hear the smile in his voice. "Don't worry, sugar, I'm gonna look after you."

Smack.

His hand against my arse shocks me.

"Owww." My cry turns to a moan when his caressing touch soothes the stinging skin.

Three more spanks come in close succession making my skin burn, and exquisite pain flows through me. Circling my clit with his fingers he teases me, stroking and caressing until I'm arching up off his lap, seeking out more. Then he stops, pulling his fingers away from my sex, rubbing his palm over the raw heated skin on my arse, chuckling.

He's torturing me.

"I hate you." I gasp as his palm cracks against my cheek, the flesh blooming with pain. Before I can process the burn he pushes two thick fingers into my pussy turning the pain into glorious, awful pleasure. "Oh my god," I cry, clawing at his leg, pushing back into his touch begging for more.

"You love this don't you Livvy? The pain, the pleasure, you're begging to be spanked and fucked. Your pussy's so wet, you're soaked, dripping." His voice drops to a gravelly rasp, and I shudder.

I purr as he roughly fucks me with his fingers, then circles my clit never quite touching it. Wiggling over his knees I squirm, wanting him to finger me harder, to rub my clit, or spank me again.

Tutting in amusement, his hand tangles in my hair, pulling sharply in warning. "No, you don't get that yet," he warns pulling his fingers from inside of me, leaving my sex empty and aching.

I hear the sound before I register the feeling. His palm spanks down against my arse once, then again, then a third time with punishing intensity. Burning hot pain bursts to life and it's almost too much, too intense, dissolving my lust to nothing more than a spark. Then two fingers push deep inside of me, his thumb finds my clit and all the hurt is forgotten, the pain just a prerequisite to the blissful ecstasy as an orgasm hurtles towards me.

"You want me, don't you, sugar?" he growls.

I'm incoherent, barely groaning as sensation consumes me. "Nhhhhh," I mumble.

He withdraws his fingers, spanking me again. "Tell me you want me, Livvy." His fingertip circles my clit then lightly glides across the top of it.

"Please, please," I chant desperately.

"I like it when you beg. But I need you to tell me you want me." His palm connects with my skin, harder this time.

"Ahhh," I scream. Heated and sore, everything tingles in pleasure, and arousal gushes out of me.

Smack.

"Tell me you want me, Livvy," he demands.

Smack.

"Tell me."

Smack.

My arse is on fire, but it's not painful. I fight against the urge to close my legs tight to stop the need building inside me, but I don't because I want him to take control, to push me over the edge. Echo's rough skin strokes my back, my arse, my pussy.

His touch is everywhere, but never enough.

"More. Please more," I beg. I need him to make this end, to stop torturing me. I need to embrace the blissful sensation when the pleasure overtakes and I lose all sense of reality.

"I want you, Echo. Please."

Thwack.

His hand whacks down on my arse and two of his fingers plunge into me. Stroking my clit with his thumb, he moves his fingers inside me, coming so close to my G spot but never quite touching.

"Tell me you're mine, Livvy." His words barely register.

I'm so close, my orgasm building then fading in waves as he teases me. My fingers and toes are tingling, my whole body tense, trying to chase the orgasm that Echo's keeping just outside my reach.

"Tell me you're mine." His voice is demanding and begging me at the same time.

Eyes screwed shut, I can see my orgasm in my mind; a ball of luminescent light, swirling and cascading over and over, almost in reach but a fingertip away.

"I'm yours, I'm yours," I scream.

His fingers pull away and the gaping sense of emptiness makes my stomach drop. Then I'm in the air and being thrown onto his bed. Ripping my panties down my legs he discards them over his shoulder, crawling up my body and hovering over me, his face above mine.

Then he kisses me.

It's only the second time we've kissed. We've fucked, we've argued, he's spanked me. But it's only the second time his lips have touched mine and now they're punishing, claiming my mouth and possessing me totally.

"Who do you belong to, Livvy?" he demands.

"I don't belong to anyone."

A growl of frustration spills from him. Crawling down the bed, he buries his face in my pussy and oh my, his tongue should be ordained a weapon of mass destruction, because it's both the best and worst thing to ever happen to me.

He licks my clit, teasing it before flattening his tongue and running it straight down the centre of my sex. He laps at me like he can't get enough of my taste, thrusting his tongue inside me, and fucking me till I'm writhing around the bed in delirious desperation.

Pulling back, he reaches up and tenderly strokes my cheek. "I love you like this, sugar, all desperate. Only I can make you feel like this, only I can do this to you. Tell me, Livvy, who do you belong to?"

Our eyes lock. He's a virtual stranger. I can't let him claim me, possess me.

His hand strokes my side, caressing my hip. He runs his finger straight down my sex, barely touching my clit. Dipping inside me with just the tip of his finger, he brings it up to his mouth and sucks the end. "You taste so sweet. Tell me who owns you. Who do you belong to?"

My mouth drops open, and I lick my dry lips. I've felt lost for so long. But looking into his eyes, time slows and everything makes sense.

"I'm yours. I belong to you," I say, my voice clear and coherent.

"Damn straight you do, sugar," he says with a smile.

Two fingers push roughly into me. "Gahhhh," I cry. My muscles clench around him, and I'm desperate for more. "Echo, please."

He grins and moves down the bed. Our eyes meet, and he smirks as he licks my clit. The sensation hits me like a bomb, and I surge off the bed, pushing my pussy into his face.

"Fuck, sugar, I'm gonna make you come so hard," he groans, nipping at my clit with his teeth. A third finger slides into me, curving upwards and finding my G spot and massaging until heat starts in my toes and consumes the rest of my body till I'm screaming in pleasure.

Sweat coats my skin, and my chest heaves as I gasp for air. Echo's arms wrap around me and he pulls me into his chest as his warm lips kiss my neck. "Sleep, baby," he whispers.

Exhaustion washes over me, my eyelids flutter shut, and I fall asleep.

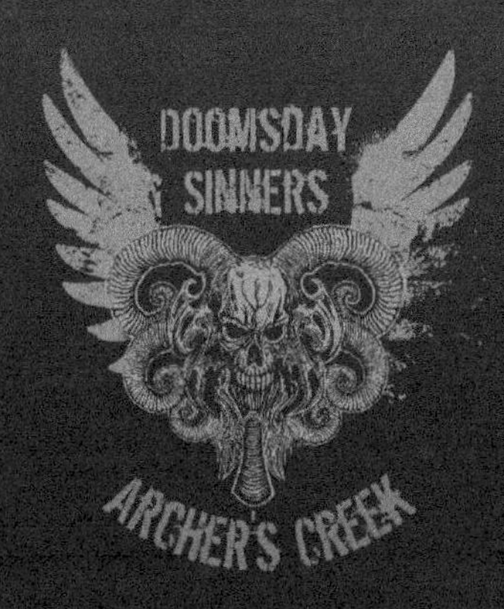

TWENTY-FIVE

Echo

I might have claimed her, but fuck, she's claimed me too.

I've never felt like this before.

I want to touch her and mark her. Hell, I want to tattoo 'Property of Echo' across her ass so everyone knows she's mine. The last time I had a woman for more than a night, I was eighteen and about to leave for the army, but seeing war and death changes you. I went in a boy and left a broken, cynical man.

I've been happy finding a willing hole to fuck for years, and I never thought I'd want anything more than that. But this girl, something about her is different. Today's been a fucking nightmare, but this right here, lying in bed wrapped around Livvy, feels right.

She's woken something inside me, a primeval need to claim her, to be in complete control. She's mine now, and I never plan on letting her go.

TWENTY-SIX

Olivia

I wake up naked and alone in Echo's bed. The sheets are cold; the dent in his pillow and his recognizable Echo scent are all that's left of him as an overwhelming feeling of emptiness in the room spreads to my chest.

Mine.

His words creep into my mind, along with memories of the possessive way he touched me. My hand reaches for my neck; I can still feel the way his fingers wrapped around my throat, how his lips kissing me is the last thing I remember before I fell asleep.

I walk to the bathroom and splash water on my face. Lifting my head, I groan at the sex-ravaged reflection that stares back at me in the mirror. His room's masculine and clean, but practically empty, and I hunt for my clothes but can't find them. His T-shirt hangs over the back of a chair, so I pull it over my head, loving how the soft cotton rubs against my naked skin, the fabric dropping to midthigh so only my legs can be seen.

I can't find my shoes, so I pad barefoot out of his bedroom and head towards the bar. The low hum of music and male chatter buzzing in the background. It's quieter than earlier, with maybe twenty or so bikers sitting in groups drinking and smoking. The atmosphere's relaxed, and no one notices me as I walk silently into the room.

Smoke's behind the bar. When he sees me, his serious eyes pin me to the spot, but quickly soften as recognition and amusement flash across his face. Taking in my T-shirt dress and bare feet, he smiles and shakes his head. He turns to a group of guys sitting on the other side of the bar, and whistles. "Echo, brother, you need to deal with her before she starts a fucking riot." He tips his head in my direction, and twenty sets of eyes turn to me.

Echo storms across the room and looms over me, his huge frame blocking me from view. "Livvy, what the fuck do you think you're wearing?" he snarls.

I shrug. "I couldn't find my clothes, so I borrowed a T-shirt."

TWENTY-SEVEN

Echo

She's standing in the middle of the clubhouse wearing a fucking T-shirt and nothing else.

I can't tell the entire fucking club to keep their eyes off my woman when she's wandering around practically naked.

When Prez called for church, I hid her clothes so she'd be forced to stay in my room. My woman's a flight risk, so leaving her naked was the only way to make sure she'd be there when I got back. I never figured she'd come find me just wearing my fucking T-shirt.

I can feel the heat of my brothers' stares on my back. All of the horny bastards are trying to get a look at what's mine. I've claimed her. I needed to hear her say the words and know she understood them.

She belongs to me, and it's time to claim her properly.

TWENTY-EIGHT

Olivia

Echo stalks closer; his hands circling my waist as he lifts me into the air. It feels like the most natural thing to wrap my arms and legs around him whilst he walks us back to his room.

He shuts the door behind us, and the lock clicks into place. Dropping me to my feet, his fingers grip the hem of his shirt and he peels it up and over my head. Completely naked, I stand as his eyes devour me from head to toe, my nipples hardening as his gaze drops to my breasts and arousal pools between my legs. The look in his eyes is territorial and predatory. I can see the hunger in him. His whole body tense and poised, ready to consume me.

"On the bed."

The command in his tone leaves no room for question and

I comply instantly, climbing onto the bed and shuffling back till my head hits the pillows. “Spread those legs wide, baby, I want to see that pussy.”

Vulnerability at being completely exposed washes over me, and a blush of embarrassment heats my face and chest. I cover my eyes with my hands and slowly let my knees fall to the sides.

“Look at me, sugar,” he growls and I let my hands fall away and my eyes meet his. “Good girl,” he praises, staring into my face for a moment, then, licking his lips before his gaze drops between my thighs to where my pussy’s open and displayed for him. His teeth pull his bottom lip into his mouth, pure sexual desire burning in his gaze, and I feel my arousal drip down my legs.

“So fucking perfect,” he murmurs.

Placing his leather waistcoat over the back of a chair, he pulls his undershirt over his head, revealing the colourful tattoos that adorn his beautiful chest. He’s a work of art. A huge chest piece flows effortlessly beneath the words ‘Honor’, ‘Love’, and ‘Freedom’, that stand proudly across his collarbones.

My mouth waters and my fingers twitch, desperate to touch him, to kiss every inch of him. His hands drop to his waist, and I watch while he opens the buttons on his jeans, popping them one by one. Defined muscles sculpt his abs, culminating in a v-shape that frames his hard cock. His jeans fall to the floor and pool at his ankles, before he kicks them to the side and straightens to his full height.

A tattooed Adonis. I barely get to appreciate the spectacular view of his naked form before he prowls towards me and I curl my legs together and sit up, desperate to reach him.

"Stop. Open your legs," he commands.

I fall back, resting on my elbows. The heat in his eyes and his gloriously hard cock fill me with confidence, and slowly I part my ankles, spreading my legs wide, and arch my back seductively.

A primeval sound escapes him as he pounces. He covers my body with his, pinning me to the bed. His hard cock slides against my pussy, and I lift my knees, desperately urging him closer to my aching core.

His kiss is a brand of ownership. He's consuming me, dominating me, all with the touch of his lips to mine, only pulling back to nip at my bottom lip with his teeth.

"I need you. Please," I beg.

A fingertip grazes my cheek, trailing a path to my chin. He tips my face up and kisses me. Echo reaches between my legs, where my flesh is swollen and dripping wet. Desperate, I wrap my legs around his back and try to draw him towards me, but he pulls my legs away and pushes them up to rest over his shoulders. His tattooed fingers grasp his impressively hard cock and tease my clit with the head.

"Ahhhhh," I moan as my hips thrust, rubbing against his swollen tip as I arch my back off the bed, pushing closer to him. I can't take it anymore. "Echo, please, please now."

Our eyes lock as he pulls on a condom, then slowly guides himself into me. My muscles stretch, accommodating his size, and the air pushes free from my lungs until he's fully sheathed inside me.

He circles his hips, and delicious pain sparks through me. I'm stretched to capacity, his length massaging every sensitive muscle as he slowly retreats. Gliding inside me again, he sets a torturous pace. Every thrust builds my orgasm in a slow burn that swirls in my stomach and heats my skin.

Pulling my nipple into his mouth, his lips wrap around the erect peak and suck tightly. He nips the pink tip with his teeth, but the pain instantly turns to pleasure when his tongue laves over the sensitive flesh.

"Sugar, I love your nipples. I could play with them all day," he says with a groan.

I moan when his teeth sink in further, biting harder, his warm tongue swirling across the hurt before he sucks my nipple deep into his mouth again. Pulling back, he changes the angle of his cock, his thrusts staying slow and steady, but his cock hits deeper. My orgasm hovers just out of reach while he plunges deep, each thrust exquisite agony. Shuddering, I throw my head back in ecstasy as he kisses a path down into the valley between my breasts, his tongue seeking out my other nipple, and taking it into his mouth, sucking hard.

"Oh god," I cry, desperately burying my hands into his hair, gripping and pulling with every thrust of his hips. "Echo," I whimper.

His eyes rise to meet mine while his teeth continue to abuse my nipple. "What's the matter, baby, do you need to come?" he drawls.

I nod frantically. "Yes. Yes. Now. Please, please."

A smug grin twitches at the corner of his mouth. My eyes follow his tongue as it dips out, flicking first one nipple then the other. "Who owns you, sugar?" he asks with a sly grin as his thrusts still, and he pulls back till only the head of his cock still inside me.

The answer slips from my lips easily. "You. I belong to you."

Firm hands grip my hips, pulling me onto him in one hard thrust. I whimper, my eyes rolling in bliss as slams back into me again.

"Who owns all your orgasms, Livvy?" Echo pauses, his cock buried deep inside of me, our eyes locked as he waits for my reply.

"You." The word flows easily, and I'm surprised to feel at peace with his ownership. He plunges back into me, and I shatter, screaming as my orgasm explodes.

My legs hit the mattress as he slides them from his shoulders. He flips me, and I land on my stomach, his fingers gripping my thighs as he lifts my arse and pushes my knees and legs under my chest. My arms drape in front of me, pliant, whilst he moves me into the position he wants and enters me from behind. My hypersensitive muscles happily stretch to allow him in; his whole body covering mine, as I surrender, completely subject to his will.

One of his hands covers my hip, while the other wraps around the back of my neck, his thumb gently stroking the skin, back and forth as he rocks in and out of me. The relentless pounding of his cock triggers another orgasm that bursts out of me on a cry and Echo tenses, groaning as his release spills deep inside me.

His cock slides out of me and I roll to my side, stretching out my legs and I watch as he pulls off the condom and throws it into the wastebasket. Collapsing back onto the bed his strong arms band around me and he pulls my head to rest on his chest. Neither of us speak, the room's silent except for panting breath and racing hearts. His fingers absentmindedly stroke the side of my breast while our legs knot together.

He's consuming me. We're practically strangers, but it doesn't seem to matter. "Oh my god, I can't believe I'm doing this," I murmur.

Echo chuckles lightly. "What do you mean, sugar?"

I reach up and cover my face with my hands. "This. I'm in Texas, getting spanked and fucked by a biker. I can honestly say, I never even dreamed this would happen to me."

Echo pulls my hand from my face. "Which part, the spanking or the biker?" he asks, amused.

Laughing lightly, I reply, "Both."

His chuckle vibrates through his chest. "You loved it. It's too late to pretend you're a good girl now."

I push off his chest and lean back on my elbow, our eyes meet. "But that's the thing, Echo, I am the good girl. I've only had boring sex with my normal, suit-and-tie boyfriends."

His eyes darken. "Fuck, Livvy. I don't ever want to think about another guy fucking you."

"Sorry." I sigh. "I just don't do this. I never expected this."

Echo pulls me back down so I'm resting on his chest again. "Livvy, I fucking love that you like me telling you what to do. I love the way your body reacts to me. I love the shade of pink your ass went when I spanked you, and the sounds you made. Sugar, you're fucking perfect, and all mine."

"This is fucked up." I groan.

His fingers still, and I try to move, but his arms clamp down, holding me to him. "There's nothing fucked up about this, sugar. You're mine," he growls.

Frustrated, I push against his hold and ask. "God, Echo, what the hell does that even mean?"

An exasperated sigh billows from his chest, and seconds later, I'm face down on the bed with his hand holding both my wrists above my head. His body weight pins me down, and rough fingertips pull my hair to the side. "Do I need to remind you again who you belong to?" he whispers.

Soft kisses rain from my jaw down my neck. "Hmm, sugar? Do I need to prove I own every inch of you?" His teeth sink into the soft skin where my neck meets my shoulder, and I shudder with need. "I don't need to prove anything, do I, Livvy? Your body knows who owns it. Your brain might be overthinking this, but your body feels this connection. Your body knows that this is exactly where we should be."

Flipping me onto my back, he straddles my waist and growls out. "Being mine means that we're together. I don't fucking understand this either, but I know that you belong to me and I belong to you. We can figure everything else out as we go along."

Filled with confusion, I shake my head and look away from him, unwilling to show him the fucked-up guilt gnawing at my chest. His fingers grip my chin and force my face up to meet his angry eyes. "Livvy," he snarls.

I want Echo more than I've ever wanted another man. Why did this have to happen now, when our time together is so limited. "We shouldn't be starting something that can't last, Echo. We have an expiry date. Eventually, I have to go home."

"No," he barks out. His lips claim mine, and the moment Echo touches me, the world around us stops. "Eyes on me, sugar. You don't question this. Us. It's new, I get that. But this connection, it's fucking real. It's happening. I gave you the chance to leave last night, but you decided to stay. So if you want out now, you need to look me in the face and tell me you don't feel what I feel."

His eyes burn into mine, daring me to deny it. I try to speak, but the lie sticks in my throat. "Yeah, sugar, that's what I thought."

TWENTY-NINE

Echo

What the hell is happening to me?

For years, women have been interchangeable, but never a long-term prospect. I've never met any bitch who ever made me feel like that could change.

Until her.

I can see a future with her. It scares the shit out of me, but for the first time, I want more from life. I thought the club and my brothers would be my future, and they are. But now the future has Livvy by my side too.

I don't know what's different about her. I want her in a way that makes no sense, but is completely obvious at the same time.

She's perfect, hot as fuck and feisty.

I want to own every inch of her, and for her to know that she fucking belongs only to me.

I lie in bed and watch her sleep, her perky tits rising and falling as she breathes, until I finally fall asleep, one hand wrapped around her tit and the other cupping her perfect fucking cunt.

When I open my eyes, daylight is creeping through the blinds, casting beams of light and shadow across the bed. She's still in my arms, her back to my chest, her ass pushed up against my cock.

My dick's awake and hard as fucking steel. Her tits are free of the covers, with her nipples hard and begging to be pinched. I can't help myself; I slide my hands up her sides, cupping both of her breasts and gently caressing. When I roll her nipples between my fingers, her breath hitches. She's not fully awake, but her body is responding, urging me on.

Relinquishing one nipple, I reach down her front and slide my hand over her pussy, spreading her lips wide and letting her arousal drench my fingers. As I coat her clit with her cream, she arches into me, searching for friction even in her sleep. Her wet cunt clenches around me, but reluctantly I remove my fingers from her perfect pussy, suck her arousal from my skin, and stare at the beautiful woman lying in my bed. My heart slams against my rib cage and a surge of possession pulls the air from my chest.

Mine.

Even in the short time we've known each other, she's gotten

under my skin; I want to wake up like this every day. I suddenly understand my anger when she snuck out after our first night together. I wanted to wake up with her. I wanted her to be the first thing I saw and touched, and I wanted to be the first thing she saw the moment she opened her eyes.

She sighs quietly in her sleep and carefully, I roll her onto her back and gently climb between her legs. I rest my body against hers, making sure my weight is held on my arms, and drop a kiss against the corner of her mouth. Her eyelids twitch, but she doesn't wake. I pepper kisses across her cheek and down her neck, watching as goosebumps pebble her skin.

Circling her nipple with my tongue, I pull it into my mouth and suck gently. She starts to stir, gasping lightly as her back arches, pushing her breast against my mouth. I reach for a condom, rip open the packet, and slide it over my hard cock. She's wet and ready for me, but I fight the urge to slide deep within her.

Her eyelids flick open and gradually she wakes, her eyes focusing on mine, and she smiles.

THIRTY

Olivia

My sleepy eyes focus on Echo.

I have no idea what's happening between us, but him being the first thing I see when I wake up is perfect. Smiling, I silently watch him; his hair's a mess, he's possessive, bossy, sexy, and… mine.

His tongue is busily licking and sucking at my breast, but when he realises I'm awake, he lifts his head and starts to speak. I interrupt him. "Hi," I say.

He tilts his head to the side, obviously amused. "Hi."

I don't know what to say to him. So far we've filled our time together with sex, but this morning feels different. I can feel his cock against my pussy, but the desperation to consume each other isn't as strong as the need to connect with him. Nerves flutter in my stomach, yesterday was so intense, and now I don't know how to act around him.

"Hi," he repeats, leaning forward until his lips meet mine. The moment his lips find mine all of my nerves disappear, his touch soothes me, and I wrap my arms tightly around him. Without a thought he pulls me into his chest holding me tight and humming contentedly into my neck.

"This is why you shouldn't have run from me, sugar. This is how yesterday should have started—you wrapped in my arms. I was so pissed that you ran off and we didn't get a chance to do this," he whispers reverently.

"Echo." I murmur, regret clear in my voice.

He loosens his embrace and silences me with a kiss. "It's done, but I wanna wake up with you every day from now on. Don't run from me again."

With a single grind of his hips he fills me, his cock sliding easily into my wet and eager core. Gasping I cling to him as he gently rocks back and forth, his eyes never breaking the connection with mine as he worships my body, arching over me, pushing me closer and closer until I splinter.

Still tingling from my orgasm, I feel the grin spread across my face. "Mmmm," I hum, totally sated, my limbs heavy. Snuggling into Echo's warm body under the blanket, I relax against his strong arms, sighing happily as he pulls me into his hard chest, and I melt against his warmth.

This man is a huge contradiction. He wants to claim me, own

me, but I don't feel like property. I feel desired and worshipped, and wrapped in his arms feels like the safest place in the world. A wave of happiness washes over me, and curled against him I let my eyes drift shut.

***

Warm fingers stroke the hair from my face. The mattress depresses and a quiet, gravelly voice calls, "Come on, sugar, time to get that sexy ass out of bed."

Groaning, I roll over and pull the blanket up to my nose. "God no, go away," I grumble.

His gruff laugh reverberates through the room. "Baby, don't make me drag you out of this bed. I promise you won't like it one bit."

Light floods the room, invading my sleep and early morning, un-caffeinated, anger spews from me. "Echo, for fuck's sake, just fuck off."

My eyes startle open as the blankets are ripped from me, cold air replacing my warm cocoon and coating my naked skin in goosebumps. Echo looms over me, grabbing me and flipping me onto my stomach so fast that I barely have time to process what's happening before his huge, rough hand thwacks against my arse cheek. "What the fuck?" I scream, kicking out at the angry man leaning menacingly over me.

"Watch your fucking tone, Olivia. I've told you before you

don't speak to me like that. Ever. I'll fucking spank your ass so hard you'll have my handprint on you for a week. You get me?"

My eyes widen in shock. It's weird to be turned on by how he just spoke to me, but arousal gushes from me, dampening my thighs.

Grabbing my hips, Echo flips me back into my back, crawling up my body and caging me in, his arms braced on either side of my head. "Let's try this again, shall we, sugar?" he drawls.

I nod, and a smug grin tips the edge of his lips. Leaning in, he presses his lips against mine, kissing me deeply, and his warm tongue forces entry into my mouth. I sigh contentedly when his lips release mine, his tattooed fingers twisting into my hair, tugging gently on the curls.

"Good morning, baby, you sleep good?" he asks, his Texas accent sweet as honey.

"Yes, thank you," I reply softly.

A smile breaks across his face, and he looks younger, happy. His eyes caress my skin, taking in my naked body. "Sugar, as much as I'd love to keep you naked and in my bed all day, it's time to get up."

"Urgggh, I hate mornings." I groan.

"You're not a morning person?"

"God no. My mum used to be up singing at the arse crack of dawn every morning when I was a kid, she ruined mornings for me." My lip curls in disgust at the memory.

"Singing. Why?" he asks, confused.

"She calls it celebrating the new day. I call it too many magic freaking mushrooms the night before."

Echo's laugh vibrates through his chest. "Magic mushrooms?"

I sigh deeply then reply. "Yep. My parents are huge hippies who're stuck in the seventies. Our house was practically a bloody commune."

Echo barks out a laugh. "A commune? Seriously?"

"Maybe it wasn't that bad. But it took me until I was a teenager to learn to sleep through her morning madness. I swear I still have nightmares whenever I smell incense." I shudder at the thought of the awful sickly sweet scent.

Echo's eyes dim and a shadow seems to cross his face before he speaks. "Sounds better than my parents. My dad used to drag my ass out of bed in the middle of the night and make me run drills for hours before I could go back to sleep. Having a drill sergeant for a dad was no fucking picnic."

I want to comfort him, but he's not telling me this for my sympathy, he's just sharing something about himself with me. "Your dad was in the army too?"

"Too? Who the fuck told you I was in the army?" he barks.

Unsure where his anger has come from, I pull in a shaky breath. "Brandi mentioned it. I didn't realise it was a secret."

Echo's eyes darken before he closes them and quickly shakes his head. When they open again, the shadows seem to have cleared, and he smiles apologetically as he cups my cheek.

"It's not, sugar. I just don't like to talk about it."

Kissing me quickly, he sits up, pulling me into his lap. I want to ask him more about his past and his time as a soldier, but before I get a chance, warm hands slide under my legs and he stands, lifting me into the air like I weigh nothing. I cling to him like a monkey, my arms and legs wrapped tightly around him as he walks us across the room.

Echo stops in front of the bathroom door loosening his grip on my legs until I slide down his body and my bare feet hit the cold wood floor. I wait with my arms still entwined around his neck and my naked body fully pressed against him as his huge erection pushes against my belly, and my skin tingles in anticipation of his touch. Dipping his head he nuzzles the hollow where my neck meets my shoulder. The air around us crackles with chemistry, and his warm tongue tastes my skin.

He exhales loudly like he's in pain, pulling my arms from his neck and separating us as he slowly steps back. Without the warmth of his body the cold air of the room hits me, making me aware that I'm still naked and chilling my skin. Still standing at arm's length, he touches my shoulders, turning me away from him and towards the bathroom, his fingertip trailing a line down the curve of my spine, right before he smacks my arse hard.

"Go take a quick shower, sugar. Breakfast's in ten," he says on a laugh when I jump away from him covering my arse with my hands.

Scowling at him I take a step towards the bathroom, pausing

for a second before glancing back over my shoulder and flashing him my most innocent smile. “Don’t you want to join me?”

His eyes darken, raking over my naked form. “Is that what you want? You want me to bend you over in the shower and fuck you from behind?”

The air in my lungs stops, and I pull in a short, desperate breath. My heart is pounding in my chest and my sex throbs with excitement, but his face is hard as he waits expectantly for my answer. My eyes roam his T-shirt-covered chest, his tight worn jeans, and the obvious outline of his hard cock. I take in every glorious inch of him, moving upward till I’m staring into his eyes. Then I nod.

His soft chuckle and mischievous smile have my skin prickling in anticipation. “We both know if I touch you right now I’ll end up fucking you so hard and so many times you won’t be able to walk by the time I’ve finished with you.”

Nodding enthusiastically, I turn toward him, waiting for him to pounce on me, feeling like his prey, only I want to be caught. His first step towards me makes me want to run to give chase, but the urge to throw myself into his arms is just as strong, so I wait for him to take the next step. But he doesn’t move.

Instead, he reaches out, his fingertips stroking my nipple softly before pinching slightly. I watch his fingers work their magic, mesmerized, until his voice pulls my attention. “I’m going to fuck you so hard your legs shake, I’m gonna own every inch of you.” He pauses, pulling at his bottom lip with his teeth.

"But not now. So stop trying to tempting me into fucking you and go take a shower."

Disappointment washes over me, and I pout, but his eyes harden, telling me silently that there's no point arguing with him, so I slowly walk away from him, throwing over my shoulder, "Echo, where are my clothes?"

His cheeky laugh confirms that he stashed my clothes last night to stop me from getting dressed. "No idea," he says, smirking.

I turn to face him and shrug nonchalantly. "Okay, no problems, I'll just go au naturel then today. I'm sure the guys in the bar will all appreciate the show," I say, cupping my breasts in my palms and rubbing my thumbs over my nipples, sighing seductively.

Echo's eyes darken to almost black as his face contorts with a scowl. "That's not fucking funny." His voice rises to just shy of shouting, "No one gets to see you like this but me. You hear me, Livvy?" His entire body is rigid with rage as he stomps away from me. "Get in the shower. Your fucking clothes will be waiting for you. Come find me when you're done." Anger fills the air, and furious eyes flash at me before he turns his back and leaves, slamming the door behind him.

Stunned by Echo's reaction, I stare at the closed door. I was hoping to provoke him into fucking me in the shower. I didn't expect his anger, but I'm incredibly turned on by his possessive reaction. "What the hell?" I say, confused.

Shaking my head, I blow out an exasperated breath and turn on the shower, stepping under the torrent of steamy water. Echo's shower gel smells like him, an intoxicating scent of clean soap and citrus. Inhaling deeply, I close my eyes and images of him bending me over, my hands pressed against the cool tiles, flash behind my eyes. My breath catches in my throat as I imagine the powerful water drumming on my back as Echo pounds into me, his body arched over mine, his possessive voice reminding me that I belong to him.

I move my hands slowly down my body, needing to take the edge off the ardent desire that Echo sparked to life. As I reach my pussy, I hear his commanding voice in my head.

"No."

Instantly stilling, my eyes widen as I realise what I've done. His dominant personality is consuming me, and I can't help liking it. Just the sound of his authoritarian voice in my memory has my abused nipples standing to attention and my sensitive sex pulsing with arousal.

Flipping the water to cold I let the freezing stream coat my heated skin, icing my libido. When I turn off the water I'm shivering from the cold shower and I drag Echo's fluffy towel over myself, drying my skin and wrapping it around me before I walk back into his room. His clothes hang messily over the back of a chair, and I drag my hand across them, strangely comforted by the familiarity of his belongings.

Finger combing my wet hair, I pull it into a messy braid,

knotting the end to keep it in place. My dress is laid out neatly on the bed, but my bra and panties are missing. I pull on my dress, smoothing down the skirt, before turning to check my appearance in his mirror. My reflection shows no hint that I'm naked beneath the fabric and I giggle, rolling my eyes and smiling to myself that Echo, my dominant man, will be the only one who knows I'm wearing a dress and no panties.

Echo's black waistcoat is laid on the bed with a note resting on top of it. I drop the note onto the sheets and instinctively reach for the supple leather. Picking it up, I realize the waistcoat is smaller than Echo's and I rub my thumbs reverently across the butter soft leather before turning it over. On the back there's a large embroidered demon face with horns and wings and eyes that stare back at me. Imposing script spells out Doomsday Sinners above the demon and Archer's Creek below it.

Turning it back over in my hands, I trace the embroidered letters with my fingers. "Property of Echo." My heart starts to race as I read and re-read the words. It's beautiful in a strange way, leather isn't really my style, but its so soft and as I bring it up to my face and inhale deeply, the rich, comforting scent of Echo fills my nose.

Carefully placing the waistcoat back onto the bed I pick up the note. Echo's handwriting is strong and concise, with each letter written in capitals.

WEAR ME – E

I reach out to grab the waistcoat, but pause with my fingertips inches above the leather. This feels significant. Echo's told me again and again since we met that I'm his, but wearing a badge that literally says property feels much more monumental than his private claims in the throes of passion.

Moments pass while I stare at the word 'property'. When I'm in his arms he makes me feel worshipped not owned, but it feels too soon to even call him my boyfriend, let alone wear a badge that tells the world I belong to him. Is this something to do with the biker club? I wrack my brain, wishing I'd paid more attention to the MC romance books my friend tried to get me to read, if I had I'd probably know if this property tag is significant.

Frustrated with myself, I quickly grab the waistcoat and slip the leather over my shoulders. It's warm to the touch and heavier than I expected. Pulling in a deep breath, I wait to see how it feels, wait for it to feel wrong only instead of being repulsed, Echo's scent surrounds me, and my lingering doubts evaporate. Trusting my instincts I hug the material around myself, quickly leave Echo's room and head into the clubhouse.

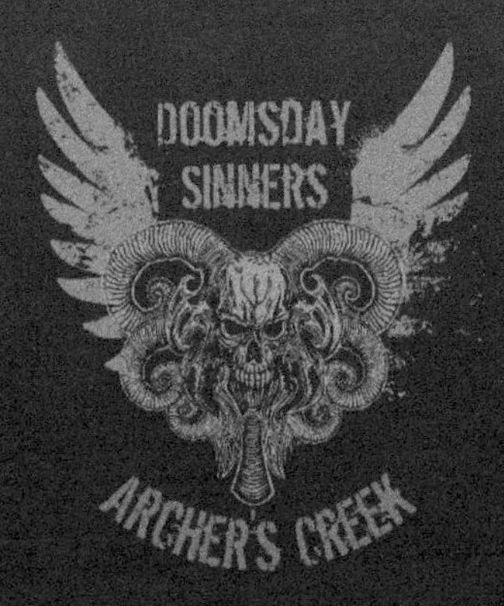

THIRTY-ONE

Echo

Morning sex with my girl is the best fucking kind of sex. But every time I fuck her it's even better than the time before. She makes my dick hard the moment she touches me. Fuck, who am I kidding? I've been walking around with a constant hard-on since the first time I laid eyes on her.

Last night I made her mine and this morning I left her my property cut for her and told her to wear it. There's a tiny part of me that knows it's wrong to ask her to wear it when she doesn't completely understand what it'll mean, but honestly, I don't fucking care. I'm taking her as my old lady, and I want the whole club to know it.

My gaze finds her the moment she walks into the bar, her long legs bare and perfect, her sexy fucking dress playing peekaboo, flashing me a hint of her smooth thighs as she walks. She's naked, her pussy bare, but the sexist thing about her is the words emblazoned across her left breast.

'Property of Echo'

Three words that tell the world she's owned, that tell the club and my brothers to back the fuck off. A smile spreads across my lips and I watch her get closer, my dick ready to take her again, to pull her onto my lap and slide into her naked cunt.

She's walking fucking sin and every single person in the room has noticed, she's so fucking sexy it's impossible not to notice her. But they also saw the cut, they saw *my* fucking property cut, and they all know what that means.

She's mine.

My old lady.

I claimed her in the eyes of the club, and no one can touch her now. Hell, if I wanted to, I could make it so none of the horny fuckers ever look at her again.

She doesn't know that the moment she put it on it branded her as mine. The clubhouse's full, so basically every member of the Sinners now knows to treat her with the same respect they treat me.

She's got the club's full protection, because she belongs to me and the Sinners now.

And she's got no fucking clue.

THIRTY-TWO

Olivia

Walking into the bar it feels like every eye in the place turns to look at me. My skin starts to tingle, and I can feel his eyes on me before I spot him. Echo's sitting at the furthest table, waiting patiently for me to come to him, but the heat in his eyes smoulders brighter with every step closer I take. Time slows, and moments feel like hours, but as soon as I'm near, his arm shoots out, grabbing me and pulling me onto his lap.

Warm lips press against my ear, his whiskey-smooth voice whispers, "Fuck, I want you naked in nothing but that cut. Feel how hard I am for you right now." Rolling his hips, his solid cock pushes against my arse and arousal pulses through my over sensitized body.

I wiggle in his lap and Echo groans against my neck, making

a girly giggle burst from my lips.

"You think that's funny, do you?" he growls, his hand sliding up my thigh and disappearing under my skirt. A fingertip circles my clit, and I jump. "Not so funny when it's you getting teased, is it, sugar," he growls into my neck.

Clamping my thighs together I push at his hand. "Stop, we're in a room full of people," I hiss.

His face falls into a scowl. "I don't give a fuck where we are, Livvy. This pussy belongs to me, and I won't let anyone see what's mine, but its mine to touch whenever the fuck I want."

Leaning in, he takes my mouth in a hard, possessive kiss, and I melt into him. My legs relax and his fingers impale me. He swallows my squeal, in his kiss before curling his fingers into me and massaging my sensitive nerves.

"Mine." The word is said on a growl with his lips buried against my neck. Pulling his fingers roughly from my pussy, he sucks them into his mouth. My stomach swirling with nervous desire as I watch him lick my arousal from his skin.

"Delicious," he murmurs, wrapping his strong hands around my waist and lifting me from his lap. My feet hit the floor, but before I can move he's behind me, pulling me into him, my back tight against his chest. His palm wraps around my throat, his fingers spread wide collaring me as he tilts my head to the side.

Warm breath heats my ear and when he speaks, his voice

is quiet and only for me. "Don't ever try to stop me touching you or your pussy, sugar. You gave yourself to me and I don't plan on giving you back."

Releasing his hold on me, he softens, urging me forward with a playful slap on my arse. Echo guides me to a long trestle table overflowing with breakfast food, and my mouth waters at the crispy bacon and fluffy eggs. Filling my plate, I skirt my way back to our table, setting my plate down at an empty spot and pulling out a chair.

"No," Echo growls, lifting me off the floor and repositioning me in his lap.

I roll my eyes at his caveman behaviour and turn arching my eyebrows in question. "Echo, what are you doing? There's plenty of chairs."

"But I want you on my lap," he says with a pout. My big bad biker's actually throwing puppy dog eyes at me, and I melt, relaxing against his chest and loving how his strong arm bands around my waist holding me in place.

The food is delicious, and after the first mouthful, I take a moment to look around the room. The clubhouse is vast, a mix of beautiful exposed brickwork and simple whitewash. Sinners memorabilia lines the walls with framed leather waistcoats hanging in a row behind the bar. A bank of leather booths run along one wall, with tables and sofas dotted in groups throughout the cavernous space. There's a pool table at the far end, then a doorway that leads to the bedrooms with more rooms leading off a balcony above us.

The place is huge, but in the daylight, it's bright and airy, completely different to the dark sexually provocative club I'd experienced at the party. The room's filled with a sea of bikers in identical leather waistcoats, the horned demon on the back and a name patch on the front. A few familiar faces lift their chins in greeting as I scan the crowd, but the majority either eye me with interest or pointedly avoid my gaze.

Fascinated, I pick out the handful of women. They're all young and attractive, but hard with too much make-up, fake boobs, and tight jeans. But unlike at the party, at least they're all wearing clothes.

Sleaze pulls out a chair and sits down at our table, nodding to Echo. "Brother." Then turns to me. "Olivia, nice to see you again," he says, with a small smile.

I smile shyly. "Morning, Sleaze."

Turning back to Echo he raises his eyebrows in question and motions to me. "So when did this happen?" he asks.

"Last night," Echo replies with a smile, his hand creeping up my thigh, teasing me as his fingers spread wide across my leg.

Sleaze nods. "And you're sure, 'cause you know what it means?" he asks pointedly.

Echo tenses beneath me, his easy-going mood dissolving. "Course I'm fucking sure," he snarls.

Confused, I look between Echo and Sleaze. "What's going on?"

Reaching up, Echo wraps his hand around my nape, pulling me in for a searing kiss. "Nothin', sugar," he assures me.

Echo's kiss silences me for a second, but I'm not an idiot, and it's pretty damn obvious that something's going on. I focus on him, waiting for him to meet my eyes, but his gaze stays locked on his plate and he refuses to acknowledge my question.

Sighing frustratedly I turn to Sleaze. "Sleaze, want to tell me what's going on?"

Echo's eyes finally lift from his plate, and he growls at me, his teeth clenched. "I just told you everything was fine, Olivia."

Ignoring Echo, I stare at Sleaze. Torn, he looks to Echo, then back to me. Sighing deeply, he runs his hand over his face before leaning back in his seat and crossing his arms over his chest. "This is between you and your man, I just think y'all are making a pretty bold statement," he finally says.

Confusion must show on my face, because Sleaze points to the leather waistcoat I'm wearing. "Echo asked me to wear this. Why's that a statement?" I ask warily.

Anger contorts Sleaze's face and furious, he turns to Echo. "What the fuck, brother? You didn't tell her what prancing about in your fucking property cut means?"

"This is none of your fucking business, Sleaze," he grits out angrily.

Pushing Echo's hands off me, I jump out of his lap, turning to stare at the two men. Echo reaches for me, but I dodge and step out of his grasp.

"Livvy, get your ass back over here," Echo warns.

Angrily, I shake my head and take another step away from him, pulling one arm free from the leather cut. "Echo, I don't know what the hell's happening here, but me wearing this," I cry, grabbing the 'Property of Echo' patch and shaking it at him. "Is obviously more significant than I think it is. You need to explain what kind of statement I just made, because Sleaze's reaction says that this waistcoat means a hell of a lot more than I think it does."

Rising from his seat, Echo towers over me, his teeth gritted together his body tense with barely restrained anger. "Olivia, don't you fucking dare take that off. I swear to fucking God, woman," he growls, his voice full of cold authority.

"Fuck you, Echo," I shout, shrugging off the cut and throwing it at his chest as I turn and walk away from him. Crossing the room I march straight for the exit door, but Smoke's leaning against it, his arms braced across his huge chest. "Move Smoke, I'm leaving."

He shakes his head. "Sorry, Liv, not gonna happen."

I widen my eyes, anger pulsing through me. "Please," I beg, but Smoke just smirks and shakes his head. "Sorry, honey," he shrugs.

Taking a step closer to the man giant I fight to keep my calm, but lose. "Smoke, I swear to fucking God, I will cut your cock off in your sleep if you don't let me out of here right now. Didn't you learn not to mess with an angry British woman the last time I kneed you in the balls?"

His eyes widen in surprise, but he doesn't get a chance to respond because my skin prickles in recognition, and I know Echo's standing behind me. Smoke glances over my shoulder and nods before moving aside.

Pushing past him I open the door, and rush away from the building, but within two steps, Echo's hands are on me and I'm lifted off the floor and spun around to meet his heaving chest and furious face. "Livvy, I've had enough of you fucking running from me. You said you were mine, and I'm making sure that every one of my horny fucking brothers knows it too."

Ripping away from his grip, I step back, but Echo follows me, stepping forward and refusing to allow me to evade him. "What does it mean?" I shout. "The waistcoat. What does it mean that I was wearing it?"

Echo straightens, pulling his shoulders back, his eyes sparkling with intensity. "It's called a cut," he replies coolly.

Rolling my eyes sardonically, I sneer at him, "Thanks, I really should have invested in that biker-to-English translation guide when I saw it the other day."

"Livvy." Echo's tone is a warning, but I'm too angry to care.

"What did you do Echo? You set this up, you got me to wear it knowing I didn't know what it meant. You owe me an explanation of just how fucked I am."

His arm curls around my spine, forcing me to stay put while he closes the distance between us until my breasts are pressed tightly against his chest. "It means you're my old lady Livvy."

"Old lady," I gasp, my eyes widening with shock, my lips parting as words form, but die when Echo speaks again and I feel the vibration of each word as he says it.

"It means you're my woman. My property. You're part of the Sinners now. They'll treat you with respect because they can't look, touch, or fucking speak to you without my okay. You. Are. Mine," he growls.

"Oh my god, what have you done," I gasp, my words barely a whisper. "This is too much, too quick. Why?"

"I don't care if it's a minute, a day, or a fucking lifetime. You belong to me and have since the moment I set eyes on you," he roars, the sound so primeval I try to arch away from him, only to have my escape stopped by the steel band of his arm.

When his lips find mine, instead of fighting, like I know I should, I surrender. The moment his hands touch my skin, my anger dissolves and I melt into his command of my body. His lips attack mine, kissing me roughly, reinforcing his claim, owning me and dominating me.

He lifts me off the ground and my legs instinctively wrap around his waist, his touch consuming me so all I can think is *more*. Something about him makes all of my resolve to keep things casual between us disappear, his controlling attitude and orders make my brain switch off and my instincts take over. All I want is to give myself over to him and allow him to consume me.

My back hits a wall, a second before his rock-hard cock

grinds against my pussy through the fabric of his jeans. Pulling away from my lips his hand wraps around my neck, collaring my throat, dominantly holding me in place as he reaches down and releases his length. Our eyes lock, and for a second he pauses, rubbing the head of his cock across my wet folds and coating it in my arousal before guiding himself to my entrance and plunging into me in one hard thrust. All the air bursts from my parted lips, but he doesn't give me a second to catch my breath before he's pulling out and slamming back into my pussy. This is more than just sex, it's brutal and raw, his fingers wrapped around my throat, the other beneath my thigh angling me so he can take me hard enough to brand me at his.

His eyes stay locked with mine while he takes me ferociously again and again. "Always," he rasps. "Forever." His voice is dark and stern, branding his claim into my brain. "Mine."

Two more thrusts and he sends me over the edge making me scream as my orgasm is forced from me in an explosion of angry, violent pleasure. Silencing me with his lips he thrusts, frantically slamming into me so hard I cry out against his mouth in glorious pain as another orgasm roars through me. Echo groans and jerks, emptying himself deep inside me, filling me so completely that my eyes roll back in my head before his body relaxes, slumping down against my shoulder.

My breath falls from me in loud erratic pants. He lifts his head, his eyes finding mine a moment before he presses his lips to mine and kisses me gently, reverently and in complete contrast to the angry, savage sex we just shared.

"Mine," he whispers, his hand sliding up from my neck to cup my cheek, gently stroking my heated skin.

The hand beneath my thigh, squeezes gently before he angles my body and slides his still semi-hard cock out of me. I wince as hot liquid runs down my thighs, then freeze, my entire body tensing, as panic washes over me.

"Fuck," I whisper, clawing at Echo's shoulders until he drops me, and I fight to stay upright on wobbly legs. "Fuck," I scream, furious at myself for my own stupidity.

"Livvy?" I barely hear him shouting, too consumed in my own thoughts. "Livvy, baby, what's wrong?"

Reaching between my legs I run my fingers through the sticky cum coating my fingers before thrusting them in front of his face. "This is what's wrong," I screech. "Your fucking cum running out of me. We didn't use a condom. Oh my god, how could we be so stupid?"

He stares at me like I've lost my mind.

"Echo, are you clean? Please tell me you're clean," I beg.

His eyes focus on my fingers, where his cum glistens in the sunlight.

"Echo," I shout.

Blinking, he looks back at me. "Lift up your skirt and spread your legs."

I shake my head furiously. “Answer the fucking question, Echo. I’m clean, are you?”

His face darkens. “Of course I’m fucking clean; I’ve never had sex without a condom. Never,” he says through gritted teeth.

My eyes roam his face, searching for a lie, but he looks sincere and I believe him. Relief flows through me, and I tip my head back to rest on the wall.

“Livvy, lift up your fucking skirt and spread your legs,” he growls.

My eyes lift, his expression is dark, intense, he’s in full dominant mode.

“Now.”

My heart pounds at his command, and I slowly lift my dress and move my legs apart. His gaze drops to my thighs; and he squats down, his face mere inches from my pussy as he watches his cum work its way from my sex and down my inner thighs. Reaching out he caresses me, stroking his fingers up and around my entrance, feeling my arousal mix with his cum and soak his hand. “I love to watch my cum drip out of you, sugar. I love knowing that I’ve been so deep in you, claiming you from the inside out,” he rasps.

Two fingers slide into my pussy as he collects his cum and pushes it back inside me. I’m so focussed on watching his fingers that his voice startles me. “I want my seed still inside you hours after we finish,” he murmurs.

Pulling his fingers free, I gasp as he collects more of the

arousal that's coating my skin and slides it back into me. Adding a third finger, he pushes up until his knuckles are almost buried, curling his fingers and forcing his cum as deep as he can get it. "I'm never using a condom with you again, Livvy. I'm gonna mark your cunt with my seed and brand you every time we fuck. I'm gonna push my cum deep back inside, so every fucking horny man who comes near you will smell me on you and know you belong to me."

As he talks his fingers work my pussy. "You're gonna come sugar, clench down hard on my fingers and let your greedy cunt suck all of my seed back into you." His dirty words and talented fingers push me over the edge and I shake and mewl incoherently when I orgasm all over his hand, my body pulsing in ecstasy.

THIRTY-THREE

Echo

I've fucked a lot of women, and putting a condom on is like second nature to me. I always wrap up; hell, the club whores spread it about so much sometimes I double wrap. I don't want my dick anywhere near their nasty cunts without a rubber.

But I was so desperate for Livvy, I didn't even think about a condom. Fuck, sliding into her perfect pussy without any barriers is the most incredible thing I've ever felt. Her pussy is mythically good, tight and hot, and fuck, now I know what she feels like bare, there's no way I'm gonna let anything stop me from feeling her heat on my cock when I slide deep inside her.

The look of panic and fear on her face when she realized we hadn't used a condom made me feel like a bastard for not taking care of her. At least until I saw my cum on her fingers and dripping out of her pussy. Then my cock saluted me and told me to bend her over and do it all over again. I'm turning into a fucking caveman, because the idea of filling her full of my seed makes my heart pulse and my pride swell.

My cum leaking out of my woman's pussy, I had no idea that it would be a massive fucking turn-on.

I should see if she's on the pill, but honestly, I couldn't give a crap. I want her full of my seed. I want, no, I need to brand her in every way possible.

My future, Livvy, her belly swollen with my baby.

Where the fuck did that thought come from?

I've never wanted a family, but Livvy pregnant.... My chest swells at the idea that she might be growing my child already.

Her voice startles me. "I'm on the pill, so we don't need to worry about me getting pregnant," she says nervously.

Fighting not to show my disappointment, I just nod, rubbing my fingers over her cunt one last time before I pull her dress down, hiding her from my view. "Come on, baby, let's go and pack up all your shit from Mimi's before work, and I'll get one of the prospects to go fetch it later," I say taking her hand and guiding her towards my bike.

"Why would I pack my things?" she asks, sounding confused.

Smiling, I throw my arm over her shoulders and pull her into my chest. "If you're moving in with me I figured you'd want your stuff," I say with a laugh.

THIRTY-FOUR

Olivia

"Echo, I'm not moving in with you," I say, not even trying to hide the horror in my voice.

Ignoring me, he lowers the helmet onto my head and busies himself fastening the strap.

"Echo, I'm serious."

Gentle fingers caress my cheek before his lips graze the corner of my mouth. Silenced, I simply stare as he effortlessly straddles his bike and waits patiently for me to climb on behind him.

The ride to Miss Mimi's is thankfully short. I hold on so tight I begin to lose feeling in my hands, my eyes stay closed and my face stays buried into Echo's back the entire time.

We stop and I jump off the bike, steading myself for a

moment before a fumble with numb fingers to undo the helmet. Echo moves my hands and unclips the strap, then pulls the helmet from my head and balances it on the handlebars of his bike.

I step back awkwardly. “Okay. Umm, thanks. I’ll see you later.” I turn to leave, but his fingers wrap around my wrist. My eyes dart up to look at him, and his smile is wide and indulgent.

“Go pack your shit. Then I’ll take you to work.”

I shake my head, trying to pull my arm from his hold, but his grip is unrelenting. “I’m not moving in with you, Echo, and I work just over the road I don’t need an escort.”

His smile twitches before he breaks into a raspy chuckle, “Go do as you’re told, sugar.”

His grip loosens, and I turn, darting towards Miss Mimi’s. Looking back over my shoulder, I blow him a kiss and shout, “I’m not moving in with you, Echo. See you later.”

The door clicks shut, and I flop back against it, shaking my head and smiling as I think about my bossy biker. Echo’s dominant personality consumes me, he breaks all my rules, but I like it, even though I shouldn’t. In the last twenty-four hours he’s made me happier than I can remember being and madder than I’ve ever been. I’ve run from him and then jumped back into his arms the moment he growls at me. He’s making me behave like a crazy person, but walking away right now would be impossible.

Pulling in several calming breaths I try to find some

equilibrium, but no matter how much I try to divert my brain, every thought flashes back to him and us.

I glance quickly at the clock; it's time to get to work, so I rush to shower before changing into denim shorts and a Strikers vest. Sassy heels are swapped for worn Converse, and I grab my bag as I head for the door.

My phone beeping distracts me, and I turn, grabbing it from the bedside table and quickly reply to a few texts from friends back home.

Home. The UK and my life there feels like a lifetime ago. Catching my refection in the mirror across the room, I'm not sure I fit into the world I left behind anymore either. The old Livvy was prim, proper, and lost. The girl in the mirror is wild, free, and happy. My American adventure might have helped me shake off the lost girl, but it's Echo and all of his maddening qualities that are responsible for the smile.

As I leave Miss Mimi's, he's leaning up against his bike just where I left him thirty minutes earlier. Blowing out a sigh I tip my head to the side, raising my eyebrows at him. He smirks in response. "Echo, what are you doing?"

Handing me the helmet he waits for me to strap it on. I stare at it, then look over Echo's shoulder at Strikers just across the street. "The bar is right there." I point behind him, but he doesn't even glance. His eyes are fixed on me, narrowing as he waits for me to concede. "Echo, this is ridiculous." I sigh in frustration.

Strong hands lift me into the air, placing me on the back of the bike before I get a chance to protest. "Echo!" I shout.

Firm lips press against mine, silencing me, and my eyes fall closed. The kiss devours me, but it's over too quickly, and I slowly open my eyes just as he places the helmet on my head.

The journey to Strikers takes less than a minute. Climbing off the bike, I remove the helmet and hand it to him, but instead of taking it, he pulls me into his chest; palming my arse with his huge hands and lifting me onto my tiptoes so he can claim my lips again.

"See how much nicer I am when I get my way," he drawls.

I raise my eyebrows in exasperation and pull away from his grasp, turning to walk away. Echo's arm wraps around my shoulders and he drags me back into his shaking chest as he quietly chuckles, leading us both through the front doors.

Strikers is busy, with people standing three deep at the bar. "Bloody hell, it's only early. Why's it so busy?"

Pulling me into his chest he kisses my temple sweetly. "The night shift just finished at the factory, darlin'. They head into town for a drink before they go home to sleep."

Brandi busily rushes from customer to customer, and I head towards her, but Echo stops me, pulling me in for a passionate kiss. Arousal swirls in my stomach, his touch leaving tingles on my skin as I slowly open my eyes, desperate to see my desire echoed in his pupils.

Instead of lust, his eyes sparkle with mischief, and warm leather hits my bare skin. I look down and find I'm wearing the contentious cut, Property of Echo bold against the black fabric. He steps back, smiles, winks, then turns and walks away.

My eyes flick from his back to the cut and back again.

"Liv, get over here. Time to work, baby girl," Brandi shouts, her voice spurring me into action.

"One minute," I shout back.

Stomping across the bar, I shout, "Echo." He pauses and turns and I throw the cut, hitting him square in the face. Holding the leather in his hands his expression darkens and he stalks towards me. I back away, but he's too quick. Thick arms band around my waist tightly as lifts my feet off the ground and walks us away from the bar and into the shadows at the back of the room.

"Let me go," I scream, but my squeals are drowned out when the house band starts to play. Lowering me to the floor in front of a booth that's dimly lit and barely visible from the bar, I struggle in his arms till his hands push down the front of my shorts and panties, crudely cupping my pussy.

"Here's your options, sugar," he rasps angrily against my ear. "You can wear this cut and let everyone in this bar know that you're mine and to stay away. Or I can fuck your sore pussy with my fingers. I'll make you come over and over until you scream so loud that the entire town hears you and knows you're off limits."

Gasping loudly, I shudder when he kisses me on the temple.

"Now I like the sound of the second option, sugar, but it's

your choice," he says, his voice smug as his finger strokes up and down my sex.

"How about you stop being a fucking caveman and let me get to work. Then you can go do whatever it is badass bikers do all day," I shout.

A growl vibrates through his chest, and he forces me forward, bending me over the table at the booth. "Option three is I pull down these tight little shorts and give you a hard reminder of exactly who you belong to," he growls.

Pushing back against him I struggle to free myself, but his weight holds me down, keeping me helpless as he teases my clit. "Echo, I'm sore from all the times you've reminded me already in the last couple of days, so don't be a dick. Let me up," I snap at him.

His laugh's dark and hard. "This pussy belongs to me, Livvy. If you're too sore from taking my cock then I'll fuck you with my tongue and kiss it all better," he purrs. "Now tell me, sugar, who do you belong to?"

I push back against him as hard as I can, but he's unmovable. "Oh, for god's sake." I groan. "You, you stupid, psychotic caveman, I belong to you. Now stop being such a nightmare, give me the damn cut and let me get to work."

I'm freed and turned to face him a moment later. He drops the cut over my shoulders and I pull it over my Strikers vest and throw my arms out to the side, posing sarcastically. "Happy now?"

His smile is smug, and he lifts the hand he just pulled from my pussy to his lips, sucking his fingers enthusiastically. "Ecstatic. I'll be over here if you need me."

Rolling my eyes, I shake my head muttering obscenities about my ridiculous, crazy, manipulative man under my breath as I make my way to the bar.

THIRTY-FIVE

Deciding

Tainted.

Ruined.

I can see the impurity on her.

I can see the sin oozing from her skin.

She allowed herself to be contaminated by him.

Do I cleanse her, purify her soul?

Or set the sin free.

Now it's time to decide.

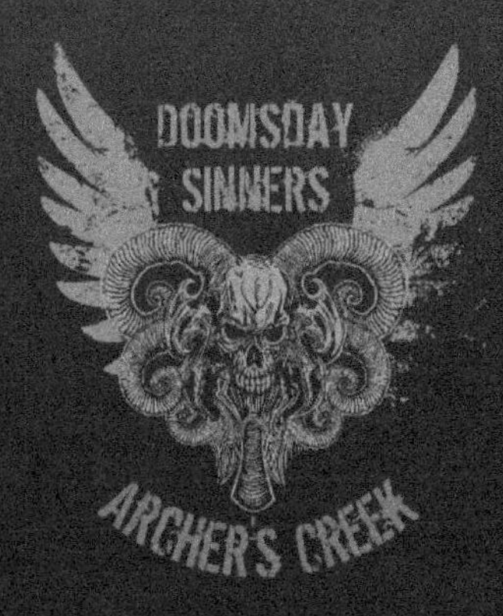

THIRTY-SIX

Echo

Sitting and watching Livvy is becoming an obsession. We always have a guy in the bar for security, usually a prospect pulling bitch duty while they earn their patch. But watching her work the bar with my name across her chest, I just can't convince myself to leave. I've got shit to do, work that won't go away just because I want to spend the day staring at my woman's ass, but my ass is still at the bar two hours after I got here.

She smiles and flirts with everyone and I swear, if I hear her laugh at one more thing these fuckers say, I'm gonna lose my shit. I can hear her giggling with Brandi, and I'm getting hornier every moment I sit and watch her. I'm seconds away from dragging her into the backroom and fucking her, my cock's so hard. Hell, if she hadn't told me she was sore, I'd have done it by now.

My phone rings, distracting me, and I tear my eyes away from her, glaring at the guy she just served as I pull my cell from my pocket. "Sleaze, what's up, brother?"

"There's trouble over at Beavers, and I need you to get over there."

Sighing I look up at the girls behind the bar. "Fuck. Send Daisy over to Strikers, and I'll meet you there."

"Why the fuck are you at Strikers?"

"I'm on security duty."

Sleaze laughs. "Let me guess, Liv's working."

"Fuck off," I hiss, scowling down at my cell. Everyone in Archer's Creek knows that Sleaze is a head case when it comes to his old lady, he marked her as untouchable years ago and there ain't many in this town who'd risk his wrath. But you bet your ass he'd be down here sitting at the bar with me if he thought anyone was stupid enough to try anything with Brandi.

"Brother, you've got it bad. I'll send Daisy down to watch the girls. See you in ten," he says with a laugh.

Shoving my cell back into my pocket, I head to the bar and crook my finger at Livvy. Sighing, she walks toward me, her eyes blazing with annoyance and heat. "I've gotta go do some work, so Daisy's gonna come stay at the bar till I get back."

"Brandi and I will be just fine. We don't need a babysitter."

"Sugar, this isn't a babysitting service. There's always a Sinner here. If these drunk bastards know there's someone from the club here, they don't start any trouble."

Nodding in understanding, she starts to take off her cut, and I growl. "Sugar, don't you dare take that fucking cut off." She glares at me, and I love the fiery, angry spark I see in her eyes; it makes me wanna fuck it out of her till she's all soft and submissive.

"Fine, you bloody caveman, I'll keep it on. Happy?" she snaps.

I reach out and grab her chin, forcing her to look at me. "Anyone touches you, and I mean anyone, I want to fucking know. Give me your phone." She reaches into her pocket and hands it to me. I program my number in and call myself before handing the phone back to her. Leaning over the bar, I pull her towards me, and kiss her till she's breathless and my dick's so hard I'm gonna be walking with a limp for the rest of the day. "Be good, baby, I'll be back soon," I say as I turn to leave.

My feet reach the door just as Daisy walks in. We shake hands, embracing with a back-slapping hug. "Prospect, I gotta go take care of some business. Look after the girls, make sure no one causes any trouble. If Livvy takes off that cut, you call me, and if anyone touches her, you fucking kill them. You hear me?"

Daisy barks out a laugh. "No problem, Echo."

I nod, taking one last look back at Livvy. Her face breaks into a smile before she blows me a kiss and I leave with a fucking massive pussy-whipped smile on my face.

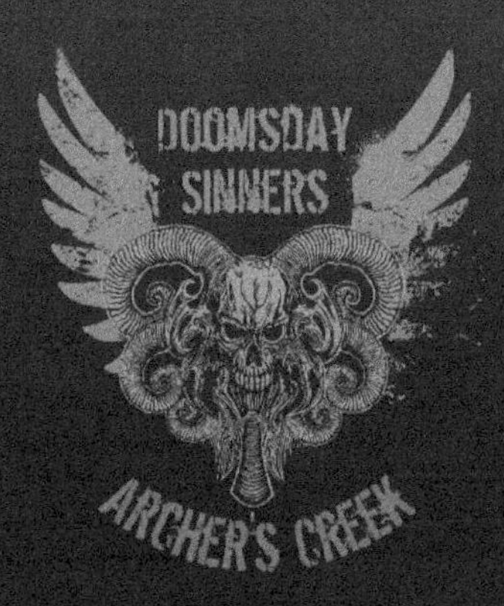

THIRTY-SEVEN

Olivia

The door's barely closed before Brandi's next to me, practically vibrating with excitement. "Girlie, you've got some explaining to do, so start talking."

Groaning I scan the bar, hoping for a customer, but the rush of night shifters has dwindled down and only a handful of guys remain. Sighing deeply, I scrub my hands over my face. "I don't even know where to start."

She tugs at the corner of the leather cut I'm wearing. "How 'bout you start with this," she suggests.

I start to shrug the cut off, but Daisy's grunt from across the bar halts me, and I turn, throwing an angry glare in his direction. "God, don't get me started on this thing," I sigh. "Echo left me a note this morning asking me to wear it. I figured he was just being his usual caveman self. You know what men are like about you wearing their clothes. So I put it on and walk straight through the clubhouse wearing it. I had no idea what he was setting me up for."

Brandi's hand covers her mouth in shock. "That bastard let you walk about announcing to everyone that you were his old lady, and you had no idea."

I nod. "Basically, yeah, that about sums it up."

She turns and jumps up to sit on the wooden bar. "So, are you his old lady? I mean, you're still wearing it, so you must be. But its been like a day how did this all happen?"

Stepping back to lean against the counter behind the bar, I sigh, lifting my hands up to clutch at my cheeks. "God, there's just something about him. I mean, I've never been around a guy like him before. He completely overwhelms me and drives me absolutely mad, but I just seem to find myself doing whatever he tells me."

Laughing, Brandi coos, "Baby girl, you found your first alpha. Don't they make them like him back home?"

Heat stains my cheeks. "If they do, I've not found one yet. Not that many alpha males in Lancashire, and Echo's like alpha on steroids. He's just so intense and dominating."

Brandi nods knowingly. "Yeah, but you love it, don't you?"

I nod and gush, "God, I really do. I've never been so turned on in my life. I've had more sex in the last twenty-four hours than I've had in the last six months. He only has to kiss me and I'm practically panting." Closing my eyes I let my head fall back and sigh loudly. "He wants me to move in with him. It's ridiculous; I only met him a couple of days ago. This is all moving far too fast and I go back to the UK in a few months' time. He's all in, and I just can't be."

Brandi jumps down from the bar and wraps her arms around me in a tight hug. "Sweetie, love doesn't happen at the same pace for everyone. Just 'cause it's quick doesn't mean it's wrong, and, girl, I've known Echo for years, and I've never seen him act like this."

I sag in Brandi's arms and homesick-filled loneliness overwhelms me. I miss my mum and my bestie. Stroking my hair, she pulls me tighter into her chest. "Oh baby girl, it's gonna be okay," she soothes kindly.

I'm so grateful for her in this moment, I need a friend and she's here acting like we've known each other forever. "I don't know what to do. When I'm near him, he's all I see. I can't stop being drawn to him, and the sex, god, the sex is out of this world." Words pour out of me in a rush. "But we don't know each other, and I'm leaving, and he's bossy and a pain in the arse, and he keeps threatening me with orgasms. I mean, seriously, what kind of threat is that? 'If you don't behave, I'm gonna make you come so hard you scream.' That's just a walking enticement for being a brat," I blurt out exasperated.

Brandi laughs so hard she doubles over, one hand on her hip, the other holding her stomach. "I'm sorry, it's just—" she explodes into another bout of laughter. I huff and grab a beer from the cooler, but before I can drink she steals the bottle from me and swallows deeply. "Okay, okay, *okay*, so what I'm hearing is that Echo is a sex machine who's trying to control you with orgasms," she says, trying not to laugh.

"Yes," I cry exasperatedly.

She barks out another loud laugh, spitting beer all over the floor. "And this is a bad thing why?"

I close my eyes, laughter bubbling from my chest. "Oh my god, there's nothing bad about that at all. What the hell am I complaining about?"

Her arms wrap around my shoulders, and her head rests on me as our laughter subsides. "Sweetie, you're overthinking this. You like him. The sex is hot. Just enjoy spending time together and fuck like rabbits. If you're meant to be together, you'll end up together. But in the meantime, have fun."

"I really should. But now he's sending biker babysitters to keep an eye on me. I mean, why the hell would I need a guard in this tiny town?" I ask exasperated.

Brandi smiles good-naturedly. "Daisy's not here for you. There really is always one of the guys from the club here. The town's pretty safe these days, but about a year ago there was this weird time when club girls started disappearing."

"What happened?" I ask.

"Well, they just stopped coming to the club."

"Maybe they decided they just didn't want a biker

anymore," I suggest. Brandi scoffs and shakes her head. "Okay, well maybe they decided that sleeping with every member of a club is not the right way to bag yourself a permanent biker, and they moved onto somewhere they won't get called whores?" I say sarcastically.

Brandi laughs loudly. "No, these girls were long-time club girls. They wore their club whore badges with pride. It was really strange, one day they were partying with the guys, the next day they were just gone and we never saw them again. These were regulars that were at the club five nights a week, and then they just never came back. First one girl, and then a couple of months later a second girl, and then a third. I think it was five girls in the end that just vanished."

"So what happened?" I ask intrigued.

"Well, Anders, that's the Sinners president, he spoke to the sheriff, and they did some enquiries but never found anything. Their families never even reported them missing, and when the sheriff contacted them, they weren't surprised, said that they probably picked up a guy and left town. The last one that disappeared was Elise, that was about seven months ago. None of them ever came back. It was strange," Brandi says, concern and sadness still evident in her voice.

"Wow, that's creepy," I say with a shudder.

"Yeah, totally. The club called all of the women and kids into lockdown for like a month, but the girls never came back and no one else disappeared."

The door opens and Gus walks in. Brandi pats my shoulder, squeezing gently before turning to serve a guy at the end of the bar. “Hi Gus, how you doing today?” I say, smiling broadly.

His glorious smile lights up his whole weathered face. “Evening, Miss Olivia. You’re a sight for old eyes, young lady.”

Heat rushes to my cheeks. “Gus, you old charmer, you’re making me blush.”

“My Millie always used to say I was a charmer.” Gus’s eyes mist over, and I reach over the bar and place my hand over his.

“Tell me about her.”

“She was an angel. She loved everyone, and she was always trying to mother those boys in the club. Not that they let her, but she was always trying. She was a kind soul, and much too good for an old geezer like me.” Unshed tears fill his eyes.

Smiling, I pat his hand. “She sounds like a wonderful person.”

“She was.”

I grab a beer and slide it across the bar to him. Tipping the bottle back, he takes a quick sip. I tense when his eyes drop to Echo’s name on the cut I’m wearing.

“I see you’ve got yourself a young man then.” I nod and look down at the property patch. Gus, smiles widely. “Echo’s a good man. He’ll look after you, but if he’s not treating you right, you come find Gus and I’ll set him straight,” he says sternly.

I relax, surprised at how much his approval means to me. “Thanks, Gus, I’ll let him know you’ve got your eye on him.”

The night goes quickly with a steady stream of customers who are all nice and chatty even though Daisy growls at every guy I serve. After a couple of hours I've had enough and stalk angrily over to him. "Daisy, what the fuck's your problem?"

He glances at my face before his eyes flick to Echo's name on my chest. He pauses for a moment then drops his gaze back to his phone.

"Daisy?"

Completely ignoring me, he focuses on his hands.

"Daisy, hello," I snap, slapping my hands against the wood of the bar dramatically. When he doesn't react, I straighten and turn my head, catching Brandi's attention and signalling to the now mute Daisy. She watches him for a second before shrugging in response. Shaking my head, I scoff and walk away from him.

By the time my shifts over, it's late, the last of the customers have left and I'm ready to take a shower and fall into bed. Daisy's still at his post at the end of the bar, watching Brandi and I as we finish cleaning and prepping for the next day, but I ignore him, grabbing my purse and hugging Brandi goodbye before I turn to leave. When my skin starts to tingle, I know he's here before the door even opens and then he's there, and I can't look away. Like a moth to a flame, I'm moving toward him and then he's puling me into him and wrapping me in his huge arms and even though it shouldn't, even though I fight it, he feels like home.

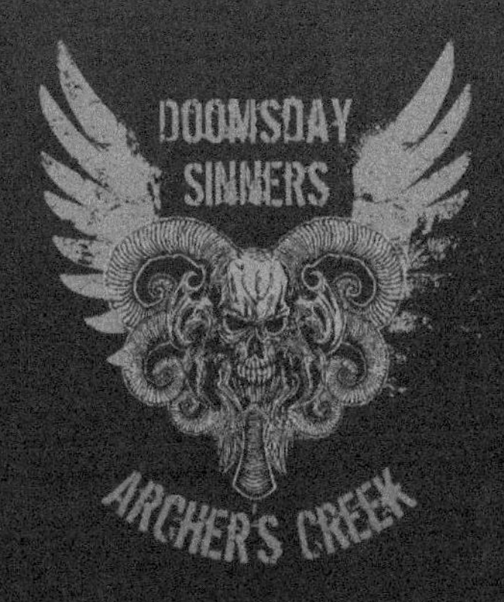

THIRTY-EIGHT

Echo

This bitch is under my skin, and I'm turning into a pussy-whipped fucking bastard. From the moment I headed out to Beavers earlier, all I've wanted is to get back to her. Every time my dick finally calms down, I end up thinking about her ass bent over in those tight fucking shorts and I'm rock-hard again. Then I think about all the drunk assholes at Strikers who are looking at my woman's ass bent over in those tight fucking shorts, and I'm so angry I can barely see straight.

I need to be inside her again. I need to remind myself she's only for me and those bastards might look, but they can only imagine how wet and tight her perfect pussy is.

Pushing open the door I walk into Strikers, and my eyes go straight to her. I know exactly where she is before I even see her. She's got her purse and I seriously fucking hope she wasn't planning on leaving before I got here. Archer's Creek is fucking remote and the town's basically run by the club, but there's still some fucking shady nutjobs out there. She needs to realize she can't go wandering around alone at night; it's not safe.

Heat flares in her the moment our eyes lock. She moves. I move. My arms reach for her and I pull her to me, holding her close to my chest until we both relax, the tension melting as our breathing syncs.

Daisy walks over. "We good?" he asks.

"Yeah, brother, you can head off now. Any issues?" I say.

He shakes his head and turns to leave as Livvy shouts, "Bye, Daisy, it was lovely talking to you."

Wrapping my hand around Livvy's neck, I turn her face to look at me. "What the fuck's that all about? Has Daisy been flirting with you?"

Both Livvy and Brandi burst out laughing. Livvy's head flops into my chest, her arms wrapping around my waist. Brandi's laughing so hard, she can barely speak.

"Hardly," Brandi says. "Liv tried to get him to stop glaring at the customers, but he wouldn't even look at her. He never spoke a single word to her all night."

What the fuck is wrong with me? Just the thought of Daisy flirting with her makes me want to beat the shit out him. I need to tone down this fucking crazy. I sound like Sleaze. Fuck, I've been busting his balls for years over how overprotective he is of Brandi. Now I know how he feels. “You ’bout ready, sugar?” I ask.

She nods, and I guide her out of the bar and lift her onto my bike. Her nose wrinkles in frustration, but ignoring her, I strap the helmet onto her head.

“Jesus Echo, Miss Mimi’s is literally a minute away. I can walk quicker,” she whines.

Ignoring her I climb onto my bike, pulling her forward so her body’s flush with mine and her pussy’s rubbing against my ass. Sliding my hand up her thigh, I squeeze gently. “Sugar, we can spend the night at that old bitch’s if you want, but I guarantee my bed’s more comfortable.”

She scoffs. “How about I spend the night in my bed and you spend it in yours?”

God, this bitch frustrates me. “Olivia, it’s late. Stop being a fucking pain in the ass and pick. My bed or yours. It don’t matter to me, ’cause either way, my cock’s gonna be deep inside you in the next half hour.”

THIRTY-NINE

Olivia

For the third night in a row, I'm back at the Sinners' clubhouse and on my way to Echo's bed.

"Livvy." His voice is full of command, and I reach for him, my skin tingling and desperate for his touch. Warm fingers wrap around the back of my neck, his thumb grazing back and forth over the pulse point as he guides me through the bar. My panties are soaked with arousal, and my heart races as I count the steps till we're alone.

Several sets of eyes follow our progress, but instead of the lascivious looks I got the first night, there are respectful nods.

His grip on my neck tightens. "You're my old lady now," he says.

I nod, and understanding dawns on me. To this brotherhood

of men, being an old lady elevates me above the women just here to get fucked. Being an old lady makes me significant, a part of this life, a part of the club.

Opening his door, he urges me through before shutting and locking it behind us. His room's tidy and impersonal, clinical almost. The last two times I've been here I've been too angry and filled with lust to really take notice.

"Do you live here all the time?" I ask. His eyebrows lift in surprise, and I shrug. "I don't know anything about you. It's not like we've done a lot of talking the last few days."

Chuckling lightly, he reaching out and collars my neck with his hand, his thumb stroking the skin on my cheek. "I live here most of the time. I've got a house just outside of town, but I don't use it that much, too quiet."

Unexpected tears well in my eyes. His answer is much more telling than he realises. "Do you have any family in town?" I ask. He narrows his eyes, his hand falling from my neck, before he shakes his head. "Do you have any family anywhere?" I swallow down the emotion in my voice.

His eyes narrow and darken. "What's with the twenty questions, sugar?" His voice is harsh, and I flinch at the accusation in his tone.

I stiffen and blurt out. "I'm just trying to get to know you a little better. Is that a problem?"

Suspicious eyes focus on me, searching my face. "You still sore, Livvy?" he questions, as heat starts to smoulder in his green depths.

I shake my head. “A little, but I’ll be okay.”

He nods, fire burning brightly in his eyes. “How ’bout we play a little game.” A cunning smile twitches at his lips, all the suspicion is gone and he’s in complete control again. Straightening to his full height, he steps into me, towering over me, purposefully intimidating me, until I’m squirming on the spot and biting at my lip nervously.

“Wh...what game?” I stutter, instinctively stepping back as he watches me, his eyes narrowed in amusement. He steps forward, and I retreat, caught in a game of cat and mouse where I’m the prey. My back hits the wall; there’s nowhere left to run. He keeps moving till his chest pushes up against mine, and leaning in, he dominates my mouth, kissing me till I’m breathless.

“How ’bout this, sugar, a nice easy game. For every question I answer, you do something for me in exchange,” he drawls seductively.

“That seems like it works more in your favour than it does in mine,” I say nervously.

He laughs, his fingers absentmindedly caressing the swell of my breast. “Okay, well, how ’bout this. You ask me a question; I’ll ask you to do something. But I guarantee by the end of the game you’ll be enjoying yourself.”

I duck under his arm and dart across the room, putting the bed between us. “Okay, Biker Boy, game on.”

A loud laugh bursts from him, and I grin in response.

Resting his back against the wall, he crosses his legs at the ankle, relaxed. “Okay then, sugar, ask away.”

Full of cocky confidence, I stand tall, my hands on my hips, and say with a smirk, “I already asked my question. Where’s your family?”

Echo’s arms are crossed across his chest, he tenses, the action so small I could have imagined it. “My folks had me when they were older. We didn’t get along that well, and they passed away a few years back. I’ve got an older sister that’s settled and living in Florida with her husband and a couple of kids. We don’t speak much.” His voice is monotone and emotionless, but the torment in his eyes betrays him. I want to go to him, to comfort him, but then the storm in his eyes clears and my alpha biker is back.

He rubs his hands together, straightens, and takes a single step closer. “My turn, sugar.” His eyes scan my body head to toe, and he bites his lip while he thinks. “I wanna see that ass. Come here, turn round, and bend over. Palms flat on the bed.”

Sashaying across the room I pause at end of the bed. Glancing over my shoulder, I smile as I bend at the waist and slowly lower myself over the bed, pushing my ass out and wiggling it a little as I get into position. My palms reach the mattress, and I pause, my eyes still locked with Echo’s, the silence filled with sexual tension.

I wait for him to pounce, to feel the weight of his body behind me, but he doesn’t move and I have to hold back my groan of frustration. For a second I felt powerful, but his inaction has turned the tables and he's in complete control again. "Is Echo your real name?"

"No, ma'am," he drawls. "My mama christened me Foster Michael Stubbs, but I haven't answered to anything but Echo in years." His voice sounds distant, even though he's only a few steps away.

"Foster," I speak out loud without realising. "Hmm, I think Echo suits you better. How did you get the nickname Echo?"

His smile is amused. "When I first joined the Sinners, I was straight out of the army. I was used to takin' orders, so when one of the guys asked me to do something, I answered 'Yes, sir.' They thought it was so fucking funny, said I was like an echo. It stuck, and I've been Echo ever since."

He chuckles at the memory and I glance away, basking in the joy of the sound. Warm hands land on my hips and startled, I jump as his fingers slide around my waist and slowly unbutton my shorts. "It's all about this ass today, baby. Let's slip these shorts off." His voice is a low growl, as he peels the shorts and panties down my legs. I groan when his hot breath hits my exposed skin, lifting my legs one at a time as he frees my shorts and drops them to the floor behind us.

Hands grab my arse cheeks, squeezing tightly, spreading me and exposing me to his unrelenting gaze. "Ummm, this ass," he groans. When he releases me and steps back, I grieve the loss of his touch, rubbing my thighs together and squeezing my internal muscles to quell the ache of desire.

Desperation laces my voice. "How old are you?" I ask breathily.

"I'm thirty-five. How 'bout you?"

"Twenty-five."

He's close behind me, not quite touching, but so close I know if I pushed back slightly my arse would hit his crotch. Shivering, I groan as his hot breath caresses a path down my spine and across my heated sex. "Clothes off, sugar, then back into position." It's an order, and all pretence of the game is gone. He's in charge, and I'm a willing pawn desperately doing what he tells me to.

I quickly comply, ripping my shirt off until I'm naked and panting, desperate for his next command. "So submissive. I love that about you. So eager to do what I tell you. I've never wanted that before, but with you, I need it." His words are laced with his smoky southern accent, and my pussy throbs, arousal so heavy that one touch from him would have me screaming.

"What's your question? Or are you bored of this game now?" he asks.

I close my eyes and gulp a deep, calming breath. "Er, how long have you been with the club?" I force the words out of my dry throat, and I can hear my own desperation.

He's playing with me; I can sense his amusement and hear the obvious smile in his voice. "I joined the Sinners straight out of the army, so 'bout seven years ago."

I hear his words, but I'm so consumed with desire that I fidget, rising onto and falling from my tiptoes. "Echo, please," I beg.

"Spread those legs wide, sugar, let me see you."

I push my legs wide and drop onto my elbows, arching my back and I push my bottom high in the air. "Do you enjoy telling me what to do, Echo?" I ask, already knowing the answer but needing to hear him tell me.

He chuckles, low and raspy. Arousal gushes from me and drips slowly down my legs. "I fucking love it. Just like you do, Livvy. I fucking love that when I tell you to touch yourself, you won't think about it. You'll just reach your hand between your legs and fuck yourself with your fingers."

My forearms are braced against the bed, and dropping my cheek against the mattress, I free one hand. The ache in my pussy pools in my stomach and my finger easily slides into my soaked sex. "Oh god," I cry, pulling my finger free to circle my clit, shuddering, so close to release.

"Fuck, you're soaked. Are you okay? Not too sore?" His voice is laced with desire, and I frantically shake my head and groan in response. I don't see him move, but I feel his lips against my arse cheek, kissing me quickly, his touch warm against my skin.

"Now two, baby. I wanna see you fuck your fingers," he orders.

I pushing two fingers into my sex, stroking my internal

walls, the flesh soft and warm. "Harder," he demands, and I push deeper, curling upwards.

A cry falls from my lips as I pump my fingers in and out until I start to tense, my orgasm rising.

"Deeper, sugar, I want you to fuck those fingers like they're my cock. Fill that greedy cunt, stretch yourself out for me." His voice is hard and unyielding and I slide in a third finger, arching my back as I bounce up and down on my own hand, chasing my release.

"Stop," he demands, his gruff voice instantly halting me.

"No, no, no," I gasp.

Strong fingers wrap around my wrist, pulling my fingers free and placing my hand palm down on the bed again. Lifting my head, I start to argue, but he turns me, gently pressing my cheek against the mattress.

A second later, his hot, wet tongue laps from my clit to my arsehole, and I twitch, almost overwhelmed with sensation. Large fingers plunge inside me, and the force pushes me further onto the bed. "Fuck my hand, sugar, make yourself come," he demands.

Arching my back, I push further onto his fingers, groaning as he stretches me, fills me. I roll forward then plunge back onto him, forcing his hand deeper into my soaked pussy. "That's it, sugar, you're so wet. You want more, harder, don't you?" His words vibrate through me, and I groan in response, moving faster. His spare hand rests at the top of my arse cheeks, circling as I fuck his hand like a dildo.

Eyes closed tightly; I feel his thumb push against my lips. "Open up," he growls. I part my lips, and his thumb pushes into my mouth. "Suck," he orders. "Get it nice and wet, Livvy."

I suck his thumb, swirling my tongue against the salty skin. "Good girl," he praises, pulling his thumb from my mouth. Drawing a wet line between my arse cheeks, he circles my sensitive opening, coating it with my saliva.

I flinch. "Echo," I say nervously.

"I'm gonna make you feel so good and come so hard, I promise," he assures me, pushing the tip of his thumb against the tight muscle of my asshole. I shudder, attacked by a barrage of sensations as hot, painful, tingling hurt powers my release towards completion. "Anyone ever taken you here, sugar?" he asks.

I thrash against his fingers and shake my head, feeling his smile when his lips touch my shoulders and kiss a path down my spine. "This belongs to me, Livvy. I'm gonna take it knowing I'm the first and only person who'll ever get the pleasure of feeling how tight your virgin ass is."

"Echo, please, please," I beg, my desperation for release all-consuming. The fingers inside me curl, hitting my G spot, and I arch back, pushing his finger further into my arse.

"Rub your clit, sugar, make yourself come for me," he demands.

The kaleidoscope of sensations is too much. My fingers find my clit and my orgasm explodes. Echo roughly pulls his fingers from my pussy and impales me with his hard cock. My hands twist the fabric of the duvet tightly as he thrusts into me, my body sparking to life again in a second orgasm as his hips drive forward and he eases his finger further into my arse.

My sensitive flesh grips his cock as he slides out till only the head is still buried inside me. Again and again he plunges into my pussy, the sharp edge of pain from his finger in my arse as it moves in time with his dick, forcing my orgasm upwards. Hard and deep, the double penetration heightens the sensation. My skin pulses, every nerve ending hypersensitive.

"Echo. Oh god. No, no. Don't stop, don't stop," I moan incoherently, the movement from his fingers and cock pushing me closer to the edge. "Oh fuck, ahhhhh."

I detonate, fireworks exploding behind my eyes, and my whole body clenches as I scream in euphoria.

FOURTY

Echo

Livvy's a screamer.

God, I fucking love that sound and knowing I can drive her that insane. I come a second after she does, emptying deep inside her.

Slumped over the bed, her beautiful body is coated in a sheen of sweat. I pull my semi-hard cock out of her and scoop her into my arms. Her eyes are closed, and her body is soft and pliant, completely exhausted.

Placing her in the bed, I strip quickly, and crawl in behind her. She climbs up my chest, burying her head into my shoulder and I inhale deeply. She smells like sex and Livvy, a sweet, fruity smell that invades my lungs. One of her legs curls over the top of mine, and I feel the wetness seeping out of her pussy. Gently, I reach down and push my cum back inside her. She stirs, mewing quietly as her pussy still contracts with the aftershocks of her orgasm.

This bitch makes me fucking primeval. I'm so fucked up, because something deep inside of me roars with pleasure at the idea that she's full of my cum. She's on the pill, but that's not one hundred percent full proof, she could still get pregnant and then she'd be unquestionably mine.

This isn't me. I'm fucking careful where I put my cock; I've never had to think about babies or shit like that. I'm not built for that kind of life. I never thought I was capable of feeling; hell, I'm not a deep fucking guy. I love my life, but it's simple, fucking easy.

I love my club, I love my bike, and I love the simplicity of the brotherhood and family that comes with being a Sinner.

Livvy is fucking complicated. She makes me feel things that I never thought I'd ever want to feel.

I want her. I fucking need her. Now that she's mine, the empty space in my chest that I didn't even fucking realize was there is filled with her. She's captured me completely.

I need to own her, heart and soul. I need to control her body and consume her heart, claim her in the most basic, carnal way, until she's so fucking tied to me she couldn't escape if she wanted to.

Because she feels like she could be everything.

My heart, my goodness.

My fucking happy ever after.

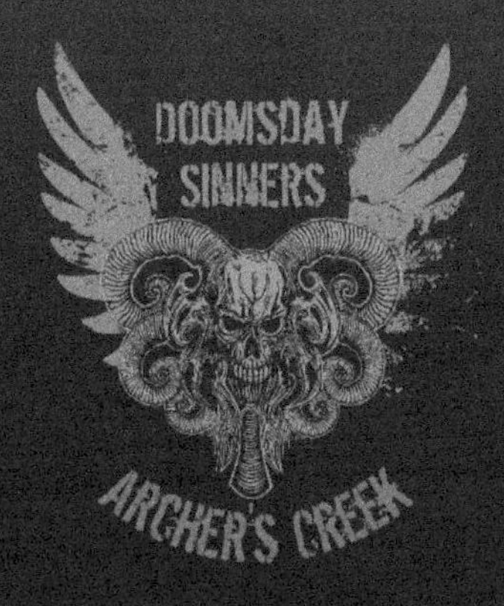

FOURTY-ONE

Olivia

Lying curled in his arms, I'm content, but overwhelmed. My head rests on his chest, his heart beating against my ear, our legs entwined. We're as close to each other as possible; his fingers plucking at my hair, pulling the curls gently before releasing them.

Peace. The silence surrounds us, the room dark except for the moonlight shining through the slats of the blinds. Neither of us need to speak; we're content with simply touching each other, our skin communicating what we can't or won't say.

I need you.

I want you.

Don't let me go.

Make me stay.

"Echo," I whisper, my voice shattering the stillness.

He sighs. "What's the matter, sugar?"

Tilting my head, I kiss his tattooed chest, nuzzling deeper into his embrace. "I don't understand this."

His hand rests against my head, holding me to him. "What's to understand?"

I spread my fingers wide, comforted by the thump, thump, thump of his heartbeat against my skin. "This isn't normal, Echo; it's never been like this before."

"Exactly, Livvy. It's never been like this before 'cause this is *it*. Me and you are *it*, sugar. I fucking refuse to believe you're not meant to be mine. I saw you and claimed you, like it was destined. You've always been mine, *always.* We just hadn't met yet. Don't matter if it's seconds or hours or fucking years since we found each other."

The determination and certainty is so clear in his voice that I stop breathing and tears flood my eyes. "How can you be so sure? What if this isn't real? What if it's too perfect? What if it's too easy, and instead, we hurt each other or burn up like a star that was too bright to last for more than a second?"

"No," he growls, lifting me up as he sits, placing me so I'm straddling his lap, our eyes locked together. "No. You're looking for reasons why this won't work, but it's already decided, Livvy. I never wanted this life, never felt like this about a woman before. Till you. I know I'm supposed to make you mine, take care of you, protect you. It's fucking built in to me."

Staring at him I try to respond, but words won't come. Desperation overwhelms me and need consumes me, daring me to make the most of every moment, because it feels like time's running out. I lean into him, our lips connecting, and for once I'm in control. Sliding my tongue into his mouth I try to provoke him, desperate for him to take over and dominate me.

"Please. I need you," I beg.

"Sugar, calm the fuck down. I know this is fucking with your head, so talk to me. I'd love to sink back into that tight pussy again, but I don't want to hurt you, so sit your ass in my lap and don't fucking wiggle," he orders.

Embarrassed and unsure, I fall forward and bury my face into his neck. His arms wrap around my back, holding me against him, but I pull my arms free and lock them around his neck, pushing myself as close to him as I can get.

Echo pry's me from his neck and encourages me to sit up in his lap, his fingers around my hips, circling patterns across my skin. "Talk to me."

"I don't know what to say," I murmur.

He chuckles lightly, and I watch his lips curl into a slight smile. "Tell me about home, or tell me what you had for lunch. Hell, tell me what you wanted to be when you grew up. I don't care, sugar, just talk."

"I wanted to be a lion tamer," I confess.

A laugh bursts from him, and he bites his lip before his mouth spreads into a wide smile. "A lion tamer, huh?"

Nodding, I smile. "Yep, my mum and dad took me to the circus when I was about five, and there was a lion in the show. The lady in the ring with it had the most amazing outfit, with a top hat and everything. So I decided then and there that I wanted to be just like her."

He leans forward and grasps my chin, holding it tightly and kissing me deeply. "I wanted to be Indiana Jones," Echo says. "He had the hat and went on cool adventures. He was awesome, and at seven, he was my fucking hero."

"Indiana Jones, wow. Harrison Ford was hot as hell in that hat," I say, laughing.

Echo's hand squeezes my hip, and I flinch, giggling at his teasing touch. "Do you like it over here in the US? Or are you homesick?"

I pause for a second. "I miss home, but I love it here. I've been on holiday for three months, what's not to love? But that's why this doesn't feel real, Echo, because it isn't. Life's easy when the only thing you have to worry about is where you're going to wander next."

"Move in with me, sugar."

I sigh wearily. "Echo—"

He interrupts me. "Listen to me, Livvy. You say this doesn't feel real, so let's make this real. Move in with me, stop wandering and set down some roots. Here with me."

"I need some time, Echo."

Gripping my chin with his fingers he turns my head, forcing

me to look at him. “I just need you,” he growls.

The words hang between us, but we still fight to be as close as possible as I slide down his body and settle against his chest, happy when he wraps me tightly in his arms. My eyes close, and I slowly drift into unconsciousness to the sound of his whispered words. “I didn’t know my heart wasn’t beating till I met you and it started again.”

***

Time seems to stand still; days pass, but nothing changes. My mornings, afternoons, and nights are filled with Echo. We don’t talk about the future; we live in the now. Stern orders, caressing touches, and mind-blowing orgasms keep me tied to him, unwilling to withdraw from my new addiction.

“Sugar, come here,” he orders.

Leaving Brandi and the group of women I’m chatting with, I make my way across the clubhouse. Echo’s eyes drop to take in the tall heels and tight jeans I’m wearing, his eyes slowly tracking a path up to my chest, pausing at my boobs that are perfectly displayed by my vest top. Heat flares in his gaze, and a wicked smile spreads across his face.

He pulls me into his lap, wrapping his hand around my throat, and tipping my chin up in a smooth practiced move. Kissing me roughly, his tongue demands entrance and my lips part instinctually so he can invade my mouth.

We don't talk, but every touch, every kiss reminds me that I belong to him. He brands me again and again, his claim so natural now it's second nature. His lips release mine, and breathlessly I stare up at him, desperately willing him to lift me up and take me to bed.

A voice shatters the sexual intensity that binds us together. "So this is your old lady then, Echo. Fuck, I never thought I'd see the day." We turn towards the voice, and I lean back to see the man it belongs to. Silver hair frames a masculine face that's weathered but incredibly handsome. His trimmed beard reveals full lips and neck tattoos disappearing below his shirt.

"Livvy, this is Blade," Echo says.

Pushing upright I reach out and offer him my hand to shake. Blade's firm grip holds me while he assesses me from head to toe. Uncomfortable with his touch and his blatant perusal of me, I try to pull my hand back, but he refuses to release me. Still holding me, his other hand reaches out and strokes my cheek, slowly moving lower as he speaks. "Such a pretty thing, we like to share here in the Sinners, so how 'bout I get you next."

Appalled I tug at my hand, parting my lips, ready to demand he fuck off and stop fucking touching me, but Echo speaks first.

"She's mine," he snarls, his voice hard and full of authority. Moving purposefully, he steps between me and Blade, forcing him to release me, pushing me behind him and pulling himself up to his full height as he towers over Blade menacingly. "Mine, Blade, you understand that? You might be the VP, but I'll fucking slit your throat if you ever put your hands on my woman again. We clear?"

A huge smile splits Blade's face, changing his appearance completely. "Echo, I'm playing with you, brother. I heard you threatened to kill Puck the other night. I needed to see how deep you are for her. Old lady isn't a title we give out on a whim," Blade says seriously.

Echo nods, his shoulders still tense. He moves back, curling his arm around my neck protectively. I peer at Blade; his smile's gentle and focused on me. "I'm sorry, sweetheart, that was a fucking shitty thing for me to do. But you understand, I had to know if you were just a fuck. I've known Echo for a long time, and he's never hinted at wanting an old lady. I needed to know if this was real. Now I do. Welcome to the Sinners," Blade says.

Blade's behaviour annoys the hell out of me and sets me on edge, as I wonder who else is going to question my sudden promotion to old lady. I don't know if Blade was being a dick as a test for Echo, or for me, but I feel antsy and worked up. Blade's words and actions have obviously provoked Echo as well, and he's more possessive than ever. We lounge on a sofa, and he keeps me on his lap, touching me constantly; holding me tight and reinforcing his ownership of me to everyone in the room.

Before I met Echo, I would have punched a guy for saying he owned me. But here in Archer's Creek in the Sinners' world, it's different. Being Echo's makes me feel safe and cherished. In this world, his claim isn't derogatory. It's an honour.

Blade's presence changes the dynamic of the room. The senior officers all gravitate towards him, and soon we're sitting with Blade, the vice president, Marley, the road captain, and Sleaze, the sergeant-at-arms.

"Echo, I've got to get to work," I say. He pulls me in for a quick kiss and nods.

"Okay, sugar, go get your shit, and I'll take you."

Reluctantly moving from the warmth of his arms, I shake my head. "Its fine, you stay here, and I'll call a cab," I say.

Echo stands quickly and steps closer, crowding me. "I said I'll take you."

A wave of frustration consumes me, and I snap at my overprotective man. "Echo, I'm more than capable of taking a fucking cab. I did it for years before I met you."

A dark scowl crosses his face and I back away slowly, but he stalks me, grabbing my hand and hauling me into his hard chest. "I don't give a flying fuck what you did before we met. If I say I'll take you to fucking work, then I'll take you to fucking work. Do you understand?"

Anger clouds my judgement, and I shove at him. "No, I don't fucking understand. You're being a stubborn idiot. I don't need a bloody babysitter."

Strong arms wrap around my waist and haul me into the air, leaving me hanging upside down over his shoulder. "Echo, what the fuck!" I scream.

Striding a few yards he drops me to the floor before quickly spinning me around and forcing me to bend over with my chest pinned to a table. His body cages me in, his weight holding me down. "Echo, get off me," I demand.

"Fuck no, sugar, you're gonna stay right here while we sort this out. Who do you belong to, Livvy?" he questions, his voice dominant and full of annoyance.

I groan in frustration and push back against him, but he's in complete control and I can't move. "Who. Do. You. Belong. To?" His angry voice growls next to my ear, his hard cock rubbing against my arse. "Livvy, you need me to fuck the answer out of you again?"

I refuse to speak, trying to find purchase with my hands. "Livvy, last chance before I pull down your jeans and fuck you till you remember who owns you," he threatens.

"Argggh, you do."

His sharp teeth sink into my neck and bite me. I feel a stab of pain then his tongue licking the marks, soothing my skin. "That's right, I own you. You're my fucking woman, mine to care for, mine to worship, mine to protect. I take that fucking seriously. So when I say I'm gonna take you to fucking work, it's 'cause I'm gonna take you to fucking work. You get me?"

Reluctantly, I nod. "Thank fuck for that. Now go get your shit, you're gonna be late," he says.

His weight moves from my back, freeing me, and I push my hands against the table and start to rise when his hand smacks against my arse in a punishing thwack. “Owwwww,” I shout and rub my sore arse cheek.

His amused voice whispers in my ear. “I think you might need a good spanking, sugar, remind you who’s in control here. Fuck, I can’t wait to take you across my knee and turn your ass red.” I shudder, my eyes widening in excitement at his erotic threat. “Later,” he smirks. “Now go get your stuff.”

FOURTY-TWO

Echo

Livvy disappears towards my room, and I wait for any of my brothers to call me out on the way I handled her. I scan the room, eyeballing my brothers one by one, but no one says a word. Respect is a huge fucking deal in the club, and as long as you're treating your woman right, people tend to mind their own business.

Fuck, she drives me crazy. She's used to being on her own, but why the fuck would she waste money on a cab when I can just take her? My momma might have died being disappointed in me and my life, but she raised me to be a gentleman. My girl needs to go to work, then I'll fucking take her.

Maybe the guys she's been with in the past wouldn't have cared, pussies who didn't know how to treat a woman, but she's mine now, and I want to take care of her. She's still refusing to move in with me, so I want every other minute she'll give me. It's only been a week, but I don't want to let her out of my sight.

Livvy's a flight risk, she freaks out over every question or doubt she has and she keeps talking about leaving, but that's not happening. She's my old lady now, and I'll do everything in my power to convince her to stay.

FOURTY-THREE

Olivia

We ride to Strikers in silence with his promise to take me over his knee still thrilling my thoughts. I'm so distracted I forget to argue as he wraps me in my cut before kissing me breathless and taking a seat at the back of the bar. Just like Brandi said, there's always one of the bikers at Strikers. Most of the time it's Daisy or the other prospect, Slow, but sometimes Echo stays.

He's slowly worming his way into my heart, asking me to tell him random things about myself. What my favourite film is—Sweet home Alabama—Vampires or werewolves—Vampires—and if I like day or night best—night. Little by little, we're getting to know each other, and beyond the caveman "*You're mine*" claims, he's sweet and takes care of me in a way that no man I've ever known has done before.

His eyes have been on me all night, teasing me with his gaze while I serve drinks to the regulars. My nipples are pebbled, eager for his attention, and my panties are soaked from the controlled intensity that pours from his stare.

"Jesus, honey, go fuck him already. The sexual tension's so thick in here you could cut it with a knife," Brandi says with a smirk.

My cheeks redden. "God, is it that obvious?"

Brandi laughs loudly. "Liv, the guys are taking bets on how long till he hauls you into the backroom."

Groaning, I cover my face with my hands. "I think there's something wrong with me. He's such a caveman. He's controlling and bossy and unreasonable."

"Let me guess. You love it, don't you?" she says with a knowing smirk.

My eyes widen in embarrassment as I nod in agreement. "God, I do. He tells me to do something, and I jump to do it. And I mean anything he tells me to do. I love that he watches me. I love that he's a control freak with me. The more he does it, the more I need."

Erotic visions flash into my mind, and my face heats in mortified arousal. "What the hell just went through your mind?" Brandi asks. I shake my head, ready to deny my dirty thoughts, but Brandi speaks first. "No, don't tell me. I don't want to know. It's quiet, so go home. Go let your man take care of you, because if you go to the party tonight this horny, there'll be a riot."

I shake my head. "No, Brandi, its fine," I assure her.

She ignores me and walks to the end of the counter and whistles loudly. "Echo, come get your girl. She's done for the day."

Echo's bike stops outside Miss Mimi's, and I jump off and unstrap the helmet. "What time's the party tonight?" I ask.

Pulling me back to him, he palms my arse, dropping kisses and nips at my neck. "It'll start sometime this afternoon and then go till it's done. Why?" He nuzzles into my neck, his lips roaming from my collarbone to the swell of my breasts before biting playfully.

"I need to know what time to be ready by. I'm assuming you're gonna come get me?"

Leaning back, his eyebrows rise in question. "Sugar, why would I need to come get you?"

Embarrassed, I cross my arms over my chest. "Oh, ah, I don't have to come if you don't want me to." I try to step back defensively, but he hauls me back to him, smacking my arse so hard I jump.

"Woman, what the fuck are you talking about? You're my fucking old lady, your ass is gonna be pinned to me all fucking night where I can keep an eye on you. But explain why the fuck I would need to come pick you up. Where the fuck you planning on going?"

Confused and unsure, I stare at my fingers, picking at the nail polish awkwardly. Strong fingers gently wrap around my throat, tilting my head till I'm looking up at him. His leg pushes between mine, rubbing against my pussy and creating a delicious friction. I shudder lightly, and my voice is breathy. "I've finished working for the day. I planned on lazing about, maybe answer some emails," I say.

Echo shakes his head, slowly grinding his leg against my sex. "No."

"What do you mean, no?" I ask breathily as he keeps the pressure between my legs, arousing me, taunting me with his lazy touch. My eyes flutter closed for a second, but I fight my body's reaction to him, forcing my lids open.

"I've got to go over to Austin to see to some business, and now you don't have to work, you're coming with me," he says quietly, his thumb brushing over the peak of my pebbled nipple.

"Well, what if I don't want to come to Austin with you?"

Echo's eyes narrow, and a knowing smile twitches at his lips. "Is that what you really want to do, sugar, sit in your room at Mimi's and check your emails?"

My lips part as a sigh slips from me. "No, that's not what I want," I breathe, squeezing my thighs together.

"So what is it you want?"

My eyes widen, and I try to hide the desperation in my voice. "I thought you were the one in control," I taunt.

His laugh is quiet and full of sexual satisfaction, like I'm doing exactly what he planned for me to do. "You wanna play, sugar? You want me to show you what I'm gonna do if you don't do as you're told?" His finger trails a path down my jaw. "I know you like it when I take charge, Livvy. So ask me, beg me, to remind you how in control I am," he drawls seductively.

My breath stops in my lungs. I'm frozen to the spot, desire and trepidation pulsing through me. "Please," I beg.

"Please what, sugar? Do you want a reminder? Do you need me to take you over my knee and spank you?" The dark intensity of his eyes hypnotises me. I'm so excited I can't find the words, so I just nod.

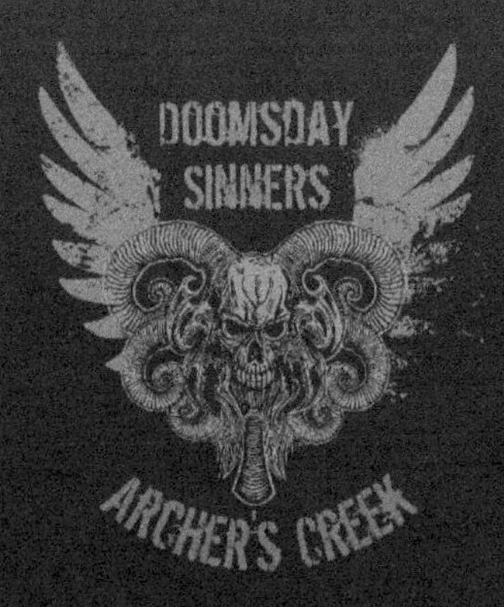

FOURTY-FOUR

Echo

Fuck, she surprises me every time.

The sex with her is fucking unbelievable all the time, but when I step up the control and really dominate her, she loves it.

But this is the first time she's asked for me to take control. I promised her a spanking, and she lit up at the thought. Fuck my cock is so hard at the idea of pulling her across my knee and reddening her perfect skin.

Grabbing her hand I pull her into Miss Mimi's house. I'm not fucking welcome here, but my woman's so turned on its either go into the house or take her outside in the yard.

Opening the door to her room, I pull her inside before shutting and locking it behind us. She's panting, and I can smell how turned on she is. Her nipples are rock hard and pushing against her bra, but she manages to wait patiently as I cross the room towards her.

"Turn around and face the wall," I order. She complies instantly; she's got no idea how perfect and submissive she is. My hands trace her rib cage and push upward to cup her breasts and caress her eager nipples.

"Arms up," I demand and she instantly lifts her arms into the air, letting me pull her tank up and over her head. Her arms fall back down to her sides and I take a moment to just look at her, discarding her tank to the floor. Her bra is sheer white, her dark nipples peeking through the lace. Reaching out I thumb her nipple, smiling when she gasps. "Take it off." Unclasping it, she lets the bra fall down her arms and drop to the floor.

"Hands on the wall." My tone leaves no room for question, and she moves till her palms lie flat against the exposed brick. Glancing over her shoulder at me, her eyes smolder with heat as I circle her waist with my hands, pushing her jeans and lace panties down her legs, sliding her shoes and clothes free of her feet until she's completely, perfectly naked.

My woman is absolute fucking perfection.

"Turn around," I rasp, my dick so hard I could come in my jeans just from looking at her.

She turns slowly, revealing her flawless tits and wet, dripping cunt. Her pupils are dilated and her chest's heaving, she wants this, she's fucking desperate. "How wet are you, Livvy?"

Groaning, she fidgets, pressing her thighs together as she

fights to keep her hands pressed against the wall behind her, following my rules without me even having to remind her. "Very."

"Show me," I demand. She's unsure, so I urge her on. "Touch yourself, sugar, let me see how wet you are."

Lifting one hand from the wall she dips it between her legs and I groan as she parts her folds and strokes down to her entrance. I grab her dripping hand, sucking her arousal-soaked fingers into my mouth. "Livvy, baby, you taste so fucking sweet. Do you want me to taste you?" She nods frantically. "Tell me, sugar. Ask me to taste you," I taunt.

"Please," she begs. "I need you; I need you to taste me. Please," she pleads, her sweet voice laced with desperation.

I shake my head. "Not yet, baby, I don't think you deserve it."

FOURTY-FIVE

Olivia

My skin's hot and desperate for stimulation. I can't wait any more, so I slip my hand back between my legs and slide my fingers into my soaked sex.

"No," Echo barks, roughly grabbing my hand to stop me. In a flash, he twists both my arms behind my back. "I didn't tell you to touch yourself again did I? Only I get to make you come. That's my pleasure now. I don't want you to touch yourself unless I tell you."

Frustration consumes me. "Then touch me, please," I beg.

His hand strokes between my legs before he roughly forces two fingers inside me. "Is this what you need, for me to fuck your wet pussy with my fingers?"

I nod frantically. "Yes, yes. Hard, make me come."

An amused grin appears on his face, and his fingers slide out of me and into his mouth. He slowly licks them clean of my arousal and sinks into an arm chair. “Come here, over my knee.”

Gasping, I shudder, a mix of excited fear and arousal ploughs through me.

“Now,” he orders.

Flinching at the demand in his tone, I take two steps towards him, but his intensity unnerves me, and I stumble. Darting his hand out he catches me before I fall, strong fingers entwine with mine, keeping me upright as he guides me between his legs.

“Lie across my lap, hands on the floor,” he says, his thumb rubbing soft circles against my hand, soothing me.

Carefully I lay down across his legs, my stomach resting on his thigh, my legs dangling as I brace my hands on the floor. I’m shaking, but its not fear, it’s anticipation.

“Fuck sugar, I’ve never spanked a woman in my life, but you spread out like this, naked waiting for me to redden your ass. It’s the sexiest god damn thing I’ve ever fucking seen,” he rasps, his hand stroking my arse.

The first hit makes me yelp in shock, then giggle as the stinging heat bursts to life in the spot his palm just landed.

The second swat of his hand is harder, landing with an audible smack and this time I don’t laugh. The pain is instant and intense and I part my lips ready to tell him to stop.

The third and fourth spanks come in quick succession, first one cheek and then the other. I feel the pain but instead of flinching away from it I arch into his hand, the burning heat morphing into a warm tingle that spreads across my legs and all the way between my thighs. My sex clenches in anticipation and a gush of arousal rushes from me.

"Who do you belong to, sugar?" Echo asks, his voice ragged as he caresses my arse.

I respond immediately. "You."

This time when his palm lands on my sensitive skin I gasp with desire as glorious, tingling sensation pools in my stomach.

"Who's in control, Livvy?"

Pushing my arse into his waiting hand I silently beg for more. "You are."

His hand ricochets against my heated skin and tears pool in my eyes, but my sex vibrates with delight. Every nerve ending in my body is poised and ready to detonate. I never thought I'd want a dominant man, I never thought I'd enjoy being spanked, but this is the single most erotic moment of my life so far.

As if he's sensing my mood Echo scoops me off his legs and repositions me onto his lap. The rough fabric of his jeans rubs painfully against my sore skin, but the moment his lips find mine, I'm consumed by his gentle, reverent kiss.

"You love me taking control, don't you, baby? You fucking loved being spanked," he whispers, his voice a low lust drenched aroused drawl.

I nod enthusiastically.

Lifting me from his lap, he stands me on my feet between his parted thighs. His hand pushes between my legs, thick fingers cupping my sex, feeling how wet and ready I am. "Up on the bed, baby, lie on your side," he orders.

I dart across the room, wincing slightly when a pulse of pain explodes through my reddened arse. Lying on my side I rest my head on my hand and turn to watch as Echo stands and slowly undoes his belt. Kicking off his boots, he pushes his jeans down his thighs, freeing his cock and letting it bounce up against his stomach. Ripping off his T-shirt, he prowls toward me gloriously naked, his dick leaking pearls of precum at the tip.

Grabbing my ankles, he yanks, pulling me down the bed until my sore arse is almost hanging off the end. Splitting my legs wide, he growls a feral growl and slams his hard length into me, filling me completely in one thrust.

His fingers wrap around my raised leg, bending it and pushing it up and into my chest to open me wider. Plunging deeper into me, he fucks me with abandon, all pretence of gentility gone as he slams into me with mindless intent.

I watch where we connect, fascinated by the way he disappears deep into me, until his wet thumb circles my tight arsehole, rubbing the sensitive skin for a second before pushing inside of me.

The pain's exquisite. "Ohhhh," I moan, arching into his hand as he fills me completely.

"Sugar your ass is so tight, I'm gonna take it. I'm gonna

own every bit of you. My dick in every hole, my hands, my tongue on every inch of you."

Closing my eyes I shudder at his words, hating that I love his dirty taunts.

"Touch yourself, baby, let me see you play with that clit," he orders.

I fumble, lost between the overwhelming sensation of his dick in my pussy and his thumb in my ass. When my fingers graze my clit I cry out and his thrusts get harder, sinking deeper into my tight flesh, pushing me closer and closer to release.

"Don't come, Livvy. If you do, I'll keep you on the edge all day and all night," he warns. Groaning in frustration, I pull my fingers from my clit, knowing that I'm close.

"Keep rubbing that clit, sugar. I wanna watch. But I say when you come. Do you understand, Livvy? Your pleasure belongs to me."

Timidly, I slide towards my sensitive clit, but my orgasm builds too quickly and I stop, waiting for the sensation to fade. Like he's sensing how close I am, Echo fucks me harder and harder, each thrust moving his thumb buried deep in my arse.

His voice is ragged and gravelly. "Are you close, baby? Are you ready to come?"

I nod frantically. "God, yes. I need to come. Please make me come."

Abruptly he stops, pulling his cock from my pussy and his thumb from my arse. My body hums, the orgasm draining from my skin, like water disappearing down a drain. "What the fuck? Why have you stopped?" I yell, my chest heaving.

His face is calm and impassive as he silently crosses the room, pulling his jeans over his painfully hard dick.

"Echo," I cry, rolling to my back, my eyes wide and horrified at being left wet and unsatisfied.

Smirking he drags his shirt over his head, and slides on his cut. Sauntering across to the bed, he leans over me, wrapping one hand round my neck and tilting my head up. "Was that a good enough reminder, Olivia? Of who's in charge?"

"ARRRRGGGHHHH," I scream in his face.

Laughing loudly, he pulls me to my feet, kissing me lightly. "Get dressed, baby, we need to get to Austin."

FOURTY-SIX

Echo

I've never seen my little hellion speechless before, and it's fucking adorable.

She wanted to play this game; hell, it wasn't my idea. My balls are so fucking blue I'm in pain. Pulling out of her was the hardest thing I've ever done, hearing her beg and watching her do exactly what I tell her is so fucking sexy.

If she gets her ass dressed without throwing a tantrum, I'm gonna pull over just outside of town and fuck her hard, bent over my bike till she screams. If she gets all bratty, we're both gonna have to wait until we get back to the clubhouse later.

I'm getting the silent treatment. Her eyes are shooting daggers at me, and she hasn't said a word since she screamed in my face. After I told her we were going out, she got dressed in a sundress so tiny her red ass is practically hanging out the back of it.

I can sense her anger, she's good and pissed at me, but hell if it doesn't make me want to start over again and teach her another lesson on why I'm the boss.

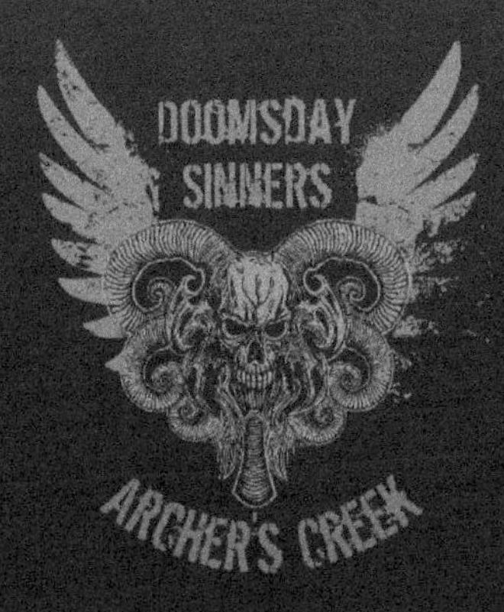

FOURTY-SEVEN

Olivia

I glare at him, every inch of me twitching with frustrated anger. The smug, amused look on his face is infuriating me, but the smell of sex that's filled the room, is so strong I'm holding my breath so I don't run back to him and beg him to fuck me.

I need to get away from him. My skin's still alight, anticipating him and the orgasms he gives me. I wanted him to spank me and fuck me. Instead, he's being an evil fucking twat. Me, my pussy, and every nerve ending in my skin hates him so much right now. "Move, please," I snarl, glaring daggers at him.

His arms are braced across his huge chest, and lazily he unfurls them. But I stare rigidly at the door till he moves, ignoring his amused chuckle as I push past him and rush away.

Still refusing to speak to him, I climb onto his bike,

squirming on the leather seat in my tiny dress. With a chuckle he starts the engine and we ride out of town, the wind whistling past us, my hair blowing behind me and my body sheltered behind Echo's broad back.

Turning off the highway, he pulls the bike onto a secluded side road surrounded by woods. Effortlessly pushing down the kickstand, he climbs off the bike and turns to face me, his intense stare dissolving my ire and replacing my anger with nervous insecurity. I fidget uncomfortably as he circles the bike, stepping forward, and abruptly lifting me into the air before moving me to the front of the seat and climbing on behind me.

"What are you doing?" I ask.

Ignoring me, he lifts my hands and places them on the handlebars, wrapping my fingers around the grips. I hear the click of his belt being undone and his zipper lowered, and I frantically search our surroundings for people. My dress is roughly pulled from under my arse, my panties pushed to the side, and I'm exposed from the waist down. Echo lifts me by the hips, holding me in the air for a moment before bringing me back down and impaling me onto his rock-hard cock.

"Ahhhh." The dry scream comes from the back of my throat as I hold on tightly to the handlebars, my legs dangling by the sides of the bike. In this position, bent forward, with his dick buried deeply inside me I can't move. He grasps me tightly, lifting my hips and slamming me back down onto his waiting cock.

“Ahhhhh. Oh god, fuck,” I cry. Again and again, he pulls me down and impales me on his hard length, fucking me mercilessly. He groans into my ear, his hardness swelling before he explodes inside me. His hot cum pulses into me, tipping me over the edge, and I orgasm, screaming in ecstasy.

Still trembling with the aftershocks of my orgasm, he lifts me off his cock and his cum immediately gushes out of me. Reaching between my legs, he drags his hand across my pussy, collecting his seed, then sliding three fingers back into my pussy, forcing his cum back into me. I whimper while my muscles clamp around his fingers and slowly, he pulls his hand free, his wet fingers spreading more of his arousal onto me, rubbing it across my clit and coating my pussy and thighs.

His voice in my ear is low and raspy. “This is my fucking pussy, Livvy. All of your orgasms, all of your pleasure is mine. Do you understand?” His fingers strum my clit while his other hand drops between my legs and three fingers push into me again. “Tell me, Livvy. I want to hear you say it.”

I nod, my eyes closed tightly. “Yours. I understand.” My head falls back so I’m lying against his chest. His fingers fuck me roughly while his thumb frantically rubs my clit and I come again, screaming loudly, but he doesn’t stop. Rubbing my clit again, his fingers curl upwards, fucking my pussy relentlessly till I fall apart on a third orgasm, twitching and thrashing. My shudders gradually subside, and boneless, I melt into his arms, finally sated and thoroughly reminded.

We sit for minutes on his bike, silent except for the sounds of our breathing and the chirping of the crickets in the grass. Echo absentmindedly strokes my arms, while my back rests against his chest and my heart pounds loudly against my ribs. I'm comforted by him but still excited by his touch.

"I can't believe we just did that," I say, giggling.

His chest vibrates as he laughs, a low rumbling sound. "I never heard you telling me to stop, sugar."

Groaning I lift my hands and cover my heated cheeks. "I know, it's just anyone could have seen us. They might have seen us. I wouldn't have bloody noticed."

Gentle fingers clasp my chin and turn me to look at him. "No one saw us, sugar, I promise. I wouldn't let anyone see you like that. That's just for me." Sincerity shines clearly in his eyes, and my heart melts a bit more for him.

"Echo, what are we doing?" I ask, desperate for clarity.

He sits up straighter, his movement pushing me upwards. "We're just enjoying a moment, Livvy."

I smile. "You know that's not what I mean. We've avoided being realistic and lived in this fantasy land for the last week. But seriously, what are we doing together? I'm leaving in a couple of weeks."

His whole body stiffens. Picking me up, he lifts me clear off the bike and places me in front of him. "What the fuck you talking 'bout, Livvy? Where the hell you planning on going?" His anger's palpable, his entire body tense and poised, ready to explode.

"Why are you so angry?" I ask. "You knew I was only here while I earn enough money to carry on travelling."

"You're not leaving, do you hear me?" He shouts, his face red, his beautiful features twisted with rage.

My lips part and eyes widen in shock. "Echo, you know I can't stay here forever."

Jumping off the bike, he paces back and forth, his hands manically raking through his hair. "That's bullshit, Olivia."

Shaking my head, I scoff lightly. "Echo, I'm only here as a tourist. I have to go home."

Echo stops pacing and turns back to face me. "So get a work visa."

"It's not that simple." Our eyes lock, and I see the hurt and anger swirling in his eyes.

"Do you want to stay?"

When I step towards him, he stops pacing and turns to face me. "Echo, I didn't expect to meet you."

Angry, his eyes drill me to the spot. "You didn't answer the question, Olivia. Do you want to stay?"

I reach up and touch his stubbled chin with my fingertips. "Yes, I want to stay. But it doesn't matter what I want. My visa runs out in less than three months, and then I'll have to go back to the UK."

Echo shakes his head, looks up at the sky, and roars. It's the most primal sound I've ever heard, and goosebumps break out instantly on my skin. When he looks back at me, the anger has drained from him and in its place is desperation.

My chest hurts. “I hate the way you look right now, Echo.”

My proud, strong, alpha man is gone.

When he speaks, even the tone of his voice sounds different. “So don’t work. I make enough money for both of us. Hell, I wouldn’t want to you to work at the bar full-time anyway. Problem solved. We move into my place, and then you stay.”

“It’s not that easy. I can’t just decide to ignore the law and stay.”

Echo grabs me and pulls me to him, wrapping his arms around me. “You can and you will. I just found you; I fucking refuse to let you go. You’re not going anywhere.”

Angry at him, I push on his chest and try to step back, but he refuses to release me. “Echo, if I don’t go home, they’ll deport me, and I’ll never be able to come back.”

His strong arms pull me into his chest, enfolding me in a tight hug. He crushes my lips with his; the kiss is so full of possession and resolution that my knees go weak.

When he speaks, his voice is so full of certainty. “I refuse to let you go, sugar. You’re not going anywhere. We can sort it out. I’ll find a way. You’re mine, you belong to me, and I’m not letting you go.” I want to believe him; I almost believe him. Then reality crashes down around me, and I nod, knowing that there’s nothing he can do but wishing he could.

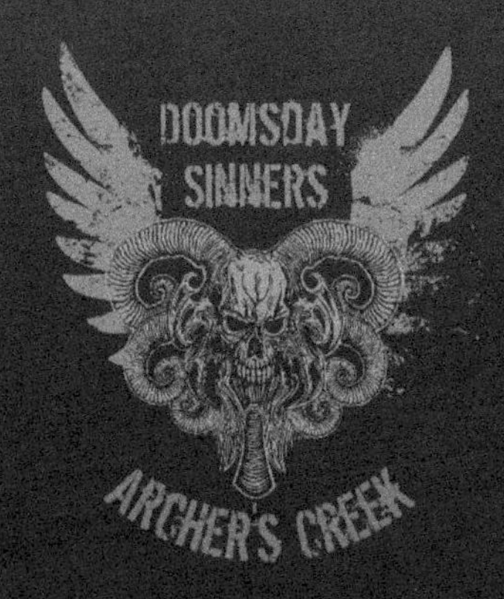

FOURTY-EIGHT

Echo

She might think she's leaving in a couple of weeks, but fuck no, that's not happening. I don't give a fuck about her stupid fucking visa; I'm not letting her go, no fucking chance.

Hell, I'll fucking handcuff her to the bed before I willingly let her leave me.

The Sinners in Archer's Creek might be a small chapter, but the network of Doomsday Sinners stretches across the whole United States. Over the years, I've met a lot of people and made a lot of connections. I've done a lot of favors for a lot of people, and I've saved those markers to call in case I ever need to. Well, now's the time to call them in, all of them if I fucking have to.

Livvy doesn't believe me yet, but I refuse to lose her.

My happy ever after is going nowhere.

FOURTY-NINE

Planning

I see the way she looks at him.

She's polluted.

It's time to act.

To purge the demons from her.

Time's running out.

He's evil. They're evil.

I can set her free.

Now's the time to plan.

FIFTY

Olivia

Austin's a beautiful city, and seeing it on the back of a bike makes it even better. We don't talk about me leaving again, or how little time we have left. My alpha man is back with a vengeance and more determined than ever to make me do as I'm told.

"Sugar, get your ass back in there and try a couple more things on for me. You know I'm gonna get my way, so just go do it," his voice is assured and a little smug.

Groaning, I pout. "This is ridiculous. You need to stop buying me stuff. I can buy my own clothes."

His eyes narrow. "Livvy, go do as you're fucking told. Now."

I scowl at him, then turn to leave, but he grabs me and

swings me over his shoulder. “Echo, put me down! This dress is short. I’m flashing everyone in the shop,” I cry.

Laughing loudly, he smacks my arse quickly before pulling my dress down. “Serves you right for trying to torture me with this tiny fucking dress.”

The shop assistant scurries out of his way, not questioning him when he joins me in the changing room. He drops me to my feet, then crowds behind me in the small space and locks the door. His eyes twinkle mischievously, and he pulls a hanger from behind his back. A pale blue lacy basque hangs from it and my hands twitch, eager to touch the delicate fabric.

Leaning into me he quietly whispers into my ear, “Strip.”

One word. One word is all it takes to have me hot and needy. Clamping my thighs together, I try to dull the ache his voice has ignited. Echo’s strong fingers part my legs easily, and pushing his hand between my thighs, he cups my soaked pussy.

“So wet, Livvy. You’re always so wet for me,” he murmurs against my ear. I arch onto my tiptoes as two fingers push deeply inside me. He teases me, massaging my sensitive sex before he pulls them out to suck his fingers into his mouth and lick off my arousal.

“Strip.” His unmistakable command is harsh, and I comply, pulling my dress over my head and dropping it to the floor. His eyes flash with a predatory gleam. “Mine,” he growls.

I nod. “Yours.”

He dangles the basque from the end of his finger, and I take it from him. The lace glides over my flesh and heightens the excited tingling that pulses along my skin. His fingertip touches my cheek before gently stroking a path down my neck to the swell of my breast. My breath shallows, and I wait for him.

“On your knees, Livvy.”

FIFTY-ONE

Echo

Fuck, my woman is perfection.

Seconds after I say the words, she sinks to the ground and sits back onto her heels. The club whores would've had my cock out and been sucking away like it was the answer to eternal youth by now. But my beautiful girl looks up at me and waits for me to tell her to suck.

Sheer perfection.

I quickly undo my pants, and grabbing a handful of her wild hair, I guide her mouth onto my dick. Her lips seal, and my knees buckle. Bracing my hands against the wall behind her I watch in the mirror while she goes to town on my cock. Sucking, she rolls her tongue up and down my shaft, driving me fucking wild.

My orgasm starts to rise, and the muscles in my thighs tense.

"Sugar, I'm close," I say, desperate to shoot my load down her throat and watch while she swallows my cum.

She pulls back, freeing my cock from her luscious mouth with a pop. Her hand wraps tightly around my length, and she starts to stroke up and down, lapping at the head with her tongue and swirling around the tip. Her face tips back till our eyes lock, and with a smile, she flattens her tongue, licking down my shaft all the way to my balls. Her fingers squeeze my sac lightly, and looking up at me, she smiles.

"Do you need to come, babe?" she asks, her lips temptingly wet.

Nodding I lean forward the air caught in my lungs, waiting for the feel of her hot mouth around my dick. She kisses the tip, then releases me, rolling back onto her feet and gracefully rising from the ground. My mouth falls open, shocked at the evil grin that spreads across her face.

"It's a real bitch when someone stops right before you come, isn't it?" she purrs.

My balls are fucking blue, and my little minx is giggling and grinning like the Cheshire cat. The blue lacy thing is off and her dress is back on, but all I can do is shake my head, I'm too fucking shocked to be pissed.

Forcing my hard dick back into my jeans I pull her to me, crushing her mouth in a demanding kiss. "I should be spanking your ass right now, or shoving my cock in your mouth and making you suck me till I come down your throat," I snarl.

Her eyes widen, desire mixed with a little fear sparkling in their depths. "What the fuck are you doing to me, Livvy?" I say on a groan, pulling her to me as she stands on her tiptoes, her lips meeting mine in a kiss that says everything. "You know this isn't over, don't you, sugar? You owe me a blowjob."

With a smile, she winks at me and rushes from the changing room. I smack her ass as she passes, and the sound of her giggle goes straight to my dick.

I'm fucking rock-hard again.

FIFTY-TWO

Olivia

Back on Echo's bike, we ride down the highway and out of the city. Sleek high-rise buildings are replaced with tall green trees framed by a cloudless blue sky. Riding past a sign for Zilker Park, we cruise along, eventually pulling into a parking lot. Echo kills the engine and motions for me to climb off; he follows suit and pulls a bag from a saddlebag I'd never noticed before. Slinging his arm across my shoulder, he leads me across the lot.

"Where are we?" I ask.

Echo pulls me closer with a smirk and says, "This is Zilker Park, sugar, home to one of Austin's crown jewels… Barton Springs."

I start to question him, but then I see the water. Still, clear water, shimmering as far as I can see. Excited, I turn to him and smile brightly. "It's so beautiful. I've never even heard of this place."

Winking, he lifts his arm from my shoulder and grabs my hand. "Come on, let's go for a swim."

I drag my eyes from the water and look at Echo. "I haven't got a bikini or anything with me."

He lifts the bag he's carrying into the air and shakes it. "All sorted, come on."

Pulling me across the lot, Echo pays our entrance, and we separate at the changing area. I open the bag Echo handed me and find a red bikini and a folded microfibre towel. Quickly stripping, I pull on the skimpy red fabric, placing my clothes and towel in a locker.

Stepping out of the changing room I self-consciously tug at the strings of the bikini, making sure the tiny amount of fabric is covering everything it needs to. Finally forcing my hands to my sides, I lift my head, and gasp at the sight in front of me. Echo's in loose board shorts, his tattooed torso broad and delicious. Leaning against a barrier with his legs crossed at the ankle, he's the picture of relaxed, sexy man.

When he notices me, he smiles widely and strides towards me. The moment I'm within reach, his hands wrap around my waist and he lifts me into the air, kissing me passionately. "Fuck, sugar, letting you out in public in that bikini might be a fucking mistake. You look edible and so fucking gorgeous." He kisses me again, gripping my chin and tipping my face up to look at his. “I’m a fucking lucky son of a bitch that you’re mine.”

The heavy weight of his arm rests over my shoulder, and he leads me across the grass towards the water. Winking mischievously he sweeps his arm under my knees and scoops me into the air. I wrap my arms around his neck, giggling as he spins in a circle.

“You ready to get wet?” he asks.

Before I get a chance to speak, he rushes to the edge of the pool and steps off. We plunge into the cool water and I surge to the surface, coughing and spluttering. “Echo, you arsehole!” I shout as I spin from side to side, searching for him. “Echo,” I shout, spotting him beneath the water just as his large hand wraps around my ankle and pulls me under again.

As I break the surface, I open my eyes and look straight into Echo’s, he’s treading water in front of me, his mischievous eyes twinkling. Laughing, I launch myself at him, throwing all of my weight on his shoulders and forcing him under the water.

He pops straight back to the surface, and biting my lip, I dive under the water and swim away from him as fast as I can. I hear his deep, gravelly laugh seconds before he grabs my leg and hauls me backwards. “Ah, ah, ah, sugar. I caught you, no escaping now,” he says playfully.

Holding me against his chest, he dips his head to kiss me, his lips briefly touching mine. Then he releases me, splashing me with water as I laugh and chase after him as he swims away. We play in the water for an hour, chasing, splashing, and swimming like kids.

When we finally clamber out of the water, I collapse on the grassy bank, the balmy air quickly starting to dry my skin. Echo lays down next to me, sliding his arm beneath my head and urging me to rest against his chest.

"This place is amazing, Echo. Thank you for bringing me here."

His fingers run through my wet hair. "You're welcome, sugar. I haven't been here in years, but I figured you should see some of Austin's highlights."

Rolling into him I stroke his chest with the tips of my fingers, chasing the beads of water that have settled against his skin. "Where did you grow up… Foster?"

Echo stills beneath me, and I feel his chest rise as he pulls in a deep breath. "Please don't call me that. I fucking hate it. The only person to call me Foster was my mama, and she always said it with so much fucking disappointment in her voice."

"Why would she be disappointed?"

Echo pulls me tighter into him, like he needs to feel me as close as possible. "We're an army family, that's what we do. I left. She never forgave me. The last time I saw her, she told me I was a disgrace to the family name."

Outraged, I sit up. "That's ridiculous! You were in the army; you served your country. She should be proud of your service, not petty about you leaving."

Echo reaches for my face, his fingertip stroking my cheek. "It's okay, sugar, her opinion stopped meaning anything to me a long time ago. I'm happy with my life and my choices. I love being a Sinner. The club and my brothers are my life, and now I have you."

I drop my eyes and try to back away from Echo, but he stops me, lifting my chin to look at him. "I'm never gonna want to give you up. We'll figure out a way for you to stay. I promise."

I don't get a chance to respond before he kisses me. His lips dominate mine, and I melt into him. Echo ends the kiss, and breathless and panting, I open my eyes and stare into his. He touches my kiss-swollen lips with his thumb and smiles. "Come on, I still have some business to take care of before we go home."

By the time we're back on the bike, the sun's started to set, the sky a multicoloured painting, and I suddenly start to appreciate the freedom of this way of life. Wind rushes past us, and life's happening all around us, yet it feels like we're floating along in a bubble.

We pull off the main road and head into a small town, stopping outside a dodgy-looking tattoo shop. Echo kills the engine, lifting me off his bike and removing my helmet. "Come on, sugar, I want to introduce you to someone."

When he pushes open the door, a bell dings and a muffled voice shouts from the back, "I'll be with you in one minute."

A red velvet sofa sits under the window, with a large

reception desk commanding most of the space. The walls are decorated with framed tattoo designs. Dime-a-dozen butterflies and flowers sit next to incredible works of art so intricate I want to walk across the room to study them. Echo sits, pulling me into his lap and nuzzling his warm lips into my neck.

A tall, skinny guy wanders from the back of the shop, removing a pair of latex gloves. His eyes scan my face indifferently but when he spots Echo, he breaks into a huge grin. "Echo, brother, how the fuck are you?" I'm shocked by his lilting Irish accent.

Echo nudges my leg, and I stand, moving out of his embrace. He strokes my shoulder affectionately as he moves past me and strides over to the guy, embracing him in a tight hug and thumping his back loudly. "Park, long time no see. When did you get back?" Echo says happily.

Park's tall with bright pink hair styled into a messy mohawk. He's wearing Converse with tight jeans and a vintage Nirvana T-shirt, and all the skin I can see is covered in tattoos from his ears to the tips of his fingers. His Sinners cut matches Echo's, but instead of pristine black leather his is distressed and embellished with studs and graffiti-style letters spelling out Park on the front.

"Not long, brother, just a couple of days ago. It's fucking good to be back," Park says.

"Livvy, come here, baby, I want you to meet Park. This fucker's done all of my tats. The bastard is a fucking genius," Echo says.

Smiling I walk forward, offering my hand in greeting. “Hi Park, it’s nice to meet you.”

“Well hello, sweetheart, is that an English accent I hear?” Park asks, seems surprised by my obvious accent.

I giggle. “It is. You don’t sound so Texan yourself.”

Park takes my hand and kisses the back of it with a flourish. “And what’s your name, sweetheart?” he asks flirtatiously.

“I’m Olivia, but you can call me Liv. I bet the American girls lap up all that Irish charm, don’t they?”

A cocky smile covers his face. “They love it. But it usually works just as well on English girlies too.”

A loud laugh bursts from me. “I think I’m immune.”

Park smiles indulgently, then leans in and raises his eyebrows in question. “And why’s that?”

“Because she’s mine.” Echo looms behind me ominously, his body inches away from mine. My eyes roll at his caveman behaviour, seconds before his strong arms wrap around my waist and pull me close. Park’s eyes widen in shock, flitting back and forth between me and Echo.

“Park, I want you to meet Livvy, my old lady,” Echo says, his voice a possessive growl.

Park’s jaw drops, his mouth gaping in shock. “Fuck off. You’re joking. You with an old lady?”

Echo nods, smiling broadly. Park’s eyes fall to me again, and his eyes narrow suspiciously. “Well, sweetheart, you must be a special kind of special to have pinned this one down.” His tone's intentionally insulting, and I open my mouth to respond, but Echo cuts me off.

"Party tonight, brother?"

Park's attention turns from me to Echo, his concerned expression morphing into an easy smile. "Hell yes. It's been too long since I've had me any club pussy."

The men chat easily about the club and the other brothers, and I zone out. Warm lips touch my temple, pulling me from my daydream. "Sugar, stay here with Park. I've got some business to take care of in the back," Echo murmurs.

I nod and Echo disappears into the private rooms behind the reception desk. Awkwardly fidgeting with the hem of my dress, Park glares at me menacingly as the clock ticks loudly in the uncomfortable silence. My eyes scan the room, and then I turn and walk to the sofa, sinking down into it while Park perches on the desk.

Finally breaking the silence, Park clears his throat. "So, what brought you to the US?"

Relieved, I blurt, "Okay, small talk, I can totally do this. I'm travelling, spending six months seeing as much of my American bucket list as I can."

Nodding thoughtfully, he smiles knowingly. "And when do you go home?"

I blow out a sigh and force a small smile onto my lips. "Ahhhh, so that's what this is about. I've got eleven weeks left."

Park jumps up to sit fully on the shop counter, his long legs dangling over the edge. “In the club, him calling you his old lady is like him calling you his wife, you know that right?”

The air leaves my lungs on a shocked exhale. “Wow wife. I knew it meant I was his, but he never mentioned wife,” I say, panicked.

Park glares at me expectantly and says, “Does he know you’re leaving?”

I smile sadly. “Yeah, he knows, but he’s not exactly taking any notice.”

His accusing stare melts into a sympathetic one. “He’s not gonna let you go. You know that, don’t you, girlie?”

Sighing, I scrub my hands over my face. “I’m not sure what you want me to say. He’s not going to have a choice. My flight’s booked.”

Park’s eyes widen and a mocking chuckle rumbles from him. “Oh fuck,” he says. I raise my eyebrows, and nod in agreement.

FIFTY-THREE

Echo

The tattoo shop's one of the club's legitimate businesses, but it's also a front for the weed grow we have in the basement. Weed isn't legal in Texas yet, so this is one of those times where the club plays on the wrong side of the law.

Park's an artist; he's fucking brilliant with a tattoo gun, and I wouldn't trust anyone else to do my ink. The guy's got a client list a mile long and plenty more clambering to get his work on them. But he's also a hell of a gardener, and the club produces and sells the best weed this side of Colorado.

We've been having some complaints that the manicured product has been low in weight, and it's my job to find out who in the hell is fucking with the club. The idiots that work for us have no idea that I've got cameras hidden all over the shop and basement to keep an eye on what goes on.

Pulling my laptop from my desk, I watch as some stoner fucking punk, barely out of school, blatantly steals from the Sinners. Stupid fuckers got no clue what he just did, but me and Sleaze can enjoy teaching him some respect later.

I've known Park since I joined the club, and I love him like a brother. He just turned up one day and never left; we prospected together and have been close ever since. When I walk back into the front of the shop, the tense atmosphere hits me in the face. My girl and my brother both plaster fake smiles on their faces when they see me, but it's obvious that something's going on. I should probably confront them about it, but I just want to get my woman home. I can find out what's got them so quiet later.

Park's watched me fuck so much pussy in the last few years that it's not a surprise me finding an old lady would come as a shock. I want him and Livvy to get along, but I couldn't really give a fuck if they don't. She's mine and Park's like blood, so they'll accept each other sooner or later.

Livvy has woken something in me, and it's not just about having somewhere to stick my dick anymore. I want her, in this fucked-up primeval way. I want to consume her. I want her in my house and in my bed.

She's mine, and I intend to keep her. My girl was more than a fuck the moment I saw her in that tiny white dress; I just had no idea that she'd end up becoming my home.

FIFTY-FOUR

Olivia

We say goodbye and I rush away, desperate to leave Park's stifling presence, but the echo of his voice follows me. *"Does he know you're leaving?"* Guilt consumes me. I know I'm leaving and Echo knows I'm leaving, but there's nothing either of us can do about it.

Rushing across the road, I brace my hand on the seat of the bike, inhaling slowly as Parks words assault me. *"He's not gonna let you go."* Tears pool in my eyes, threatening to fall, but I blink them away.

I don't want to leave.

Tears fill my eyes and this time I don't try to fight them. Closing my eyes I let them fall, feeling the heat of my despair like its scolding me. Quickly wiping away the signs of my anguish, I whisper a prayer to God or anyone else who might be out there. "Please let me find a way to stay with him. I want to stay."

As we ride home, I wrap myself tightly around Echo, not questioning him as we coast straight through town and out towards the edge of Archer's Creek. Beautiful cottage-style homes, painted in creams and whites, line the streets and Echo pulls to a stop outside a house at the very end of the road. Instead of the bland pallet of the neighbouring properties, the house is painted a pale blue with a covered porch that curves around the front and seems to wrap around the whole building. It's the last house on the row with a separate garage set back from the house and dense trees fringing the garden on two sides.

Echo turns off the engine and we sit, silently looking at the impressive house in front of us. Slowly climbing off, Echo holds out his hand to help me, not releasing me once my feet are on the driveway.

"This is your home?" I ask. He nods, and for the first time since I met him, he looks unsure. I turn back and look up at the house, taking in the white shutters on the windows and the swinging chair hanging from the porch. "It's beautiful, Echo. Why would you live at the club when you could be here?" I whisper.

His lips crash into mine, kissing me long and deep till I'm wide-eyed and breathless. Swinging me into his arms, he quickly unlocks the front door and carries me through, placing me on my feet just inside the hall.

The house is bright and airy but practically empty, completely bereft of anything that would make it a home. Beautiful hardwood floors flow from the front door straight to a gorgeous sweeping staircase, but the place feels lifeless, like it's just waiting for someone to claim it.

"Do you want the tour?" he asks. I nod, and grasping my hand, Echo pulls me down the hall and into the lounge room. A huge TV and two armchairs sit in the middle of the otherwise empty room.

Light pours in through large windows and warms the barren space and I wander away from Echo and stand for a moment just looking at the view of his beautiful, peaceful gardens. I can feel him watching me, uncertainty pouring from my normally bossy, overbearing man. He observes me quietly before crooking a finger at me. "Come here, sugar, I'll show you the rest of the house."

Echo tows me from room to room, each one empty, unlived in, and void of life. The modern kitchen is brand new, all of the appliances still covered in the protective packaging and unused. I drag my hand across the granite worktops and caress the cool smooth surface.

Glancing at Echo for a moment, I scan the unused kitchen and cross the room to the huge American-style fridge sitting in the corner. Intrigued, I pull open the doors to look at the contents. "Beer and bottled water. That's it?" I ask. Echo shrugs then reaches around me to shut the door. "You've really never lived here, have you?"

I've never seen Echo look nervous before, but I can see it on him now as he avoids my gaze. "I tried once, but it was just too quiet."

"You've never thought about having one of your women move in?" I ask, raising my eyebrows.

He scoffs lightly and smiles. "I've had lots of women, sugar. But you don't ask women you fuck to move in with you."

"You're fucking me."

Ignoring me, he shakes his head, takes my hand and leads me out of the kitchen and onto a gorgeous covered patio that overlooks a lavish, but empty pool. "So what do you think?"

Lost in my daydream of living here, of lounging by his pool or cooking in his kitchen, his questions startles me. "It's a beautiful house, Echo. I just don't understand why you'd choose to live in one room at the club when you could be here instead."

Smiling, he reaches out, tucking an errant strand of my hair behind my ear. "Because it was missing something."

I laugh. "Yeah, it's missing furniture, but that's an easy fix. You have IKEA over here, don't you?"

Pulling me into his arms, he kisses me, his touch consuming and dominating, but sweet and loving as well. "Sugar, it's not missing chairs. It's missing you."

I stare at him, my heart pounding in my chest, frozen to the spot, as his warm fingers collar my throat gently.

"Nothing to say, Livvy?"

I shake my head, and he chuckles quietly, taking my hand. "Come on, I'll show you the rest of the house."

My hand held tightly in his, he leads me through three large, airy, and empty bedrooms, all with gorgeous attached bathrooms and then pauses outside the fourth door. Turning, I look up at him questioningly, but he just winks at me a moment before I'm swept off the floor and into his arms. A giggle bursts from my lips and I wrap my arms around his neck as he pushes open the door and walks us into the room.

Without him having to tell me, it's obvious this is his bedroom. Its stunning, with floor-to-ceiling windows that flood the room with light. His bed's raised on a platform with steps that lead to the dark wooden bed frame and crisp white bedding. Doors step out onto a balcony that overlooks the gardens below.

Echo moves behind me and wraps his arms around my waist. "Move in with me," his raspy voice says into my ear.

I don't respond. Instead, I stare through the glass at the peace outside.

"Move in with me, Livvy." His voice takes on a demanding tone; he's not asking anymore, and I waver, so tempted to agree.

"I can't," I sigh, defeated, my eyes falling closed as my head drops forward. Silence engulfs us and I cross my arms over my chest, hugging myself.

His guttural growl shatters the quiet, his anger and frustration palpable in the air. Squeezing my eyes closed I try to hide from everything I'm feeling, but I should have known that Echo would never let me hide from him. I hear his footsteps a second before I'm airborne and weightless. My back hits his soft bedding with a thud and my eyes pop open.

Echo's above me, dominance sparkling in his eyes. "Echo, you can't sex a yes out of me. I can't move in when we both know my time is limited. It's too cruel to both of us. We should be taking a step back, not a massive one forward," I cry.

"No," he snarls. My mouth forms a reply, but he cuts me off. "If you didn't have to leave, would you say yes?"

Anger explodes from me, and I push at his chest, but he barely moves. "But I do have to leave," I shout.

Leaning in he silences me with a punishing kiss. "If you didn't have to leave, would you say yes?" he asks again.

I study him. He's so strong and determined. He says I'm his. He protects me and cares for me. He worships my body and brings me more pleasure than I could ever have imagined.

He makes me happier than I've ever been.

I'm falling in love with him.

Echo watches the emotions flash across my face, his fingers stroking my cheek. "I know you'd say yes, sugar. I know because I feel it too. So say yes."

My eyes fill with tears, and I hear Park's words loudly in my head again. *"He's not gonna let you go."* Closing my eyes,

I block out my thoughts and start to nod, but he interrupts. “No, fuck this, Livvy, you don’t get a choice. You’re moving in. Now let’s go get your shit.”

A laugh bursts from me and tears fall down my cheeks. “Okay.”

His face sobers. “Yes?”

I nod. “Yes. I’ll move in with you.”

FIFTY-FIVE

Echo

I kiss her breathless then reluctantly pull her from the bed.

"Come on, sugar; let's go get your shit." I'm not giving her the chance to come up with some fucked-up reason why she can't live with me. I'm taking her to get her stuff now, and then I plan to fuck her over and over in our bed till she can't imagine being anywhere else.

I drag a giggling Livvy behind me and throw open the doors to my garage, waiting for her reaction to my baby. Her eyes light up when she spots my completely restored vintage 1953 Chevy truck. I open the door for her, and she slides along the bench seat, her small hands stroking the original polished wood dash. I climb in and haul her back along the seat till she's next to me with my arm draped over her shoulders.

It takes us about five minutes to drive to Miss Mimi's, and Livvy disappears inside to pack up her clothes and girly shit. Mimi fucking hates the club, so Livvy asked me to stay out here, but I'm bored and I want my girl, so maybe if I help I can get her home and naked quicker.

I walk up to the front door, open it, and immediately hear voices. Livvy's British accent is soft, and my dick hardens just from the sound of her. "Miss Mimi, thank you so much for renting me the room, but I'm actually going to be moving out today."

Mimi's snooty voice is obnoxiously loud. "Miss Olivia, you shouldn't be going anywhere with that riff-raff. They're nothing but thugs and criminals."

"Thank you for your concern, ma'am. I appreciate your advice, but Echo's a good man," Livvy says in a polite but confident voice.

Mimi's laugh sounds maniacal. "A good man? Was he being a good man when he broke my darling Wyatt's nose, or when he gave him two black eyes and a fractured cheekbone? That vagrant Echo is a psychopath who needs to be thrown in jail with the rest of the criminals in that godawful motorcycle club."

I quietly step into the hall. Livvy's standing with her back to me, and the old bitch is standing in front with her evil crimson fingernails gripping Livvy's arm. Mimi screeches, and I watch Livvy flinch in shock. "You're just another one of their whores, spreading your legs for those awful bikers. You should be ashamed of yourself. May God have mercy on your soul," Mimi shouts.

I stride forward and touch Livvy's back, and she shrinks into me.

"*Whore,*" Mimi screeches.

Turning my woman, I guide her out of the house while Mimi screams at us.

"*Whore*."

Keeping Livvy sheltered in front of me I spin back to the evil old bag. "Hey, you crazy old bitch, get back inside and keep your mouth shut. What the fuck is wrong with you?"

I lift a shell-shocked Livvy safely into my truck, load her stuff in the back, and drive quickly away with the echo of Mimi's voice chanting "*Whore, whore, whore,*" receding as I finally take my old lady home.

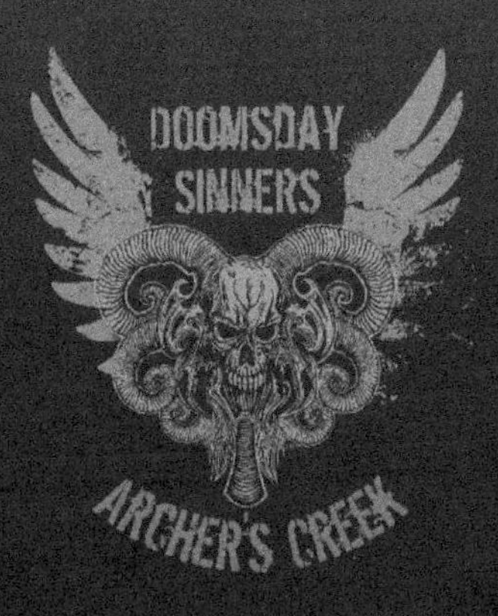

FIFTY-SIX

Olivia

My hands are gripped tight over my ears, but I can still hear Miss Mimi's shouts.

"Whore."

Lifting my feet onto the seat, I bury my head into my knees as Echo pulls away from the curb. Mimi's words hit hard. It's only words screamed by an angry, bitter old woman, but I can't shake the insult.

"Sugar, you okay?" Echo asks.

I shake my head and pull my knees up closer to my chest, curling into as tight a ball as I can. An arm reaches across my shoulders, drawing me into the safety of his embrace. His touch and the heat of his skin calms me, and I unfurl, climbing into his lap as he drives.

"I didn't realize she hated the club so much. Fuck, it's been ten years since her old man left with one of the club skanks," Echo says, stroking my back soothingly.

After a moment we fall silent. I'm in his lap, his arms wrapped around me, holding me close to him while my heart gradually slows, and my muscles relax.

"Thank you," I whisper.

"What are you thanking me for?"

Still clinging to him, I lift my head and softly kiss his neck. "You stepped between us. I should have walked away, or told her to fuck off, but I just froze. I've never been called a whore before. She was just so angry and mean."

Echo's body stiffens beneath me. "You don't need to thank me. She shouldn't have said a word to you. If I'd sent a prospect to collect your stuff, none of this would have happened."

I lift my head from his shoulder just as we pull onto his driveway. He turns off the engine and starts to open the door, but I reach for his hand, stilling it. "Echo, you protected me from her. I've never had someone other than my parents do that for me."

His fingers lift my chin, forcing me to look at him. Intensity and possession flare in his eyes and I have to swallow back the emotion that's building inside of me. "I'll always protect you, Livvy, always. It's my job to look after you, to keep you safe."

I nod, understanding for the first time what his claim really means. He lifts me, and I wrap my arms and legs around him tightly. Our lips meet and we kiss, but his lips don't dominate mine; instead they reverently whisper his promises. That he'll look after me, protect me, and keep me safe.

Echo carries me upstairs and sets me down on the bathroom counter, kissing me quickly before he turns on the taps and starts to fill the gloriously large claw-footed bath.

"Strip."

For once, it's not an order. His voice is soft, and his eyes are filled with concern. But one word is all it takes; my breathing shallows and my heart races. I watch him, then slowly remove my clothes till I'm standing naked, waiting for him. Heat fills his eyes as he takes in my bare skin, my breasts heaving, aroused.

His hands slide along my skin from my hips and over my ribs. Holding me gently, he lifts me into the bath, and I submerge into the water. Kneeling on the floor at the side of the tub, his rough, callused hands cupping my cheeks, he takes my lips, claiming me, owning me.

Desperate for more, I track his movement when he stands and turns to leave. "Aren't you getting in?" I ask.

He smiles but shakes his head. "Not yet. You relax. I'm gonna get your stuff out of the truck. Then I'll come wash your back."

Winking at me he heads to the door, pausing he turns and looks at me over his shoulder. "Welcome home, Livvy."

Home.

I close my eyes and lay my head back against the side of the bath, smiling widely.

My phone bursts to life, the sounds of Blake Shelton's 'Kiss My Country Ass' blares loudly, refusing to be ignored. Groaning, I lean over the side of the bath and grab my phone from the pocket in my dress.

The screen flashes "James Calling." And I squeal with excitement; it's been far too long since I spoke to anyone from back home.

"Bestie," I say as I answer the call.

James makes an audible sigh. "Thank fuck, Liv we thought you'd been murdered or abducted by aliens or joined a cult or something. It's been nearly two weeks since the last time you called." The relief is obvious in his voice, and I feel like the worst kind of friend.

"Shit, I'm sorry, hon. It's just kind of been an insane couple of weeks."

James's reply is instant. "Why, what's been going on?"

With a groan, I sink back into the water. "God, I don't even know where to start. I'm not sure you'd believe me if I told you."

Chuckling, he prods, "Come on, Liv, spill. What's happened?"

I blow out a long, laboured sigh and respond, "Okay, so here's the short version. You know I was going to El Paso?"

"Er, yeah," he replies, sounding confused.

"Okay, so my bus broke down. Then it left without me, leaving me stranded in this little town called Archer's Creek, in

Texas, of all fucking places."

"Shit, Liv, are you okay?" James asks, concern edging his voice.

"Yeah, yeah, I'm fine," I assure him. Then I blurt out quickly, "But I met a guy who turned out to be in a biker gang, who got me a job at the bar they own. Well, he's kind of perfect, and I'm kind of falling for him. He asked me to move in with him, and I said yes, then the guesthouse I was living in, the owner turned out to be a psycho and she chased me out of the house today calling me a whore. Oh, and I guess I'm kind of a biker's old lady."

James's voice rises. "Wait, wait, wait. A biker gang as in *Sons of Anarchy*?"

"Yes."

Speaking slowly and cautiously, he says, "Liv, do you need to see a doctor? Are you in a hospital? Because I hate to tell you this, sweetie, but you sound like you're living the plot of a bad soap opera."

I laugh loudly and sit up quickly, making water splash over the side of the bath and onto the floor. "Oh my god, it does sound like a bad TV show, doesn't it? Echo's turned my life into a melodrama."

I pull the phone away from my ear as he shouts, "Echo, who the fuck is Echo?"

"Echo's the guy I've met."

"And he's a biker?"

“Yes.”

“And he’s called Echo?” James’s voice is slightly incredulous.

“Yes.”

“And you’re living with him?”

“Yes.”

James goes silent for a second. Then I hear him shout, “Dan, Liv’s lost the fucking plot! Can you see how much flights are to Archer’s Creek, Texas.” James’s boyfriend Dan responds, but I can’t hear what he says.

Laughing, I quickly reply, “I haven’t lost the plot, you daft sod. I know it sounds like I’ve made it up, but I swear to fucking God it’s all happened.”

The indulgent affection in his voice is so clear, I can picture his face. “Bloody hell, Liv, it’s only been two weeks. This could only happen to you.”

I chuckle. “Tell me about it.”

James laughs lightly. “So this guy, you like him?”

I sigh dreamily. “I like him.”

“Is that all?” he questions.

“No, I more than like him. I think I’m falling for him.”

His voice goes all girly when he asks, “Soooo, what’s he like?”

Groaning, I pull my hands from the water and cover my eyes. “He’s not my normal type at all. He’s huge, muscly, and covered in tattoos.”

He giggles. “Sounds perfect.”

My face breaks into a huge smile as I think about Echo. “He’s bossy and domineering and so intense. But he makes me feel safe, protected. When I see him, it’s like I’m drawn to him, like he pulls me in, and the thought of not being with him makes my chest hurt.”

“You love him,” James says.

“No.”

James’s voice is soft. “Liv, you love him.”

Sitting up straight, I gasp. “Fuck, I love him.” James laughs loudly, and I fire back, “Don’t laugh, you bastard. I’m leaving in a couple of weeks.”

“So stay,” he says, like it’s the simplest thing in the world.

“I can’t. It’s not like I can just stay.”

“Why not?” The question in his voice almost makes me question myself.

“My visa.”

“Oh shit. So what you gonna do?”

“Enjoy the time I’ve got and fall apart when I leave.” My voice cracks on the word leave, and I feel my heart banging against my chest as panic starts to creep inside me.

“Oh Liv, I’m sorry.” I can hear the sympathy in his voice. Tears fill my eyes, and I nod even though I know James can’t see me through the phone. “It’s all gonna work out, Liv, you’ll see. Just please don’t leave it this long without even a text. Because we really will be on a plane to track you down next time.”

Clearing my throat quickly, I try to hide the obvious tears in my voice. “I promise, love you.”

“Love you too, Liv. We miss you,” James coos.

“Miss you too, bye,” I say, the words filled with emotion.

The call ends, and I’m filled with an overwhelming sense of homesickness.

I miss my friends.

FIFTY-SEVEN

Echo

Unpacking Livvy's stuff is easy; she's travelling really fucking light. The sight of her clothes hanging in my wardrobe gives me a massive hard-on. I only keep a few things at the house, but her tiny dresses next to my stuff makes my heart pound.

God, I'm turning into such a fucking pussy.

I want her to make this a home, our things mixed together. Fuck, that's something else I never thought I'd want—someone else's shit cluttering up my house.

The thought of her naked in the bath, the water glistening on her skin, is driving me crazy. I'm already pulling off my shirt and walking towards the bathroom when her phone rings. Some godawful country song screams out till she answers it and starts talking. I don't know who's on the other end, but I try really hard not to listen—till she says my name.

Her voice gets soft and breathy. Fuck, this girl destroys me.

Time to call in those favors; I need to find a way for Livvy to stay or for me to go with her.

Either way, I can't give her up.

FIFTY-EIGHT

Olivia

My skin's starting to prune by the time Echo comes back into the bathroom. Completely naked, he saunters across the room, and my breath hitches when he turns towards me. I don't know where to look first. My eyes start at his smug grin and track a path over his tattooed chest and his perfectly defined abs to his hard cock. Standing aroused, his large shaft begs for my attention, and I grab the side of the bath, pulling myself upright.

"No," he says. I pause and watch him walk closer, the muscles in his stomach rippling as he walks. "Move forward, sugar." I shuffle forward, and Echo slides in behind me, his legs on either side of my body. His hands slide down my arms entwining our fingers as he urges me backward till my back hits his chest and I melt into him with my head against his shoulder.

His worshipping embrace is unexpected. Usually when he touches me, it's commanding and forceful and I love him taking control; but the way he's touching me now, caressing me, almost cherishing me, makes my heart stutters in my chest.

He kisses the back of my head, and I feel the heat of his lips through my hair. "I'm so glad you're here, Livvy." His voice is quiet.

"Me too."

We lapse into silence, just us in our cocoon where the outside world and real life can't reach us.

I lie in his arms, my fingers drawing circles on his hand. "How long were you in the army for?" I ask.

"Long enough."

I'm so desperate to know him, but I don't want to push him, especially about this. "You don't want to talk about it?"

He exhales. "Not really, sugar. It's my past. I saw a lot of stuff I wish I hadn't, and I lost too many friends."

Turning my head I press a kiss to his bicep. "I'm sorry," I whisper.

His chuckle is dry and hard. "What are you sorry for? It's not your war." We fall into silence, and his tense muscles slowly relax. "Tell me something about you instead," Echo says.

"What do you want to know?"

His hands, dip into the water briefly, pulling the warm liquid up to drip onto my stomach. "What's your family like?"

he eventually asks.

Laughing, I picture my parents in my head. “They’re eccentric old hippies who smoke too much weed and listen to far too much Hendrix.”

Echo chuckles. “You don’t get along?”

“No, we get on. I adore my mum and dad, but we don’t exactly have a lot in common.”

“Oh yeah, how come?”

I feel like I need to be able to see him while we talk, so I roll over and turn to straddle his legs. “Well, back home, before coming here, I was kind of stiff. I had a boring job and a boring life. I was boring. No one believed I was going backpacking.”

His eyebrow raises in question. “Why not? It’s not an unusual thing to do.”

I scoff. “It was for me. Plus, it’s not like you can exactly backpack in Prada heels.”

His chuckle vibrates through his chest. “You don’t strike me as a designer girl, sugar. You spend more time in shorts and flip-flops.”

“I’m not anymore,” I say. “This is me now. But my parents have never been more proud of me than the day I told them I was going on this trip.”

“Yeah?” he prompts.

“Yep. My mum told me to find freedom and embrace it, that if my old life wasn’t making me happy, to find a new one.”

I roll my eyes dramatically.

Echo's mouth twitches into a small smirk. "And you found me."

I nod and smile shyly. "I found you."

His voice gets louder and determined. "I'm gonna find a way for us to stay together, sugar, one way or another."

Bracing my hands on either side of him, I lean down till our lips meet in a gentle touch; pushing everything I want to say but can't, or daren't, into the kiss.

I want to stay. Come with me. I love you.

"I spoke to my friend from home earlier. He called me panicking because I've been so distracted by you I haven't called home since we met," I say.

Echo's face hardens slightly. "Oh yeah, what friend?"

"James," I say. "He's my oldest and best friend; we grew up together. I think we've known each other since we were three. At one time, I thought we'd end up being family, when he was engaged to my cousin Juliet."

"What happened?" he asks.

A chuckle bursts out at the memory. "It's kind of a messed-up story."

Smiling indulgently, Echo settles into the warm water. "I've got time."

I lean forward and plant a quick kiss on Echo's lips. "Okay, well, I'd always suspected James was gay, and when I finally asked him about it, he came out as bisexual. He always said he was an equal opportunity lover, guys, girls—he even went out with a guy who insisted he was a fairy for a while. But it was still a surprise when he got together with Juliet, even more so when they got engaged. I love my cousin, but Juliet is an intense girl, super high-maintenance, not at all what James normally went for, guy or girl. But anyway, I was seeing this guy called Dan."

Echo tenses beneath me and groans. "Fuck, I don't want to think about your exes. It makes me fucking violent."

I giggle. "I wouldn't worry. This isn't one of those stories." Echo's hands settle on my arse, and he nods, indicating for me to continue. "Well, I was seeing Dan, and the four of us were close, and I mean we spent a load of time together. It was Juliet's birthday, and we were all going out to a pub for a meal. The whole family was there, and we're all drinking and having a great time. I nipped back to my car to grab my jacket, and there were Dan and James dry humping against a wall."

Echo's eyes widen. "Hang on, sugar. Your ex and your best friend?"

"Yep. I mean, obviously, James with a guy wasn't exactly a shock, but finding Dan with his tongue in James's mouth was a bit of a surprise," I say, laughing.

Echo sits up, shocked. "I thought James is still your friend?"

I smile and shrug. "He is. They both are. Obviously, I was pissed at the time, but Dan and I weren't serious. Honestly, I think I was angrier with James, but that was ages ago. James and Dan have been together ever since, and I love them both."

Echo shakes his head, nonplussed. "Fuck, that's messed up."

Laughing, I lean in and kiss him. "I know, but they were meant to be together. I can't hold a grudge and stay angry just because they found their soul mates in a fucked-up way."

Echo smiles indulgently and lifts me from the bath. "Come on, sugar, time to get ready." Wrapping me in a huge fluffy towel, he quickly dries himself, then painstakingly slowly dries my skin, caressing me and teasing me. He smacks my naked arse and nudges me out of the bathroom, throwing himself onto the bed. Stark naked he settles himself against the pillows, crossing his arms behind his head and watching me with a smug smile on his face.

My things are all unpacked, and the few bottles of product I had in my bag are arranged on top of his bureau. Grabbing a tube of moisturiser I exaggeratedly smooth it over my naked skin, glancing over my shoulder at him, an innocent expression on my face. "Don't you need to get ready?" I ask.

His bottom teeth peek out, pulling his lip into his mouth and nibbling at it gently. My breath catches in my chest and my hands still. Releasing his lip, he shakes his head slowly, his eyes focussed intently on me. "I'm enjoying the show. Don't let me stop you."

I flash him a coy smile and start to coat every inch of my skin in cream. I bend over and slowly caress my ankles, my hands rubbing the lotion in circles until it disappears. Next I straighten, rubbing my hands over my chest, circling first one breast and then the other.

Echo's eyes are wide and amused as he watches me walk away from the bed and back to the bureau. I reach for the moisturiser, but his hand stops me. Pinning my arms to my sides, he sweeps all the bottles to the floor and pushes me down, forcing me to bend over the unit, my nipples pressed flat against the cold wood.

"Do you think you're clever, Livvy? Do you think it's fun to tease me?" His voice is gravelly and rough, barely restrained desire evident in every word. "What should I do with you, sugar?" His fingers tiptoe down my arse cheeks and dip between my legs.

"Should I fuck you here?" Two fingers plunge roughly into me, pulling out quickly and tiptoeing back up to circle my arsehole, pressing gently against the tight hole. "Or shall I fuck you here?"

I gasp, and he chuckles in response. "I can't wait to fuck this ass, Livvy. Fill you up with my cock, knowing it's the first time you've ever been taken there." Panting loudly, I shudder. Arousal and fear mix headily at his touch and his words. "You want it, don't you? Your ass full of my cock, my cum dripping out of this tight little hole."

I groan, then nod, pushing back onto his fingers, willing him to ease the burn of desire.

"I know you do, baby. But not tonight," he drawls.

His hard cock lines up with my pussy, and he slowly pushes inside. Holding on tightly to the wood of the bureau, I meet him thrust for thrust as he rocks in and out of me, forcing me onto my tiptoes with every punishing thrust.

"Fuck, sugar, what you do to me," he rasps, holding my hips roughly as he pulls me back harder onto his cock.

"Oh god, I'm so close. Echo, please," I pant. Bending his knees, his cock changes angle and a pulse of pure pleasure crashes through me, sending me flying over the edge into oblivion. The intensity of my orgasm buckles my knees and he tightens his grip and he follows, sending his seed pulsing deep inside of me.

I'm pulled upright, his strong arms turning me into his chest, and our lips meet. My breathing evens, and Echo's hold loosens. His hand cups my chin and he tilts my face to look at him as he forces his hands between my legs, collects the cum leaking out of me, and rubs it across my breasts and pussy.

"Echo, I haven't got time to take a shower," I whine.

Echo smiles smugly, lifting his eyebrows cheekily. "I know." My mouth drops open, but he leans forward and kisses me sweetly before swatting my arse. "Get dressed, sugar. Wear the black dress."

Stepping away from him on shaky legs I scoff lightly as I make my way to the wardrobe. Finding the dress he asked me to wear, I pull it from the hanger and slip it over my head. Black with a sweetheart neckline, the skirt falls to midthigh and instead of straps, there's a criss-cross pattern of thin ribbons across my shoulders and chest, so all my skin is still visible, but the ribbon makes a peekaboo pattern across my cleavage. It's simple yet incredibly sexy. I tame my hair into a fishtail plait that falls across one shoulder, throw on my leather ankle boots, and finish my look with a swipe of mascara and cat's-eye flick eyeliner.

It takes Echo less than five minutes to get dressed, but even just in a black T-shirt, jeans, and his cut, Echo's beautiful. His colourful tattoos are framed against the dark material and my nipples pebble in appreciation.

His eyes roam me from head to toe. "Sugar, you look like fucking sin."

I smile coquettishly. "Is that a good thing?"

In a second, he's across the room and I'm pulled back into his chest with his hand disappearing down my panties. "A fucking great thing. Except my dick's gonna be hard as steel all night."

"Do we have to go to the party?"

He laughs, but reluctantly releases me, licking his arousal-covered fingers. "Come on, let's go." With a pout, I let him guide me down the stairs and into his truck.

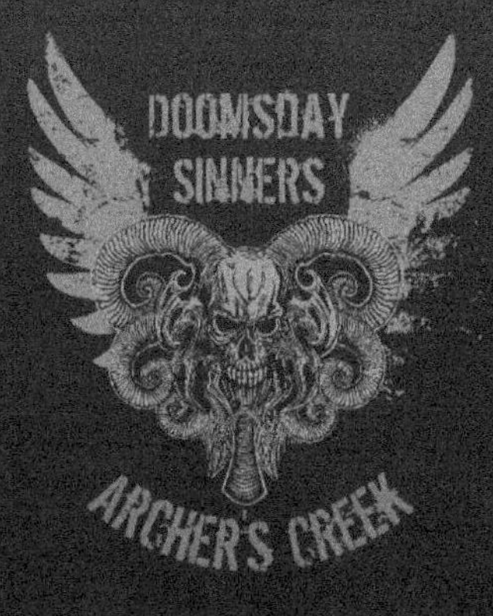

FIFTY-NINE

Olivia

The party's much bigger than the last one, and people spill out of the clubhouse to dance around bonfires lit on the car park and grounds. Strangers fill the bar, hedonistic, sensual self-indulgence freeing them to forget their inhibitions. Naked women dance on podiums with their heads tipped back, lost in the music.

Overwhelmed, I shrink into Echo's embrace, allowing him to guide me through the room. A path clears for Echo as he walks. His naturally intimidating presence is dangerous enough for people to instantly recognise he's not someone to fuck with. We stop at a table, and I'm grateful to spot the familiar faces of Sleaze and Brandi.

"Liv, you look hot. I love this dress on you," Brandi says,

leaping from Sleaze's lap and pulling me into a hug.

"Thanks, hon, you look gorgeous too," I say. She's wearing super skinny, high-waisted jeans and nude heels, her top's got a high neck with panels of fabric cut out to hint at the skin beneath.

Brandi twirls and laughs. "Sleaze thinks so too," she says, winking at me. Sleaze growls, and his hands snap out to grab her around the waist, pulling her into his lap. I laugh loudly as Sleaze drags her closer and kisses her passionately.

Echo hands me a drink and lifts me to sit in his lap. Sipping it, I watch the revellers for a moment thoughtfully. "It feels like such a long time since we were at the last party, but it's been less than two weeks," I say.

His hand slides up my leg before dipping beneath my dress. When he speaks, his voice rumbles sexily in my ear. "I wanted you so bad that night."

I turn to look at him fully and smile. "You ignored me the whole night, then threatened to kill that guy and dragged me off to your room."

His laugh vibrates through his chest. "I didn't take my eyes off you all night, sugar. I tried to leave you alone, but the moment Puck touched you, I knew you were mine and he needed to keep his hands to his fucking self."

People start to join our table. Park arrives first, his assessing eyes watching me cautiously. Two bikers I don't know arrive, then Blade, and finally Puck. I freeze, my whole body tensing. Echo's grip tightens, and he pulls me closer into his arms before he turns to Puck and growls ominously.

Puck strides straight up to Echo and holds out his hand. "Brother, I didn't know she was yours. I'm sorry."

Echo leans forward, grasps Puck's outstretched hand, and shakes it. "Apology accepted, brother. I'll still fucking kill you if you touch her again."

Puck smiles and nods. "No worries."

Puck tilts his head in my direction, silently seeking permission to speak to me. Echo nods and Puck turns and kneels in front of me. My eyes widen, unsure what he plans to do. I expect him to touch me; but his hands stay resting on his knees. "Olivia, please accept my apology. I'm sorry."

His words sound sincere, and when I glance at his face, his eyes urge me to believe him. Nodding, I lean forward slightly. "That's okay, but I appreciate the apology. I'm sure he doesn't actually mean he'd kill you."

His laugh alters his features completely. "You're his old lady, I'd deserve it."

I shrug and wrinkle my nose slightly in agreement. Puck laughs and rises, moving to the other side of the table and sitting next to Blade. Brandi catches my eye and signals that she wants to dance. I climb out of Echo's lap, but his hand grabs mine, halting me. "Where you going?"

I lean down and kiss him lightly. "To dance," I say. He nods, slapping my arse playfully before turning back to his friends.

I manage to down the rest of my drink before Brandi grabs my hand and pulls me into the crowd. The music's so loud it's impossible to talk, so we both throw our hands in the air and grind to the music, laughing and basking in the freedom. Thirsty, I touch Brandi's arm. "Drink?" I shout. She mouths something in response, but it's too loud to hear her. Confused, I lean in and shout in her ear. "I need a drink!" Nodding, she fans herself and gradually we force our way through the crowd back to our table.

My eyes land on the back of Echo's head, my skin heating just from knowing he's close. Smiling I pull Brandi behind me, eager to get to him. We weave around people, gradually edging closer to the table—and I stop dead. A blonde woman's practically sitting on top of him, a brunette flanking his other side, her hands resting on his shoulder.

Brandi walks into the back of me, shoving me forward. She catches me before I fall, and her eyes find the threesome on the sofa before turning a sympathetic look on me. Angry, I pull in a deep breath, push out my chest, march up to the table, and glare at Echo and his companions.

I act before I think, grabbing a handful of the blonde's cheap extensions and violently yanking her head back. Screaming, she falls from the sofa, her shocked eyes turning angry when she sees that I'm her attacker and scrambles to her feet.

We stand toe to toe. "Get the fuck away from him," I snarl,

my voice hard and lethal.

Breathing heavily, she screams in my face, "Who the fuck are you?"

My eyes flick to Echo for a second before returning to blondie. "I'm his old lady, so I suggest you get your skanky fucking arse away from him right now or I swear to God I will break your ugly fucking nose."

Her eyes widen for a second, then she snarls, "Echo doesn't have an old lady. Go find another Sinner to fuck, 'cause me, Ebony, and Echo are gonna have some fun tonight, and we know just how to keep a man happy." Smiling triumphantly she starts to turn away from me but I grab her shoulder and haul her back to face me. My vision turns red as I pull back my elbow and punch her in the face.

Blood spurts from her nose and she screams, but I ignore her, scanning the rest of our group and finding a new-found respect on all of their faces. Brandi cheers loudly, "Woo, go Livvy." I laugh at her and curtsy briefly, shaking my head at myself. Skank one and two step towards me, and I feel Brandi at my shoulder, silently supporting me.

Echo steps up behind me, his arms wrapping around my waist, his body tense. "Sugar," he rasps, pressing a kiss to my cheek, before turning back to the skanks in front of us. "I see you've met my old lady and from what I just heard I think you might need a reminder of exactly what your place is here. You pair are club whores; you're here to get fucked. You're easy, free pussy for those who want it. We get to pick you up or drop you whenever we want. You girls let us fuck you anyhow, anywhere, in any-hole, and you love it, you beg for the scraps that the Sinners give you. But when a Sinner decides to make a woman his old lady, it's because she's a fucking lady, someone that we respect and that deserves the respect of everyone in or involved with the club. That means that the whores don't ever disrespect someone who's been honored with the position of old lady. You need to fucking apologize to my woman, right fucking now."

Shocked, I stare at Echo, then at the thoroughly reprimanded skanks. Their eyes narrow on me even as they both apologise. Echo leans in and kisses my temple before he speaks, "Right, girls, you have two choices. You can get the fuck out of the club and never come back, or you can become Puck's playthings for the next week." Their eyes widen at the mention of Puck's name and Echo chuckles, "I take it you both know about Puck's… preferences." Silently they both nod. "So, what's it gonna be?"

The girls look at each other, then the one called Ebony turns and walks away, quickly scurrying through the crowd. All eyes turn to the remaining girl. She walks to Puck and sinks to her knees at his feet. He leans down and whispers in her ear, her eyes close for a second, then she nods. They stand, and Puck wraps his hand around the back of her neck as he leads her towards the bedrooms.

Puck and the girl disappear, and seconds later, Echo spins

me to face him, lunging at me and claiming me in a brutal kiss. His lips consume me, and I melt into him—until images of women pawing him flash into my mind and I push at his chest till he steps back, freeing me.

"What the fuck was that?" I shout.

Echo looks confused, reaching for me again, but I quickly step back. "Skanky and slutty pawing all over you," I say pointedly. He ignores me, trying to pull me into his arms, but I bat his hand away.

Scowling, he grabs me, holding me tight to his chest. "That was nothing, sugar," he coos.

Anger pulses through me, and tilting my head to the side, I raise my eyebrows in question. "Oh, that was nothing. I just got into a fist fight with a girl who informed me I could go home because her and her skanky friend would be keeping you happy with a dirty little threesome tonight. Is that nothing? Oh, okay, then shall I go sit in some guys lap and offer him a lap dance? Would that be nothing as well?" I say sarcastically.

Echo's whole body tenses and fury explodes in his eyes. "Don't fucking move, Livvy," he growls.

I bark out a dry laugh. "Yeah, not so funny when the tables are turned, is it? If you want those skanks, that's fine, I'll leave. If not, then I suggest you keep your hands to yourself and any fucking sluts away from you, okay?"

He nods once, his hand collaring my throat, gently stroking the pulse point there. "I'm sorry," he whispers.

Apologetic eyes lock with mine, and I get lost in his gaze. My muscles relax one by one and as if sensing my acceptance, he guides me into his chest, wrapping me tightly in his strong arms. Dipping his head to my ear he whispers, "I'm yours, you're mine. That's it, sugar."

Echo hands me a drink, and tentatively sits, watching me and waiting for my reaction. I tip back the glass and swallow deeply, the cool beer soothing my throat.

As he studies me, I smile mischievously at him, grabbing Brandi, and leading her back out to the dance floor. Feeling his eyes on me, I dance, swaying provocatively to the music. Brandi winks conspiratorially before pulling me close. Our legs entwine, my arms resting over her shoulders, hers on my waist. Our bodies rub against one another, the music fuelling our provocative routine as we move closer, dancing, smiling and laughing loudly.

Dropping her lips to my ear, she speaks, but I can barely hear her over the loud bass. "Ten, nine, eight, seven, six, five, four, three, two, one."

Echo and Sleaze materialize in front of us, both intense and determined as they reach out and pull us apart. Sleaze pulls Brandi in close, whispering in her ear. The music hides what he says, but Brandi's eyes widen and then glaze over with a lust-filled haze.

I pause, unsure what Echo will do, expecting to be hoisted into the air, or forced into a position where he can reinforce him claim on me. But instead his chest touches my back, swaying against me to the music. “We’re dancing?” I say in shock.

Hearing the surprise in my voice, he wraps one of his arms across my stomach and guides me to move to the rhythm. His hips rotate, grinding with the pulse of the bass and I relax as my body sinks against his, allowing him to move me as he pleases. His large, tattooed hand rests on my thigh, edging my dress up inch by inch as the other pushes against my stomach, holding me tight against him.

Lost in him, I reach back and wrap my arm around his neck. My eyes drift closed as his touch and the ethereal pulse of the music hypnotise me. His fingers edge under my dress and slowly climb up my leg. As he brushes against the fabric of my panties; my breath hitches and a small moan escapes me.

Sliding his fingers under the damp fabric of my panties, he circles my clit once, before pushing one thick finger inside my wet pussy. The music disguises the noise of my pleasure, gasps and moans lost in the pulse of the song. He grinds against my arse as we dance with his finger buried deep inside of me, curling up, pressing on my sensitive flesh.

“Did you enjoy teasing me, Livvy?” his voice, smooth as whiskey, growls in my ear, his thumb rotating against my clit. “Shall I tease you now?”

I shudder, his words affecting me. “No, I need you.” A second finger slides inside me. “Ahhhh,” I moan. Desire pools in my stomach, and my hips unconsciously circle into his hard cock. He laughs, the sound drowned by the music, but I feel it vibrating through his chest. "Please," I beg, my voice wanton and desperate.

"That's it, sugar. Let me hear you. This body belongs to me," he growls as his fingers slide deeper, stretching me deliciously.

"Echo," I cry, so close to release, my body tenses, and I fight to tamp down the orgasm that's threatening to explode.

"Come for me. No one but me can hear you," he rasps, as his thumb presses down on my clit, and I detonate, biting my lip so I don't scream. I shake, my knees go weak, and I cling to Echo, his lips nuzzling and kissing my neck.

Eyes closed, I collapse against his chest with my legs wobbly and my skin still tingling. Echo bends, scooping me into his arms, and walks us straight out of the clubhouse and back to the truck. Wrapping my arms around his neck, I breathe deeply and inhale his uniquely Echo scent. He opens the door and places me on the seat before climbing in. Needy, I climb straight back into his lap, desperate to be close to him. Warm lips touch my temple, and we leave the madness of the clubhouse in a cloud of dust.

The journey home flashes by in a series of touches. His hands and lips caressing, stroking, and pinching. My mind is a jumbled mix of sensation with only one clear thought.

Echo.

He places me down on the floor once we reach our bedroom, lifts my arms into the air, and pulls my dress over my head, dropping it to the floor. My bra and panties are ripped from me, and I'm naked, waiting.

He quickly discards his clothes, lifting me into the air as his lips find mine and I wrap my arms around his neck. Carrying me to the bed, he lowers me till my back touches the cool sheets, his eyes swimming with desire, as I shudder in anticipation.

Quickly crawling down my body, he hovers over my pussy, so close I can feel his warm breath on my skin, then pauses. Our eyes meet, silently staring as tension buzzes and crackles in the air. "I want to memorize this moment, Livvy, the way you look. So fucking desperate, so fucking perfect."

Reluctantly releasing my gaze, he peppers reverent kisses on my thighs and mound, slowly working towards my clit and pussy. His breath warms my skin, and I shudder in anticipation. The seconds that pass feel like hours till his tongue strokes along my fevered flesh.

"Oh god," I cry.

His movements are lazy, licking my clit then lapping the full length of my pussy, only for his tongue to dip inside of me a moment later. His actions aren't intended to make me come, more to build up my pleasure, driving me insane with need. I want to touch him. My hands find his hair, desperate fingers entwining in the strands and pulling frantically.

"What do you need, sugar?" he asks.

"You. I need you. I want to touch you. Please."

He crawls up my body, and my frantic hands rake his back,

trailing a path over his spine and shoulders. I push one hand between us and grasp his hard, eager cock, sliding my hand up and down his length. His skin's warm and velvety smooth; drops of cum create a wetness my thumb collects as I move up and down.

Standing abruptly, he reaches for me and I take his outstretched palm, letting him pull me to my feet. He sits back down on the side of the bed his feet flat on the floor, his hand gripped around his cock, lazily sliding up and down his length. "Come here," he beckons.

Cautiously, I go to him. Strong fingers spread across my hips, guiding me to turn around and sit in his lap, my back to his front. I look up, and our reflection stares back at me from the mirror.

Echo's eyes lock with mine, and we watch ourselves in the glass. "Don't look away. I want you to watch while I touch you."

Curling his ankles underneath my calves, he slowly spreads his legs and I stare into the mirror as my pussy's revealed, my legs supported by his. "Watch," he orders.

Tattooed fingers cover my breasts, his colourful skin contrasting with my paler flesh, the erotic scene playing out in our reflection. Pinching my nipples, he rolls the sensitive peaks between his fingertips and unable to help myself, I let my eyes drop from the mirror, drawn to where his skin touches mine.

He stops.

Arching my back, I try to push into his touch, but his fingers cuff my neck and squeeze lightly. “Watch,” he says. The single word a demand that I’m helpless to deny.

I lift my chin and find his eyes in the mirror again. Watching him touch me heightens each sensation, and I flinch as he rolls and pinches my nipples. The pain morphs into a burning ache, and my skin tingles in pleasure as his hands trail over my ribs and dip between my legs.

He moves his knees, widening our legs until I’m completely on display. Fingers run up and down my pussy, spreading my dripping arousal and teasing my swollen flesh. My breath catches in my throat. His eyes are focussed on me as he watches me watch myself. Our eyes clash, lust and passion sparking till his eyes dip, and I follow his gaze in time to see him push two fingers deep inside of me.

Spreading my folds, he displays my pulsing clit; rubbing and squeezing the sensitive bud as I arch my back, purring and mewling, consumed with sensation. “That’s it, Livvy, watch me make you come. I wanna hear it, sugar. I wanna hear you scream for me.”

He buries a third finger into my tightness and my muscles clench onto him, keeping him inside of me as he pinches and rubs at my clit. My entire body tenses, as sensation explodes beneath my skin and I arch off his lap, screaming his name as I climax.

Echo’s hands rest lazily on my legs, his damp fingers absentmindedly drawing patterns on my skin. I slowly open my eyes; our gazes meet in the mirror and the heat between us surges.

"You're mine; nothing else could ever be enough," Echo whispers.

Wrapping an arm around my stomach, he lifts me, guiding his hard cock into my soaking core. We watch in the mirror as his cock disappears inside of me, the erotic reflection heightening the sensation. Echo takes control, sliding my body up and down his length. My inner muscles tighten and grip him, pulling us both over the edge as we come together, joined as one.

SIXTY

Echo

I never wanted a woman until her.

I never needed a woman until her.

She's fucking perfect.

She's mine.

Our eyes meet; I'm still buried deep inside her, connected.

Words I've never said to a woman before, words that need to be said, flash through my mind.

I've never wanted to say them till now.

I've never needed to say them till now.

"Olivia." Turning her to face me, I wait until she's focused. "I love you."

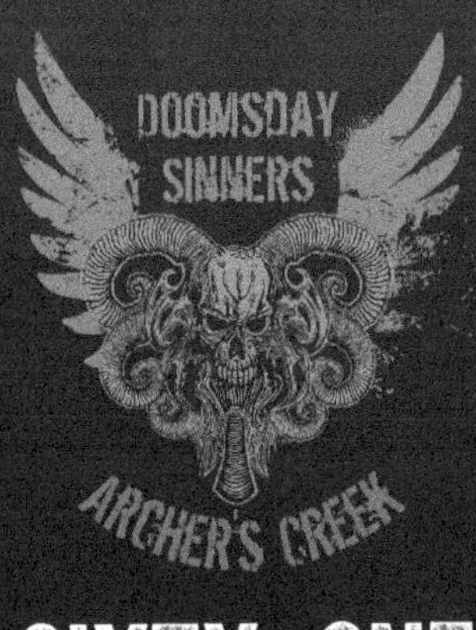

SIXTY-ONE

Olivia

My heart pounds, and my ears buzz, white noise consuming me.

I hear his voice, his words, and everything stops.

"I love you."

Do I deny the way I feel? This might not be forever, but right now, in this moment, it's perfect. And really, how many truly perfect moments do we get?

This could all blow up in my face tomorrow, but I don't have to lie to myself now. If I only get to keep this feeling for a fleeting moment, then it'll be worth all the heartache I have to suffer for it.

So I fall and let fate catch me; after all, that fickle bitch obviously has plans for us.

"I love you, too."

***

We fall asleep entwined together, and hours later, light floods through the windows, warming the room. My eyes drift open and reality overtakes my surreal dreamland. I'm unsure of the time, but its feels early; the world silent except for the sound of the birds serenading the dawn. The reassuring thud of Echo's heart beats beneath my head, and his heavy arms are wrapped around me. Happiness and contentment wash over me. Smiling to myself, I burrow deeper into Echo's chest, closing my eyes and allowing sleep to drag me under again.

Gentle kisses pepper my neck and cool air wafts over my skin, urging me to open my eyes. "I love you," Echo whispers.

I wasn't looking for him. I came here to escape the monotony of my real life. Instead, I got something I had no idea I even needed.

Echo.

I feel his fingers drawing patterns on my skin, willing me to wake up. I'm happy. I've been stumbling through life from one day to the next, just trying to make the best of things.

But then something or someone will come along and shatter the illusion, making you realise that simply making the best of things is not the best you could be doing with your life. Sometimes you'll be lucky enough to find someone who makes the highs higher and lows easier, and that's what I've found.

Opening my eyes I stare at the man who has me ruminating on all the great questions in life. In our bubble, in his home, in his bed is the happiest I've ever been, and I want to hold fast to this feeling for as long as I can. "I love you," I say.

His eyes light up at my words. "I love you too, sugar."

Echo claims my mouth, his kiss saying a thousand different things. His lips are possessive and loving, dominant and gentle, claiming me again and again with every touch. And I bask in it, matching his intensity kiss for kiss. An instant later, we go from loving to desperate.

My phone alarm beeps, shattering the intensity, and we both groan in frustration. "Echo, I've got to get ready for work," I say.

He rolls on top of me, resting his arms on either side of my head, and pouts. "Don't go today."

I laugh. "I have to go. Now let me up please."

His eyes glint playfully as he lowers his head and pulls one of my nipples into his mouth, nipping at it with his teeth. The bite of pain sends a jolt of pleasure through me, and I close my eyes, basking in the sensation. Inhaling sharply, I force them open and push against his chest. "Sweetie, I need to shower, I'm sore, I'm walking like John Wayne, and I smell like sex."

A growl comes from deep in his chest, and his lips claim mine possessively. "I want you to smell like me, that way everyone'll know your mine," he says.

Turning away from his dangerous mouth I giggle. "Yeah, or I'll just make everyone horny and thinking about sex."

Dramatically, he pushes off me and flops onto his back, covering his face with his hand. "Fuck, sugar, now I don't want you anywhere near any of them drunken idiots." Still giggling, I squeal as he hauls me off the bed, carrying me into the bathroom and placing me onto the counter while he turns to run the shower.

Completely naked, his muscles ripple and contract as he reaches for the dials and starts the water. His toned shoulders begin a path down his spine to his toned arse. Tight, firm, and round, he's so perfect I refuse to look away.

"Like what you see?" he asks.

Caught, I look up and nod. "I do, your arse is perfect."

His chuckle is deep and so incredibly sexy that I shudder. Shaking his head, he reaches for me, pulling me off the counter and slapping my arse before guiding me into the shower. He follows me in, watching as I rub shampoo into my hair and clean my skin. Once the water has washed the last of the suds from my hair he closes the distance between us, sliding his hands around my waist and pulling me close.

"Now you're nice and clean all I want to do is dirty you up a bit," he growls into my ear.

Turning my head, I kiss him, sliding my hand down his back to his perfect arse and feeling him smile against my lips.

"I want you so bad," he says between kisses.

"So take me."

"You're sore," he rasps, reaching for my hand and pulling it down to wrap around his cock.

Gripping him tightly I pump his dick, feeling it swell as he claims my lip in a punishing kiss. "Fuck," he hisses as I work him, stroking up and down. My pussy starts to pulse, I'm sore but I don't care.

"I need you," I whisper against his neck, licking a path up to his ear.

"No," Echo groans.

"Yes," I hiss. Releasing his cock I turn around, bend over and spread my legs wide, pressing my hands against the cold tile for balance.

"I don't want to hurt you," he snarls as he rubs his dick against my pussy lips.

"I love you Echo," I coo, smiling widely as my words push him over the edge and he fills me with his dick. Pulling back, he plunges forward, hitting the bundle of nerves deep inside of me as he fucks me hard and fast, his movements frantic as he races us both towards completion.

"God, I'm so close. Oh god, I'm going to come." I shiver, the intensity of my impending orgasm pulsing through me.

"Together, Livvy, let me hear you," he snarls, roughly ploughing into my pussy; two, three thrusts, and we come together, shuddering and moaning in unison.

Wincing a little I dress quickly, taking his hand as he leads me out of the bedroom and into the kitchen. Lifting me onto the granite counter, he chuckles when I wince again. "If you're sore it's your own fault, I told you no, you're the one who fucking insisted," he mock scolds, heading to the fridge and pulling out two bottles of water before handing one to me.

My eyes fall to the brand new oven, still covered in the plastic wrap. "Are you ever planning on using this cooker?" I ask, jumping down from the counter and running my hand across the oven, my mouth watering at the thought of the breakfast we could cook.

Echo smiles. "Feel free. I don't have a fucking clue how you even turn the damn thing on. The saleswoman told me it was the best available, so I bought it. But I eat at the club, so I've never had any use for it."

Laughing excitedly, I rip at the plastic, freeing the oven and searching for the switch to heat it up. "Do you have any food?" I ask.

Sheepishly, he shakes his head. "Fuck, sugar, I don't keep anything here. But we can go get some groceries and anything else we need later."

Nodding disappointedly, I grab my bag and follow him out of the house. I head towards Echo's bike but his loud whistle stops me. "Can you drive?" he asks.

Surprised, I raise my eyebrows. "Erm, yeah, of course I can drive."

Echo smiles indulgently and lifts his hand, a set of car keys dangle from his finger. "You wanna take the truck?"

My eyes widen in shock, and I stutter, “Wha-what? Me drive?” He nods. Squealing, I run to him and grab the keys from his outstretched finger, holding them to my chest. “Seriously, I get to drive the truck?”

He nods, a huge smile stretched across his face and I launch myself at him, jumping into his arms and hugging him tightly. “Oh my god, thank you. This is so cool. I love this truck,” I shout excitedly.

Leading me over to the garage, he opens the truck door and lifts me in. “I’ll follow you. I’ve got to work this afternoon,” he says.

Window down, wind blowing through my hair, and music blaring, I drive the short distance to Strikers. The truck’s amazing, and my face is covered in a huge grin as I pull up outside the bar. Echo stops his bike next to the truck and opens the door for me. I jump at him, and he catches me, grinning as I wrap my legs around his waist and kiss him playfully. “You like the truck?” he asks.

Smiling broadly I cradle his cheeks in my hands. “I love the truck, and I love you.”

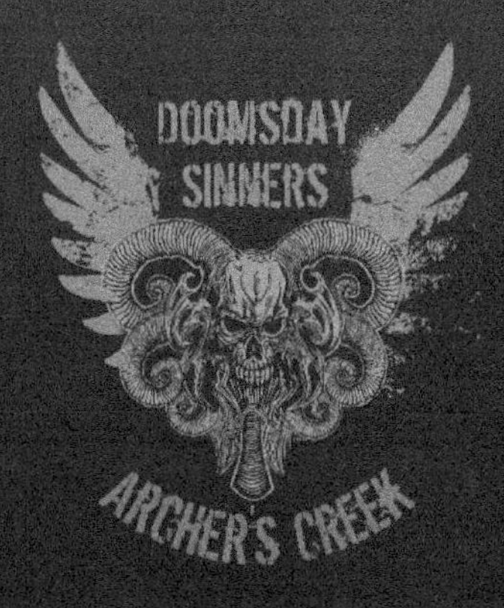

SIXTY-TWO

Echo

She loves me.

Fuck if I know why, but it changes everything.

Hearing those words coming out of her mouth has me growling and more fucking possessive than I've ever felt.

She loves me, and she's mine. I'm a fucking caveman through and through; everything in me screams to keep her safe and protected.

I'll never let anything hurt her.

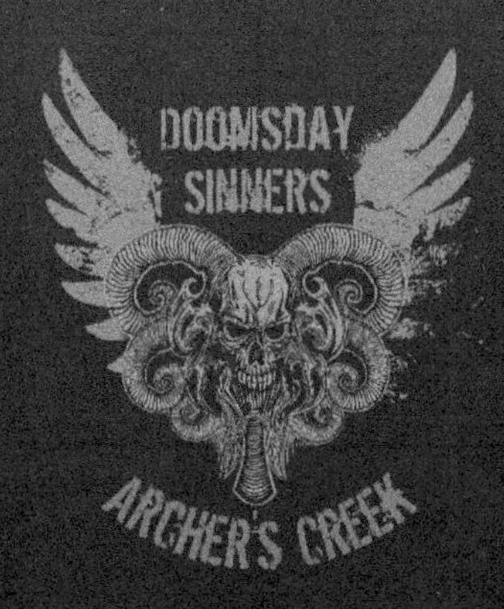

SIXTY-THREE

Acting

Her fate is sealed.

Our destiny entwined.

Perhaps I can save her, drain the devil from her blood.

Or maybe I'm the executioner sent to free her from her sinful existence.

I've watched.

Waited.

Decided.

Planned.

And now it's time to act.

SIXTY-FOUR

Olivia

Echo sits at his booth in the back of the bar and glares at every guy I serve. Striding across the room he rounds the bar, scooping me into his arms and kissing me. When he pulls back, we're both breathless and panting loudly. "What was that for?" I ask.

Fire burns in his eyes. "To remind them, and you, that you're mine," he growls.

Laughing, I shake my head and push at his chest. "Oh my god, you really are a caveman. I don't need reminding, and neither do they. Literally everyone in this town knows I'm yours."

His lips reach mine in a sweet, consuming touch. "Maybe I just like kissing you?" he teases.

Wrapping my arms around his neck I purr, "Well, I suppose I can work with that."

He sits me on the wooden bar, while his fingers play with my curls absentmindedly. "What time do you finish today, sugar?"

Grabbing my phone from my pocket I check my schedule. "I'm on till five."

He nods, his lips nuzzling into my neck. "I've gotta go take care of some stuff. Daisy's on his way, but I'm not sure if I'll be back before you finish. Will you be okay to drive the truck home?"

I roll my eyes at him. "I have no idea why this bar needs a biker security guard. I've never even seen a drunken scuffle here."

Scowling he grasps my chin and squeezes. "Livvy," he warns.

I sigh loudly. "Fine, whatever. I'll be fine getting home. I'll stop and grab some food so I can break in that oven of yours as well. Is there anything you don't like?"

His smile is huge. "I'll love anything you cook me. The house key on the ring is yours anyway, so call me if you need me."

"I will," I reply.

Lifting me from the bar he pulls me into a swoon-worthy kiss and my heart is racing by the time he sets me back down. Our eyes lock, his sincere and serious. "Love you, sugar. Be careful."

"Love you too." I whisper, as our lips touch once more, and he leaves just as Daisy walks through the door.

The rest of my shift finishes quickly. "Bye, guys," I shout, as I grab my bag and wave to Abe and Daisy who nod their heads in acknowledgment. Darting out the door towards Echo's truck, I pause to admire how pretty, big, red and shiny it is before I jump in and drive the short hop to the grocery store.

Running in, I wander around the shop grabbing some basics as well as some steak for dinner. After paying for my stuff, I head back outside and load my bags into the box in the back of the truck. My skin prickles, a shudder running down my spine, and pausing, I turn around and scan the street. Several empty cars are parked in the lot, their drivers busy shopping, but the feeling of being watched doesn't disappear.

Cautiously, I push the rest of my bags into the truck, checking over my shoulder every few seconds. I scan the street again, then shake my head and laugh at my overactive imagination. Climbing into the truck, I turn the music up loud and head back to Echo's.

After pulling into the driveway, I kill the engine and the music silences, but I carry on singing loudly, jumping from the truck and dancing to the front door. Unlocking it, I throw the door open wide and wander back to the truck, flip down the tailgate, and start pulling my groceries from the storage box.

Feeling eyes on me, the pit of my stomach clenches and I spin around, looking up and down the street. Cars are parked outside houses, and a few children play at the far end, their squeals muted by the distance. Paranoid, I grab some of the bags and rush inside. The house is comforting, quiet but welcoming. Pulling in a steadying breath I talk to myself in the silence. "God, Liv, get a grip."

I place the bags in the kitchen, tamp down my nervous fear, and walk back outside. Leaning over the side of the tailgate I grab the last of my shopping and grunting from exertion, I mutter to myself, "God, how much did I buy? These bags weigh a ton."

As I turn to head back inside pain explodes through my shoulder; I drop my bags as strong arms wrap around my chest and cover my mouth.

A thousand thoughts flash through my mind.

What's happening to me?

Am I going to die?

Echo.

Mum and Dad.

Please don't hurt me.

Please don't rape me.

Frozen in fear, I'm dragged backwards with my heels scraping along the ground.

Time seems to stop.

"Fight." I hear Echo's voice in my head, and I'm jolted back to reality.

Fight.

I bite down on the hand across my mouth, my teeth sinking into the skin with as much force as I can. My attacker grunts in pain and the hand falls from my face.

"Help. Help! *Help!* Someone help me please!" I scream. I thrash, my fingernails clawing at skin, feet kicking, arms flailing. I fight for my life.

Dropped to the ground, I scramble to my feet. Disoriented, I spin, searching for the way to safety.

"Wyatt?" I gasp, as my gaze falls on my attacker.

Wyatt's eyes sparkle with insanity, a maniacal grin spreading across his face. Fear prickles my skin, my heart thuds in my chest and I step back, pull in a deep breath, and prepare to run. Filled with adrenaline, I force all of my energy into my feet and surge forward, darting past Wyatt and towards the street.

Pumping my arms, I sprint. His steps are loud behind me, and I dare a look over my shoulder. He's so close.

Screaming, I forge forward, running as fast as I can as fingertips scrape at my back. I'm thrown forward; my arms instinctively going out in front of me as his weight hits my back, knocking the air from my lungs.

I dig my fingernails into the dirt and try to claw myself from beneath him. But he roughly flips me to my back before climbing on top of me. "Ahhhhhh, no! Get off me! *Get off!*" I scream in his face.

His fist slams into my cheek, and the force throws my head to the side. "Shut up," Wyatt snarls. Heat surges through my face, my vision blurring as the surrounding skin starts to swell. He leans forward, his putrid breath blowing into my face. "I am the executioner. Time to face your fate."

Pain explodes through my face, and everything goes black.

***

Pain.

Darkness.

Fear.

Hushed voices usher me towards consciousness. Pain pulses through my head, dizziness and nausea hitting as I struggle to open my eyes. Blinding light invades my pupils and I try to lift my arm to shield myself from the glare, but it won't move.

I can't move.

I pull at my other wrist. Straps hold me down. My legs are spread, but something tight is wrapped around my ankles.

I'm tied down.

I force my eyes open. My stomach churns, and throwing my head to the side, I vomit, fear and bile emptying onto the floor.

Wyatt's face appears above me, disgust lining his mouth.

"What on earth's that smell?" a female voice asks, and I twist my neck to see who it belongs to.

Wyatt turns to speak to the woman, and longing and fear flash across his face. "She threw up."

"It's the devil in her, trying to break free. We need to release it so we can kill it. She's beyond saving now," the woman says.

Instantly, I recognise her voice and try to speak, my voice scratchy and dry. "Miss Mimi?" I gasp.

Her prim, poised face comes into view, only the violent anger in her eyes making her seem different from the southern belle I'd met the first day I went to her guest house. "Foul, evil whore. Be gone, devil. How dare you speak to me. I won't be polluted by your nefarious ways," she screams.

Hatred twists across her face, the pearls at her throat jumping when her fist rises and smashes into my cheek. The impact of her punch forces my face to the side, and I close my eyes for a second, defeated. I force my lids to open and glance at my surroundings. I'm in a copse of trees; forest surrounds us, and only the blue sky above taunts me with the thought of freedom. I pull at my bindings, but both my wrists and ankles are tied down. I'm completely immobile.

"Temptress," Wyatt's voice calls me, and I turn to him. Mania glitters across his face, a wide grin spread across his mouth. "Temptress, it's time."

Fear fills my chest, and my breath comes in short, frightened bursts. "Time for what?" I ask.

He lifts a silver knife, the shiny blade glinting in the dappled light and reverently strokes the tip of the blade with his fingers before running the flat length of it across his cheek. "It's time to save you. The Sinners have infected you, tainted your very soul. Made you into a whore who spreads her legs for that filthy biker."

Open-mouthed, I stare at him. I'm going to die.

"I can save you, Olivia. God spoke to me. He said you were meant to be mine. That this was a test for me. I have to save you, and you have to be pure enough to be saved," Wyatt says.

I shake and tremble in shock and fear and helplessness. Miss Mimi appears above me, her hand caressing Wyatt's shoulder. Staring at me, she speaks. "She's just like the others, darling. Filth and sin consumes her. She's not good enough for you, my sweet. You need someone pure, someone who hears God and understands his call."

She wraps her arms around Wyatt and turns him away from me, her old wrinkled hand cupping his cheek. "I understand you, sweetheart. I'm all you need," she coos, pulling him toward her and kissing him, her hand dropping to rub his erection through his trousers.

I gag, disgusted.

"No," he shouts, pushing her away; she falls back, landing on the floor next to me. "No. God said Olivia was mine. A gift for all my hard work and devotion. Praise for the souls I've set free, all those girls whose blood ran out before they were truly pure," he rants. Wyatt steps closer and runs the knife along my cheek, the sharp tip piercing my skin. Heat surges to the cut, blood pooling to the surface. "You're my reward, Olivia. He should never have touched you."

His fists rain down on me, punching my face, chest, arms,

and legs. I scream and try to curl my limbs up to protect myself, but the bindings hold me still and exposed to his punishment. Pain screams from my skin and Miss Mimi's loud laughter is the last thing I hear as I drift into unconsciousness.

SIXTY-FIVE

Echo

Today has been a fucking good day.

I woke up wrapped around my girl, had her screaming in the shower; watched her prance around the bar for a few hours and now I'm thinking about all the dirty things I plan to do to her when I get home.

When I got called out to go sort some club shit, the bouncers at Beavers had managed to catch one of the motherfuckers who've been causing trouble, and me and Sleaze taught him a couple of broken bones worth of lessons.

All in all, a fucking good day.

I'm cruising my bike back towards my house and my girl and I can't wait to get home. My cock's so fucking hard, I plan to bend her over the kitchen counter as soon as I walk through the door. Then maybe I'll eat her perfect little pussy on the stairs, and then I'm gonna claim that ass of hers.

My truck's parked in the driveway, so I ride past it and park my bike in the garage. Walking past the truck I see an apple on the ground, then another a few steps further along. Circling around the back of the truck I see the tailgate's still down and there's grocery bags on the ground, food spilling from them.

The hairs on the back of my neck prickle. Something's not right.

I rush to the house and find the front door wide open. "Livvy!" I shout. As I move from room to room, my shouts become more frantic. "Olivia. Livvy, you here, sugar?" The house is empty, so I pull my phone from my pocket and call her cell. The stupid country song she's set as a ringtone screams to life and I follow the noise, finding her phone next to her purse, covered in dirt on the ground beneath the truck.

Panicking, I call Sleaze.

He answers after the first ring. "Brother."

"Is Livvy with Brandi?" I ask.

His response is immediate. "No, Brandi's with me. She's been home all day. Why, what's up?"

Growling, I hold the phone away from my ear and pull in a breath. "I don't know. Livvy said she was going to get groceries then come straight home. The truck's here, the groceries are dumped all over the driveway. The door to the house's wide open, but Livvy's not here."

I hear him mutter to Brandi in the background. "On my way, brother," he says and ends the call.

The sight of the bags scattered on the ground pushes me over the edge, and throwing my head back, I roar. Frustration, anger, and fear filling me.

Gus, the old guy across the street is sitting in his rocking chair on his porch, quietly watching the world go by. I stomp across the street and shout up to him, "Hey, you seen Livvy?"

He stands and makes his way to the railing. "Why hello, Echo. No, I haven't seen her since you two went into the woods earlier. Why? Did she say she was coming to call on me?"

Fear takes hold of me, my heart slowing so quickly the breath in my chest falters. "You saw her going into the woods with me?"

"Well, erm, I wasn't prying or nothing. Just after all that screaming an' shouting the kids were doin' earlier, I came out to see what all the fuss was about."

"Gus!" I shout, and the old guy jumps, shocked. "Gus, are you sure it was Livvy?"

Gus reaches up and scratches his head. "Well, my eyesight's not what it used to be, mind you. But it sure looked like a man and a woman walking from your driveway and disappearing into the trees."

Dread fills my stomach; I haven't felt fear like this since my first day on deployment in Iraq. "And you heard screaming?"

He nods slowly, his eyes sharpening, like the pieces are

beginning to fall into place in his mind. “You don’t think it was kids doing all that screaming?” he says morosely.

I shake my head, my eyes narrowing. “My house is wide open, bags full of groceries scattered all over my driveway. You heard screaming and then saw people disappearing into the woods behind my house.”

Gus straightens, the frail old gent gone and in his place an angry man. “You think someone took her?”

I nod and look him in the eyes, needing him to see the fear there. “I think so, yes. I don’t know why anyone would target her, but I think they did. Can you show me where they went into the woods? There’s a few paths that run from my house. I need to know where to start searching.”

Slowly backing away, he opens to door to the house. “Yes, I can show you. I’ll be right out.”

I watch him disappear into his house, and grabbing my phone, I call Sleaze again. He answers on the first ring. “I think someone took her,” I say. “Gus, the old guy from across the street, heard screaming and then saw two people walk into the woods at the side of my house. It’s too much of a coincidence for it not to be related. I’m going to look for her.”

Sleaze growls. “Wait for me. I’ll be there in ten.”

I shake my head, and reply, “I can’t, man. I don’t know how long she’s been gone or how far into the woods she is. I need to get going.”

Sleaze’s voice is full of worry when he speaks. “Echo,

brother, don't go in there alone, who knows what you're gonna find."

"She's my fucking world. I love her. I need to find her. I'm *going* to find her," I say emphatically. I end the call as Gus rounds the corner of his house, two shotguns resting across his shoulders. "What the fuck you got there, old man?" I say, surprised.

Gus scowls and racks the slide on the shotgun, loading the weapon. "Less of the old man. I'm coming with you. If someone's got Miss Olivia, I'm gonna help you find her. I was in the army for fifteen years. I might be old, but I still know how to shoot a gun."

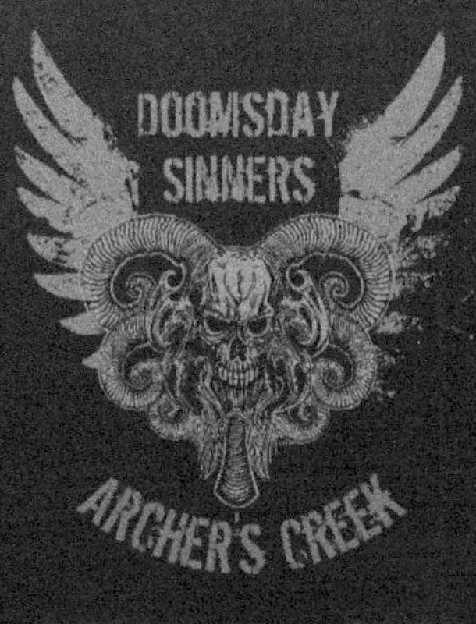

SIXTY-SIX

Olivia

Cold air coats my skin, and everything hurts. Pain thuds through my head and my face is stiff. I force my eyes open, but my vision's blurred, and I blink to try to clear it.

"Welcome back, temptress," Wyatt says.

Unwelcome memories surge to the surface. Wyatt and Miss Mimi, pain, fists, knife. I clench my fingers and pull in vain at whatever holds my arms.

Miss Mimi's face appears above me. "It's time, whore. God punishes those who sin. It's your time to be tested," she snarls.

She raises the knife in the air and runs the flat blade down my neck and across my chest. Slicing into the fabric of my dress, she cuts straight down the middle to the hem, and the material falls to the sides. "Whore, look at yourself. You disgust me," she spits, anger and fury pouring from her in waves.

Terrified, I pull at my bindings, the straps ripping into the skin of my wrists and ankles. Wyatt stands over me, his eyes scanning my body. "You were made to tempt, Olivia; I can see the sin under your skin." He draws the tip of the knife across my breast; blood droplets pool on my skin. "I want to see you, my temptress. My reward."

He slices my bra and panties with the knife, then removes the fabric and leaves me naked and exposed, his eyes burning with arousal. My stomach churns and vomit surges up my throat and out.

Burning heat scorches across my thigh, and I scream as blood drips down my leg. The knife slices over my other thigh, and I feel my blood running across my skin. My throat feels raw from screaming, the sound echoing in the silence of the woods.

"That's it, whore, the sin runs free with your blood!" Miss Mimi screams as she takes the knife, scoring my arms and stomach.

Tears fall down my face. "Stop, please stop," I beg.

Wyatt ignores me, a blissful longing etched across his face while his hands are on his cock, stroking himself through his trousers. He pulls his shirt over his head and stares at me in a trance-like state; licking his lips as he watches the blood run from my wounds. Finally naked, his swollen cock protrudes from between his legs. Smaller hands wrap around his waist, and Mimi starts to stroke his aroused flesh.

Disgusted, I close my eyes, unable to watch whatever happens next.

"No!"

Wyatt's shout shocks me, and my eyes fly open. Miss Mimi's on the ground, her eyes shut, unmoving.

"Temptress, you're my reward. My penance for doing God's work. I can see the sins and impurities running from your blood, but I can't wait. The devil's inside you. I know I shouldn't touch you, but I need to."

Working his hard cock with his hand, he walks towards me and kneels between my legs, his fingers sliding up my blood-soaked thigh towards my sex. Repulsed, I scream, my throat raw as I thrash against my bindings. Pain roars through my wrists, and I kick and pull my arms with every ounce of energy I have.

The strap around my ankle loosens, and pulling my leg free, I kick at Wyatt. Hope builds in my chest when I hear the crack of impact as my foot crashes against his head. Pain burns through my ankle, but buoyed, I ignore it and pull at the straps on my other limbs, determined to free myself.

"You little bitch," Wyatt snarls as his eyes narrow and anger glows red across his face. Blood trickles from his temple, his fists clench, and cocking back his arm, he punches me in the face.

Everything goes black.

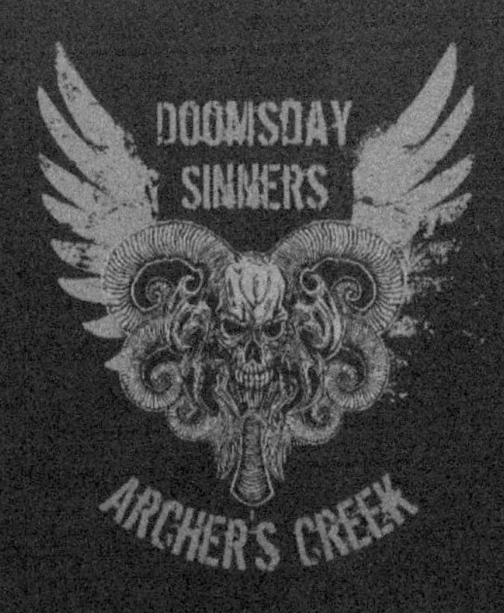

SIXTY-SEVEN

Echo

Gus leads me to a path at the edge of the woods and hands me one of the shotguns as we make our way into the trees. Silently, we creep along the path, hoping to hear something to point us toward Livvy.

Dense forest surrounds us. Fear trickles along my spine, every footstep bringing me closer to finding her. I move quickly, refusing to think about what could be happening to her right now; forging forward, Gus following quietly behind me.

A noise makes me pause; Gus's hand rests on my shoulder, assuring me he heard it too. Laughter, followed by a piercing scream.

I run.

Gus falls behind, unable to keep pace. The noise stops, then screams burst through the silence again as we dart towards the sound.

The path opens into a clearing in the woods. White stones form a circle with a low wooden table positioned in the middle. Livvy's tied down, straps around her wrists and ankles.

She's naked and beaten, blood covering her perfect skin as she screams, thrashing against her bindings. I see the naked man between her legs, and an angry red mist descends. I surge forward, breaking out of the trees just as Livvy's foot gets free and she kicks him in the head.

Startled, he rights himself and punches her in the face.

Like an animal, I roar with anger. I drop the shotgun and fly forward, tackling Livvy's attacker to the ground.

His face comes into view. "Anderson?" I say, shocked. Wyatt takes advantage of my surprise and punches me in the face, his fist grazing my jaw. I launch myself at Wyatt and wrestle him onto his back, throwing my fist forward and hitting him again and again. My fists keep swinging, anger and fear fueling me as his hands claw at the ground, his face a bloody mess, one eye swollen shut.

He grabs something from the dirt, swinging his arm up, and fire burns through my ribs. I fall to the side, pressing my hands to the blood oozing from a wound on my skin. Wyatt's face changes to a smug grin, and wrapping his hand around the hilt, he raises the knife above his head, laughs and lunges at me again.

An ear-shattering boom pierces the air.

Wyatt's eyes widen, and his gaze drops to his chest as blood splutters from the hole in his torso. Life slips from his face, and he slumps, falling backwards into the dirt.

I turn and find Gus standing behind us, his shotgun still pointed at Wyatt, smoke pluming from the barrel. Our eyes lock. He gives me a single nod, and I nod back. It's the most I can do at the moment to acknowledge that he just saved both mine and Livvy's lives.

Livvy.

Scrambling to my feet, I run to her and fall to my knees by her side. I throw my phone to Gus and shout, "Call 911! Tell them to get police and an ambulance to meet us at the house."

My hands shake as I frantically try to free her from the straps holding her to the table. I falter, unsure where to touch her bruised and bloody skin. The open wounds on her arms, stomach, and legs are running with fresh red blood. Bruises are already starting to cover her entire body, and her beautiful face is barely recognizable, one eye swollen completely shut.

I touch her neck; her pulse is weak, but there. Relief pours from me, and lifting her carefully into my arms, I stand and cradle my brave woman against my chest.

When I turn around, Gus's gun is still pointed at Wyatt's dead body. His eyes don't move when he speaks to me. "She—she alive?"

I nod. "Yes."

Gus's eyes close briefly. He turns away from Wyatt's corpse, slips off his jacket and covers Livvy's naked skin. Tormented tears pool in his eyes, and he lifts his hand to reach for her, but stills inches above her damaged body. "Take her. I'll stay here with him till the police get here," he says, his gruff voice cracking with emotion.

Nodding I start to walk away before pausing to look back at Gus. "Thank you," I say. He nods, and I quickly turn, rushing along the path towards the sound of sirens.

I emerge from the trees as the shrill call of sirens shatters the peace of my sleepy neighborhood. Doors open and people peer out, eager to see what's going on, but their eyes never look to where I'm hidden at the end of the row of houses.

The sirens get louder, and flashing lights herald the ambulance's arrival. It screeches to a stop at the bottom of my driveway. Two paramedics jump out and rush towards us.

Livvy's cradled to my chest, covered by Gus's jacket but still exposed. Everything in my gut tells me to shelter her, not to release her in case she disappears. That this is all just a dream and she's still with Anderson, being tortured and abused.

I tremble, fear and anger so closely mixed I'm unsure what I'm feeling.

"Sir, we need to look at the girl," a young paramedic says, his hands held out towards Livvy. Instinct has me pulling her further into my chest. "Sir, what's her name? Can you tell me what happened?" the paramedic asks.

"Her name's Olivia. She was kidnapped. He hurt her." The paramedic nods and holds his palms upwards and towards me in a gesture of surrender. I stare down at Livvy, her bloods covering my arms, my shirt soaked and red. "Help her. Please help her," I beg.

A female paramedic pulls a gurney from the back of the ambulance before rushing towards us. "Sir, you need to lay her on the bed so we can look at her," she says. I nod, but my hands won't release her. "Sir, we can help her. But only if you let her go."

Reluctantly, I lay her on the stretcher, her pale body marred by bruises. The paramedics swarm around her, prodding and poking at my girl. "There's a pulse. It's weak, but I can feel it. We need to stop this bleeding fast," the man says as the female rushes to the ambulance and comes back with a bag full of supplies.

My knees buckle. I'd felt her pulse, but hearing them confirm it, my legs give way and I fall to the ground.

More sirens blare, and the sheriff pulls alongside the ambulance. "Echo, what's going on?" the sheriff asks.

Not taking my eyes from Livvy, I speak, my voice robotic. "Wyatt Anderson attacked my girl. He kidnapped her and took her into the woods. Tied her down and beat her, cut her with a knife over and over. He was about to rape her." The words die in my mouth, and reality crashes down on me.

I reach for Livvy's hand and grip her cool flesh between my

fingers to reassure myself that she's really here.

"Where's Anderson now, son?" The sheriff asks.

I point in the direction of the woods. "Dead. Gus killed him. He's in the woods guarding the body," I say.

The sheriff signals to his deputies, sending them off into the woods. "Echo, you know I'm gonna need you to come in. Give a statement," he says gently. I nod, and he places his hand on my shoulder, squeezing lightly.

"Sir, are you family?" the paramedics ask.

I reluctantly drag my eyes from Livvy's still body and face the ambulance crew. "She's mine," I say.

They look at each other in confusion. "Are you family?" the female paramedic asks again.

My gaze moves back to Livvy as I answer. "Yes."

The woman shrugs and turns to grab the end of the gurney, knocking off the brake. "You can come in the ambulance, or follow behind. But we need to take her now; she needs to be at the emergency room."

"I'm not leaving her," I growl.

They nod and start to wheel her towards the ambulance. I hear the roar of Sleaze's bike as soon as he turns into the street. "Echo," he shouts, running across the yard, reaching us in seconds. His eyes scan Livvy, and he pales. "Fuck, what the hell happened? Is she okay?"

"She's alive."

"We need to go. Now," the paramedic shouts. They hold

the doors of the ambulance open, and I turn to leave, but Sleaze pulls me in for a tight hug.

"I'll follow you to the hospital," he assures me. Grateful, I climb into the ambulance, my eyes locking with Sleaze's as they close the doors.

SIXTY-EIGHT

Echo

At the emergency room, they pull her away from me. "Livvy. Livvy! Where the fuck are you taking her? I need to be with her," I shout.

The paramedic reaches for me. "Sir, she needs to be treated. You can't go back there, I'm sorry. Someone will be out soon to let you know what's happening."

I'm not sure how long I wait. It feels like hours, but it could be minutes as I sit and stare at the doors, waiting for my beautiful girl to walk through them, back to me. Instead, doctors and nurses come and go, always rushing, always solemn.

Sleaze and Brandi arrive. Brandi runs at me, sobbing and I wrap her in my arms, my body trembling.

"Oh god, Echo. I can't believe this happened. How is she?" she cries.

Defeated, I drop my arms from her shoulders and scrub my hands across my eyes. "I don't know. They took her, and no one will tell me what the hell's happening. Just that they're treating her and they'll come and speak to me once there's an update."

Sleaze pulls Brandi into his chest; our eyes lock, and he grips my shoulder in a silent show of support.

"Echo, what the hell happened to your side? You're covered in blood," Brandi asks, her voice filled with concern.

I glance down at my T-shirt, it's wet with blood, the stain so dark it's almost looks black. "I'm not sure whose blood it is. Anderson slashed me right before Gus killed him. It's only a scratch, I'm fine."

Brandi shakes her head and grabs a nurse, pointing out the wound. "Sir, I need to take a look at that," the nurse says.

Shaking my head I refuse. "I'm not going anywhere till I know what's going on with my girl. They took her through those doors, and no one will tell me what's happening."

Brandi and the nurse look at each other briefly before turning their attention back to me. "Sir, if you let me have a look at that wound, as soon as I've finished, I'll go and get an update on your girlfriend. Okay?" the nurse asks.

Reluctantly, I agree. "I'm not moving, so if you want to look, you're gonna have to do it right here." Pulling off my shirt, I sit on one of the waiting room chairs and carry on staring at the doors, waiting for Livvy.

True to her word, the nurse stitches me up and then disappears behind the doors. Ten minutes later, she comes back. "Your girlfriend is stable. They've stopped the bleeding from the knife wounds, but she's pretty beaten up, so they're having to run some tests to check for internal bleeding. She's still unconscious but often the human body stays asleep to give itself time to heal," she tells us.

She leaves, and my head falls forward into my hands. Brandi's arms wrap around me, and we both cry quietly, comforting each other.

Time passes. The receptionist forces forms into my hands and asks me to fill them out for Livvy but I can't answer most of the questions. I don't know her address in England, or what blood type she is. I don't know her medical history or if she's allergic to anything.

There's so much we still have to learn about each other. But I know the important things: she's mine and I'm hers.

Time passes, the minutes ticking by as Brandi and Sleaze sit beside me, and all of us watch the doors for more news.

"Echo," a voice calls. I turn and see a crowd of my brothers filtering into the waiting room. Park, Smoke, Daisy, Puck, and Blade stand stoically, their hands buried in their pockets. Nodding, I acknowledge their arrival but turn back to my vigil, waiting for the doors to open.

Sleaze gets up and speaks to our Sinners brothers. I hear their hushed voices, but I tune it out. They're not important. All that's important is my girl, behind those doors.

The police arrive, and since I refuse to leave my post, they take my statement in the waiting room. I tell them what happened, recounting how I found her.

Bruises.

Blood.

Knife.

Dead.

Visions of Livvy tied to that table while that sick fuck tortured her fill my mind, and rushing to the trashcan, I vomit, acid burning the back of my throat.

SIXTY-NINE

Olivia

Beep.

Beep.

Beep.

Noise flickers at the back of my brain, tempting me to consciousness.

Beep.

Beep.

Beep.

My fingers lie against a scratchy sheet. I curl my hand, and my limbs cooperate and twitch to life.

Beep.

Beep.

Beep.

Light bleeds through my closed eyelids, and I try to open my eyes.

Beep.

Beep.

Beep.

I pry my eyelids apart. The brightness hits me, and my head clenches in pain.

Something beeps softly in the unfamiliar, clinical room. Breathing hurts, moving hurts, simply shifting my eyes hurts. In a barrage of images, I remember everything. Wyatt, pain, Miss Mimi, disgust. Fear, agony, blood, darkness.

I'm in a hospital. I'm not sure how I got here, but hospitals are safe, so I'm safe.

Wyatt. I shudder in revulsion. Where is he? How did I get here?

Echo.

I need him.

A nurse walks in, smiling when she sees me looking at her. "Welcome back, darlin'. My name's Darlene, and I'll be your nurse. Just give me two secs and I'll page the doctor and let her know you're awake."

"Echo." My voice is raspy, but she hears me.

"What's that, sweetie?" she asks.

I try to clear my throat, but it comes out as a raspy cough. "Where's Echo?"

She smiles brightly. "Is that the hunk of a man that's out in the waiting room? The tall, tattooed drink of water?" she asks.

A single chuckle escapes me before I dissolve into a gravelly cough. "I need him. Please," I beg.

She nods, understanding flashing in her eyes. "Of course, hon. I'll page the doctor then go grab your man for you." I smile gratefully and she leaves the room.

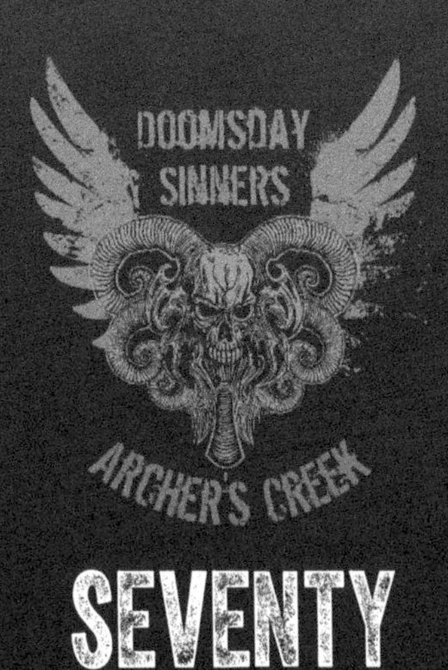

SEVENTY

Echo

I've been sitting out here for hours. It's somewhere in the middle of the night, but I've lost track of the time. It means nothing while Livvy's stuck behind those doors.

I owe Gus everything. He saved our lives, and I'm gonna spend the rest of my days trying to pay back that debt.

This was my fault.

She got attacked 'cause of me, 'cause I let her run from me that first night. The next morning, she ran straight into him. I knew Wyatt Anderson was a stupid little bastard, but I had no idea he was a fucking psycho.

The sheriff doesn't think this is the first time he's done this. Apparently, they found other blood at the scene, older blood.

He's dead.

I'm so fucking angry that I wasn't the one to take that bastard down. When Livvy needed me, I was on the ground.

I didn't protect her.

I let him take her. I let him hurt her.

This is all my fault.

I haven't taken my eyes off the door. The nurse told me that she's stable, but that's it. I want to rage and shout. I want my girl. But security have already warned me they'll kick me out if I try to force my way in again.

So I wait.

The doors open and a nurse walks through. She scans the room till she sees me, and her face breaks into a glorious smile.

"Are you Echo?" she asks. I stand and nod. "She's asking for you."

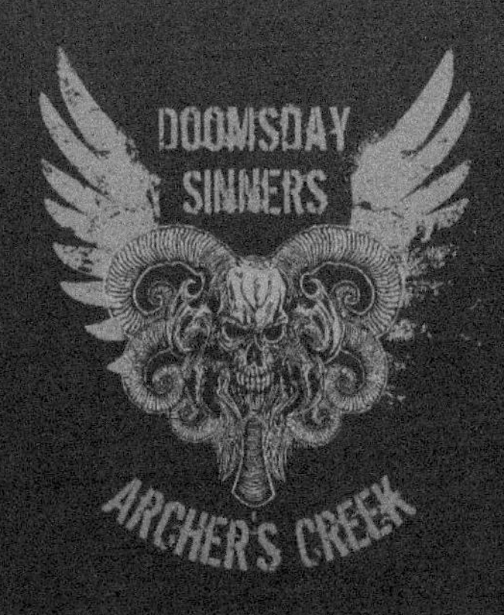

SEVENTY-ONE

Olivia

Echo barrels through the door and as our eyes lock, emotion rushes to the surface. Air stutters in my bruised lungs, and I start to sob. Tears blur my vision and I flinch when he touches me, but he gently wraps me in his arms.

"It's okay, sugar, you're safe now," he says, stroking my hair and peppering gentle kisses on my head. "I'm so sorry, Livvy. I'm so sorry."

Shaking uncontrollably, I can't stop crying. I hurt. My skin's tight, purple bruises mottling everywhere I can see. My right eye is swollen shut, but I see him as tremors rack his chest and silent tears track down his cheeks. I pull my head back from his chest and look at him properly. "Echo," I cry.

He reaches out, stopping an inch before he touches my face.

"Please," I beg. Pain is etched across his features, but he cups my chin and leans in until his lips touch mine. It's barely a kiss, but the sensation stings the broken skin, and I hiss with pain.

His beautiful face pales. "Fuck, I'm sorry." He pulls away, but I stop him, grabbing hold of his shirt. He stills, and I snuggle in close to his chest, waiting while he settles cautiously back against the bed. Nestling into his arms I sign with relief; his lips kissing my hair and forehead like he's reassuring himself that I'm really here.

"I love you." My voice sounds weak and small, but I need to say the words and for him to hear them.

His whole body relaxes, his arms tightening and holding me to him. "I love you so much, Livvy. I'm so fucking sorry."

The door opens and a doctor walks in, followed by Darlene the nurse. "Olivia, I'm Dr Ericson. It's nice to see you awake. How are you feeling?"

"I'm okay. I can't open one eye, and I hurt, but I'm okay," I say.

The doctor looks at Echo. "Sir, would you mind stepping out? I'd like to talk to Olivia in private."

Echo moves, and panicked, I grab his shirt and shout, "No, I want him to stay."

The doctor looks from me to him but eventually nods. "Okay, well, Olivia, you lost a lot of blood. We've stitched up your wounds, and hopefully, the scarring shouldn't be too bad, but we have a great plastic surgeon on staff that is going to come take a look in the morning. You've been badly beaten, so you're going to be in some pain, which we can help with. Your eye is very swollen, but in a day or two, that should reduce and you should be able to open it again. You're showing no signs of internal bleeding, and all of the tests we've run have confirmed that."

I nod and try to take in all of the information she's giving me, but the pain starts to overwhelm me. "Olivia, when we examined you, we found signs of sexual activity. We need to know if you were sexually assaulted. If you'd prefer to speak about this in private, that can be arranged," the doctor says, her voice calm and emotionless.

Feeling Echo holding his breath beneath me I shake my head. "I don't know. He hadn't touched me. Like that. I think he was going to, but I got free and kicked him in the head. He punched me, and I don't remember anything after that," I say, my voice cracking.

"No, he didn't rape her," Echo says firmly.

"Echo, you don't know that," I say quietly.

"I do," he says. "I saw you kick him. He knocked you unconscious just as I got there. He didn't go near you again after that." Relieved tears spill down my cheeks, and Echo kisses my head. "It's okay, sugar, it's okay. He's never going to hurt you again."

The doctor clears her throat, gaining our attention. "We're going to give you something for the pain. We weren't able to contact a next of kin, so would you like us to call anyone?"

I shake my head. "No, that's okay. Echo's here, and the rest of my family are back in the UK."

Her head flips between me and Echo. "Olivia, because of the nature of your injuries, I can't release you without someone to care for you," she says sternly.

Echo tenses. "Doc, I'm gonna fucking take care of her."

The doctor looks at Echo and then at me. "Olivia, is that what you want?"

I nod. "Yes. Echo will look after me."

The doctor tips her chin in agreement, and turns to speak to Darlene for a moment before leaving.

The door closes, and I carefully sit up and turn to look at Echo. "What happened, how did I get here?" I ask.

His face blanches and a darkness filters across his eyes. "What do you remember?" he asks cautiously.

When I close my eyes, Wyatt's face is there and I quickly open them again, my heart racing, fear pulsing through me. Echo holds me closer. "Get some rest, sugar. You're safe now. That's all that matters," he says, his hands running up and down my back lovingly.

I shudder, the images of my attack playing on repeat in my head. "Was he arrested?" I ask.

He shakes his head, reaching out to run a gentle finger over my battered cheek. "He's dead, sugar. Gus shot him."

Overwhelmed with relief, a sob escapes from my lips. "And

what—what about Mimi? Is she dead too?" I ask as tears stream down my face.

Echo stills beneath me, tensing. "Mimi? What's she got to do with this?"

Pulling myself out of his arms I carefully twist to fully face him. "Mimi was there, Echo. She's completely insane. They were working together."

A few moments later, Darlene the nurse re-enters the room and injects something into the drip that's attached to my hand. My pain recedes, and my eyes start to get heavy. I let my body succumb to the tiredness and fall asleep in Echo's arms.

Wyatt's there every time I close my eyes, and flashbacks haunt my dreams as I fight them in my sleep, thrashing and punching, fighting with everything I've got.

I bolt awake. The room's dark and I'm alone.

Echo.

He's sitting in a chair by the window, and my breathing begins to settle the moment I see him. Slowly rising, he crosses the room, pulling me into his arms and settling back against the mattress. His eyes are tortured, darkness shadowing his usual brightness. "I'm so sorry, Livvy."

"Why?" I ask, confused.

I feel his chest sigh when he exhales. "This is all my fault," he says, anger and pain so clear in his voice.

I try to sit up, but Echo's arms tighten carefully around me, holding me in place. "How is any of this your fault? I got attacked by two deranged people who thought they were executioners sent from God. None of this is your fault."

"No, Livvy. I should have protected you. You're mine. I promised I'd look after you, and I failed. I let you down and you got hurt. Fuck, you could have been killed. I don't deserve you. You should fucking hate me, Livvy. I'm so sorry."

I shake my head vehemently. "The only people to blame are Wyatt and Mimi. You didn't cause this, you and Gus saved me. Without you, God knows what would have happened. You have to stop blaming yourself."

Both Echo and I fall silent, the darkness of the room surrounding us. Wrapped in his safe arms, I relax into Echo's chest and sleep pulls me under again.

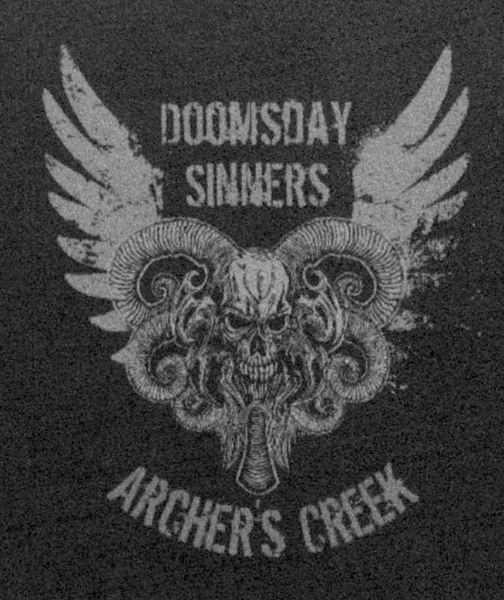

SEVENTY-TWO

Echo

I thought I'd fucking lost her today; feeling her chest moving up and down is the most fucking amazing thing in the world. I watch her sleep, curled in my arms as nightmares plague her. I fucking hate that I let her down, because no matter what she says I know It's my fault she's here, like this.

That crazy old bitch Mimi is still out there. She was there with Anderson, encouraging him to hurt my girl. I'm gonna make her suffer for every bruise on her body and every tear Livvy cries. I didn't protect her from them before, but I'll never let anything happen to her again.

***

Livvy's been in the hospital for two days. Her body's starting to heal, and her bruises are started to fade. Her snooty-ass doctor keeps telling me to go home, but that's not fucking happening. I haven't left her side; she wants me here, she needs me here, and I need to be near her too.

She's quiet and in pain but she doesn't want to take the painkillers because she says they make her feel drowsy; I keep insisting, and she does as she's told. Livvy's scared, she's putting on a brave face, but I see the fear in her eyes every time the door opens and watch her thrash and fight every night in her dreams.

The police came by to take her statement. She cried the whole way through as she told them what happened, how they beat her and sliced her skin with a knife, the same knife Anderson stabbed me with.

Wyatt's dead, and Mimi's still missing. How the fuck did a woman in her sixties just disappear without anyone seeing anything, I don't know, but I'm not leaving it up to the police to find her. Every fucking Sinner is out there searching for her. She won't be able to hide for long.

I'm finally taking my girl home today; I want to sleep in our bed with her in my arms all night. All her spark's gone; she's a shadow of herself, and I fucking hate it. She needs to feel safe and relaxed, and I'm gonna make sure she does.

I let this happen to her. I should have looked after her. I should have kept her safe.

I failed her.

SEVENTY-THREE

Olivia

Leaving the hospital is like being able to breathe fully after days of struggling. As soon as I step outside, fresh air fills my lungs and I instantly feel better.

I need to call home. James is going to freak out. He's going to want me to come home or to come see me, and I can't deal with that yet.

I'm scared. So fucking scared ever since Wyatt grabbed me, and I can't shake it. I know I went through a traumatic event, but I didn't think I'd feel this way. I feel weak, and I refuse to allow Wyatt to have that power over me.

He's dead and he can't hurt me or anyone else now. But he's dead because of me. He was insane, he was going to kill me, but a person is dead because of me. I'm not sure that's something

I'll ever get over.

Echo lifts me gently and places me into the truck. There's a distance between us that I hate, I'm bruised and battered, but I'm fine and his hands are so tentative and unsure. He doesn't want to hurt me or scare me, but I need to be close to him. It's the only time I feel safe.

I miss my alpha, bossy, unreasonable Echo, but since the attack, he's changed. From the moment we met, he's refused to leave me alone, but now when I need him to keep me close, he's putting distance between us.

We haven't kissed since he rushed into my hospital room. His hands hold mine and stroke my hair, but he's detached and distant.

I miss him.

Climbing into the truck, he starts the engine, and pulls away from the hospital. I'm sitting on the opposite side of the seat, staring out the window at the scenery, but I've never been in this truck and sat this far away from him. Holding my breath, I wait for my controlling Echo to wake up and demand I slide over to him, but all I see is the anger and frustration etched so clearly across his face.

The moment we pull up to the house, my eyes lock on the woods. Uncontrollable shudders wrack my body and I throw open the door, racing from the car, straight across the street and bang on Gus's front door.

The door opens and there stands lovely, charming Gus. He

saved me. He killed another human being to save me. Launching myself into his body, I wrap my arms around his neck. He steps back from the force of my embrace, steadying himself as he cradles me in his arms, hugging me tightly.

"Thank you," I gasp.

Chuckling softly, he pulls back just far enough to pat my cheek. "Olivia, my dear, I'm so glad you're okay. I wanted to come to the hospital, but Echo said you'd asked people not to visit."

"I'm so sorry," I say, through a barrage of tears.

"It's okay, sweetheart," he assures me.

I shake my head. "It's not okay. You killed him, Gus. You killed someone to save me. I'm so sorry."

Gus pulls me into his arms again and pats my back. His touch is so paternal that my heart swells with affection for him. Cupping my face with both of his hands he smiles softly. "You listen here, sweetheart. You have nothing to be sorry about. I'd do it again in a heartbeat if it saved you or anyone else from being hurt by him. This isn't your fault. It was his."

I nod and straighten, trying to pull myself together. "Thank you, Gus, you saved my life."

Gus smiles warmly. "You're very welcome, Olivia. I'm so very glad to see you okay and home."

Leaning in I press a kiss against his cheek, then slowly walk across the street to where Echo is leaning up against the tailgate of his truck, his arms crossed, watching me. I take his hand, gripping it tightly as he lifts our entwined hands to his lips, gently kissing my skin.

Wordlessly, he leads us into the house, his huge body sheltering me from the woods. Without me having to tell him, he instinctively knows that I'm not ready to deal with confronting the demons of what happened yet. Echo walks me upstairs and into his bedroom. The bed's unmade, the sheets tousled from the night we spent here.

"Get into bed, sugar. The doc said you need to rest," Echo orders gently. I start to argue, but he silences me when he grabs the hem of my shirt, slowly lifting it over my head. He peels my shorts off, then quickly undoes my bra and pulls my panties down, holding me steady as I lift my legs free.

Naked, I wait for him to touch me, to remind me that I belong to him. My breath comes in short bursts as anticipation pulses through me. I watch as he drops his cut onto a chair, pulling his shirt over his head and revealing his glorious chest. When he steps towards me, my nipples pebble in awareness and he leans in, his lips touch my forehead, and he drops his warm shirt over my head.

Stunned, I stare at him.

"You need to sleep," he growls.

I push my arms through the sleeves, and the hem of his shirt falls to my knees. Sweeping me from my feet he cradles me to his chest, holding me with one arm, as he pulls back the sheets and places me in the bed.

I grab his arm. He tries to pull away, but I hold him tightly. "Echo." Uncertainty pours from my voice, and his eyes avoid mine. He straightens and backs away, scanning me from head to toe, his assessing eyes taking in every cut and bruise.

"Sleep," he says firmly and backs away, leaving me alone and insecure in his huge, empty bed.

The silence descends around me the moment he shuts the door, and a barrage of unanswered questions shout at my subconscious, refusing to be ignored.

Why won't he kiss me?

Doesn't he want me anymore?

Is he repulsed by all the scars and bruises?

Where's my controlling alpha who's determined to own me?

Sitting against the pillows, my mind swirls at a hundred miles an hour, and I stare into space, tears spilling down my cheeks. I need Echo to make me feel normal. He says he loves me, but I need to know if the attack has changed things for him.

I'm just not brave enough to ask him, in case it has.

The door inches open, and seeing me sitting up, Echo walks in. "You okay, sugar, you in pain?" I shake my head and he moves closer. "Come on, Livvy, you need to try and get some sleep."

I hold out my hand to him; my voice small and begging. "Please don't leave me."

Worry shrouds his eyes. "Never," he says climbing into bed and pulling me into his arms.

A relieved breath collapses from my lungs and crawling into his lap, I wiggle into his chest until he surrounds me. Safe and protected, I finally close my eyes.

SEVENTY-FOUR

Echo

Livvy pulls my arms tight around her and my whole body relaxes for the first time since I realized she was missing. It doesn't take long for her to fall asleep, but I lie wide awake, listening to her breathe and reassuring myself that she's okay and here.

But she's not okay. Her face is a fucking mess, her beautiful skin marred with bruises where those psychos punched her and cut her. Her perfect lips are red and broken and one of her eyes is still swollen shut.

I'm terrified of hurting her. She's so fucking delicate and so small compared to me. She's suffered so much, and she's still so frightened, so I'm trying to keep my hands to myself.

Every fiber of me wants to wrap her in my arms and mark

her as mine so the universe knows not to fuck with her again. But I can't, because every time I look at her I can see the fear in her eyes. She's not scared of me, but she's still fucking scared, and I don't have a fucking clue how to take that fear from her.

My phone rings, and I curse the fucking club or anything that'll pull me away from her. "What?" I snarl.

"Brother, how is she?" Park asks.

Since she woke up in the hospital, she hasn't wanted to see anyone, so I've kept the club away from her. We're all big fuckers, and I don't want to frighten her any more than she is already. "She's okay. In pain and tired."

"She back home?" Park asks.

I sigh deeply. "Yeah, we just got back an hour ago."

"Fuck. Man, I'm sorry, but a shipment of weed's gone missing, and I need you to do your thing and find it," Park says. I can hear the apology in his voice, but it does nothing to stem the anger that bursts from me.

"Fuck!" I shout. "Why does this have to happen now. There's no way I can leave Livvy alone."

Park remains silent, knowing this is fucking with my head. He's only the messenger, and if I say no, it will be Prez on the phone next.

"Arghh," I roar, then snap. "Fine, give me ten to sort someone to come sit with Livvy." I cut the call off before he gets a chance to respond.

Pulling up Sleaze's number I call him and he answers on the

first ring. “Echo,” he answers, his tone anxious.

“Brother, I need a favor. Where’s your old lady at?”

He doesn’t get a chance to respond before Brandi shouts loudly in the background, “Is that Echo? Tell him I’m coming to see Liv today and I’ll cut off his balls if he tries to stop me.”

I smile; Sleaze’s bitch is a good woman and a good friend to Livvy. “That’s what I was calling for. I’ve got club shit to deal with. Can you and Brandi come sit with Livvy till I get back?”

I’d forgotten how close they live until the doorbell rings a couple of minutes later. Brandi rushes in, and after giving me an evil glare, she disappears upstairs in search of Livvy. Sleaze waits for me to invite him in before following me to the family room.

I’ve known Sleaze for years. I’ve seen him angry, in pain, and frustrated as fuck, but I’ve never seen that look of sympathy on his face before, and it cripples me. “I’m sorry this happened, brother. How you doin’?” he asks.

I blow out an exhausted breath and rub my hands back and forth through my hair. “It’s fucked up. It’s my fault this happened to her. She’s mine, and I let her get attacked. I failed her. I don’t deserve her.”

Sleaze doesn’t usually waste words, so I’m shocked when he reaches out and grips my shoulder. “This isn’t your fault. None of us had any idea that Anderson was gonna lose his shit,” he growls. I shake my head. I know this is on me, but Sleaze’s grip tightens. “This wasn’t your fault. Your girl is gonna be fine."

I nod, and he nods back.

Coughing to clear the emotion that's making a lump build in my throat I grab my keys. "Her meds are in the bathroom if she needs them. I'll be back as soon as I sort out this fucking shitstorm."

SEVENTY-FIVE

Olivia

When I wake up I'm cold, shivering. The covers are pooled around my waist, but Echo's gone. His side of the bed is warm but empty.

Irrational tears well in my eyes. He's pulling away from me.

The first tear runs down my cheek and is quickly followed by a second and third. Echo and I crashed into each other's lives, but in a short space of time, he's become completely vital to me.

My tears are pouring freely down my cheeks when Brandi appears in the doorway. Rushing to me, she cocoons me in her arms. "Oh Liv, come here, sweetie."

Words pour from me as I sob into her shoulder. "He's gonna leave me. I can see the look in his eyes. He doesn't want me anymore, and I don't know what to do. All he sees when he looks at me is the bruises, and I need him to touch me. I love him."

I pull in a deep breath before looking up into the sympathetic eyes of my friend. "Sweetie, calm down. Echo loves you. He hasn't left your side since the attack, but those psychos really did a number on your face and I think he's just gonna need some time to figure out how to deal with this," she says, her hands stroking my hair. "Now, how you feeling? You need some pain meds?"

Her genuine concern heats my cheeks and tears pool in my eyes again. We may be new friends, but we've forged a connection that will last long after I leave Archer's Creek. "No, I'm fine. It looks worse than it is."

She smiles sadly and sighs. "I doubt that, honey."

Wiping the tears from my cheeks I pull in a deep, calming breath. "Where's Echo?"

"He had to go deal with some club stuff, so he asked me and Sleaze to come stay with you till he got back," Brandi tells me, as she fusses around the room, picking up my discarded clothes and folding them onto a chair.

"Oh, okay," I say quietly. My shoulders slumped, my disappointment obvious.

"He wasn't happy about going, but he was the only one who could sort out whatever the problem was," she assures me.

I nod, unconvinced, pull on my shorts and follow Brandi downstairs. Sleaze is watching TV in one of the Barca Loungers.

Seeing me, he jumps up and pulls me into a tight hug, kissing my hair. I cling to him, a few more tears escaping before I can pull back and wipe them away. Sleaze doesn't speak, just returns to his seat and carries on watching the TV.

Brandi and I walk into the kitchen, and she fills the kettle, searching the cupboards for tea. My phone sits on the counter, charging and I grab it and see the message icon flashing wildly. There's several texts from friends back home and one from James.

James: Hey Liv, how goes the biker sex? I want lots of hot stories when you get home so get kinky baby lmao!!! xx

A laugh bursts from me, and Brandi turns glancing at me in question, so I show her the message and she laughs. "You need to call home, baby girl, let them know what happened," she says, rubbing my shoulder.

Sobering, I nod. "I'm not sure where my parents are, but James is going to lose his mind. He's going to want to come here, or for me to go home."

She hands me a cup of camomile tea and lifts her own to her lips, blowing at the steam that billows from it. "What do you want to do, Liv?"

I tip my head back and pull in a breath. "I want Echo."

Brandi smiles warmly then steps back. "Well then, you call your friend, tell him what happened. Then you tell them that the big bad biker you love and your friends here are taking real good care of you," she says with a smile.

Feeling brave, I excuse myself and walk into the garden. I sit down on one of the chairs on the back patio and dial his number. The phone rings out for a few minutes before James answers. “Hey Liv,” he says brightly.

“Hey.”

“What’s happened, what’s wrong?” James asks quickly. He can tell just from my voice that something’s happened. I pause, silently steeling myself to tell him. “Liv, I’m freaking out here. What the hell’s going on?” he shouts, his voice filled with concern.

I pull in a deep breath and speak quietly. “Something happened.”

“Was it that fucking biker, Liv, because I swear to God, I’ll beat the shit out of him if he did something to hurt you,” James explodes.

“No, never. Echo would never hurt me. Something else happened,” I quickly blurt out.

“Fuck, are you pregnant?” James says.

“*What?* No!” I shout. Then I inhale deeply, exhale, and say. “I don’t really know how to say this. I was attacked.”

Silence.

“Are you still there?” I ask.

“Yep, I’m booking flights. I can get a direct flight to Houston, and I’ll be with you by tomorrow night. Can you get to the airport?” James asks, his voice filled with emotion.

“Sweetie, I’m fine. You don’t need to come here,” I say,

tears pooling in my eyes.

James scoffs. "Liv, you're daft if you think I'm not coming to get you."

"James, I'm fine. I'm out of hospital, and it's just bruises left," I assure him.

"*Hospital!*" he roars. "Right, I'm booking it now."

"No, James, honestly, don't come. Echo and my friends here are taking care of me. I'm fine."

"What happened, sweetie? Oh fuck, did someone rape you? Please don't say you were raped." his voice trembles.

"No, no, I wasn't raped, I promise," my voice cracks.

"So what happened?"

"I met this guy, Wyatt, and he asked me out. It was his aunt who owned the guesthouse I was staying at. Anyway, he was a dick and the date didn't go well, so I was leaving when Echo turned up and went all alpha on him. I hadn't seen him since, not once in weeks. Then I got home the other day and he and his aunt kidnapped me. It was all kinds of fucked up. They beat me up pretty bad. But Echo and Gus, the guy from across the street who comes into the bar, they saved me. He's dead, the guy who attacked me. Gus killed him," I say. Tears stream down my face.

Even though I wish James were here right now, I'm not ready to leave Echo. James is my oldest friend, but he wouldn't understand why I need to stay.

"Fucking hell, Liv. Be honest, are you okay?"

I clear my throat and try to sound as okay as possible. "I'm fine. I mean, I'm not, obviously I'm not fine, but I'm going to be okay."

"I really want to come get you, Liv. I need to see that you're all right."

"I know you do, but I have Echo, and he's looking after me," I say, desperately wanting, needing to reassure James that I'm safe and cared for.

"Is he there? I want to speak to him."

I balk. "Er, no, he's not here. He had to pop out."

James voice hardens. "Sounds like he's taking great care of you, Liv, leaving you alone."

"I'm not alone," I say quickly. "He had Brandi and her husband, Sleaze, come stay with me while he went out."

"Oh, yeah, well I suppose that's okay," James reluctantly concedes.

"It is, it's fine."

I hear James's anguished sigh. "I want you to FaceTime me, Liv, not once a week, but every day. If not, then I'm coming to get you. I don't care what you say, sweetie."

"Okay, I'll FaceTime you starting tomorrow. I promise, if I need you, I'll ask you to come, or I'll come home. But this is where I need to be right now, okay?"

I can hear how unconvinced James is when he finally speaks. "Okay. I love you, Liv. Thank God you're okay."

"Love you too, speak tomorrow," I say, then cut off the

phone. Holding it in my hands I breathe out a sigh of relief. I pull up the photos of my friends back home and feel torn. A part of me wants to go home. James and Dan would look after me, or my mum and dad would come home. But my chest hurts just thinking about leaving Echo; we don't have that much time left together, and I want to make the most of every moment.

I just wish I was still sure Echo felt the same way.

***

My bruises are almost gone; the vivid purple has faded to sickly yellow and soon there'll be nothing left to say that I was attacked. Small scars mar my arms, stomach, and legs, but the plastic surgeon assures me they'll fade with time.

Wyatt and Mimi fill my unconscious mind. If I fall asleep alone, I fight for my life every night until Echo crawls into our bed and protects me from my nightmares. His touch shelters me, and I sleep dreamlessly until he leaves every morning and the dreams wake me up soaked in sweat and screaming.

Weeks have passed since the day everything changed. I'm caged in this house, living with the man I love who's become a stranger.

Brandi's been my sanity; at Strikers or here, she listens to me babble and vent. "Liv, sweetheart, it's only been a few weeks. Just give him some time," she says.

"I can't do this anymore. He doesn't want me here, he just

hasn't got the balls to tell me to go."

Brandi scoffs. "That's ridiculous. The man's obsessed with you. He loves you."

"Brandi, he hasn't touched me in over a month. We don't sleep together. We don't kiss. He's more like my jailer than my boyfriend. He's gone from sexy controlling to insane controlling."

Brandi rolls her eyes. "Liv, you're being dramatic."

"I'm not," I say and throw my hands in the air in frustration. "I haven't had a minute's privacy since the day I came back from the hospital. He's never here, but he sends you and Sleaze or Smoke or Daisy to babysit me. Puck and Blade were even here the other day. He doesn't want to be around me, so he's palming me off on anyone he can."

"Liv," Brandi says doubtfully.

I turn my eyes at her imploringly. "Brandi, I wish it wasn't true. But it is. I don't want to leave, the thought of never seeing Echo again makes me feel like I can't breathe. But with the way things are between us, I think leaving's the best thing for both of us."

Her arms wrap around my shoulders and pull me in for a tight hug. "I don't want you to leave, Liv. You're my best friend," she says quietly.

Tears pool in my eyes. "I feel the same way. I'm really going to miss you," I say, sniffling.

Dropping her arms, she moves back. "So don't go. I don't

want you to go and I promise you Echo doesn't want you to go. If you leave, you'll regret it."

"I can't live like this anymore, Brandi. He used to constantly have his hands on me, and the sex was out of this world, but now he doesn't touch me. He holds my hand and strokes my hair, but that's as intimate as we've been since the attack. To start off, I was okay with it. I hurt and I was still a bit freaked and he always cuddled me as I slept, but that's stopped too now."

I stand up and start to pace, frustrated and angry. "What I don't understand is, if he doesn't want me here, why isn't he giving me the opportunity to leave. My bossy alpha man is gone, and instead he's a distant control freak. I just wish it was the control freak that was telling me to take off my clothes and spread my legs. He's cold and growly. When I kiss him, he pulls away. God, one night I was so frustrated I jumped on him and straddled his lap. He lifted me off him and left the house, saying he had club business to sort out, then he sat on his bike in the driveway till Daisy got here."

Brandi sits silent, her eyes wide with shock.

"He doesn't want me anymore, but he's more jealous than usual. If I'm working, he sits at the bar intimidating anyone who looks at me the wrong way. It's like he doesn't want me but no one else can have me either."

Sympathy floods her eyes. "Have you tried talking to him about it?"

Defeated, I slump onto the sofa, my head in my hands. "I've

tried asking him what's going on, but he evades my questions. He says I'm still delicate and need more time to fully recover."

Her arms surround me, and she pulls me into a tight hug. "Oh Liv, I had no idea things were this bad."

I cry silent tears against her shoulder. "I can't do this for much longer. The pretence is exhausting. I'm not running, but I need to get away from him and give us both a chance to move on with our lives. I just need to figure out how I'm going to leave."

SEVENTY-SIX

Echo

I keep letting her down. She got attacked because I didn't protect her.

I don't deserve her.

I crave her in my arms, but I need to earn the right to claim her again, prove to her that I can look after her for the rest of our lives better than I've done since we met.

I'm a fucking pussy.

She's slipping away from me, but I can't seem to pull my head from my ass long enough to make things better.

The need to protect her at all costs is consuming me. The police think Wyatt and Mimi assaulted and killed five other girls, all of them beaten, drained of blood, and buried in the clearing in the woods. Even though her bruises are almost gone, every time I look at her I see her strapped to that table, bleeding and unconscious.

The guilt's eating me alive. Wyatt's dead, but I still feel like I let her down.

I'm searching for Mimi. The insane old bitch has disappeared, but I'm determined to find her. No one can hide forever, and the sooner she's found and either dead or locked in a prison cell, the sooner Livvy will finally be safe.

Maybe then I can claim her again.

I don't deserve her love, but I fucking crave it. I'm a walking hard-on, and it's getting harder and harder not to take her every moment I'm near her. But I haven't earned her back yet.

I'm her man, and it's my job to protect her, but I failed, and she was attacked because of it. I'm hurting her and she's angry at me, but she needs to be safe above everything else. I can't touch her anymore, but my hands itch to hold her and bring her pleasure. I can sense her arousal whenever I'm near her, and it's intoxicating. She's like a drug to me.

But I don't touch her.

She was almost raped because I didn't protect her like I should.

I failed.

SEVENTY-SEVEN

Olivia

Echo left two days ago. He texted me to say that he was busy with the club, but I know he's avoiding me.

Daisy's on babysitting duty, he follows me as I walk from the living room into the kitchen, his quiet presence constantly lurking behind me. Grabbing a bottle of water from the fridge I walk to the patio with my biker shadow a few paces behind me. Anger bubbles to the surface, and spinning to face Daisy, I scream, "Stop fucking following me!"

His impassive expression infuriates me.

"Speak. Say something, for fuck's sake," I yell at him. I know he hears me, but he refuses to respond. Raking my hands through my hair, I tip my head back and scoff quietly to myself. "I can't do this anymore," I whisper and shake my head as tears fill my eyes.

Stomping past Daisy I'm walking into the living room just as the door opens and Echo strides in. His face is etched with intensity, and my pussy clenches in response. Without a word, Daisy leaves shaking hands with Echo on his way out and then it's just me and Echo and the suffocating silence that descends around us.

"Where've you been?" I ask, then wince. I've become the clichéd nagging wife, and I hate myself for it. He looks up but doesn't speak, walking past me into the kitchen, his shoulders slumped and defeated. The intense glint in his eyes is the only promise that the Echo I knew before the attack still lurks inside him.

Guilt overwhelms me; I did this to him. "Echo, we need to talk."

His back stiffens. "Not tonight, Liv, I'm beat," he says, his voice strained.

Tempted to stay silent, I pull in a deep breath and straighten, buoying myself to speak. "I can't do this anymore, Echo."

He spins round, anger morphing his face. "What the fuck are you talking about?" he snaps.

Shocked by his outrage, I step back. "I can't keep doing this. It's obvious you don't want me here."

"You're my woman, of course I want you here," he shouts.

I sigh. "You haven't touched me in weeks. You avoid me as much as you can, and you pawn me off on babysitters who follow me round all the time. It's ridiculous, and I can't do it anymore."

His eyes widen and a hint of my alpha man flashes back at me. “What are you saying, Olivia?” His words are slow and full of warning.

I take a deep breath and force the words out. “I’m saying you need to let me go.”

Anger flares in his eyes. “Never, I’ll never let you go,” he growls.

“Arrrrr,” I scream. “I’m not a toy that you get to play with when you choose and then ignore the rest of the time.” He scoffs at my words but doesn’t respond. “I refuse to be babysat all the time. Wyatt’s dead and Mimi has disappeared. They can’t hurt me again, and I refuse to be a victim anymore!” I shout.

Echo pulls in short, angry breaths. His anger’s barely held, his voice stern and unyeilding, “I didn’t protect you once, Livvy. I refuse to let that happen again. Mimi is still out there, and until she’s found, you will have someone with you at all times. You are mine and you will do as I fucking say. Do you understand?”

Stunned, I stare at him. “I don’t even know how to start to respond to that. I refuse to be followed permanently, that’s absurd. And Wyatt and Mimi going crazy and trying to kill me wasn’t because you didn’t protect me. It’s because they’re freaking nutjobs.”

His expression is guarded, but his hands go to his hair, pulling the strands as he shakes his head. “Echo, me being attacked wasn’t your fault.” He turns his face away and refuses to acknowledge me. I grasp his face between my hands and force him to look at me. “It happened because Wyatt and Mimi are ill. They lost the plot, and I got caught in the fallout, but that has nothing to do with you,” I say passionately, desperately hoping that he will believe me.

Moments pass as I silently wait for him. His head lifts, and he looks at me. Really looks at me for the first time in days. I stand on my tiptoes and kiss him, desperately willing him to kiss me back, and my heart breaks when he firmly moves me away from him.

His head drops, his voice gravelly and rough. “I love you, Livvy, but it’s my job to keep you safe. He hurt you because I allowed that to happen. I should have protected you and made sure no one could hurt you. I failed you.”

Tears run down my face as I shake my head. “Do you think this is my fault? I encouraged him. I went out on a date with him.”

Echo grabs my chin, and I feel the anger vibrating from him. “Don’t be fucking stupid, of course this isn’t your fault,” he snarls.

Wrapping my hands around his forearms, I nod. “Exactly. I know I’m not to blame, but neither are you. This isn’t your fault.”

He turns his back to me and shuts me out.

I’ve lost him. He’s so blinded by misplaced guilt that nothing I say or do will make a difference now.

Staggering upstairs, I rush to the bathroom and turn on the

shower before my legs give way and I sink to the floor. The water drowns out the sound of my sobs. As I shake uncontrollably, I pull my knees to my chest and rock backwards and forwards, consumed by grief.

I'm toxic to Echo, and it's time to let him go.

Wiping the tears from my face, I turn off the shower and walk back into the bedroom to find my phone. My hands shake as I dial Brandi. She answers immediately. "Hey doll, you okay?"

The words catch in my throat. "I need your help."

I hear Brandi's intake of air. "Anything, just name it," she instantly replies.

"I'm leaving him," I whisper.

***

I lie in bed and stare at the ceiling. The plan's in place, and tomorrow night I won't be here in this bed or in this town. I'm going to leave the man I love. I always knew that eventually I'd have to, but rubbing my chest, my heart physically hurts, like deciding to leave has finally split it in two.

Unable to stay still, I throw off the covers and slide out of bed. Echo never comes to bed till after I'm asleep, but I can't sleep with him even for a couple of hours knowing that it will be the last time I ever do it.

It's dark outside, but I see the orange glow of his cigarette and the silhouette of his broad shoulders sitting by the pool. Grabbing a blanket I curl up in one of the BarkaLoungers, pulling the warm fleece tightly around me. Silent tears fall, staining my cheeks as the TV murmurs quietly in the background, lulling me to sleep.

Strong arms curl under me, lifting me from the chair and hoisting me against a warm chest. I can't see him in the blackness, but his familiar scent surrounds me, and I burrow into him as he carries me up the stairs and gently places me in the bed. The sheets are cold against my skin, and I roll towards the wall, expecting him to leave, but the mattress depresses and Echo's warmth settles against my back. Its heaven and hell rolled into one.

SEVENTY-EIGHT

Echo

Fuck!

I'm fucking this up so badly.

She wants me to let her go. Never.

I'll never let her go. She's mine; it's as simple as that.

The woman is blind if she thinks I don't want her anymore. That's impossible. My cock's so hard it's straining at my jeans whenever I'm near her. I need to sort my shit out and find a way to keep her safe and keep my sanity.

I won't let her run from me; she's my fucking happy ever after, and I refuse to lose her.

If she runs, I'll chase her.

I can't lose her.

I've never felt more like a coward than I do today. The

women I love is in our bed, and I'm hiding outside. Finally growing some balls, I walk back into the house and find her fast asleep in a chair, the blanket that's pulled up to her chin not hiding the tears that are still streaked down her cheeks. She cried herself to sleep. Lifting her into my arms, her soft body against mine is the worst kind of torture. Her perfect Livvy smell intoxicates me, and all I want to do is strip off her pajamas and claim what's mine.

I meant to put her into bed and then leave again, but I can't drag myself away. Instead, I climb in with her, hating that instead of coming toward me she instantly rolled away, like she expected my rejection. I reach out and pull her against my chest, stifling the tortured groan that builds in my chest when she relaxes against me. I should leave, but I can't tear myself from her. I miss the physical connection we had. I know that I'm to blame for losing it, but I haven't done enough to deserve it back yet.

Her words from earlier chime in my head. *"Echo, me being attacked wasn't your fault."* The conviction is clear in her voice; she really believes that this isn't on me. I just wish I could believe it too.

Burying herself further into my chest, she kicks off the covers in favor of my body heat, wrapping her leg around my thigh and sighing happily when she's plastered to me with no space between us. With her in my arms I'm finally at peace too. Exhaling raggedly, I blink into the darkness of the room, wishing I had any idea what to do to fix things. I thought I was okay before I met her, but since she turned up I'm more than happy. I'm complete. She's my missing piece, and I don't know what I'd do without her in my life.

Fuck that. I refuse to know what I'd do without her. I'm never gonna be without her again.

I'm so fucking angry that she wants me to let her go. For weeks while she's been healing, I've tamped down my need to control her body. But when shit about her leaving comes out of her mouth, I have to fight the urge to throw her over the bed and spank her ass.

I watch her sleep, planning, no, needing to stay with her all night and watch her wake up all rumpled and sexy. But as light starts to filter through the blinds, I just can't face her, knowing she's still in danger. I need to make her safe again, and until Mimi's found, she's not. So as dawn breaks, I skulk out of bed like the coward I am.

In the solitude of the house, I try to reflect on Livvy and how I can start to make things better with her. I need her safe, but I don't want her to be unhappy. Maybe I could have one of the guys guard outside the house when she's home, so she doesn't feel so watched.

Fuck, I've got to claim her again soon, 'cause my balls are so fucking blue that I can't take it anymore. I don't fucking deserve her, but if she's forgiven me for failing her, maybe I can figure out a way to make peace with myself for letting her down as well.

I know her leaving isn't a fucking option and I think I've figured a way for her to stay for good, so it's time to stop acting like a fucking hormonal pussy and man up.

My woman needs her man, and hell, that's one job I can definitely do.

My phone rings, shattering all thoughts of reconnecting with my old lady. Fuck, why now? "What's up, Sleaze," I say as I answer.

"Sorry, brother, Prez called church, non-negotiable. Daisy's on his way to you, should be there any second."

"Why today? Do you know what's going on?"

"Nah, just that it's serious and we need to go," he replies.

"Fine, I'll be there once Daisy gets here for Livvy."

I've never been this reluctant to leave her before. The feeling in my gut is telling me I should stay, and I wish I could. Fuck, I could just slide inside her wet heat and be back in fucking paradise. Instead, I'm dragging my ass away from my girl and getting dressed.

Climbing the stairs, I lean against the doorframe and watch her. My world is lying in our bed. She's the reason I wake up in the morning. She belongs to me, but fuck she owns me heart and soul.

Turning to leave I take a last look over my shoulder and my heart fucking stutters—she's everything.

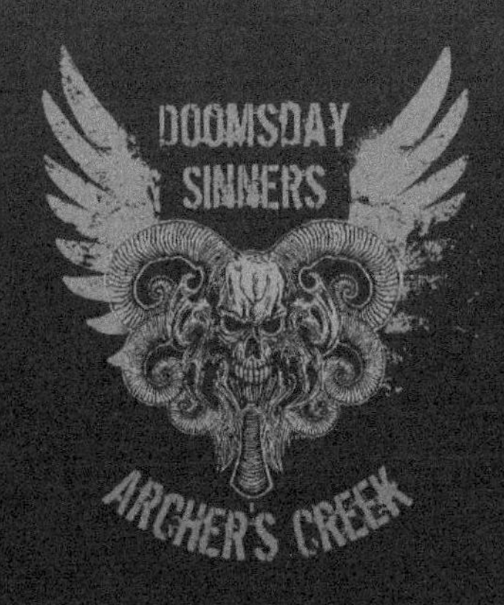

SEVENTY-NINE

Olivia

Morning comes quickly and hope blossoms in my chest, but when I open my eyes to a cold and empty bed it dissolves. His imprint in the pillow is the only way I know I didn't dream him being here. With my resolve tightened, I quickly pack all of my stuff into my backpack and push it to the back of the wardrobe.

I dress for my shift at Strikers then open the bedroom door to find Daisy standing guard in the hallway and his silent presence is exactly the sign I need to bolster my shattered heart.

Hope is a fickle bitch. I'd hoped that Echo would know I'd planned to run. I'd hoped he would be here to stop me. Instead, I'm being babysat again

The silence is deafening. Since the day I met Daisy and he

mouthed off to Echo about me, I haven't heard him speak more than one word consecutively in my presence, no matter how much I needle him. But today his quiet is both a blessing and a curse. Instead of infuriating me, today Daisy's silence gives me room to think and to reason why leaving is the right thing to do.

He patiently watches me as I grab a cup of coffee and when I don't attempt to engage him like I normally do, I can see the question in his eyes, but he still never says a word.

Placing my cup in the dishwasher, I run back upstairs, close the bedroom door behind me and lean against it. I nervously drag my backpack from its hiding place and drop it out of the bedroom window, wincing when it makes a quiet thud as it hits the ground. I hold my breath and wait for Daisy to burst through the door, but as minutes pass and nothing happens, I blow out a breath of relief and text Brandi.

Liv: Bag's ready for you. x

The plan is for Brandi to wait for us to leave then drive here and grab my stuff. Simple but effective. Scanning the room, I take in the familiar details; this will be the last time I see it. I drop to the bed and pull Echo's pillow to my face, inhaling deeply, locking his fresh Echo smell to memory. Slowly, I walk to the door, pausing with my hand on the handle as I take one last look behind me before I leave.

It's time to go.

I signal to Daisy, and he follows me out to the truck, opening the door for me to climb in. Across the street, Gus is standing on his porch, drinking a coffee. Jumping from the truck I race across the street; I can't leave without saying goodbye.

I can hear Daisy's heavy footsteps behind me, but I don't stop until my feet hit Gus's porch steps, and I glance over my shoulder. Daisy stops in the middle of the street, shakes his head, and starts to walk back to the truck. Since Gus saved mine and Echo's lives, he's been completely embraced by the club. The Sinners take care of their own, and the brothers regularly drop by to visit with him now.

"Everything okay, sweetheart?" Gus asks, his smile radiating warmth, as I dash into his waiting arms.

"Gus, you're one of my people. You know that, don't you? Not just because you saved me, but because you brighten my life." I hold onto him tightly and he wraps his arms around me, hugging me back. Once I leave, I doubt I'll ever be able to come back here, so I need him to know how important to me he is. "You make my day every time I see that smiling face of yours."

His cheeks stain red, and I smile widely, knowing that he secretly loves the praise I shower on him. "Young lady, I swear you deliberately try to make me blush."

I laugh softly. "I'm so glad I met you."

Gus wipes his fingers under his eyes discreetly. "Me too, sweetheart. We were never blessed with children or grandchildren, but my Millie would have loved you."

"Oh Gus," I cry, as tears well in my eyes.

He chuckles and steps back. "Go on, get yourself off to

work. And stay safe. I'll see you later."

Nodding, I lean in and press a kiss to his wrinkled cheek. "See you later, Gus."

Head held high, I walk back to the truck. Daisy holds the door for me and I climb in as a single tear escapes and silently rolls down my cheek. I'm leaving so much more behind in Archer's Creek than just Echo.

Time ticks by slowly; the bar's quieter than normal. My escape plan's simple, but we need Strikers to be busy. I'm nervous and the sadness that fills Brandi's eyes every time she looks at me, isn't helping either of us look less suspicious.

Daisy sits guard at the far end of the room, so I walk to the opposite corner and beckon Brandi to me. "Sweetie, you have to stop looking at me like that," I say.

She grabs my hand and squeezes lightly. "Liv, honey, I think you're making a mistake."

"I can't do it anymore, Brandi. We're making each other miserable. All he feels towards me now is guilt, and it's breaking my heart." Tears start to fill my eyes, but I blink them away, refusing to let them fall.

"Are you sure, Liv?" she asks. "Because I think he's gonna lose his shit when he realizes you've gone. I think that man loves you, and in his stupid caveman head, he feels like he let you down when you got attacked."

I sigh and push my hands through my hair. "I know he thinks this is his fault, but I don't feel that way. He says he loves me, that he owns me, but if that were true, he'd keep me close not push me away. He doesn't even want me to touch him. It's done. Finished. Now I just want to leave quietly with a little bit of dignity."

With an understanding nod, she pulls me in for a hug. "Okay. Just in case I don't get to tell you later, I'm really gonna miss you," she says and then rushes away, wiping a stray tear from her cheek.

Pulling in an emotion filled breath, I whisper, "I'll miss you too."

The bar gradually starts to fill up with people, and my nerves kick in. The clock hits four fifteen, and catching Brandi's eye, I nod and she smiles sadly as she nods back. Spinning to hand a customer a bottle of beer she swipes a tray of glasses off the counter, knocking them to the floor.

The glasses shatter into a thousand pieces, shards flying everywhere. "Oh my god, I'm so clumsy. That was a whole tray," she cries dramatically. Quickly handing the beer to her customer, she rushes off to grab a broom.

"I'll go grab a new box of glasses from the stockroom," I say. Brandi nods, grabbing Daisy and insisting he man the bar as she tidies the broken glass.

I slip into the stockroom and laugh at the irony of the situation. In seven weeks I've come full circle, the day I arrived in Archer's Creek, I left my backpack's stacked up against the storeroom shelves and it's here again now. Only this time I'll be leaving behind the man I love, good friends, and a place I could have called home.

It's time to leave, but my legs won't move. My breath stutters in my chest and agonizing pain pulses from my heart. Closing my eyes for a second I pull in a harsh breath, then another, forcing a second gasp of oxygen into my lungs. Tears escape from the corners of my eyes, but ignoring them, I will my limbs to work and sling my backpack over my shoulder.

Throwing open the back door I leave Strikers and Echo behind. Just like we planned, an out of town taxi's waiting for me, and I slide inside with tears soaking my cheeks. I practically hold my breath the entire way to Austin, my ears pricking every time I hear a motorcycle. Watching the road behind us, I'm desperate to see Echo barrelling down behind us to stop me from leaving. But far too soon, we pull into the airport, just like Brandi and I planned.

Taking out my phone I text her.

Liv: I love you for being such a good friend. I'll text you soon. xx

My hands shake and a sob vibrates in my chest as I power down my phone and remove the SIM.

EIGHTY

Echo

This day has been a fucking nightmare. It started with Prez calling an urgent church this morning, because the Nevada chapter of the Sinners wants us to start running guns for them. The money's good, but the risk's high, and as far as I can see, it isn't worth the reward.

The club president is in charge, but for stuff like this a unanimous vote from all of us is needed, and we spent three fucking hours debating if we should get in bed with the Nevada brothers. In the end, we all decided that it wasn't worth it; none of us want to end up locked up.

I got another fucking phone call the moment church finished from a frantic business owner that we provide security for. Someone had broken in and stolen a load of jewelry, and I had to go over and check the video feed.

Now it's late afternoon and the pull to go find my girl is fucking overwhelming. Jumping on my bike I head back towards Strikers. Livvy's shift runs till ten tonight, so I know she'll still be there. I'm fucking desperate to get to her. I've had a nasty feeling in my gut all day that something's wrong, and until she's in my arms, I won't settle.

When I slow at an intersection my phone rings, so I pull over to answer it. Daisy's name flashes on the screen and my heart starts to pound. I texted him earlier to tell him I was on my way, so he wouldn't be calling unless something was wrong.

"Is she okay?" I ask. I can hear him breathing, but he doesn't speak, and the sick feeling in my stomach intensifies. "Daisy, what the fuck's going on. Is she okay?"

"She's gone."

"What? What the fuck do you mean, she's gone? How the fuck can she be gone? You're watching her. Why the fuck weren't you watching her?" I shout.

"I don't know what happened, man. One minute she was here, then she was gone," Daisy says, worry clear in his voice.

"Well, look for her," I snarl. "Fuck, do you think someone took her?" I say, suddenly terrified that Mimi got to her.

"I've searched, man, but she's not anywhere."

"Did you go back to the house? Maybe she went to Gus's. She and him are close now," I say, panicked.

"No, man, I've been all over town; I've even been to the

club in case she went there."

"Fuck. I'll go check the house. Hopefully she's there and she's just trying to make a point to me. She's pissed off at being babysat all the time." I sigh, a slither of hope filling my chest that she's just done this to be a fucking brat.

"Echo, brother, I'm so fucking sorry. I should have been watching her better."

I can hear his remorse and fear, but I don't care. She's missing, and it was his fucking job to make sure that didn't happen. "Yeah, you should have," I growl.

Kicking my bike started I race across town, breaking every speed limit as I fly towards home. If she did this just to be a brat, I'm gonna tan her ass so hard when I find her, she won't be able to fucking sit down for a week.

Pulling onto the driveway, I kill the engine and jump off. I search the house, but she's not here. Panicked, I run back to our bedroom and frantically search for something to help me find her. I open our wardrobe door and instantly stop. It's empty; all of her clothes are gone.

She's gone, not taken by someone or playing games with me.

She left me.

"*Fuck!*" I bellow, slamming my fist into the wall. Shards of plaster fly everywhere, and a fist-sized hole remains in the aftermath of my anger. I slide down the wall. My ass hits the floor, and I cradle my head in my hands.

She's gone.

Frozen, I sit on the floor in shock.

She left me.

My phone starts to ring in my pocket, but I can't seem to find the energy to answer it.

She's gone.

Rubbing my eyes, I blink, forcing them to focus. The sun glints off something just under the bed, and prying my ass off the floor, I crawl towards it. The fine silver chain dangles from my fingers, the heart-shaped charm swinging.

Touching something of Livvy's jolts me into action. It's time to fucking pull myself together and go find my girl.

No way am I letting her run from me. She's mine. I own her fucking ass, and I plan on bringing her home to me. I love her and she loves me. She's gone 'cause I'm a fucking idiot, but we're forever, so I need to find her so I can make sure she knows that too.

By the time I walk into Strikers, I'm so fucking angry I'm seeing red. Marching straight over to Daisy, I grab him by the neck and pin him against the wall, screaming in his face, "How the fuck did this happen? You're supposed to watch her, and yet she's fucking gone. You're gonna wish you were dead by the time I'm done with you."

Daisy's hands scrabble at mine, his fingers clawing at my skin, trying to get me to release my hold. But I'm not thinking clearly; my mind's consumed by Livvy and the fact that she ran from me.

Brandi's shouts break through the red mist. "It's not Daisy's fault she's gone, Echo."

I drop Daisy and his ass hits the floor as he rubs at my fingerprints on his throat. I turn on Brandi, and she steps back in the face of my anger. “Where is she, Brandi?” I snarl, as I stalk towards her.

Fear crosses her face, but bracing herself, she shakes her head, “Gone.”

I step towards her and she steps back. “Gone where?”

“I don’t know.”

“Bullshit. You know where she is and you’re gonna tell me. Right fucking now,” I roar.

Brandi cowers from my rage, her face paling with fear. I didn’t even know he was here, but Sleaze steps in front of Brandi, shielding her completely from me. “Echo, you need to back the fuck away from my old lady before I fucking put you down.” His voice is quiet, but I can hear the violent threat in his words.

Pulling in a deep breath I grit my teeth and focus on him. “Livvy’s gone, and *she* knows where she is,” I say as I point menacingly to Brandi.

Sleaze eyeballs me until I back up a couple of steps, and then he turns to his woman. “Is that true, baby, do you know where Liv is?” Sleaze asks her.

She shakes her head. “She’s gone, but I don’t know where.”

Sleaze steps closer to her, grabbing her chin and forcing her to look at him. “Don’t you fucking dare lie to me. Do you know where she is?” he snarls.

Her eyes widen, but she shakes her head. “She got in a cab. But I don’t know where she’s going. I promise.”

Sleaze turns back to me. “She doesn’t know, man, I’m sorry.”

“Where was the cab taking her?” I ask.

Brandi’s eyes widen. She looks at Sleaze, whose expression hardens. Then she turns to me again, “The airport.”

EIGHTY-ONE

Olivia

I tried to buy my plane ticket this morning; I had my phone in my hand, but I couldn't convince myself to click on the website. Now standing here in the middle of the airport, it feels like I'm at a crossroads. Figuratively and metaphorically. If I head one way, I can buy a ticket back to the UK, but the other way leads me to a ticket to Canada, where I'd always planned to go as the last stop on my backpacking adventure.

Wiping away the errant tears that refuse to stop falling down my cheeks, I try to rationalise my decision. I should go to Canada; my plan shouldn't change just because I met a man and fell in love. But just the thought of being on the same continent as Echo seems too tempting. I love him, and that doesn't just stop and go away. Leaving him is the best thing for both of us.

So I need to be as far away from him as possible.

My breathing gets shallower with every step closer to the British Airways ticket desk, until I'm virtually hyperventilating.

"Good afternoon, how may I help you?" the lady behind the desk asks.

Staring at her, I force out the words. "I was wondering when the next flight to Manchester is?"

She clicks at her keyboard. "There's a flight leaving at 6.50 pm. today," she says, flashing me a bright smile.

I glance at the clock behind the desk. "That's in two hours."

She nods. "Shall I see if there are any seats left? It's a busy flight, but you might be in luck."

I pull in a decisive breath, and answer, "Yes please." As she clicks at her keyboard again, I glance over my shoulder and scan the crowd. My heart's screaming that I shouldn't be leaving, but I ignore it, forcing myself to stay still as my skin tingles with the urge to run from the desk and back home to Archer's Creek.

I feel like I'm drowning, fighting the current that's dragging me under and holding me beneath the surface. My heart hurts, and I rub at my chest, trying to soothe the ache.

"Ma'am?" the sales clerk says.

Lost in thought, it takes me a moment to realise she's speaking and turn back to the desk. She looks back down at her computer, then up at me. "You're in luck. There's just one seat left available on that flight. It departs at 6.50 pm, arriving in London at 10 am There's a three hour, fifteen-minute layover at

Heathrow. Then you'll arrive in Manchester at 2.20 pm"

I hear her speaking but barely absorb any details. I just nod and hand over my parents' emergency credit card to pay for the ticket. Checking my bag at the counter I head through to security, wishing, hoping, that Echo will turn up to stop me, but he doesn't.

It only feels like minutes later that I'm buckling my seatbelt as the plane taxis down the runway. I watch through the window as Texas becomes smaller and smaller. We break through the cloud, and I lose sight of my home completely.

EIGHTY-TWO

Echo

My girl's running at a hundred miles an hour, but I hope I'm quicker.

Jumping on the back of my bike, I make it to Austin airport in record time. I even buy a fucking ticket so I can get into the departure lounge, but she's nowhere to be seen.

I knew it was a fucking long shot, thinking I could find her in an airport filled with thousands of people, but if there was even an ounce of hope, I had to fucking try.

I don't remember riding my bike home or pulling up to the house. Mine and Livvy's home. But something inside me snaps, and I explode. Tearing through the house, I smash and pulverize everything in my path. Until finally, I'm staring at our bed and all my anger disappears, in its place is crushing devastation.

I've lost her.

She's gone, and I've no idea where.

I need to find her, but where the fuck do I even start? She might have gone back to the UK or she might still be in the States somewhere, but she's a needle in a haystack and I have no idea where to begin.

Pulling out my phone, I call her for the hundredth time. It doesn't ring, just goes straight to voicemail. Her sweet voice sings out and my chest hurts, knowing that I may never hear it in person again.

The beep to leave a message jolts me back to the present. "Livvy, where the fuck are you? You ran. You fucking promised you wouldn't run anymore. I love you. I fucking love you, Livvy. It's not safe for you to be out there on your own, so get your ass back home. Just fucking call me and tell me where you are. I love you, Livvy. Come home to me."

Ending the call I slide to the floor, sitting with my phone cradled in my hands, praying for her to call. The light starts to fade and shadows take over the room. Time passes, but I'm unsure how long I've sat here, long enough to know she hasn't called.

The doorbell rings, followed by an insistent knocking that doesn't seem to be going away. Sighing loudly, I force myself off the floor; my stiff muscles protesting as I make my way downstairs. I throw open the door and brace my arm against the frame. "What do you want, Gus?" I say, my voice hollow and lifeless. I must look like shit, because Gus's eyes widen and he pulls in a shocked breath.

"Where is she?" he asks.

Letting go of the door I walk away, leaving Gus to either follow me or go back home. What little furniture I had is now destroyed, the TV's smashed and upside down on the floor and the Barca Loungers are in pieces strewn all over, courtesy of the baseball bat I found in my rage.

Gus's eyes roam over the destruction, but he merely steps over the mess and follows me into the kitchen. "Echo, where is she, son?" he asks again.

Ignoring him, I open the fridge, pull out a couple of beers and hand one to Gus. I twist off the cap, lift the bottle to my lips, and down it in one long swallow. Grabbing a second bottle, I open it, and take a long sip. "She's gone," I finally say.

The sympathy in his eyes almost breaks me. "Where?"

"I don't know. Away from me." Weariness flows over me, and I sigh, rubbing my face. "She got on a plane to somewhere, but even Brandi doesn't know where she's going. She took everything. She planned it. She left me."

Downing my beer, I open and close the cupboards, searching for something stronger. Finally, I find a bottle of whiskey, open it and swig straight from the bottle. The liquid burns as I swallow, my chest heating as the alcohol settles.

Gus silently waits for my attention. "Surely you're not just gonna let her go?" he says angrily.

I pause for a second and pull in a calming breath before I turn to face him. His angry expression mirrors my own and a diatribe bursts out of me. “I love her. She’s my fucking woman. My fucking old lady. Of course I’m not gonna just let her go,” I shout.

Fire sparks in his eyes. “Thank God for that. So how we gonna find her?”

Sighing I shake my head, defeated. “I don’t even know where to start. I went to the airport and searched for her, but she was gone. There were about fifty flights that left this afternoon. I figure she’ll go home eventually, but she could be anywhere in the world by now.”

Gus’s fist slams down onto the counter. “So that’s it. You’ve given up before you’ve even tried,” he shouts.

Growling, I straighten and square up to the old man in front of me. “She’s my woman and it’s my fault she’s run away. I’ve been a fucking idiot since the attack. She’s my fucking forever; that’s not something you just walk away from. I’ll find her, and I’ll figure a way for us to be together. I just have no idea where to fucking start.”

He nods, approval clear on his face. “Okay then. Lick your wounded pride tonight. Then tomorrow we track down your woman. That girl loves you too. You need to find her and bring her back home where she belongs.”

EIGHTY-THREE

Olivia

The flight's a blur of tears and guilt.

Should I have left?

Have I made a massive mistake?

I spend three hours in Heathrow, questioning every decision, almost convincing myself to get back on a plane to Texas. On the flight to Manchester, I eventually cry myself to sleep, only waking up as the plane hits the runway.

As I look out of the window, the view of cold and rainy Manchester is a sobering one.

Home.

The familiar skyline feels alien as I shuffle off the plane, through the airport, and out into the cold British daylight. The airport's just like I remember, a concrete jungle dotted with travellers smoking desperate cigarettes the moment they pass through the doors.

Dropping my backpack at my feet, uncertainty overwhelms me. My parents are somewhere in the middle of Eastern Europe, Russia, or Belarus, and our house is sold with new people now calling it home. I pull out my phone and go to dial James, but the black screen reminds me that I turned it off.

It's been hours since I ran away from Archer's Creek. Echo will know I'm gone by now. My fingers hovers over the power button, but I pull back, fearful of what I'll find when I turn it on. A hundred messages demanding I come back, or nothing except silent relief that I've left?

I think the silence would be worse.

Sliding my phone back into my pocket, I walk over to the taxi rank. "Piccadilly Gardens, please," I ask the taxi driver. Nodding, he waits for me to climb in, then pulls out of the airport and into the traffic towards the city centre. When reach the gardens the driver slows. "Whereabouts, love?"

"Anywhere here's fine."

He pulls to the side of the road, and I pay him before he speeds away, lost into the flow of cars. It's afternoon and the gardens are bustling with life. A myriad of people fill the urban oasis, some simply passing through the city, others standing to admire the burbling fountains.

Slinging my pack over my shoulders I walk quickly, leaving the gardens behind me and heading into the maze of tall hotels and apartment blocks. My feet know the route, and minutes later, I'm standing outside the Greek restaurant that James and Dan live above.

I push the buzzer and wait, but no one answers. Pushing again, I hold my finger on the button, letting the shrill sound sing out. "Bloody hell, you only have to press it once. Who is it?" James's voice makes tears instantly pool in my eyes; it's been a long time since I saw my best friend.

"You should be more polite. It could be someone important," I say.

"Liv?" James asks, shocked.

"You gonna let me in or what?" I say. Feet stomp quickly down the stairs, and then I'm airborne. James's arms are wrapped tightly around me, and tears stream down both of our faces.

"God, I missed you," I say.

"Me too," James says, pulling back and wiping the tears from my cheeks with his thumbs. "Tea?" he asks. I nod and let him guide me upstairs.

Slumped on James's old battered sofa, I watch him busy himself in the kitchen. "Liv?" Dan says as he wanders from the bedroom. I stand and rush towards him to be pulled in for a tight hug. He holds me away from him and smiles broadly. "Bloody hell, Liv. What the fuck happened to you?"

I look down at my jeans, trainers, and hoodie, mentally calculating if any of my scars are visible, but they're not. "What do you mean?" I ask.

With a laugh, Dan kisses my forehead and walks into the kitchen, quickly wrapping his arm around James's waist and moving him to the side to take over the tea making. He hands me a steaming cup, and both men sit opposite me on the loveseat.

Dan stares at me again. "I mean, look at you, Liv. If that's even still your name? You're practically a different person. The curls, the trainers, everything. Bloody hell, I don't think I've ever seen you out of heels, and I was sleeping with you for six months."

Pulling a cushion from beneath me I fling it at Dan's head. "Dan—" I cry, outraged, I start to speak, but James cuts me off.

"Liv, what are you doing here? You're not supposed to be home for another five weeks," he asks.

My mouth drops open, the words frozen on my lips. A tear spills down my cheek. Another follows, and then the floodgates open and my chest shakes, sobs racking my whole body.

"Oh, sweetie," James cries, scooping me into his arms. Cradling me in his lap, he slowly rocks back and forth as I sob into his chest. Dan leaves, gently kissing my head before slipping out the front door.

"It's okay, Liv. It's all going to be fine, I promise." James's soothing voice calms me, until my sobs subside and silent tears replace them. "Whatever's happened, it's going to be fine."

Shaking my head in denial I bury myself against my best friend and closing my eyes, I eventually fall asleep.

I dream of Echo, only for my heart to break when I wake up

alone and remember that the man I love is hours away and not mine anymore. I did this. I broke my own heart. I was unhappy in Archer's Creek, but I left half my heart with Echo and I feel desolate without him.

He blamed himself for my attack, and I should have tried harder to make him believe that it wasn't his fault. I love him, and I walked away instead of fighting for us. I still had five weeks with him, and maybe I could have found a way to stay. Instead, I ran, and I've got no one to blame for how I feel now but myself.

I spend the next four days on James and Dan's sofa.

"Enough. Get your stinky bum off my sofa and go have a bloody wash," James shouts. I pull the duvet over my head and groan at his intrusion. "The pity party's over, Liv. Time to tell me what the bloody hell happened."

James rips the quilt from me and hauls me over his shoulder before unceremoniously dumping me under the running shower. The water washes away the grime and tears, until I feel almost human. Walking out of the bathroom, I find James and Dan waiting expectantly for me. Kissing me gently on the forehead, Dan hands me a plate of toast and a hot cup of tea.

They silently watch me, until finally James leans forward with his hands steepled in his lap. "Time to talk, sweetie. What happened out there? Where's Echo?"

A single tear escapes, but I quickly wipe it away. "Echo and I were just a holiday thing. It's over."

"Bullshit," James exclaims.

My head shoots up, and I throw him a shocked look. "What?"

"I said bullshit Liv. I've known you for years, and I've never heard you speak about someone like you did about him. You love him. So stop talking crap and actually tell me what happened," James demands.

I pull in a deep breath. "After the attack, he started to pull away. I was pretty beat up, so I just thought it was the bruises, you know? But when they started to fade, he just stayed away. He felt like my attack was his fault, that he didn't protect me. By the time I decided to leave, he was just keeping me there out of a misplaced sense of responsibility."

A look of sympathy flashes across James face. "Oh sweetie, did he tell you to leave?"

"God no," I blurt. "But I never saw him. He'd have the other biker guys guard me and then come back in the early hours. He didn't touch me. He didn't want me to touch him. I just couldn't do it to either of us anymore."

James tilts his head to the side quizzically. "Why would you need a guard? I thought Wyatt was dead?"

I nod. "He is, but Mimi, who helped him hurt me, she disappeared."

"Do you love him Liv?" he asks.

Wide-eyed, I stare at James, unable to answer.

"It's not a difficult question hun. You either love him or you don't. So do you love him?"

I sit up straight and try to lace my voice with certainty. "It doesn't matter if I love him or not. He didn't want me there, so I left."

Dan's hand shoots into the air, and he suddenly speaks. "Did he tell you that he didn't want you there?"

My eyes flit from James to Dan before they drop to my hands and focus on my chipped nail polish. "No. He didn't have to tell me."

James hangs his head as Dan speaks, "Oh Liv. What have you done?"

"I did the best thing for both of us," I say, blinking back tears again.

James stands and walks across to me, kneeling at my feet. "You're an idiot. Liv, I don't know Echo, but I can tell you now that he didn't want you to leave. He feels responsible for Wyatt attacking you and he's terrified that Mimi is still out there and could hurt you again."

Shaking my head, I try to deny his words, but he interrupts me.

"Do you love him?"

"That's irrelevant," I say.

Dan laughs softly, his eyes flitting to James for a second before returning to me. "Olivia May Townsend, love is never irrelevant." Standing, he grabs my phone from the front pocket of my backpack and hands it to me. "Stop being an idiot Liv and phone your man."

Turning the phone over in my hands I stare at it. “What if he hasn’t called?”

Two sets of sympathetic eyes look back at me but it’s James who speaks first. “He will have. But if by some very slim chance he hasn’t, then Dan will break out his emergency vodka stash and we’ll get you absolutely plastered.”

A grin twitches at the side of my lips. “God, I missed you guys,” I say.

Dan’s smug face grins back at me. “Yeah, yeah, we missed you too. Now stop stalling and turn your phone on,” he orders playfully.

Pulling in a deep breath, I slide the SIM back into my phone and press the power button. My phone surges to life, and the silence is deafening.

He didn’t call.

Tears stream down my face, and I turn to James, unable to look at my silent phone any longer. The first beep makes me jump, then a chorus of beeps burst from my phone as messages and voicemails appear.

***

James and Dan left an hour ago, and I’m still just looking at my phone, trying to build up the courage to do more. Finally, I urge my fingers to move and click on the texts. Eleven new messages. Eight are from Echo, two from Brandi, and one is from Gus.

I click on the one from Gus first and read it quickly.

Gus: Young lady, what have you done? We're all worried about you so please call.

Shame consumes me, and I drop my phone into my lap. I never really thought about how my leaving would affect the people I left behind. I feel so selfish. I was so consumed with leaving Echo that I never gave my friends a chance to say a proper goodbye.

I miss Archer's Creek and my life there.

Lifting my phone again, I click onto Brandi's messages.

Brandi: I love you too. I'm gonna miss you so much. I wish you didn't have to go ☹.

Tears well in my eyes, and I blink them away to look at her second message.

Brandi: Echo knows. He's lost it. That man is so in love with you. You need to come home.

Gasping, I cover my mouth with my hand. I'd convinced myself he didn't care, that I was leaving for him. Frantically, I open his messages. All eight are from the day I left.

Echo: Livvy, call me.

Echo: Where the fuck are you?

Echo: This isn't fucking funny. Call me.

Echo: Livvy I'm freaking the fuck out. Call me.

Echo: I'm at the airport. Don't run.

Echo: I love you. Please don't leave.

Echo: You're mine and I'm yours. We're it sugar. I understand why you think you need to run but your life is here with me. I was an idiot and I'm sorry. I'm coming for you sugar. You're my forever.

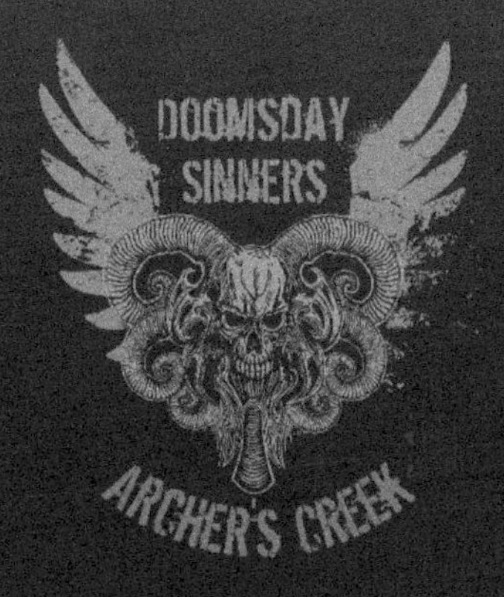

EIGHTY-FOUR

Echo

It's been five long fucking days since she left me. The worst five days of my life.

The day Gus found me smashing our home to bits, I drank myself into oblivion. The next day he was at the door at eight in the morning, and we've been searching for her ever since.

If she went back to the UK, to Manchester, then at least I'll have a place to start, but she could have carried on travelling, and fuck knows where she might be by now.

I'm so fucking angry. I need her back, but every day that passes feels like forever.

The club whores are circling me like fucking vultures, but my dick doesn't even twitch in their direction. I wish it would; it'd be so much easier to just forget her and go back to fucking anything with a willing pussy.

Who am I kidding? Even if my dick was on board, the rest of me wouldn't be. Now that I've had perfection, cheap skanks are never going to do it for me again.

Brandi fucking hates me. Sleaze has her on a tight leash since Livvy took off. He took her phone off her just in case Liv contacted her, but so far there's been nothing.

I've exhausted every way I can think of to track her down. Normally I can find anything or anybody, but that takes time, and I'm running out of patience.

I want my girl back.

I ran a check for credit cards using her name, old address, and date of birth, but she never bought a plane ticket. She hasn't used any of her cards at all since she left. She hasn't accessed any social media or emailed anyone and her phone's turned off, so we can't track her.

I moved back to the club two days ago. The cleaner I employed to keep the house clean while Livvy was recuperating came by and changed our sheets. I lost my shit and fired her. Livvy's smell is completely gone, and now it's just a big ole empty house again. I can't stand living there without her, and at least at the clubhouse I'm not alone.

When I'm alone, images of me and Livvy flash through my brain. It doesn't matter how much I drink, they don't stop. Most nights end with my hand wrapped around my hard cock, imagining all of the dirty things I want to do with her when I get her back.

But she's gone.

She hasn't contacted Brandi or Gus.

She's just fucking gone.

My phone rings, and I pull it from my pocket. "Blade."

"Echo, we've got something," Blade says.

"Livvy?"

"Yeah. Puck hacked the security cameras from the airport. We've got her buying a ticket from the British Airways desk and then disappearing through security."

My heart feels like it's beating out of my chest. "Do we know where she went?"

"Yes. British Airways only flies from Austin to London Heathrow. So she's definitely in the UK, but where she went from London we don't know."

"Thanks, brother. Is there any way we can see if she got a connecting flight from Heathrow?" I ask. If I had to guess, I'd say she's gone home, but I don't want to waste time in Manchester if she's with her parents in fucking Russia.

"Puck's working on it," Blade says. "The moment she turns her phone on, we'll track her and get you on a plane to go get your old lady back."

"Damn right," I say, feeling more hope than I have in the last five long fucking days. I hear Blade chuckling as I end the call.

Rolling Livvy's silver chain through my fingers, I stare into space. Airline websites are open on the laptop in front of me, a ticket to Manchester just waiting to be bought. I've never been to the UK, but even I know that London and Manchester are huge fucking cities.

Livvy grew up in a village outside of Manchester, but her parents don't live there anymore. Her friend James lives in Manchester, but I have no idea where and I don't know who else she would go to.

My phone rings and I grab it, answering quickly. "Blade."

"We've got her, man," Blade says, his voice triumphant.

Relief billows through me, my taut body relaxing for the first time in days. "Where is she?"

"She just turned her phone on. She's in Manchester. We've tracked her to somewhere within a quarter of a mile from the cell tower at a place called Piccadilly Gardens. According to Google Maps, it's a park in the middle of the city, surrounded by hotels. I'm sorry, Echo, but we can't get a closer location than that."

Turning to my computer I click buy on the airline ticket. "It's a start. I really appreciate it, brother."

"Bring her home," Blade says sternly.

"I will."

She's my fucking woman. I was an idiot, and I let her forget that. I need to remind her that she belongs to me, and she needs to remember that I belong to her too. My girl's run home, but a fucking ocean isn't gonna stop me getting to her.

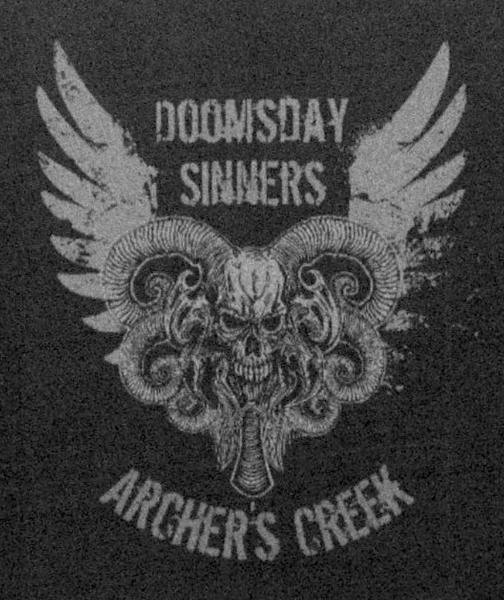

EIGHTY-FIVE

Olivia

The voicemail icon on my phone flashes, taunting me. Finally finding the courage, I tap the icon and put it on speaker. The robot voice informs me there's six new messages.

Echo's southern drawl pours through my phone. "Livvy, where the fuck are you? You ran. You fucking promised you wouldn't run anymore. I love you. I fucking love you, Livvy. It's not safe for you to be out there on your own, so get your ass back home. Just fucking call me and tell me where you are. I love you, Livvy. Come home to me."

Tears start to track down my cheeks and the pain in my chest that I've been ignoring, explodes the moment I hear his voice. My breathing becomes erratic and I ache to be near him; the pull to him so overwhelming, I start to rise from my seat.

Forcing myself onto the sofa again, I select the next message and brace myself for his words. "I need you. Our bed's empty, and I don't want to be in it without you. I'm broken, Livvy. You broke me, and I need you. Where are you? I need you."

Even through his drunken slur, I can hear the pain and hurt in his voice. I pause the messages, drop my phone, and quickly edge away from it. Loud, anguished sobs rack through me, and tears run in torrents down my cheeks. Glaring at my phone, I contemplate stamping on it to save myself from the rest of the messages, but my desperation to feel close to him, even if it's only listening to his voice, wins.

Cautiously, I gather my phone and select the next message. "Livvy, you can run, but we both know that I own you heart and soul. Come back to me now before I have to start looking for you. You own me too, sugar, and you left me behind. I need to find you, Livvy. I don't want to be without you. You're my home. I have to find you." His voice is full of command and my body responds instantly, shuddering with arousal.

Moments later, I contemplate the implication of his words. "*I need to find you, Livvy. I don't want to be without you.*" The message was left the day after I left, four days ago. Excited nerves flutter to life in my stomach.

He's looking for me.

I quickly select the next message, desperate for more of his words. "I miss you. I know things haven't been good the last few weeks, but I love you. And you love me. I know you do.

So I don't understand why you're doing this. You woke me up, sugar, and made me want more. Then you took it all away. I don't know what to do without you. I love you, Livvy, and I want you with me."

Frantically, I move to the next message. "Where the fuck are you? You're mine and you better not forget it. Get ready, sugar, 'cause I'm gonna spank your ass so hard when I find you, you won't sit down for a week. But I tell you what, you'll never forget who you belong to again. Call me right fucking now, Livvy. I'm not fucking joking."

I'm tingling all over, my lips twitching into a smile at his threats. The anger and frustration in his voice seems to escalate with each message and each day that passes. "You don't get to walk away without talking to me. You want to end things, then stop being a fucking coward and answer your phone."

I reluctantly select the last message. "It's been four days, sugar. Four days since I held you in my arms. Four days since I talked to you. Four days since I slept with you wrapped around my body. I don't know where your head's at. I don't fucking understand why you left. I refuse to think I'll never see you again. You're my happy fucking ever after."

Shell-shocked, I let my phone fall from my hand and drop to the floor. He loves me. Three words with such a big meaning, and he says them again and again. I thought his love had changed, that it had become an obligation out of guilt. But the passion in his voice removes all of the doubt from my mind.

He loves me, and he's looking for me.

He's coming for me.

Fuck.

***

In the last twenty-four hours, I must have picked up my phone a thousand times. I want to call him. I'm so desperate to hear his voice and beg him to come get me. But that won't solve anything. My visa will still run out, and I'll have to leave him all over again.

I want to go to him, but if the pain of leaving him when I thought he didn't love me is hard, leaving him knowing that he should be my future would be devastating. There've been no new messages, but like an addict, I listen to his voicemails obsessively again and again.

"Liv, if you don't call him soon, I'm going to," Dan shouts from across the room.

"Dan, I can't."

Shaking his head, he settles onto the loveseat opposite me. "You're an idiot. You love him and he loves you."

"But my visa!"

Raising his hand in front of my face, he silences me. "Liv, they're just excuses. Apply for a permanent immigration visa. You still have a month left on your tourist visa, go back and figure it out when you get there. There are options, but you're just running away. So stop being a coward and figure out how to get back to your man."

Slowly, I lift my eyes until they lock with Dan's. "I'm scared," I whisper.

Dan nods and smiles. "Love is scary, Liv. That's how you know it's right. If you weren't scared, I'd be worried, but use the fear, don't let it overwhelm you."

EIGHTY-SIX

Echo

Austin to Manchester is a fucking long-ass flight. I've forgotten what it's like to sit in a fucking cramped airline seat, trying to sleep but having the person next to you talk your fucking ear off for hours

Fuck, it's cold here.

It's been two days since I got to the UK. After I got off the plane, I checked into a hotel near Piccadilly Gardens and slept for eighteen fucking hours. Manchester's a fucking huge city, and apart from knowing what area her phone's in, she's yet to use her credit card or make even a single phone call that might help me to find her.

My girl's gone to ground.

Since I got up yesterday morning, I've been leaving her

messages every couple of hours. I tell her what I'm feeling. How I love her and how I hate her. How I want to make her scream so hard she won't know if I'm the devil or God himself.

For two days, I've walked the urban gardens and the city blocks that surround it, hoping she'll appear.

She hasn't.

I've figured out her visa issue, and now I just need to find her.

Then I'm taking her home where she belongs.

I miss her. It's time to find my woman.

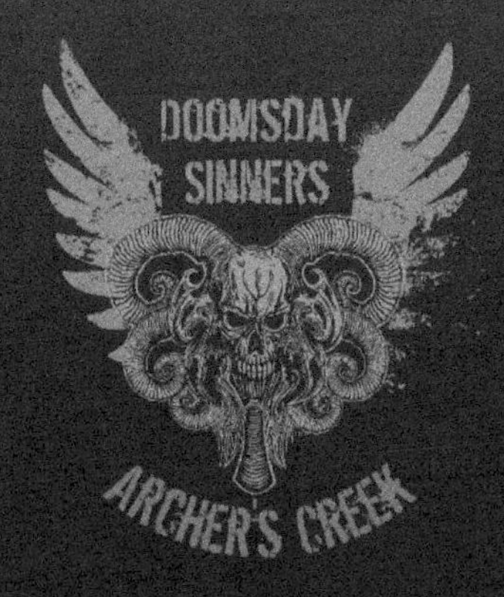

EIGHTY-SEVEN

Olivia

For two days, my phone's been barraged with calls from Echo. I love him, but every time he rings, I force myself not to answer. I've spent hours searching for a way for me to stay with Echo in Archer's Creek, because I can't go back to him until I know there's a way for it to be forever. But I don't think I can hold out much longer.

I miss him.

His calls always end with him leaving me a message and torturing me with his words.

Day One

"I don't understand why you're doing this to us, sugar. You love me. We both know you love me, so why would you want to leave? I know I caused this. That my guilt caused this. But you ran away without even trying. You're mine, Livvy, and I'm yours. Don't you see there won't ever be anyone else for me but you?"

"Do you remember that day when I reminded you why you belong to me? Do you remember how your body craved it? You begged for me to take over and remind you why you're mine. You pleaded for me to touch you and make you feel the pleasure only I can give you. Nothing else will ever feel the way it does when you give yourself over to me completely. This is my fault. I haven't reminded you in too long, and you've forgotten. When you come back to me, I'll make sure you never forget again. I'll make you come so hard and so many times that you'll orgasm screaming my name for the rest of our lives."

"I miss you. I miss your smile when you wake up. I miss those tiny shorts you wear. I miss the way you sound when I kiss your neck. I miss the way you smell when you're turned on. I miss the way you smile at everyone who comes into the bar, but when you look at me, it's brighter and happier than for anyone else. I miss the way you used to stare at me when you thought I wasn't looking. I miss the way you love me and the way you're surprised that I love you back. I just miss you, sugar. Please come home."

"I hate you for doing this to us, Olivia. You're stronger than this, but you're behaving like a coward who runs at the first sign of a problem. I hope you're as fucking miserable as I am. You turned up and showed me what it was like to want to spend the rest of your life with someone, and then you just up and walked away without giving a fuck about the carnage you left behind."

Day Two

"Sugar, it's been too long since I kissed you. When you were hurt, I worried that I'd hurt you more, so I stopped. I was scared to touch you. I know that was stupid of me, and I promise it won't ever happen again. When I get you back, I'm gonna worship your body. I'm gonna kiss your gorgeous lips, then all the way down your neck. I can't wait to feel your pulse race when I put my hands on you. I can't wait to feel the hard peaks of your nipples against my fingertips, or hear your breath hitch when I suck and bite on them. I can't wait to stroke every inch of your soft skin or push my hands between your legs so I get to see that perfect pussy of yours. I can't wait to taste you again. To run my tongue through your cunt and find your clit ready and waiting. I can't wait to push my fingers inside you and feel your tight heat clench around them when you come all over my hand. I can't wait to finally plunge my cock back inside you and feel you milking my dick as I spill my seed as deep inside you as I can. I can't wait to reclaim every inch of you as mine."

"I love you."

"I miss you, sugar. I miss how you argue with me and defy me. I miss the way you smell and how you kick off the covers and sleep on my chest. I miss your snarky fucking attitude. I miss the way you laugh when you're doing your girly shit with Brandi. I miss you. Stop this and come back to me."

"I can't wait to see the shade of red your ass goes when I take you over my knee. This time I might bend you over a chair so I can watch the cream drip from your pussy as you beg for me to spank you harder. I love it when you push your ass into my hands, so desperate for more. Either way, I'm gonna punish you so good for running away. I'm gonna fuck you till you're on the brink of screaming. Then I'm gonna stop and let your orgasm fade and start all over again. I'm gonna come all over your reddened ass and watch as my seed drips down your skin. I still need to claim that ass of yours. That tight virgin hole's just waiting to be taken by me. You're my perfection. You make everything better, and every fucking inch of you belongs to me. When I get you back, we're gonna have our forever, sugar, our happy ever after."

Seven days without him, and I'm miserable. I'm a stupid, stubborn idiot. I love him. I want to be with him, but it could take months or years to get a work visa, and I would have to come home again. I'm torturing myself with the future and wasting the time I could have with him now.

"Olivia, you need to get out of this flat. It's been a week, honey, it's time to pull yourself together. Either go back to him like you know you want to, or sort out your life here. You need to find a job and somewhere to live," James says as he passes me a cup of tea, sinking down next to me on the sofa.

"I know. I do. I can't stay here forever. I just don't know what to do anymore," I say.

My phone rings and both James and I look to the screen. "It's Echo."

James nods enthusiastically. "Answer it," he prompts.

I reach for the phone, pause and pull back, then reach for it again. The ringing stops just as my fingers finally wrap around the case. "Call him back, Liv. Do it now before you talk yourself out of it," James says.

My hands shake as I tap the screen and start to call him. Before I can press the button, the phone beeps, informing me that there's a voicemail. Quickly selecting it, I lift the phone to my ear and wait for Echo's words.

"I can't get you out of my head, sugar. I moved out of our house and back to the club. I've tried running from your ghost, but no matter where I go, the images in my head never go away. I wish I'd never met you. I was okay till you steamrollered my heart. But then I'd never know what it was like to love someone so completely that a piece of you is missing when you're not together. I'm searching for you, sugar. I wish I could give up and let you go, but I can't. I want forever with you."

Silent tears fall from my eyes, and I swipe them quickly away. "God, I'm so pathetic. I need to stop crying," I say, sniffling.

"What did he say?" James asks. I hand my phone to him and he listens. His eyes soften with Echo's words, and he passes the phone back to me.

Holding the phone tightly between my fingers I look up at James. "I don't know what to do." He smiles sadly at me. "I miss him. I'm torn, because my head's telling me that this is for the best, that suffering now will save me from an even worse heartache in a month's time. But my heart's telling me I'm an idiot, and I'm starting to agree. I'm wasting valuable time I could have with him. Oh god, I should be spending my time just being in love and making a lifetime of memories."

James smiles as he watches me make my decision. "I need to go home. Back to Echo and the rest of my Archer's Creek family. I miss them, and not just Echo. I miss Brandi and Gus. Hell, I even miss Daisy and his silence, and Sleaze in all his stoic wisdom. I miss my life there. But most of all, I miss my man. He's right. A part of me is missing when I'm not with him. My heart feels empty, and I'm a bloody idiot for wasting all this time being miserable without him."

Clapping diverts my attention from James to Dan as he walks towards us. "Thank fuck for that, Liv. It took you long enough to figure it out," he says, smiling broadly. "It's a good job I've already booked you tickets back to Texas tomorrow night, isn't it?" He says, fluttering a flight confirmation email in his hand.

I throw myself into his arms. "Thank you."

James's arms wrap around me from behind, squishing me in a hug surrounded by my best friends.

"Right, let's go and celebrate. Pastiche for food, and then onto the Glory club for some goodbye drinks," James announces.

Nodding, I grab my jacket and with James's arm wrapped around my shoulders, I leave the flat, smiling for the first time in a week.

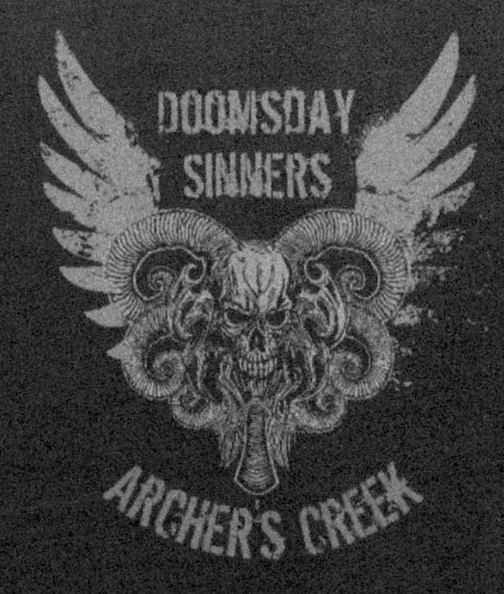

EIGHTY-EIGHT

Echo

I've been circling Piccadilly Gardens for three fucking days, and there's no sign of her. I've spoken to every hotel, but no one will tell me if they have an Olivia Townsend staying there. Puck's hacking their systems one by one, searching for her, but he's found nothing so far.

I'm sitting in a bar on the outskirts of the gardens that has a panoramic view of the square, nursing a warm fucking British beer. I've just left Livvy another fucking message. She knows I'm calling, and she's refusing to answer. I should give up, go home, and lose myself in whiskey and whores. But I can't. I need her to look me in the face and tell me that she doesn't love me.

How do you give up on the woman you're meant to spend

the rest of your life with?

Signaling the barman for my bill, I throw a note down and stand to leave. That's when I see her, walking with two guys, laughing and smiling. Anger prickles my skin when one of the guys drapes his arm across her shoulders and *my* girl looks up at him and then wraps her arm around his waist.

Fury.

Anger.

Betrayal.

Pulling my hood over my head, I leave the bar and follow her. Head down, I try to be inconspicuous and blend in with the flow of people walking the gardens. Never losing sight of her, I follow them to a restaurant and watch as they're seated near the window.

The men sit on one side of the booth and Livvy on the other. Something in my memory prickles and nags, but I ignore it. Instead, I wait quietly in the shadows and stalk my girl as she laughs and flirts with two other men.

Hidden, I watch her hug them.

I watch them leave.

Then I follow her.

I know I shouldn't; I should walk away, but I can't. My heart started beating again the moment I saw her. She's my everything, and I can't just leave.

She walks through the gardens and down a side street. Outside a rundown Greek restaurant, she pulls a key from her pocket and opens a door hidden on the side of the building.

I planned to stay outside and wait; instead I dart forward and stop the door from shutting. Quietly closing it behind me I climb the stairs. There's another door, and I pause, staring at the glass.

The woman I love is on the other side of this door, and I'm fucking terrified. I've flown halfway round the world for her, and until this moment, I hadn't considered that I might have to go home without her.

Fuck that. I love her and she loves me.

Time to get some answers.

If she can stand in front of me and tell me she doesn't feel anything for me, I'll leave.

But if she loves me, I'm claiming what's mine and taking my girl home.

EIGHTY-NINE

Olivia

I'm happy for the first time since I left Archer's Creek as James, Dan, and I celebrate my epiphany and toast my departure.

A sense of lightness has encompassed me since I decided to go home. My skin keeps tingling in excited awareness and my body's on high alert and desperate to get back to Echo.

"Come on, Liv. The Glory Club. It's two-for-one cocktails tonight," James says.

Shaking my head I pull each of them in for a tight hug. "I just want to go pack and get a good night's sleep before the longest flight in the history of man tomorrow. I can't wait to get back to him."

They both smile smugly, but Dan wiggles his eyebrows. "I bet you can't, you dirty bitch." I smack his arm playfully, smiling as the boys head towards the club, and I make my way back to the flat.

As soon as I get into the flat, I head to the bathroom and turn on the shower. Goosebumps coat my skin and I rub at my arms, quickly stripping out of my clothes and stepping under the stream of hot water. Steam quickly fills the bathroom as scented bubbles slide down my legs and swirl down the drain.

Refreshed and still smiling, I turn off the water and dry myself with the warm, fluffy towels Dan and James always buy. I wrap the towel around my flushed skin and drag a brush through my hair. A gust of cold air engulfs me as I open the door to the living area and quickly walk into the kitchen to turn on the kettle.

There's a knock at the door, figuring it's one of the boys I rush across the kitchen, mug-in-hand and throw open the door.

"Hello, sugar," Echo drawls.

Screaming I drop the mug and it hits the floor and smashes at my feet. "Echo?" I gasp, throwing myself into his arms and kissing him. The moment my skin touches his, the unsettled feeling I've had since I got into the taxi a week ago finally calms.

He's frozen beneath me, and pulling back, I look questioningly into his eyes. "Echo, what's the matter?"

"Why don't you tell me, sugar?" he asks darkly. His voice is hard and angry, and lifting me from his arms, he walks into the flat and stands menacingly in front of me. Fury is vibrating from him, his back ramrod straight, his fingers are clenched into tight fists.

“Echo, what’s going on?” I ask. I don’t understand. I’m so happy to see him I want to throw myself at him and tell him how much I love him, how much I’ve missed him. But Echo doesn’t look pleased to see me. He doesn’t look like he’s in love. Right now, all he looks angry.

Echo’s mouth twitches into a sardonic grin. “You tell me, Livvy. You fucking run from me. I travel half the fucking world to find you, and when I do, you’re all over another guy,” he snarls.

Stunned, I open my mouth to speak but no words come out.

“Is that what this was all about? You decided you wanted to be with some pussy from back home?” Echo growls, his dominant presence filling the small flat.

Shaking my head, I stand and move until I’m directly in front of him. “Echo, I don’t know what you’re talking about.”

Towering over me, he shouts, “Bullshit, Livvy. I saw you tonight with that guy. He had his arms all over you.”

Confused, I stare at Echo and search my mind for what he might have seen. When it dawns on me, I almost laugh. “Was I with two guys? A blond and a redhead?”

“What the fuck, Livvy? One cock not enough, so you need two now?” he roars.

Anger flows through me, and I slap Echo across the face, gasping in shock as pain pulses through my palm.

Echo’s eyes darken and his arms snap out and lift me into the air. Spinning, he pushes me over the back of the sofa, my arse high in the air as he rips the towel from me, leaving me completely naked.

"Echo, what are you doing?"

"Fucking reminding you who owns this pussy and this ass and you," he yells.

Shuddering in anticipation, I wiggle, urging him to touch me.

Echo inhales audibly. "Fuck, sugar. I take it those pussies have no idea how to keep you satisfied? Even two of them can't make you feel how I do," he rasps, his voice pained.

His huge palms lands against my arse with a loud smack, and I mewl in painful delight. "Echo," I cry.

"What? You got something to say? Say it now, 'cause in a minute, I'm gonna be spanking your ass so hard you won't be able to speak."

"Oh god," I moan.

"No, not God, sugar. Your man. This is why I won't let you leave me, Livvy. You belong to me, and I refuse to let anyone else have you," he snarls, his voice is hard and unyielding.

"Never. I'll never want anyone else," I promise.

"That's good. Because I was stupid to allow you to run this time, Olivia. That won't ever happen again." He spreads my arse cheeks wide, and his hot tongue licks a path from my arsehole straight down to my pussy before finding my clit and sucking punishingly.

His palm smacks down onto my arse again and again,

releasing all of his anger, fear, and frustration against my skin. The pain morphs into a burn that heats my flesh till it vibrates.

He stops unexpectedly, and I arch my back, searching for his punishment.

"God, that's a fucking beautiful shade of pink, sugar. You fucking love it. Even when your skin's heated, you still want more. Is this how they make you feel? Do you crave their control? Do you beg to be dominated by them?"

Shaking my head, I try to deny his words, to tell him that they're my friends, not my lovers, but sensation overwhelms me and the need for his touch takes the words from me.

"Did they steal that virgin ass from me, Livvy? Did one of those pussies push his small dick into that untouched hole?" Echo snarls.

Shaking my head I turn to look over my shoulder and lock eyes with him, imploring him to believe me.

"Good. 'Cause it's mine. My cock's gonna be the first one buried so deep inside your asshole it feels like you're splitting in two," he says, his voice a delicious promise.

Shuddering, I beg him with my eyes. I beg him to take me, to own me. Echo shakes his head. "No, I say when. Now I'm gonna fuck you and then cover you in my cum. I'm gonna rub it all over every inch of you, so you're branded deep into your skin with my scent."

Nodding frantically, I roll onto my back and spread my legs wide. He bends down until his face is level with my pussy and looks at me. "Fuck, Livvy. You're gushing, and I haven't touched you yet. I can't wait to see your pussy soaked with my seed," he groans.

"Please," I beg.

Unbuckling his belt, he pushes his jeans and they drop to the floor. His hard cock pops free, and I groan with desperate need. "Hold your legs wide, sugar. I don't plan on being gentle with you."

I wrap my hands around my shins and spread my legs as high and wide as I can. His cock slams into me, almost pushing me back over the sofa and we both groan in unison.

His punishing thrusts force me over the edge, and I scream as my inner muscles clench and an orgasm ploughs through me. Pulling out of me, he climaxes, spraying long lines of cum over my stomach, breasts, and pussy.

Flipping me over, he slams back inside me again. Echo grabs a handful of my hair and yanks painfully. My back arches upwards, and I'm forced deeper onto his cock as he tightens his hold on my hair, grunting as he ploughs in and out. My pleasure builds quickly, and as he slides his thumb into my arse, I tense, screaming in pleasure.

"Fuck, Livvy, I can't wait to watch my cock slide into this ass. You're gonna love the burn. The pain mixed with pleasure will drive you fucking crazy." His voice pushes me over the edge, and I orgasm again. My body clenches before spasms overwhelm me and I twitch in pleasure with every slide of his cock.

Pulling his thumb from my arse he spreads my cheeks wide with his fingers, slips his cock from my pussy, and releases his cum all over my arse and back.

Drained and languid, I flop across the back of the sofa, my breath coming in exhausted bursts, as I wait for him to come to me. His fingers draw patterns across my skin, rubbing his cum into my flesh just as he promised. Stroking my pussy, he plunges two fingers inside of me. I moan at his invasion, but he ignores me and curls his fingers deep inside my abused pussy.

"You're gonna come again, sugar, and maybe again after that. Because I fucking own you and I say you will." He adds a third finger, filling me to capacity. "That's it, Livvy. I can feel your muscles pulsing around my hand. I'm gonna fuck you with my fingers, and I'm gonna tell you when to come. Do you understand, sugar?"

Managing to lift my head enough to nod, I see the approval in his eyes. My body melts into pure sensation, and all I feel is pleasure, as he moves his fingers within me.

"That's it. Now. Come for me," he orders. His thumb circles my clit, and I scream when the orgasm rips through me. My body shakes so violently, Echo wraps his arms around me to stop me from falling. I must pass out, because when I come to, I'm alone and lying on the sofa wrapped in a blanket.

NINETY

Echo

Sitting on the other side of the room, I watch her sleep. I'm filled with regret; my head slumped wearily into my hands.

I shouldn't have taken her like that. If she's really moved on with either or both of the guys I saw today, then she's not mine anymore. I won't fucking like it, but if that's what she wants, I'll learn to fucking deal with it.

I'm still fucking furious. I thought I could fuck the anger out, but taking her without her truly being mine has left me feeling hollow.

I should leave, let her get on with the life she chose. But I can't force myself to go.

As I watch she stirs and starts to wake up. Her beautiful body stretches like a cat's, slowly unfurling, her eyes blinking open. Bolting upright she scans the room, fear and pain etched across her face.

"Echo," she cries.

I rush towards her, and she wilts with relief when she sees me. Tears are running down her face and she launches herself into my chest, the impact knocking us both to the floor. With her head buried into my neck, she sobs, her chest shaking as she cries.

Wrapping my arms around her, I hold her to my chest. "Shhhh, sugar, it's okay," I soothe.

She pulls back from me and shakes her head. "It's not okay. Nothing's been okay since I left. I'm so sorry, Echo. I'm so sorry."

My palm flattens against her head. Her hair's still damp, but her wild curls are starting to pop up here and there. "Shhhh," I say.

"No, Echo. I shouldn't have left, but I didn't think you wanted me anymore. I freaked out and I left. I ruined us. I'm so sorry. Can you forgive me?"

Dejected, I sigh. "Livvy, this was my fault. I just got so consumed with my own guilt over you getting hurt. But if you've moved on, I'll deal with it. I'll leave you alone to get on with your life. I'm sorry about tonight. I should never have touched you like that if you're not mine to touch anymore."

Her small palms cup my cheeks, and her eyes look into mine. "I'm yours. You own me, remember? I'll always be yours, and I was coming back. I know I don't have much time left on my visa, but I'm booked on a flight back to Austin tomorrow night."

I scowl and hold her at arm's length. "So who the fuck are the guys you were all over, then?" I snap. She starts to speak, but the door opens and in walk the two fucking guys who are trying to steal my girl.

NINETY-ONE

Olivia

"God, Liv, put some fucking clothes on," James screeches, quickly closing his eyes and covering Dan's with his hands.

I'm completely naked and straddling Echo's lap. His face hardens and his eyes move from me to my best friends, a glimpse of uncertainty crossing his face as tries to understand what's going on.

"Echo, can I have your shirt? I'm kind of naked here," I say. His attention moves back to me and he quickly lifts me from his lap. Standing, he pulls his shirt over his head and drops it over my naked body. Shirtless, he crosses his arms across his chest, and I gulp as arousal washes over me again.

"Liv, are you decent?" James's voice pulls me away from

"Yes. You can stop freaking out now." I laugh.

Scoffing slightly, Dan pulls James's hand from over his eyes and both guys' heads dramatically turn to my half-naked biker.

Gawping slightly, James's mouth drops open before he slowly turns to me. "Liv, you lucky bitch."

Laughing, I turn to Echo, only to find angry eyes are on me. "Sugar, want to tell me what the fuck's going on here? 'Cause my mind's pulling up some pretty fucked-up thoughts and I'm about to lose my shit."

I pull in a panicked gasp and nod. "Echo, let me introduce you to James." I point to James and see the recognition dawn in Echo's eyes. He turns to me and I nod. "And this is Dan. His boyfriend."

All of the tension leaves Echo's body, and he pulls me in tightly against his chest.

James and Dan silently watch our exchange before turning to look at one another and bursting into laughter. Fighting my own laughter I snuggle against Echo's chest and scowl at the boys. "You pair are fucking arseholes. Stop laughing." My words only make them laugh harder, so reaching behind me, I pull a cushion from the sofa and throw it at their heads.

James sobers first, and tilting his head to the side, he assesses Echo. "I'm assuming you're Echo?" he asks. Echo nods, and releasing me with one arm, he reaches out, offering James a hand to shake.

James winces and pulls his hand back. “Easy there, tiger. Liv’s like a sister to me, so there’s no need to go all caveman on me.”

Sniggering, I slap Echo’s chest. “Play nicely. These boys are my best friends.”

Echo relaxes slightly, then says, “Didn’t you say you used to sleep with one of them?”

Dan sheepishly raises his hand. “Yeah, sorry, dude, that was me. But she totally turned me gay, and now I’m in love with a guy. No threat from me,” he says quickly.

A loud laugh bursts from me, and I fling another cushion at Dan’s head, hitting him in the face. “I did not turn you gay,” I shout.

Dan shrugs and smiles. “You kinda did, Liv. Sorry.”

Echo chuckles, and sits down on the sofa, lifting me into his lap. The guys settle on the opposite sofa, and we descend into an awkward silence. James clears his throat then speaks. “So, Echo, did Liv finally call you?”

Echo looks at me expectantly before turning back to James. “No, she didn’t. I got to Manchester three days ago.”

I gasp and swing around to gawp at Echo. “You’ve been here for three days and you only came here tonight?”

His fingers snap out and grasp my chin tightly. “I had no fucking clue where you were, sugar. You fucking disappeared, and I’ve been searching for you ever since. I saw you in the gardens tonight and followed you back here.”

Silence descends again, and Dan speaks, trying to lighten the tension. "You could have stayed in Texas, Echo. She was coming back tomorrow. Saved yourself the journey."

Echo audibly growls before turning to Dan. "When my woman decides to run, I'm gonna fucking chase. She's mine. I don't take that lightly."

Stunned, Dan's mouth drops open, but wisely he doesn't speak. James mumbles under his breath, "Bloody hell, that's hot."

Unsure what to say, I stay quiet and tense in Echo's lap.

James taps Dan's knee. "Right, I think it's time for bed. Are you guys staying here?" he asks.

"No." "Yes." Echo and I both speak at the same time. He ignores me and speaks to James. "No. I'm at a hotel around the corner. We'll come back in the morning for Livvy's stuff before we go home, if that's okay?" James nods, stunned by Echo's dominant tone.

"Get some clothes on, sugar, it's late," Echo orders.

Hopping up I disappear into the bathroom and dress, quickly returning to the living room where the boys in my life are sitting in awkward silence. Seeing me, Echo stands and closes the distance between us, cupping my chin and tilting my face up. His lips meet mine in a demanding kiss of ownership. "I need to make a phone call. I'll see you outside," he says, nodding once at the guys before leaving.

As soon as the door closes James wilts into the sofa

dramatically. “Bloody hell, Liv, is he like that all the time?”

I giggle and nod. “Pretty much.”

James laughs. “Do you guys have a *Fifty Shades* sort of ‘yes, sir’ thing going on? Because he’s so bloody intense, I wanted to do whatever he told me to do, and I’m not even fucking him. Christ, your fanny must be bloody dripping constantly.”

“James,” I gasp, shocked.

James eyes widen dramatically. “Liv, I’m serious. He’s insanely hot, and he’s got that controlled sexiness that makes you want to suck his cock all day just to get him to stroke your hair. How are you not bow-legged?”

Burying my face in my hands I giggle. “I don’t want to talk about this with you,” I say, my voice muffled.

“Come on, Olivia, spill. You have a BDSM thing going with him, don’t you?” James asks excitedly.

“No,” I cry.

“Liar, liar, pants on fire, Olivia Townsend,” James chants.

My cheeks are bright red with embarrassment and I move my hands from my face and look at James again, a wicked smile twitching at my mouth. “We don’t. I swear. I’ve never called him sir. But bloody hell, now I’m thinking about it and I kind of want to.”

James bursts into laughter. “Ha. You totally found a Mr Grey. You lucky bitch.”

Dan’s been quietly watching our conversation. “James, baby, you can call me sir later,” he says, biting his lip.

James winks at him. “Yes, sir.”

Groaning, I wince. “Ewww, I don’t want to hear that. I need to go. I’ll see you in the morning, okay?” The guys take it in turns to kiss me goodbye, and I leave, finding Echo waiting in the street.

He reaches out, and I take his hand. “Come on, sugar. I’m nowhere near finished with you yet.”

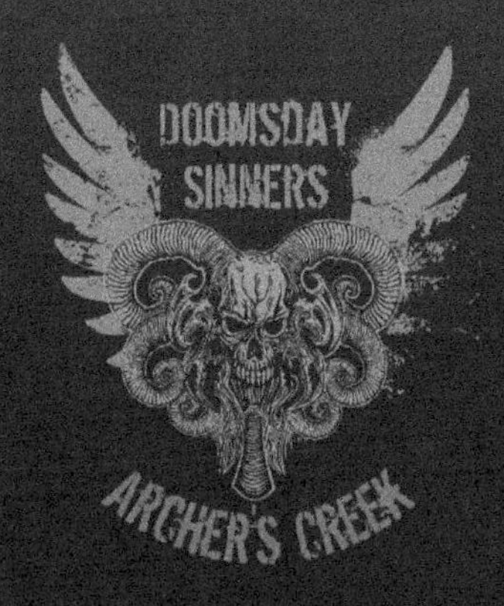

NINETY-TWO

Echo

I'm angry.

Taking Livvy settled the beast for a time, but the pain of her leaving me has bubbled to the surface again and I need to be alone with her. I should have realized that the two guys were a couple and the best friends she spoke about, but I was blinded by another man touching her and I couldn't see past that.

I pull Livvy behind me and walk quickly towards my hotel. A doorman opens the doors for us, never giving me a second glance as I drag my girl towards the elevators. "Echo, slow down," Livvy cries. The elevator doors slide open the moment I push the button, and I pull Livvy in behind me and stab at the button for the fifth floor.

"Echo," she shouts again.

Ignoring her, I wait for the elevator to stop, and silently pull her down the hallway until we reach my room. Unlocking the door, I push her inside and close it behind us. The moment the lock clicks into place a long breath escapes me, and my shoulders relax for the first time in days.

"Echo, what's going on?"

Dropping my chin to my chest I close my eyes and pull in a deep, calming breath. Once I'm reasonably calm, I look up to find Livvy's concerned face watching me.

"You ran," I say.

A pained look crosses her face. "I'm sorry."

I can't keep the anger out of my voice. "You planned to go. It wasn't a spur of the moment decision. You planned it. You packed all of your stuff and left me."

A tear runs down her cheek as she swallows visibly. "I'm sorry," she whispers.

I explode and all of my anger and fear and desperation bursts free from me. "Bullshit. What are you sorry for, sugar? You sorry for running away from me? You sorry for making me a fucking fool for thinking when you said you loved me it actually meant something? Or you sorry for being such a cold-hearted bitch that you could disappear and never look back? 'Cause a week ago, you couldn't give a fuck," I roar.

Shaking, she sinks to the floor, and I have to fight the instinct to go to her. When she speaks, her voice is quiet and full of tears. "I thought I was doing the right thing. I thought you just felt guilty. I couldn't stay with you when I was in love with you and you didn't even want me to touch you."

Livvy slowly rises to her feet, her voice gets louder and angrier. "You left me first. I got attacked. I was beaten and hurt, and I needed you. I needed you to make me feel whole again. I needed to know that you still wanted me, but instead you ignored me. So I left, because I couldn't stand living with you but being alone."

Toe to toe, I tower over her. There's so much we should have said before. If we had, none of this would ever have happened. So I let the anger and hurt that's pulsing through me overflow. "When you left, I broke, and I don't know how to fix that. I love you, Livvy. More than fucking life. You were hurt, beaten and cut. I couldn't let you touch me, 'cause every time you did, I wanted to claim you again, and I was terrified that you wouldn't see me. I was so fucking scared that you'd see him and that it would ruin us. I saw your fear. I watched you scream every night, fighting for your life in the nightmares that haunted your sleep," my voice cracks with emotion.

She's trembling, tears running down her face. "Wyatt and Mimi haunted my dreams because you weren't holding me in my sleep. I felt like the bruises and scars made me ugly to you. Every time you pushed me away, it was you telling me you didn't want me anymore. The last few weeks, I didn't see you. You became my jailer, not my boyfriend, and I couldn't live like that anymore. I felt like you were keeping me there out of guilt and a sense of responsibility. So I made a choice that I thought was the best thing for both of us. I was gonna have to leave eventually anyway, so I went before we started to hate each other." Her voice is barely above a whisper, but it's strong and clear.

My girl is standing in front of me, her back straight, fire shooting from her eyes and the rage and anger in her mirrors my own feelings. Grabbing her, I force my lips against hers, loving that her small hands grab my arms and desperately hold me to her. Ravishing her lips, I claim her anger, taking it with my own.

She suddenly pushes me away. Her lips are ripped from mine, and she screams in my face, "No!"

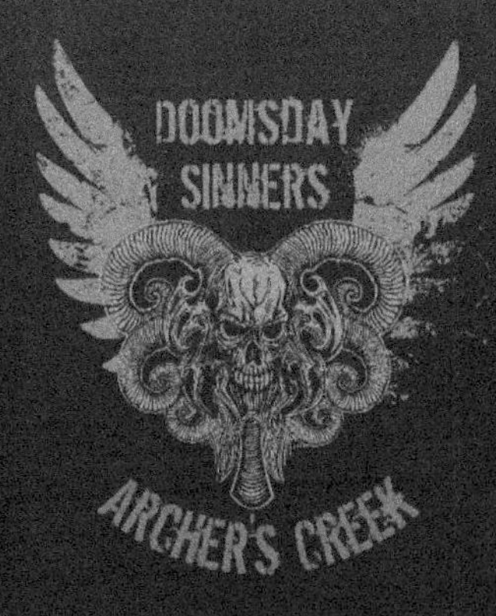

NINETY-THREE

Olivia

Echo stills immediately, and I step back and allow myself some distance. "We can't just have angry sex. We need to actually sit down and talk about this," I say, my voice hard.

Clearly fighting the urge to take control, Echo nods angrily and crosses the room to sit on the chair at the dressing table. I lift myself onto the bed and turn to face him, crossing my legs beneath me. "Can we try to talk without screaming at one another or ripping each other's clothes off?"

Echo scoffs lightly but nods. "We can try, but no promises," he drawls.

I smile and feel a blush heat my cheeks. "Do you want to start or shall I?"

Echo goes to speak but stops and closes his mouth before

opening it again. "I'm so fucking pissed at you. You ran from me. And my gut instinct is to spank your ass until you learn never to fucking run away again. Every controlling tendency you bring out in me is telling me to throw you over my shoulder and lock you in a room where you're safe and I don't have to worry about you disappearing again."

I shudder at his words, my mind consumed with filthy images.

"Sugar, you wanted to talk. I was down for the angry fucking. But if you carry on looking like your pussy's getting wetter by the second, I'm gonna have to fucking take you again. And that talk you want to have won't be happening for a while, you understand?"

Nodding I pull in a deep, cleansing breath, forcing my body to calm. "Sorry," I mutter. Echo's intense eyes watch me closely, and crossing my arms over my chest, I try to hide my hardening nipples.

Closing my eyes for a brief second, I wait for my body to calm. "I'm sorry for leaving, Echo. I know it was a stupid, impulsive choice that just made us both miserable. But all the guilt you were feeling is absurd. I can't live with the distance you put between us. We're physical. You touch me, you're bossy and controlling and nothing that I ever thought I'd want, but I crave your control. I love that you're unreasonable in your love for me. I love that you're intense and dominant, that you take charge of us. That's our dynamic. It works because it's what we both need, but if you take away all of the intimacy, and I'm not just talking about sex but everything, then what do we have left? I felt alone and lonely. I never want to feel like a guilty burden, and that's what I was."

"I'm sorry," he whispers sincerely.

My head snaps up, finding his earnest eyes looking back at me, and I know in this moment that what we have is stronger than both of our stupidity.

"I love you, sugar."

Sighing, I smile and walk to him, placing my hand on his stubbled cheek. "I love you too."

Standing, he lifts me, carrying me to the bed and lying down with me in his arms. I don't know how long we stay like that, entwined together, minutes, hours, but in the darkness, he reaches for my shirt and pulls it over my head. Unhurriedly we remove each other's clothes, rediscovering the others body until we're both naked. Our lips touch, gently caressing, our tongues stroking against one another, our kiss reaffirming the promises we made. That we belong to each other, that we're forever.

Echo's weight settles on top of me, and I squirm as his hard length rests against my sex. The kiss continues but never escalates, and desperate and aroused, I lift my hips and try to guide his cock towards my centre, but he pulls back.

"Livvy, you didn't want this to be about sex."

"I want you to claim me again. I missed you so much," I beg.

His lips dip to the hollow of my neck, and he licks my skin. "I love you, sugar."

Guiding his cock into my heat, I pull my knees up and wrap my legs around his back. He slides deeper, and I cry out as his penetration hits my sensitive inner walls. “God, I missed this. I love you,” I tell him again and again.

Echo’s eyes never leave mine as he slides in and out of me. His hands rest on either side of my face, and I feel all his concentration focussed on me. His pace increases, and our breaths change to panting. His hands move under my thighs, and he lifts my legs from behind his back, pushing them against my chest as he rocks into me.

Unlike earlier, it isn’t desperation or anger guiding us. It’s love, and the desire to reconnect. Our touches speak without words. We tell each other over and over that we love each other, that we missed each other, that we’re stronger together. This connection silently confesses that we’re each other’s futures, that we were meant to be and will fight to never be apart again.

I moan as he surges deeper. His movements become harsher, the strain showing on his face while he waits for my orgasm to build. Tipping his chin down, he circles my nipple with his tongue before pulling it into his mouth and biting gently. The hint of pain forces my orgasm to the surface, and I gasp as my body tenses and sensation flows over me. Echo’s lips connect with mine, and I swallow his groan as he climaxes, spilling his seed deep within me.

Finally at peace, I fall asleep with him still buried inside of me.

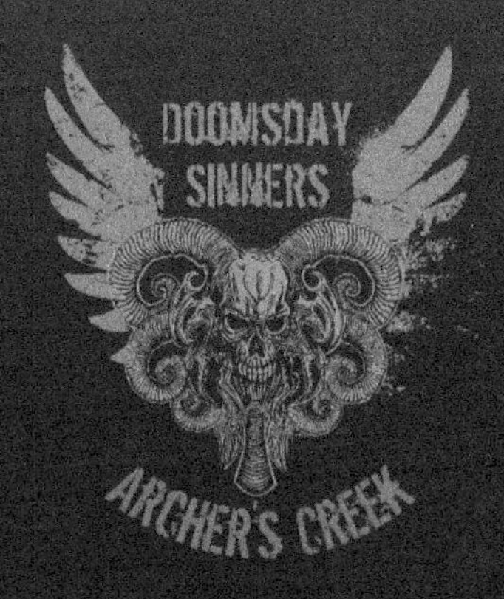

NINETY-FOUR

I wake up surrounded in Livvy. Her arms and legs are wrapped around mine, and her head rests against my chest. It's early, just after six, and the sunlight is starting to peek through the curtains.

Possessiveness barrels through me. This woman speaks to my baser urges, and I want to beat my fists against my chest and declare her my property.

Mine.

Carefully rolling her underneath me I lift her arms above her head. Dominant thoughts flow through me, and rolling onto my knees, I take in her perfect body. Her creamy skin begs to be bitten and licked. Her perky breasts tease me, her nipples pebbled and hard. Her pussy's wet with arousal and glistening in the beams of light that streak across her body.

Moving between her legs, I spread them apart and stare at her perfect sex, all wet and smooth. I can't resist any longer and drag my tongue along her parted folds. Goosebumps pepper her skin, and she shudders in her sleep. Addicted to her taste, I spread her wide and lick again, dragging as much of her juices onto my tongue as I can. Her eyes flicker open as shudders wrack through her, and she reacts to my touch before she's even fully awake.

"Echo?" she rasps, her voice full of sleep.

Crawling up her body I kiss her passionately. "Can you taste yourself on me, sugar?" I ask. Her tongue dips out to lick her lips before she smiles shyly and nods. "Do you like the taste of your pussy?"

Heat glistens in her eyes. "Yes."

"Hold onto the headboard. Don't let go. Do you understand?" I demand.

Her eyes widen in excitement before she nods. "Yes, sir." Her voice is quiet but full of desire.

"Sir?" I laugh. "Is that what you want, Livvy? Do you want me to take control?"

She nods. "Yes, sir," she says seductively, winking at me.

I smile. "This body belongs to me, Livvy. You took it away from me, and that made me incredibly angry. You're going to spend a lot of time on your knees with my cock in your mouth while I try to forgive you. Do you want to earn my forgiveness?"

Her eyes sparkle with desire, and she nods quickly.

"Good girl. I expect complete obedience. Do you think you can do that?" I ask playfully. A mischievously coy look crosses her face before she shakes her head. I laugh. "I don't think you can be obedient either. So perhaps we'll have to come to some kind of compromise. What do you think?"

She tilts her head to the side, "What kind of compromise?"

Suddenly, the playful atmosphere evaporates and our sexy game is forgotten. My voice is serious, and I realize I mean every word of what I'm about to say. "I need to take ownership of you, Livvy. I need to know you'll never run from me again."

Tears well in her eyes. "I promise I won't," she whispers.

"A promise isn't good enough." My voice sounds harder than I intended.

A single tear falls down her cheek. "Then—then what is?" she asks.

Gripping her chin with my fingers, I hold her face level with mine to ensure she hears and understands me. "You're going to marry me. You're going to promise till death do us part. Forever."

"Forever," she whispers. "Yes, I'll marry you."

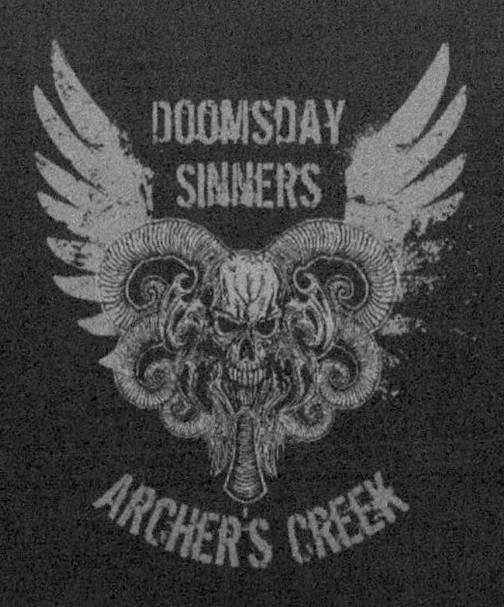

NINETY-FIVE

Olivia

Echo drags me into his arms and kisses me. "I love you, so fucking much," he says against my lips. A huge smile spreads across my face, and lifting my arms, I wrap them around Echo's neck.

"Ah-ah-ah, arms back above your head. What are those vows? Oh yes, to honor and obey. Time to start behaving like a good little wife," he says playfully.

Giggling, I lift my arms into the air and exaggeratedly wrap my fingers around the headboard. He leans forward and whispers, "I think I'm going to enjoy that particular vow. A lot. I'll honor your body every day, in every dirty way I can think of, and you can obey me." His lips touch mine, and deepening the kiss, he presses me into the bed. His tongue invades my mouth and owns the kiss, until I'm left panting, arching towards him and begging for more.

Hovering over me, his body is barely touching mine, but I moan when his hot breath scorches a path down my chest. "Fuck, sugar, I've missed that noise."

His gravelly voice vibrates straight to my clit, which pulses and throbs in response.

"Echo. Please," I beg. I feel him chuckling against my heaving breasts, then his hot tongue licks my erect nipple and I shudder.

"Patience, Livvy. I want to savour you," he warns.

Squirming, I close my eyes, tightening my grip on the headboard to distract myself. "Ow," I cry when his sharp teeth nip at my nipple. The pain turns to pleasure as it hums through my skin, and widening my legs, I wrap them around his hips, crossing my feet at the ankle. His cock pushes towards my sex, and he slides deep within me.

There's an exquisite pain as he stretches me to capacity. My back arches, and I surge upwards, groaning loudly.

"Mine. Forever. My Wife," he growls, his voice muffled where his head is buried against my neck. But I feel the importance of his words and warmth pulses straight to my core.

He rocks into me; each thrust deep but gentle.

He consumes my body, but not by force or dominance, by overwhelming my senses with words.

"You."

"Are."

"Mine."

"Never."

"Running."

"Again."

"Forever."

I brace my hands against the headboard and close my eyes. I hear every word and feel his vow behind them.

He's my forever. My husband. My life.

I try to speak, but a tide of sensation overwhelms me. An orgasm builds from nowhere, and I scream, wrapping myself around Echo and urging him deeper, until he tenses and releases deep inside me.

"I missed you," I say.

His body tenses at my words, and holding my breath, I bite my lip and brace myself for his anger. "You have no idea how much I missed you too," he replies.

Rolling onto his back he moves me until I'm lying on his chest, and sighs. "I'm still fucking pissed at you, Livvy. It's gonna take me some time to get past that."

I sit up and nod. "I know. I'm gonna give you so many 'I'm sorry' blowjobs," I say earnestly.

A loud laugh bursts from him. "Mmmm. I like the sound of that, sugar. But first we need to get you home, where you belong."

"Home," I say wistfully. Tears fill my eyes, but I blink them away. "I already have a ticket to Austin, so we need to see if we can get you on the same flight."

"The sooner the better, sugar," Echo murmurs.

I pause, unsure how to broach the subject of me returning to Archer's Creek without destroying the happiness we're both feeling right now. "Echo, I can't wait to go home with you, but I still only have a month left on my visa. I've been applying for jobs that will sponsor a visa for me, but it could be months or even years before I get one."

I expect Echo to tense and argue with me, but instead he shuffles up the bed, resting against the headboard, and I lie against his chest. "I promised you I would find a way for us to stay together, and I've been sorting it. The week we met, I applied for one of the companies the Sinners owns to sponsor a visa for you."

Blinking in shock, I'm unsure what to say. Echo cups my cheek, and his gaze locks with mine. "Even before I told you I loved you, I knew that you were *it* for me. I want forever with you, and I don't ever want us to be apart again," he says.

Lifting me from his lap, he places me on the bed and crosses the room, pulling on his jeans as he rummages in his bag. "I knew after a week together that you were mine and I was yours. I knew then that we belonged to each other, so I bought you this." He drops to his knees and opens a velvet box, revealing a stunning princess cut diamond.

My hands cover my mouth, and I gasp. Pulling my left hand

free, he slides the ring onto my finger. "I love you, and I want to marry you," he says, pressing a kiss to where his beautiful ring sits.

Throwing myself into his arms I kiss him passionately. Pulling back, I cup his face in my hands. "I love you too. So much."

Reaching into his back pocket, he pulls out some papers and hands them to me. "You might have doubted my feelings, Livvy, but I always knew. You're my forever. I had to pull a few strings to get it pushed through quickly, but I refuse to be without you again."

Cautiously, I unfold the paperwork. "Application for K-1 Fiancée visa," I read aloud. Confused, I look from the papers to Echo. "I don't understand, what does this mean?"

His smile is blinding. "You still have to have an interview, but it means that you can come home with me and we can get married. We can be together while we wait for your green card."

I walk into Echo's arms, tears streaming down my face. "You're mine, Echo. My forever, my happy ever after. I love you so fucking much."

Dragging him onto the bed I snuggle against his chest, my muscles slowly relaxing as I stare at the gorgeous ring on my finger. Bolting upright, I shout, "Oh shit. I need to try and get hold of my parents before we leave and let them know we're engaged."

"Engaged. I fucking hate that word. I don't want to be

fucking engaged to you. I want you as my wife," he grumbles.

I laugh and slap his chest lightly. "I know we're getting married, but that's not gonna be for a while. I need to tell my parents before the actual wedding."

Echo rolls quickly, pinning me beneath him. Holding my wrists down, he spread my legs with his knees and settles between them. "Listen here, sugar. I told you we're getting married, and we are. You want to get married in church, then I'll speak to the preacher when we get home. If not, Brandi can help you put something together at the club. But either way, you're gonna be my wife as soon as possible." His voice is a demanding growl, and I roll my eyes at him.

"Echo, that's insane."

"Enough!" he shouts. I freeze. "Enough, Livvy. You said forever, and that's how it's gonna be. We're getting married as soon as possible. You want your parents to come, then I'll fly them in. But there will be nothing that'll stop me from claiming you completely. And I mean nothing, Livvy."

Fire burns in his eyes, and I truly see the pain I've caused him. I love him, and I want to be with him for the rest of my life. It doesn't matter if I marry him today or in ten years' time. But it matters to him.

I pull at my arms and he reluctantly frees me. "I want to marry you. I want forever with you. I want to wear a white dress and get married in a garden. None of the other details are important," I whisper.

Echo kisses me, and we lose ourselves in a perfect moment in time, the only two people in the world, happy, in love, and going home to start our forever.

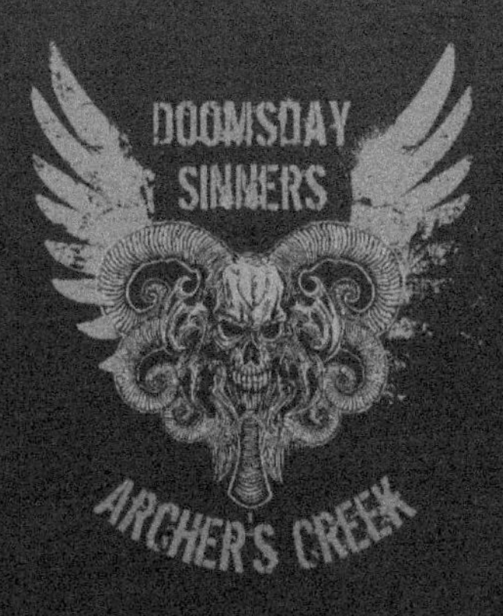

NINETY-SIX

Echo

I fucking hate airplanes. I'm too fucking big for the seats, and the food always tastes like crap.

The only good thing about this flight is that my woman's asleep in my lap. The moment the seatbelt light went off, she crawled into my arms and fell asleep.

I can't wait to get her home and marry her.

I want to tie her to me in every way. I want to give her my name so everybody in the fucking world knows she's my wife. Mine.

The need to brand her is worse than ever. She's run from me once, and I refuse to let her run again. I'm still so fucking angry at her. I'm hoping this rage I'm feeling will die down when she's sleeping in our bed every night and wearing my ring.

Glancing down, I smile at the huge diamond on her finger that glistens in the light. Fuck, my chest swells every time I look at it on her finger.

We're getting married as soon as fucking possible. I'd do it tomorrow, but she still needs to have her visa interview and she wants a dress and a garden. All I want is her as my wife. I want to start our life together without a timer hanging over our heads, so the sooner I legally tie her to me the better.

My mind flashes back to the conversation she had with her parents before we left the UK.

Livvy's fidgeting in the chair, watching the laptop as her fingers twist nervously in her lap. The screen flashes to life, and two older people appear on the screen. Livvy's smile is wide, and I instantly see her resemblance to them.

"Mum, Dad. It's so good to see you. How's Russia?" she asks.

Her mum smiles widely before replying. "Olivia, darling, you look serene." Barely pausing for breath, she launches into a conversation without letting Livvy get a word in. "We left Russia about two weeks ago, and we're in Latvia now. I'm sure I sent you an email with our new location. Latvia's such a devastatingly beautiful country, and Daddy and I just felt drawn to it. We just jumped in the camper and drove straight here. We found this amazing commune where you can camp for free as long as you help tend the gardens. They grow the most fantastic weed here, and Daddy and I have been helping to harvest the pla—"

"Mum!" Shouting loudly, Livvy interrupts her mum, who

pauses mid word. “Mum, I’d like you to meet someone. Mum, Dad, this is Echo.” She turns towards me, and I nod to her parents. “Echo, this is my mum, Ruth, and my dad, Neville.”

Neither looks intimidated by my tattoos or biker cut. They simply smile brightly at me. Livvy nudges me, and smiling briefly, I speak. “It’s a pleasure to meet you both.”

Neville leans forward and finally addresses his daughter. “Princess, you look beautiful. I love your hair like that, all wild and free. I always hated when you ironed it. Are you okay?”

Livvy beams at her father, blushing at his praise. “Hi, Daddy. I’m perfect. We have something to tell you.”

“What’s that, princess?” her father asks.

Livvy takes a deep breath and then says, “Echo asked me to marry him, and I said yes.”

Ruth pushes Neville back and moves in front of the camera. “Oh Olivia, how wonderful. Are you pregnant, sweetheart?” her mother asks excitedly.

Rolling her eyes, Livvy sighs. “No, Mum, I’m not pregnant. There are other reasons to get married, not just a baby.”

Ruth visibly sags. “Oh well, never mind. I got quite excited, thinking I was getting a grandchild.”

“Daddy,” Livvy says. Neville moves forward again, and blowing out a ring of smoke, he passes a lit joint to Ruth, who inhales deeply. “Daddy, could you just listen to me for a minute and get stoned later?” Livvy asks, obviously frustrated.

Neville nods silently, his eyes starting to glaze and gradually closing. "It's a natural experience, princess, you really should try it sometime. I can give you the number of our dealer at home if you want," he slurs.

Livvy rolls her eyes. "I think two stoners in the family is plenty, Daddy," she says sarcastically. "So we're getting married as soon as we can, in the next few weeks in Texas. Do you think you and Mum could fly out for the wedding?"

A smug grin slowly stretches across Neville's face. "God, this is good shit. The Latvians really know how to cross-pollinate," her father murmurs. Frustration shows on Livvy's face before she finally shouts, "Daddy. The wedding, can you come?"

Neville's eyes close, and he leans away from the camera.

"Mum. The wedding?" Livvy cries.

Ruth focuses on the camera before pulling in a deep drag of the joint. "Oh no, dear. There's no way we can leave Europe at the moment. I had an epiphany, sweetheart. Did I tell you? This vision came to me one night, and we're needed here. No, sorry. There's absolutely no way we can go to America."

"I'm your only daughter and I'm getting married, and you can't come because you had a dream!" Livvy shouts.

"No, dear. Not a dream, a vision," her mother answers.

Livvy sighs deeply, her shoulders sagging, and pulling her into my lap, I address her parents. "Sir, ma'am, Livvy would like you to come to the wedding. I'd be happy to pay for your airfare from Latvia to Texas and back again," I say.

Her mother smiles serenely. "Echo, please call us mum and dad. It's not about the money. It's the vision. Olivia will tell you I'm a very spiritual person, and if this vision came to me, then this is where we need to be."

I start to speak, but Livvy interrupts me. "It's fine, Mum. I'll send you some pictures, and I'll try and video call again sometime next month."

Smiling, Ruth and Neville nod. "Lovely, dear. Oh, and, Echo, try doggy style. That's how I got pregnant with Olivia, and I'm sure it'll do the trick for you as well," Ruth says.

Livvy's cheeks burn red, and she quickly rushes to end the call. "Bye Mum, bye Daddy. I love you."

"Love you, darling," Ruth says.

"Bye, princess," her father calls.

Closing the laptop, she collapses against my chest. "So that's my parents."

Smiling down at the girl in my arms, I try to imagine what she would have looked like before she left to travel the States. She told me she's different now, but I can't imagine her being anything but the girl I've fallen in love with.

James and Dan plan to fly in for the wedding. I don't fucking like that she ran from me and straight to them, but they're her closest friends, so for her sake I'm gonna learn to put up with them. James grew up with her, but Dan is her fucking ex. I don't care that he's in love with another guy. I still want to smash my fist into his face simply because he's seen my wife naked.

The stewardess insists that Livvy has to sit in her own seat for landing, so I reluctantly lift her from my lap and fasten her seatbelt.

She wakes up just as the plane lands. “Perfect timing baby, we’re home.”

NINETY-SEVEN

Olivia

It takes forever to get through security. I have to answer questions about why I left the US before the end of my visa, and why I'm back again, but eventually we make our way out of the airport and into the stifling Texas heat. We took a train to London so we could take a direct flight back to Austin, so it's only a short cab ride back to Archer's Creek and home.

Before we left England, I packed up and shipped all of my stuff over to the US, so we don't have any luggage to collect, but it feels strange to fly somewhere without any bags. The bright Texas sunshine beams down on us, and pulling my sunglasses off, I tip my head back and bask in the heat.

Echo's arms wrap around my waist from behind, and his voice rumbles against my neck. "Come on, let's go home."

Nodding, I take Echo's hand and let him lead me away from the airport. We walk towards the car park, and I look at him in question. Smiling, he winks playfully. "Smoke and Park brought my bike over for me this morning," he says.

A huge smile spreads across my face, and I bounce up and down with excitement when the black and chrome of his bike appears as we turn a corner. The Harley's still huge and scary, but it looks amazing shining in the sunlight. "Hop up, sugar," he says, handing me my helmet.

Taking his hand, I throw my leg over the seat, climbing on behind him and wrap my arms tightly around his waist as the bike roars to life. Echo pulls away and accelerates towards the highway as I squeal in exhilaration. The wind rushes past my face, and snuggled into Echo's back, I silently watch the world go by. Mile by mile the road passes us, until we pull onto a back street sheltered by a copse of trees.

"Why are we stopping?" I ask, confused.

Echo smiles at me for a moment; then his face deadpans. "I think it's time to collect on one of those apologies, sugar," he says, fighting to keep his face stern.

Closing my eyes briefly, I smile. "Oh, do you?"

"Yes ma'am. On your knees. I want to feel that hot mouth of yours around my cock," Echo drawls. I drop to my knees and smile up at him before unzipping his jeans and pulling out his cock. Circling the head with my tongue, I suck him into my mouth, swallowing him as deeply as I can. I pull back and release him with a pop.

“Is that what you want?” I ask, as I look up at him from my position on the floor. His eyes harden; one hand cups my chin whilst the other grabs a handful of my hair. He squeezes till I open my mouth then pushes two fingers inside.

“Suck,” he snarls. It’s an order, and I instantly comply. “That’s it, Livvy, now open up.” I open my mouth, and he removes his fingers and plunges his cock right to the back of my throat.

My tongue wraps around his length, and I hollow my cheeks and suck enthusiastically. “Fuck, I love the way you suck my cock. Your mouth’s so hot and wet. I can’t wait to come right down your throat,” he groans.

His fingers tighten in my hair and the hint of pain pulls a groan of pleasure from the back of my throat. Guiding my movements, he fucks my face till his cock swells inside my mouth. His hot, salty cum pours down my throat, and I swallow as fast as I can.

Panting hard, Echo pulls his cock from my mouth and I sit back on my heels, wiping the drops of sticky liquid that escaped from my lips. “God, Livvy, you’re fucking perfection,” he says reverently, pulling me to my feet and kissing me, tasting his release on my tongue.

Reluctantly he ends our kiss, carefully tucking a strand of hair behind my ear. “Come on, let’s go home. I need you in our bed.”

I see the cars outside our house the moment we pull into the street and there's a banner covering the front porch. 'Welcome Home Liv' is written in black with the Sinners' logo filling in the gaps. "Oh my god," I cry.

"This is how the club welcomes home one of its own. You're a Sinner now," Echo says.

Killing the engine, he kicks the bike onto its stand and climbs off. Grabbing me, he lifts me over the saddle and then stands behind me, his arms wrapped around my waist. "You didn't just leave me, sugar. You're a part of the club, and they missed you too."

Tears pool in my eyes, but pulling in a breath, I blink them away. "I missed them all too. I didn't realise how much I had here until I didn't have it anymore," I say, swallowing the lump of emotion in my throat.

I feel him kiss the top of my head, and then his arms release me. "Come on, let's go say hello to everyone and then tell them to leave so I can fuck you senseless in our bed."

Echo opens the front door and holds it for me to walk through. The hall's empty, but I can hear voices in the lounge room at the back of the house. I slowly walk down the hall and brace myself for the reaction to my return. I've missed them all, but I'll understand if they're still angry with me.

"Liv." Brandi's scream is quickly followed by her barrelling into me and hugging me tightly. "Liv. You're here. I'm so glad you're back."

Releasing me, she pulls back, and I can see the tears in her eyes. “God, Brandi, I missed you too,” I say as my own tears start to fall.

Her eyes lock with mine, begging me. “Please don’t leave again,” she says.

“I won’t. I promise,” I say solemnly.

Brandi nods then slings her arm around me and pulls me into the room full of bikers. Several sets of eyes turn to me, then to Echo as he moves behind me, sheltering me with his body.

Sleaze moves forward and pulls me into a tight hug, kissing the top of my head quickly. “Welcome back, Liv. Don’t fucking run off again,” he orders. His reprimand makes me feel like a naughty child, and my gaze drops to the floor in shame. He steps back, dragging Brandi into him, his hand wrapped around the back of her neck. My eyes lift and connect with Brandi’s and she winks at me conspiratorially.

The bikers all approach one by one. Smoke, Park, Puck, and Blade all hug me and welcome me back. All four tell me off for running away, before their eyes move to Echo and silently communicate something.

Daisy walks over to me, and I’m unsure what his reaction is going to be. Before I left, we had a strange relationship. Daisy’s a prospect, which means he’s not a fully patched-in Sinner, and so he got most of my babysitting duties. He pissed me off because he refused to speak to me, so I’d spent a lot of time talking at him hoping to provoke him into answering.

As soon as I'm within arm's reach, he pulls me into his body and hugs me tightly. Shocked, I freeze in his embrace with my arms hanging at my side. "Fuck, Liv. You scared the shit out of me," Daisy snarls. He steps back and my mouth drops open in shock.

"You spoke to me," I gasp.

Laughing, his hand going up to the stubble on his cheek. "Fuck, I'm not a mute. I just don't want Echo to beat the crap out of me for saying something stupid."

Spinning to Echo I raise my eyebrows in question, but he just shrugs in response. The amusement in Daisy's face fades and his eyes narrow. "Don't you fucking dare run off like that again, Liv. It was fucking stupid. Your man over there needs to take you over his fucking knee and spank some sense into you. But hear this, sweets, we've all got our eye on you. You're a part of the club now, and we won't lose you again." Pulling me to him, he kisses my forehead, only releasing me when Echo growls.

Gus waits patiently in the back of the room, his calm, grandfatherly presence out of place in a room full of bikers. Cautiously, I approach him, fidgeting with my hands while I wait for his reaction. His eyes soften when they land on me, and he pulls me into his arms the moment I'm close enough. "Young lady, you're a sight for sore eyes," he says softly.

"Hi, Gus."

Pulling away from me, anger hardens his face. "Don't you

'hi, Gus' me, Olivia. I'm so angry with you. Do you know how worried we were when you ran off? I'm so disappointed. If you needed help, why didn't you come to me instead of just disappearing? I'm too old to be losing years off my life with worry."

Thoroughly reprimanded, I stare at my fingernails. "I'm sorry. I know it was the wrong thing to do, but at the time it felt like the only option. I missed you, Gus. I really hope you can forgive me," I say, as a fresh batch of tears runs down my cheeks.

"Oh, sweetheart. Of course I forgive you. Just promise me you won't run off again."

I nod quickly and agree, "I promise. This is my home. I'm not going anywhere."

The gathering of people quickly escalates into a raucous party. Anders, the club president, arrives with the rest of the bikers and a truck full of beer. Echo keeps me in his lap or held against his chest. On the rare occasion that he has to leave me, Daisy takes up guard position. I'm obviously still considered a flight risk, and it's gonna take time for them to trust me again.

Fire pits are lit in the garden, and we move outside and settle into mellow groups around the flames. Echo sinks into an Adirondack chair, and I snuggle into his arms. Brandi sits at Sleaze's feet with her head resting in his lap. His hand strokes her hair absentmindedly, and I watch as her eyes flutter closed. Relaxed, I sink further against Echo's chest; the rhythmic movement of his breathing lulling me to sleep.

"Livvy," Echo softly calls. My eyes flutter open as he places me onto our bed. The pillows are soft and comfortable underneath me, and stretching contentedly, I close my eyes again. "No. No. No, Livvy. You can sleep in a while," Echo says, stripping my clothes from me before crawling up my body and kissing me breathless.

Fully awake, I squirm when his hot tongue licks a path down my neck to my pebbled nipples. His eyes meet mine before his teeth wrap around the peak and bite down. The sting of pain intensifies when his teeth sink further into my skin, but just before it becomes overwhelming, his teeth release me and his wet mouth soothes the burning tip.

"Who do you belong to, Livvy?" he asks, biting down on the other nipple. I moan, unable to speak. "Uh-uh. That's not the right answer, sugar," he drawls. Tugging on my nipple with his teeth, he stretches it, and I hiss at the sharp sting of pain.

Releasing me, the blood rushes back to the tip and searing pain roars to life, morphing into a burn of delicious pleasure. Echo moves down my body until his face is level with my sex. "Spread your legs wide, sugar," he orders. I pull my legs apart and Echo's approving groan has me gushing with arousal. "Fuck yeah, Livvy. Just look at that pussy. So wet and pink. Just begging for me to play with it."

His tongue swirls around my clit, and my back arches, searching for more friction.

"Who do you belong to, Olivia?"

The answer dies in my mouth when his lips seal over my clit, sucking harshly.

"I didn't hear you, sugar. Do you need to be reminded who you belong to? I know you love a good reminder, don't you? Roll onto your belly and get your ass in the air."

Shuddering in anticipation, I comply, pushing onto my knees with my arse held high in the air and my chest resting on the bed. "Good girl. Now, who do you belong to?" he taunts.

"You," I reply.

His hands caress my arse cheeks, stroking them and then spreading them slightly. "That's right. I own you, body and soul."

I jump as cool liquid runs down the crease of my arse.

"What are we?" he asks, circling the lube over my tight hole.

"Forever," I gasp.

"That's right, Livvy. We're forever. Now don't move. I'm gonna make this so good for you," he growls. Dipping his fingers into my pussy, he thrusts deeply before pulling out and moving up to my arsehole, making me shudder as his thumb probes at the tight band of muscles. "It's okay, sugar. I'm gonna stretch you out as much as I can, but when I get my cock in there, it's gonna hurt to start off with, okay?"

I nod and shudder in fear and anticipation, feeling the pressure as he presses against the tight hole. Slowly, his finger breaches the muscle and sinks inside me. Instinctively, I push back on his fingers, moving him deeper into me.

His hand slaps stingingly down on my arse cheek. “Who’s in charge, Livvy?” he demands.

I respond immediately. “You are.”

His finger pulls out and then pushes back in, and I sigh at the feeling of fullness. Pulling out completely, he quickly pushes against the muscle with two fingers, sinking back inside me, as I hiss at the slight burn.

“Fuck, Livvy. Your ass is gonna strangle me. I can’t fucking wait to see my cock disappear inside you for the first time.” His voice is a pained rasp. Groaning, I push back against his hand as he stretches his fingers apart within me. Pushing a third finger inside my arse he starts to fuck the tight hole, slowly sliding in and out of me, spreading his fingers and stretching the constricted muscle. His fingers leave my arse, and I push back towards him, hating the empty feeling he’s left behind.

“Fuck, I’m gonna be as gentle as I can. It’s gonna hurt so good, sugar, I promise.”

“Please.” I beg, watching over my shoulder, fascinated as he pours lube into his hands and coats his cock till it’s glistening. Lining it up against my arsehole, he starts to push against the puckered band of muscle. The head gradually sinks inside of me, and I whimper at the burn.

“You okay? The head’s nearly in, then it won’t hurt as much,” he promises. I nod and push back against his intrusion. “Play with your clit,” he rasps.

Reaching underneath my body, I connect with my clit and quickly start to rub the mound of nerves. Echo pushes slowly into me, until his cock is seated deep inside of me. Leaning forward, he gently kisses my spine. "I love you, Livvy."

"I love you too."

When he pulls back, his cock slides against my internal walls, and I mewl with pleasure. "Oh god." My orgasm hits like an explosion, and stars fill my vision. Echo moves in and out of me, prolonging my pleasure with every push and pull of his cock. After two more thrusts, I orgasm again. Sensation splinters from me, and my skin tingles, beginning at the centre of my torso out to my fingers and toes.

His cock slams into me one final time, Echo tenses and climaxes on a groan, spilling his seed deep inside me before collapsing onto my back. Slowly pulling out, he rolls to the side and drags me against him.

"I love you. I can't wait to make you my wife," he says, wrapping his arms tightly around me.

I smile and turn my head for a brief kiss before sleep drags me under.

***

Echo wakes me up by rolling on top of me and nibbling on my nipple. His wet tongue laves at the sensitive tip, and heat starts to pool in my stomach. The doorbell calls out, and Echo groans loudly. Lifting his head from my breast he kisses me quickly on the lips. "Time to get up, sugar. You've got a wedding to plan," he says brightly.

I groan and roll onto my side, pulling the cover back over my body. Echo rips it off me and smacks my bare arse.

"Echo, you bastard," I scream, hearing him chuckle as he leaves our bedroom and goes downstairs to open the front door.

"Liv, get up, we need to find you a dress," Brandi shouts as she thunders up the stair and into the room.

"I'm jetlagged," I grumble, reluctantly dragging myself into the shower while Brandi yells at me to hurry up.

"Come on, Liv, we need to find a dress and get everything else sorted today if you're gonna get married in the next month. When's your interview with the visa people?"

"It's next week. I don't know how Echo managed to get it pushed through so quickly, but I love the fact that I could have a visa by the end of the month." Rubbing my hair with a towel, I open the wardrobe, expecting it to be almost empty. Instead, there are hangers full of clothes. "What the fuck? Where the hell did all these clothes come from?"

Brandi walks over to me and pulls a vintage style band vest and a pair of denim shorts from the rail. She throws them at me and pulls the doors shut. "Who cares? Just get dressed so we can go," she snaps. I laugh at her impatience, but still dress quickly and let her drag me from the room.

Walking over to Echo, I stand on my tiptoes, and kiss him.

Quickly taking control, his lips dominate mine as his hands caress my arse.

"Where did all the clothes come from?" I ask.

"Remember that day we went shopping? I had someone grab some of the things you liked but wouldn't let me buy you. They got delivered just after the attack, and I forgot about them."

A soft smile covers my face, and reaching for him, I pull him in for another kiss. "I love you," I say.

"Love you too, sugar," he says, slapping my arse lightly as he grabs his cut and pulls it on.

"Are you coming dress shopping with us?" I ask.

"No, baby. Daisy will be here in a minute in the new car I bought you. He's gonna go to the mall with you, but I'll be here when you get back."

"Why can't we take your truck?" I ask.

Echo grabs me by the arse and pulls me into his chest, grinding his cock against me. "You can drive my Chevy whenever you want, but the new car is the safest on the market, and I figured you'd want something with a few more mod cons."

"But I love the truck," I pout.

Collaring my neck, he leans close and whispers into my ear. "Time to practice that obeying, my stubborn fiancée."

I shudder at his hot breath on my cheek and nod briefly. "Okay," I acquiesce.

Surprise and then suspicion show on Echo's face. I'm pulled into his arms again, and his fingers grip my chin. "What's going on, sugar? You're not arguing about the new car or Daisy going with you. What the hell are you up to?" he snarls.

"If I argue, are you going to let us go on our own, or take your truck?" I ask.

"Hell fucking no," he shouts.

"So what's the point of me arguing then? I don't think I'm in any danger, but you do. I'm not ready to talk about you buying me a car. But if Daisy following me makes you feel better, then I'll stop moaning about it," I say with a shrug.

His arms wrap under my legs, and he lifts me onto the kitchen counter. His hard cock pushes against my sex, and I groan before he swallows the sound in a passionate kiss. "God, Livvy, I want to fuck you so bad right now. I want to lay you back against the counter and slam inside you. I want to hear you screaming my name."

My eyes fall shut, and I lose myself in the sensation of his words.

Brandi's voice breaks the spell. "Oh for god's sake, Echo. Fuck her later once we've found her a wedding dress."

Turning his angry eyes on Brandi, he reluctantly releases me. Seizing the opportunity, she quickly ushers me away from Echo, steering me toward the front door. I glance at him over my shoulder, but he just laughs when I flash him my sulky face, his mouth breaking into a wide smile.

"Have fun, ladies. There's a credit card in your purse Livvy. Brandi, make sure she uses it," he orders.

Brandi lifts her fingers to her head, saluting Echo before she walks me out the front door.

NINETY-EIGHT

Echo

I woke up in my bed, in my house, with my woman naked in my arms.

Fucking bliss.

Bringing my coffee cup to my lips, I watch Daisy drive away with the girls in the SUV I bought for Livvy. It's the safest one on the market, and even though she loves my truck, I'm happier with her in the new car.

The ride to the clubhouse flies by, and I park in front of the building and walk inside. Heading through the bar, I acknowledge all of the greetings from my Sinners brothers, pausing for a moment outside the Prez's office, before knocking.

"Come in," a voice calls. Anders is sitting behind his large desk, and when I enter, he rises, walks towards me, and pulls me in for a hug. “I’m so glad you managed to track down that old lady of yours. I suggest you don’t lose her again,” he says, smiling.

I laugh and nod. “Never gonna happen, Prez. She’s planning the wedding with Sleaze’s old lady right now, and I intend to shackle her to me as soon as possible. Your guy in immigration really came through, she’s got her interview next week, and he doesn’t think there’ll be a problem getting her visa approved.”

Anders slaps me on the back and chuckles before moving back behind his desk. “No problem, brother. A good woman like Olivia is hard to find. I’m glad it’s all working out for you both. Take a seat, the others will be here any minute.”

I sit in one of the large chairs that circle in front of his desk. A knock at the door signals the arrival of Blade, Puck, Sleaze, and Park. Anders gestures to the chairs. “Brothers, have a seat.” The guys file in and sit down; we all wait as Anders leans forward over his desk, his hands steepled together in front of him.

“So what’s the news on Mimi? That old bitch must have poked her head out of whatever hole she’s been hiding in by now,” he says.

Puck speaks up. “She finally withdrew some cash from a bank in Austin the day before yesterday. We’ve got most of the club searching for her, but so far there’s been no sign of her. I pulled the video footage of her at the ATM, and she looks like a fucking psycho.”

Anders brightens before speaking again. “So she’s back

near Archer's Creek. She'll come home sooner or later. We need to keep someone on the guest house so we can grab her the moment she surfaces," he orders.

Sleaze speaks, his gruff voice laced with anger, "I've got two guys taking shifts outside the guest house. I can't wait to end this fucking nightmare and deal with her crazy ass." Five grunts of agreement sound in the small office.

Anders runs his hand over his face. "Who knew we'd be hunting down a crazy woman in her sixties? That's a fucking new one, eh? If we can, we hand her over to the police in one piece, but I don't think anyone would complain if the old bitch became collateral damage."

Once the meeting is over, we all file out of Anders office and into the bar. Sleaze's phone rings, and he answers it. As he listens, a frown pulls at his face and he nods then ends the call and turns to me. "Fucking Mimi's vanished again. The guys watching her house haven't seen her, and she hasn't used her cards again or made a single phone call," he growls angrily.

Enraged and frustrated, I stalk through the bar and kick open the door. Mimi's gone, and fuck knows how long it will be till she surfaces again. She doesn't have any other family. She doesn't have any friends.

All I do know is that my girl isn't safe until that bitch is either dead or behind bars.

NINETY-NINE

Olivia

I find my dress in the first shop we go into. Simple, white, and perfect. The summer dress is a floaty dream of chiffon with Grecian-style plaited straps that wrap underneath my breasts.

Brandi helps me plan a simple service. The ceremony will take place in the meadow behind the clubhouse, under an archway of ivy and wildflowers. We'll take our vows, then celebrate with a family-style barbecue and music courtesy of the fantastic band that plays at Strikers. James and Dan will arrive the night before the wedding, and then I'll marry the man I love surrounded by the important people in my life.

There's just one thing left to do.

Standing on Gus's porch, I lift my hand and force myself to knock. The lump in my throat pushes tears into my eyes, but I refuse to let them fall and force them down while I wait for Gus to answer his door.

I see him coming down the hall, the door inches open, and then he's revealed. "Olivia, is everything okay?"

I nod. "Yes, it's fine. I actually have something to tell you and a favour to ask," I say, biting at my lip nervously.

Concern fills Gus's eyes. "Okay. Should I be worried?"

I laugh and shake my head. "Echo asked me to marry him, and I said yes."

Old weathered hands cup my cheeks. "Congratulations, sweetheart. I'm sure you'll make each other very happy," Gus says, smiling widely.

"Thank you," I say, wiping a tear from my eye. "The favour I actually wanted to ask was about the wedding. My parents aren't coming, so I was wondering, well, hoping really, if you'd mind giving me away." I feel the slight shake in his fingers and watch as emotion passes over his face.

"Oh, sweetheart. I'd be absolutely honored," he says, his voice cracking with emotion.

***

I officially have a K-1 Fiancée visa, and it's two days till my wedding. Two days till I tie myself to Echo for the rest of my life. I'm not stupid; this is forever, and once I say "I do," I know he'll never let me run again.

I love him.

I love the life I have with him.

I love the family and friends I've found in this tiny town in the middle of nowhere, Texas.

Seated on the bar at Strikers, I chat to Brandi whilst she works. "Liv, when do your parents get here?"

Sighing deeply I swing my legs backwards and forwards. "They don't. My mum had a vision, and apparently that means they can't leave Latvia. Honestly, I think they're just bloody stoned and don't want to leave all the free weed."

"God, I love your parents." Brandi laughs.

I roll my eyes and scoff. "They're a bloody nightmare. Mum tried to give Echo pointers on how to get me pregnant quicker, for god's sake. Honestly, I'm kind of relieved they're not coming," I admit.

"Pregnant. Fucking hell," Brandi cries.

"Tell me about it," I say, my eyebrows raised.

Echo's working, so Daisy's my guard for the day. He speaks to me now. Mainly when Echo's not around, but it's so much better than his silence. The door swings open, and Echo and Sleaze march into the bar. I jump down from the counter and run towards my man, throwing myself into his arms.

"Fuck, sugar. You okay?"

Giggling, I wiggle in his arms and lean in to kiss him quickly. "I'm fine. I just missed you. Did you realise we get married in two days?" I say, excitedly.

He presses his hips into my sex, and I groan when his hard cock rubs against my pussy. "I know. Two days, and you're mine in every fucking way," he growls.

Lifting me into the air he kisses me; holding me in his arms as he walks us across the room, seating me on the counter. "Give me two minutes to talk to Daisy, and then we can go home," he says.

Brandi smacks my leg affectionately. "Bloody hell, Liv. Watching you two makes me a little horny."

I laugh lightly and lean back with my arms braced behind me.

"Shoot, I'm out of whiskey," Brandi cries. "Watch the bar for a second, while I run and grab another bottle will you," she says.

Shaking my head, I jump from the counter. "I'll go. You carry on serving."

I slip inside the storeroom and reach for the light switch. The smell of gasoline assaults me, and I pause, my fingers touching the plastic switch. I hear the grunt behind me, just as someone grabs my hair and viciously slams my head against the wall.

Pain bursts from my forehead and stars flash behind my eyes. My head is yanked backwards by the hair, almost pulling it out at the roots. I fumble blindly in the darkness, throwing my hands forward and frantically reaching out for the wall in front of me.

Goosebumps prickle across my skin when I hear a familiar

maniacal laugh right before I'm shoved into the wall again. I catch myself on my arms and use all my force to push backwards and thrust my elbow into my attacker. A momentary sense of pride consumes me when Mimi groans in pain, and spinning, I flick the switch and the room floods with light.

Confronted with the crazed eyes of Wyatt's aunt, I scream, shrinking back against the shelf. Gone is the perfectly groomed southern belle and in her place is a deranged murderer. My eyes water from the gasoline fumes, and I quickly search for the source of the smell.

Mimi pulls a large knife from her pocket and smiles at me. "Hello, whore. Wyatt should have killed you, but my weak nephew was too obsessed with his lust for you to finish the job."

Her eyes are overly wide, and her hair is dirty and matted. Her clothes are stained, and she looks like a demented psychopath.

"Mimi, you're ill. Don't do this. Let me help you," I cry, trying to calm her.

She cackles manically, then picks up a jerrycan and throws the fuel at the walls, liberally dousing them in gas. "God tasked me with ridding the world of evil-filled whores like you. But now it's time to get rid of the filthy, criminal bikers as well. I'm going to burn this place to the ground, and you and those disgusting bikers along with it," she snarls.

Placing the fuel can on the floor, she raises the knife in the air and launches herself at me. I reach behind me and desperately search the shelves for something to defend myself with. Finally, my fingers wrap around the neck of a wine bottle, and roaring, I swing it, smashing it into her head.

The bottle shatters into a thousand pieces, and blood coats Mimi's face as she screams and doubles over in pain. Using her distraction, I turn and run to the back door. Franticly, I twist the handle, but the door refuses to open. Turning my back to the locked door, I search for a weapon or a way to escape, but Mimi's blocking the other exit.

She slowly rises from the ground, blood dripping down her cheeks as she stalks towards me. "You bitch," she screams.

I scramble along the wall and stumble into the fuel can, struggling to stay upright. Mimi screams, launching towards me and slashing with the knife. Quickly grabbing the metal fuel can, I swing it towards her, knocking the knife from her hand. Gasoline splashes from the can as I hit her, covering both of us in the foul-smelling liquid.

Mimi recovers quickly and pulls a lighter from her pocket. "It's time to die, whore," she screams, her crazy eyes shining with excitement.

I run towards the door.

The click of the lighter is ominously loud, and bright flames burst into life. I'm fighting to open the door when Mimi's screams draw my attention.

Fire has consumed her whole arm, and we both watch as the flame quickly spreads into her hair and across her gasoline-soaked clothes. In the blink of an eye the gasoline catches fire and the room is quickly engulfed in flames. My eyes widen in shock and I watch, frozen, as the flames build until they cover her whole face. Her screams echo through my brain, and shell-shocked, I barely notice being lifting into the air, my eyes locked on Mimi's burning body as Echo carries me to safety.

Dazed, I watch in silent slow motion as the fire crew and ambulances arrive and head for Strikers. Fire consumes the bar, firefighters battle to control the flames as the building explodes, the windows shattering and showering the sidewalk in glass. A crowd grows; bikers and locals standing together, watching the fire be gradually brought under control.

It's dark by the time the body bag is carried from the building.

Mimi.

Dead.

My knees give way, and I fall to the ground, but Echo's strong arms catch me, holding me to his chest, as I sob uncontrollably in fear and sadness and relief.

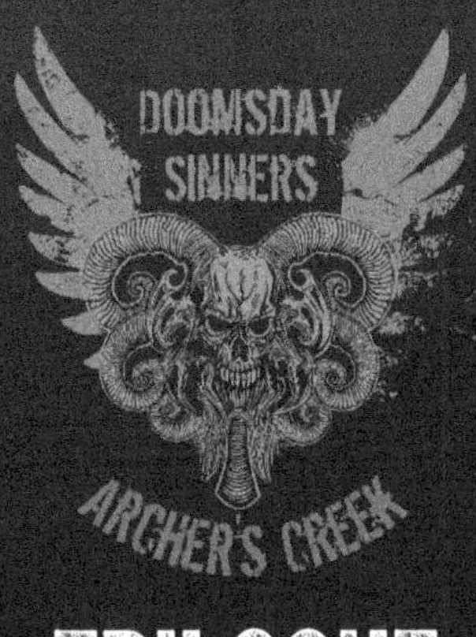

EPILOGUE

Echo

Mimi's dead. She's gone and she's never coming back.

Burned alive.

She suffered horrifically.

I want to feel bad, but I don't.

The sheriff found five other bodies in the woods. Mimi and Wyatt were psychopathic serial killers, and they almost killed me too.

I hope they rot in hell.

I'll never forget what happened. I'll never forget the look in Mimi's eyes as the flames consumed her.

My time in Archer's Creek has changed everything in so many ways. Good and bad, it all led me to Echo.

ONE MONTH LATER

Olivia

Today's the day. It's taken longer to get here than I expected, but it's finally here. Our wedding day.

Standing in the front of the mirror, I smooth down my dress, my hands pausing over my stomach. With a smile, I step outside where Gus waits patiently for me.

"You look beautiful, young lady," he says. I blush and take his hand, letting him help me into the car.

Echo thinks I don't know he still has people guarding me, but I do. My man's a control freak, and I wouldn't want him any other way. We pull up to the meadow behind the clubhouse, and Gus helps me out of the car. I loop my arm through his, and we walk to the end of the aisle. That's when I see him.

Echo.

My sexy biker is everything I never wanted.

Our eyes lock, and my hand unconsciously falls to my stomach and the baby that's starting to grow there.

Smiling, I walk towards him and the rest of my life.

My Echo.

My future.

My forever.

Echo

We stand in front of each other and promise forever. Till death do us part.

She thinks I don't know that she's carrying my baby, but I do and I can't wait to see her with our child.

I don't worry about her running from me anymore, she's tied to me in every way possible and she knows I'll never let her go. She wouldn't let me go either.

As much as I insist she belongs to me, she owns me heart, body and soul and I wouldn't have it any other way.

She's everything I never knew I needed.

She's my world.

My Livvy.

My love.

My happily ever after.

The End…

For Now.

ACKNOWLEDGEMENTS

Finishing this book is actually a dream come true. I wrote a book! How fucking cool is that!

My friends and family have listened to me talk about this for so long. I've been telling my husband I was going to write a book for about ten years, and he finally just turned around and said, "Stop talking about it and just bloody well do it." So I did.

I think I will always be a reader first and foremost, but writing may come a very close second. These characters have been talking to me for a very long time, and it's amazing to actually bring them to life. I've lived and breathed this book for the best part of two years, and I need to thank my husband, Martin, and my beautiful babies for letting me ignore them and hide in my office for the last year while I actually finished.

I've had so many crises of faith during this whole process, and I've abandoned this story completely on more than one occasion. Without the help and support of some really amazing people, I'm honestly not sure I would ever have gotten this far.

Samantha Rodgers, you were the first person to ever read my words. You were the cheerleader I needed, and you helped me believe I could actually do this.

Sybil Bartel, I adore your words and I can't thank you enough for helping me to find mine. You have held my hand, shouted at me, given me endless support and advice, and called me on my shit when I needed it. Thank you.

To all of my wonderful beta readers and friends that I have forced my book upon, I'm so sorry! But thank you so much.

Finally, to anyone who reads my story, thank you for taking a chance on a brand new author. I hope you enjoyed the story and fell in love with Echo and Livvy just like I did.

This isn't the end of Archer's Creek, so if you'd like to keep up to date on the next book in the series, then pop over to Facebook and like my author page. https://www.facebook.com/GemmaWeirAuthor/

ABOUT THE AUTHOR

Gemma Weir is a half crazed stay at home mom to three kids, one man child and a hell hound. She has lived in the midlands, in the UK her whole life and has wanted to write a book since she was a child. Gemma has a ridiculously dirty mind and loves her book boyfriends to be big, tattooed alpha males. She's a reader first and foremost and she loves her romance to come with a happy ending and lots of sexy sex.

For updates on future releases check out my social media links.

ALSO BY GEMMA WEIR

The Archers Creek Series

Echo (Archer's Creek #1)

Daisy (Archer's Creek #2)

Blade (Archer's Creek #3)

Echo & Liv (Archer's Creek #3.5)

Park (Archer's Creek #4)

Smoke (Archer's Creek #5)

The Scions Series

Hidden (The Scions #1)

Found (The Scions #2)

Wings & Roots (The Scions #3)

The Kings & Queens of St Augustus Series

The Spare - Part One

(The Kings & Queens of St Augustus #1)

The Spare - Part Two

(The Kings & Queens of St Augustus #2)

The Heir - Part One

(The Kings & Queens of St Augustus #3)

The Heir - Part Two

(The Kings & Queens of St Augustus #4)

OTHER WORKS FROM HUDSON INDIE INK

Paranormal Romance/Urban Fantasy

Stephanie Hudson

Sloane Murphy

Xen Randell

Sci-Fi/Fantasy

Brandon Ellis

Devin Hanson

Crime/Action

Blake Hudson

Mike Gomes

Contemporary Romance

Eve L. Mitchell

Elodie Colt

DOOMSDAY
SINNERS
ARCHER'S CREEK

Lightning Source UK Ltd.
Milton Keynes UK
UKHW010100130822
407231UK00001B/3